Curse of the *Arctic Star*

MW01088619

Nancy Drew DIARIES™

Curse of the *Arctic Star*

#1

CAROLYN KEENE

Aladdin
NEW YORK LONDON TORONTO SYDNEY NEW DELHI

This book is a work of fiction. Any references to historical events, real people,
or real places are used fictitiously. Other names, characters, places, and events are products of the
author's imagination, and any resemblance to actual events or places or persons,
living or dead, is entirely coincidental.

ALADDIN
An imprint of Simon & Schuster Children's Publishing Division
1230 Avenue of the Americas, New York, NY 10020
First Aladdin paperback edition February 2013
Copyright © 2013 by Simon & Schuster
All rights reserved, including the right of reproduction in whole or in part in any form.
ALADDIN is a trademark of Simon & Schuster, Inc., and related logo
is a registered trademark of Simon & Schuster, Inc.
NANCY DREW, NANCY DREW DIARIES, and related logo are trademarks of
Simon & Schuster, Inc.
Also available in an Aladdin hardcover edition.
For information about special discounts for bulk purchases, please contact
Simon & Schuster Special Sales at 1-866-506-1949 or business@simonandschuster.com.
The Simon & Schuster Speakers Bureau can bring authors to your live event.
For more information or to book an event contact the Simon & Schuster Speakers Bureau
at 1-866-248-3049 or visit our website at www.simonspeakers.com.
Designed by Karina Granda
The text of this book was set in Adobe Caslon Pro.
Manufactured in the United States of America 0316 OFF
10 9
Library of Congress Control Number 2012949338
ISBN 978-1-4169-9072-7 (pbk)
ISBN 978-1-4424-6610-4 (hc)
ISBN 978-1-4424-5162-9 (eBook)

Contents

Dear Diary,

I DIDN'T ACTUALLY BELIEVE THAT A luxurious cruise ship could have any *real* mysteries onboard.

Boy, was I wrong!

The minute we set sail, we were in mysteries up to our ears. I don't think I'll have any time to enjoy Alaska, and I've always wanted to visit the Last Frontier and pan for gold or even go dog sledding. . . .

Gotta go—George just yelled my name!

It's always something!

CHAPTER ONE

Bon Voyage

"NAME AND CABIN NUMBER, PLEASE?" THE efficient-looking porter asked, reaching for the large green suitcase sitting on the dock beside me.

"Nancy Drew. Hollywood Suite." I shrugged and shot a glance at my two best friends. "That's all they told us—I don't know the number."

The porter smiled. He was a short, muscular man dressed in a tidy navy jacket with silver piping and matching shorts, with a name tag identifying him as James. Every employee of Superstar Cruises wore some variation on that uniform, from the driver who'd picked us up at the Vancouver airport to the woman checking people in over at the gangway.

"That's all I need to know, Ms. Drew," James said. "The Hollywood Suite doesn't have a number."

I watched as he scribbled the letters HS on a bright purple tag, then snapped it onto the handle of my bag. He lifted the suitcase as if it weighed nothing, even though I knew that wasn't the case. I'm no fashion plate, but a girl needs plenty of clothes for a two-week Alaskan cruise! Then he set my bag on a metal cart along with at least a dozen other suitcases, trunks, and duffels.

Meanwhile my friend Bess Marvin was staring up at the ship docked beside us. "Wow," she said. "Big boat."

"Major understatement," I replied. The *Arctic Star* was absolutely massive. We don't see too many cruise ships in our midwestern hometown of River Heights, but I was pretty sure this one was even larger than most.

Just then I heard a scuffle nearby. "Hey, give that back—I don't want to check it!" George Fayne exclaimed as she grabbed a grungy olive-green duffel bag out of another porter's hand.

George is my other best friend. She's also Bess's cousin, though most people find it hard to believe they're related, since the two of them couldn't be more different. Exhibit A? Their luggage. George's consisted of that ugly duffel, a sturdy brown suitcase that looked as if it had been through a demolition derby, and a plain black backpack. Definitely the functional look, just like her short dark hair, faded jeans, and sneakers. Bess, on the other hand, had a matching set of luggage in a nice shade of blue. Tasteful and pulled together, like her sleek, shoulder-length blond hair and linen dress.

The porter took a step back. "Of course, miss," he told George politely. "I only thought—"

"Relax, George," Bess said. "I think you can trust him to get your toothbrush and your days-of-the-week underwear onboard safely."

"My underwear, maybe." George already had the bag unzipped. She scrabbled through the mess inside and finally came up with her laptop and smartphone. "This stuff? I trust no one."

Bess snorted. "Seriously? We're going to be cruising the gorgeous Alaskan waters surrounded by amazing scenery. You're not going to have a lot of time to look for cute kitten videos on YouTube, you know."

"Maybe not," George retorted. "But if we need to research something for Nancy's—"

"Hi, Alan!" I said loudly, cutting her off as I noticed a guy hurrying toward us.

"It's my lucky day!" the guy announced with a big, cheerful grin. "I found my sunglasses. I must've dropped them when we were getting our stuff out of the airport van." He waved the glasses at us, then slid them on and wrapped an arm around Bess's shoulders. "Actually, though, *every* day is my lucky day since I met Beautiful Bess."

George rolled her eyes so hard I was afraid they'd pop right out of her head. "Sooo glad you found your shades, Alan," she said drily. "I was afraid you'd be so busy searching you'd miss the boat."

I hid a smile. About a month earlier, Bess and George and I had been having lunch at one of our favorite cafés when George noticed a guy staring from a nearby table. He was maybe a couple of years older than us, with wavy brown hair and wide-set gray eyes. When he realized he'd been caught, he came over and introduced himself as Alan Thomas, a student at the local university. He apologized for staring and explained that it was because he couldn't take his eyes off Bess.

That kind of thing happens to Bess all the time, so I didn't pay much attention. She's not the type of girl who gets swept off her feet by just anybody.

But apparently Alan wasn't just anybody. He'd taken her on a romantic picnic for their first date, and the two of them had been together ever since. It was nice to see Bess so happy, even if I secretly thought Alan was a little goofy and overly excitable. George thought so too, though with her it wasn't such a secret.

"Need some help with those, buddy?" Alan asked as James returned for Bess's bags. "I can give you a hand. Should I just toss it there on top of Nancy's suitcase?"

"It's quite all right, sir," James replied. "Your entire party is in the Hollywood Suite, right? Just leave your luggage here and we'll take care of it. You might want to head over to the check-in line so you can start enjoying all the fine amenities of the *Arctic Star.*"

"Thanks," Bess said. "Come on, you guys. Let's go."

Alan nodded agreeably. "This is so amazing," he said to no one in particular as we headed toward the end of the line. "I never thought a poor college student like me would be taking an Alaskan cruise!"

He wasn't the only one. Just a few short days ago, I'd been wondering what I was going to do with myself for the next month while Ned was off being a camp counselor and my dad was busy with a big case. River Heights is kind of sleepy at the best of times. This summer? It was downright catatonic.

Then Becca Wright had called, sounding frantic. That was my first clue that my summer was about to change. See, Becca is just about the *least* frantic person I've ever known. Just a couple of years out of college, she'd already landed the plum job of assistant cruise director for the maiden voyage of the *Arctic Star*, the flagship vessel of brand-new Superstar Cruises. Having known Becca for years, I was sure that was mostly due to her work ethic and friendly, upbeat personality. Although I'm sure it didn't hurt that her grandfather had been a bigwig executive at the venerable Jubilee Cruise Lines. He'd retired a few years back, but he still knew just about everyone in the business.

So why the frantic call? Some suspicious things were happening at Superstar Cruises, and Becca was afraid someone might be up to no good. Naturally, that made her think of me. See, my thing is solving mysteries. Big ones. And small ones, like the case where I'd first met Becca, which had involved finding her family's runaway dog. And everything in between.

So which kind of case was this? I wondered, glancing up again at the gleaming white ship looming over the dock. Was someone really out to mess with Superstar Cruises like Becca seemed to think? Or was it just new-job jitters and a little bad luck?

"Earth to Nancy!" Alan waved a hand in front of

my face, grinning. "You look a little nervous. Not worried about getting seasick, are you?"

"Nope." I smiled back at him. Real mystery or not, I was glad that Becca had called. My friends and I were about to set out on the all-expenses-paid cruise of a lifetime!

The four of us joined the line waiting to board, which was growing with every passing second. George stood on tiptoes, hopping from one foot to the other as she tried to see how many people were in front of us.

"Hey, shouldn't there be a special VIP line or something?" she complained. "I mean, we're in the Hollywood Suite! We shouldn't have to wait in line with everyone else."

"Yeah." Alan chuckled. "Plus, we're contest winners! That should count for something, right?"

"Um, the line's moving pretty fast. I'm sure we'll be aboard soon," I said quickly. The last thing we needed was for Alan to start blabbing to the ship's employees about the whole contest-winner thing. Mainly because it wasn't true.

Bess shifted her handbag to her other shoulder and pulled out a packet of paperwork. "Does everyone have their tickets and passports handy? Nancy?"

"Why are you looking at me?" I said. "I'm not *that* forgetful, even when I'm—" I caught myself just in time, swallowing the last few words: *even when I'm investigating a case.* "Um, even when I've just crossed a couple of time zones," I finished lamely, shooting a look at Alan.

Luckily, he wasn't paying attention. He was digging into the pockets of his Bermuda shorts.

"Uh-oh," he said. "I think I left my passport in one of my bags. I'd better go grab it before they load it onto the ship."

He rushed off, disappearing into the throng of passengers, porters, and bystanders on the dock. George watched him go with a sigh.

"Okay, this is already getting old," she said. "Shouldn't we just let him in on the secret already? Alan's a huge goody-two-shoes nerd—I'm sure we can trust him not to tell anyone we're really here to solve a mystery."

"Shh," I cautioned her, glancing around quickly.

"Don't call him a nerd," Bess added with a glare. "He's just . . . enthusiastic about things."

"Yeah. Like I said. Nerd," George said.

I ignored their bickering, realizing I didn't have to worry about anyone overhearing us at the moment. A red-haired young man had just arrived at the dock, and about a dozen other people, from little kids to an old woman with a walker, were pushing and shoving and laughing loudly as they all tried to fling themselves at him at once. Almost every single one of them had bright red hair and freckles.

Bess followed my gaze. "Family reunion?" she murmured.

"Brilliant deduction, detective." I grinned at her, then turned to George. "We can't tell anyone why we're really here," I reminded her quietly. "Not even Alan. We promised Becca, remember? Besides, we've really only known Alan for a few weeks."

"Oh, please." Bess shook her head. "What do you think he's going to do? Call the *New York Times* so they can publish all your clues?"

"No, of course not." I glanced over my shoulder to make sure Alan wasn't returning yet. "But he's not exactly Mr. Introvert. We don't need him blurting out something at the wrong time, even by accident."

"Whatever." George didn't look entirely convinced. "Guess we'd better talk about the case while we can, then. What's your plan?"

"The first thing I need to do is talk to Becca," I said. "All she told me on the phone was that there'd been a few troubling incidents in the couple of weeks leading up to this cruise, including some threatening e-mails or something. Oh, and the Brock thing, of course."

Bess sighed dreamily. "I can't believe we almost got to be on the same cruise ship as Brock Walker!"

"No, we didn't," I said. "That's why Becca called us in to help, remember? According to her, Brock Walker was supposed to put the 'superstar' in Superstar Cruises. I guess that's their gimmick—passengers being able to rub elbows with superstars. So when he canceled less than five days before departure, she knew it was bad news. Then when she heard it was because someone was sending threatening e-mails to his family . . ."

"Sounds like a mystery to me," George agreed, kicking at a loose board on the dock.

I nodded slowly, still not entirely convinced. Brock Walker was an A-list actor who'd starred in a popular series of bad-boy comedy-action films. But in real life he was supposed to be a hard-working, down-to-earth family man, married to his high school sweetheart, with a couple of kids. Definitely *not* the type to flake out on a commitment, at least according to his reputation.

"I wonder what they told the paying passengers." Bess glanced around. "Especially since the rest of the entertainment is C-list at best."

George patted her laptop, which she'd slung over her shoulder in its case. "I checked earlier today— Brock put out a statement saying it was a scheduling conflict."

"Yeah." I shuffled forward as the line continued to move. "But Becca said he's really mad about the threats. He told the CEO of Superstar Cruises that if the company doesn't figure out who did it, he'll tell everyone the truth."

"Bummer." George shrugged. "But that sounds like a job for the cops or the FBI or someone like that."

"I know." I sighed. "The trouble is, the CEO is afraid that any bad publicity involving police investigations might scare off passengers and sink the company." I chuckled, realizing what I'd just said. "So to speak. Anyway, that's why we're here—undercover. The CEO used to work with Becca's grandfather, so I guess she and Becca are practically like family. Since it was too late to re-book Brock's suite, Becca talked her into flying us out and letting us stay there while we keep an eye on things."

"Which is totally awesome," George said with a grin, shooting a look up at the ship. "I'm not sure about this whole cruise thing, but I've always wanted to see Alaska!"

"So what else did Becca tell you?" Bess asked me. "You said there were some other suspicious incidents."

I nodded. "That's what she said, but she didn't go into much detail. Just mentioned something about threatening e-mails, and some prelaunch mishaps. She's supposed to fill me in when I see her. Once we know more, maybe we'll be able to—"

I stopped short as Bess cleared her throat loudly. A moment later Alan arrived, apologizing to the people in line behind us.

"Found it," he announced, holding up his passport. "I got there just in time—that porter was about to roll our cart away."

I forced a smile. Having Alan along was definitely going to make things more difficult. That hadn't been part of the original plan.

But when he'd heard that the three of us had won a free cruise to Alaska in a four-bedroom suite—cover story, remember?—he'd begged to come along. As an environmental studies student at the university in River Heights, he'd pointed out that Alaska was the perfect place to get a jump-start on his sophomore-year research project, and he'd never be able to afford that kind of trip on a college kid's budget. Especially when he lavished what little spare cash he had on his new girlfriend, Bess.

Okay, so he hadn't *actually* mentioned that last part. He hadn't had to. Bess had invited him along and told us we'd just have to deal with it. The girl seems sweet and agreeable most of the time, but she's got a backbone of steel when the situation calls for it.

Soon we were inside, being checked in and issued our ship ID cards. "Enjoy your time with Superstar Cruises!" the smiling employee told us.

As we thanked her and stepped away, I nudged Bess in the side. "Can you distract you-know-who for a while?" I whispered. "I want to look for Becca."

"Leave it to me," Bess murmured back.

Alan had just moved away from the check-in desk to tuck his ID into his wallet, but he looked up quickly. "Did you say something?" he asked Bess.

She stepped over and looped her arm through his. "I was just telling Nancy we'd meet her and George at the suite later," she told him with a flirty little tilt of her head. "Want to go for a walk to check out the ship?"

She didn't have to ask twice. Seconds later they were strolling out of the check-in area hand in hand. George shook her head as she watched them go.

"That guy's got it bad," she said. "I really don't know what Bess sees in him, though."

"That's a mystery for another day." I headed out after them. "Let's not waste time. Becca said we'd probably find her on the main deck."

George glanced around as we emerged into what appeared to be a sort of lobby area. It was carpeted in red, with murals on the walls depicting famous Hollywood landmarks. A pair of winding, carpeted staircases with gleaming mahogany banisters led upward, with a sign in between that showed the layout of the entire ship.

I barely had time to glance at the sign before a smiling young female employee rushed toward us. She was dressed in shorts and a piped vest and was holding a tray of tall, frosty glasses with colorful straws and umbrellas sticking out of them.

"Welcome to the *Arctic Star*," she gushed. "Would

you ladies care for a complimentary Superstar smoothie? They're made with a refreshing fruit mixture, including real Alaskan wild blueberries. A specialty of the ship!"

George was already reaching for a glass. She's not the type to turn down anything free. "Thanks," she said, then took a sip. "Hey, Nancy, you've got to try this! It's awesome!"

"Thanks, but I'm not thirsty," I told the waitress. Grabbing George's arm, I dragged her toward the stairs. "Focus, okay?"

"Whatever. A girl's got to stay hydrated." George took another big sip of her smoothie as we hurried upstairs.

A couple of flights up, we found the lido deck. It was a partially shaded area spanning the entire width of the ship, and appeared to be where all the action was at the moment. As we emerged out of the stairwell, we almost crashed into another employee. This one was a lean, tanned man in his late twenties with slicked-back brown hair.

"Welcome aboard, ladies," he said with a toothy grin.

"My name's Scott, and I'm one of your shore excursion specialists. Our first stop the day after tomorrow will be Ketchikan, where you'll have the chance to experience anything from a flight-seeing trip to the fjords to the Great Alaskan Lumberjack Show or . . ."

There was more, but I didn't hear it. I'd just spotted Becca halfway across the deck chatting with some passengers, looking trim and professional in her silver-piped navy jacket and skirt.

"Sounds great," I blurted out, interrupting Shore Excursion Scott's description of kayaking in Tongass National Forest. "We'll get back to you on that, okay?"

"Save me a spot on those kayaks," George called over her shoulder as I yanked her away.

"Ladies!" someone called out cheerfully. Suddenly we found our path blocked by yet another uniformed employee. This one was a short, skinny guy with a wild tuft of blond hair and a slightly manic twinkle in his big blue eyes. "Hollywood Suite, right?" he asked.

"Yeah." George sounded surprised. "How'd you know that?"

"Oh, they send us photos of our guests ahead of time. You're Nancy and you're Georgia, right?"

"George," George corrected with a grimace. She hates her real name. "Call me George."

"George it is!" The guy seemed as if he couldn't stand still. He sort of bounded back and forth in front of us. It reminded me of my neighbor's over-enthusiastic golden retriever. "My name's Max. Oh, but you probably figured that out already, right?" He grinned and pointed to his name tag. "I'll be your personal butler."

"Our what?" I said.

"Whoa!" George exclaimed. "Seriously? We get a *butler*?"

"Absolutely." Max nodded vigorously. "Each of our luxury suites has its own dedicated staff, including a butler and two maids, to make sure your trip is as pleasant and comfortable as possible. You can call on me day or night for all your needs."

"Cool," I said briskly. Max seemed like a really nice guy, but I was feeling impatient. Over his shoulder, I could see Becca moving on to another set of passengers. "We'll get back to you, okay?"

But Max had already whipped out a handful of pamphlets. "Here's a partial list of our available services to get you started," he said brightly. "Our room service menu, the shipboard activity schedule, spa services, our exclusive pillow menu . . ."

George was already examining the pamphlets eagerly. I could see that it wasn't going to be easy to shake Max.

Then I had an idea. I grabbed one of the pamphlets. "Er, the pillow menu, huh?" I said. "Come to think of it, I can't sleep well on anything but a . . . um . . ." I quickly scanned the list. "A buckwheat pillow. Do you think you could find me one right now? I might need to take a nap soon."

"Certainly, Ms. Drew!" Max beamed as if I'd just asked him to be my best friend. "I'll take care of it right away. Just text me if you need anything else." He handed us each a card with his name and number on it, then scurried away.

"Wow," George said. "A real butler! This is awesome. Maybe I should tell him to get me a special fancy pillow while he's at it."

"Forget it," I said, slapping her hand as she reached for her cell phone. "Becca. Now."

This time we actually made it over to her. I hadn't seen her in a couple of years, but she looked pretty much the same—curly dark hair, sparkling brown eyes, a quick smile. She was chatting with a rather weary-looking couple in their thirties. The man wore a T-shirt with the Canadian flag on it, and the woman was keeping one eye on the eight-year-old boy dribbling a soccer ball nearby.

"Careful, Tobias," she called, interrupting something Becca was saying about the dinner schedule. "We don't want to be a bother to the other passengers."

"Maybe *you* don't," the boy retorted, sticking out his tongue. "I told you I didn't want to come on this stupid ship!" With that, he kicked the ball into a column. It bounced off and almost hit a passing woman.

"Wow," George murmured in my ear. "Brat much?"

Becca's smile never wavered. She glanced toward me and George briefly, then returned her focus to the parents. "We have lots of activities for our youngest guests," she told them. "Perhaps your son would enjoy checking out the rock-climbing wall or the arcade. There's also a kids' tour of the ship scheduled for first thing tomorrow morning. One of our youth activities coordinators can give you all the details if you're interested."

She gestured toward a good-looking young Asian guy standing nearby. Tobias's parents thanked her, then grabbed their son's hand and dragged him toward the youth coordinator.

"Nancy!" Becca exclaimed as soon as they were out of earshot. "Thank goodness you made it. Hi, George." She glanced around. "Where's Bess?"

"She's, uh, busy right now." I didn't want to waste time explaining about Alan. I knew we probably only had a few seconds before Becca had to return to duty. "So when do you want to meet to talk?"

"Soon." Becca shot a cautious look around, her smile fading. Then she lowered her voice. "Something else has happened, but I don't have time to fill you in now. Can you meet me at my office later?"

"Sure. Where is it?"

She was writing the deck and cabin numbers down on her card when a sudden, shrill scream rang out from somewhere farther along the huge deck area.

"What was that?" George exclaimed.

Becca instantly looked worried. "I don't know, but I hope—"

Before she could finish, someone let out a shout. "Help! There's a bloody body in the pool!"

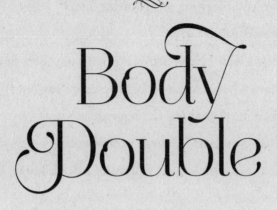

CHAPTER TWO

Body Double

"WHAT?" BECCA BLURTED OUT, HER FACE going pale. Without another word, she rushed off in the direction of the commotion.

I traded a worried glance with George. "Come on," I said. "Let's go see what's happening."

We followed the crowd and soon emerged onto a sunny, open-air part of the deck dominated by a large free-form pool. It was a riot of fountains, slides, and potted palms.

But nobody was looking at any of that. Everyone's focus was on the blond woman's pale, still form floating facedown in a widening reddish circle!

My heart pounded, and for a second I felt dizzy. I've been involved in a lot of mysteries. But very few of them involved bloody bodies of any kind. Somehow I'd just about convinced myself that Becca was imagining trouble where it didn't exist, that this was really just going to be a fun, free vacation with a little sleuthing on the side. But now? Maybe not so much.

"Oh, gross," George exclaimed, watching as a lifeguard-looking guy in silver-piped trunks dove into the pool and sliced through the pinkish-tinged water. "There's a ton of blood!"

Before I could answer, the lifeguard reached the body. He grabbed one arm, then jumped back. "Hey, it's not a real person!" he called out, sounding confused. "It's just a mannequin!"

Realizing I'd been holding my breath, I blew it out in a big *whoosh*. "Thank goodness." I glanced around for Becca and spotted her nearby. Hurrying over, I touched her on the arm. "Do you have any idea what this is all about?"

She shook her head, looking grim. Meanwhile George was staring at a young couple nearby. A pretty, willowy blonde in her midtwenties was huddled in the arms of a tall, handsome, broad-shouldered man around the same age.

"Whoa," George commented. "Looks like that girl is pretty freaked out."

Most of the people near the pool looked more excited or curious than scared now as they chattered and laughed about what had happened. But the young woman was shaking and moaning, looking really upset.

"I just met those two a few minutes ago," Becca said. "They're honeymooners. Vince and Lacey, from Iowa."

Pasting a smile on her face, she hurried over, George and me on her heels. The woman—Lacey—looked up as Becca approached. Her big hazel eyes were brimming with tears.

"Oh, this is terrible!" she moaned. "What kind of cruise *is* this?"

"It's okay, sweetheart," her husband said, stroking her hair gently. "It'll be okay."

"No!" Lacey cried, sounding borderline hysterical. "It's a bad sign, I know it!" She glanced up at Vince. "I knew we should have gone with Jubilee Cruises after all!"

Becca bit her lip. "Please don't be upset," she said. "This is just a, um, misunderstanding. Of some sort. I think."

I cringed. Becca was one of the most tactful and gracious people I'd ever met. But she had her work cut out for her. Sure, maybe Lacey was overreacting a little. But who expects to see a body—even a fake one—on their honeymoon cruise? Or *any* cruise, for that matter?

Becca was still trying to soothe the hysterical honeymooner when a handsome man in his forties arrived. He was wearing a crisp navy-and-silver uniform and a name tag that read MARCELO: CRUISE DIRECTOR.

"I guess that's Becca's boss," I whispered to George.

Within moments Marcelo had assessed the situation and hustled the couple off for a complimentary beverage. Becca and the other employees started shooing the rest of the hangers-on out of the pool area.

"Should we take a look around while everyone's distracted?" George whispered.

"You read my mind."

We hurried closer to the pool. The lifeguard had just dragged the mannequin to the edge.

"So where'd that thing come from?" I asked him, keeping my tone casual.

He hoisted the mannequin out of the water by the straps of its floral bikini, brushing off his hands as it landed on the concrete edge with a clatter. Then he glanced up at me.

"It's nothing to worry about, miss," he said politely. "Looks like it came from one of the onboard shops."

As he dove back in to retrieve the floating wig, I leaned closer to the mannequin. There didn't seem to be anything unusual about it that I could see. It was just a plastic figure with a blank white face, like the ones occupying the picture windows of countless stores all over the world.

George was staring out at the water. "So that's

obviously not real blood, either," she said. "What do you think it is?"

"It looks kind of pink, actually." I stepped to the edge of the pool and leaned down for a closer look "Hmm. Smells like raspberry?"

George stepped back and glanced around. Spotting a shiny silver trash receptacle nearby, she hurried over and peered inside.

"Aha!" she said, reaching in and pulling something out. "You were close. It's cherry, actually."

I looked at what she'd found. It was a large plastic tub of powdered drink mix. Cherry flavor. Empty.

"Fake blood to go with a fake body," I mused. "Why would someone do that? And then leave the evidence nearby?"

"Who knows?" George said. "Maybe . . ."

She let her voice trail off. Someone was hurrying toward us. It was a short, pointy-chinned woman in her twenties. She was wearing a man's fedora and a thrift-store floral granny dress, along with bright purple plastic earrings and thick, square-framed black glasses. A snazzy-looking laptop was tucked under one thin, pasty-pale arm.

"Isn't this crazy?" she exclaimed, shoving her glasses up her nose and grinning at us as if we were her best friends. "It's like one of those murder-mystery cruises or something, except nobody knew it was going to happen! Bonus, right?"

"Um, yeah, okay," George said.

"By the way, I'm Wendy. Wendy Webster." She stuck out her hand. "I'm a travel blogger. Wendy's Wanderings—maybe you've heard of it? It's like the coolest new travel blog, according to the coolest bloggers."

"I'm Nancy, and this is George." I shook her hand. "Sorry, I don't really follow blogs too much."

That seemed to take her by surprise. She stared at me over the tops of her glasses for a second, studying me as if I were an alien species.

Finally she shrugged. "Oh. You're retro, huh? That's cool," she said. "Anyway, I thought this was going to be just another boring cruise, you know? Did you guys, like, see what happened?"

"Nope," George said. "We're clueless."

I shot her a look, and she smiled back innocently. I was already trying to come up with an excuse to get away from Blogger Wendy. We weren't going to be able to do much investigating with her hanging around.

Just then a pair of young men in Superstar uniforms hurried over. "Excuse us, ladies," one of them said. "Could we ask you to please vacate the pool area? We just need time to clean up, and will reopen the pool as soon as we can."

The second young man nodded. "They're serving complimentary smoothies in the atrium lounge," he added, gesturing.

Wendy's eyes lit up. "Free smoothies?" she said. "I'm so there! Come on, girls!"

I grabbed George's arm to stop her from following. "Let her go," I hissed. "You already had your free smoothie, remember?"

We drifted toward the lounge slowly, staying behind the rest of the crowd so we could talk. "So that was weird," George said.

"What? Wendy?"

She laughed. "Yeah, her too. But I meant the pool thing. Think they'll call the cops?"

"I don't know." I shrugged. "If they do, it could delay our departure. Based on what Becca told me, I don't think the CEO would like that. Bad publicity, remember?"

"Yeah. Plus, nobody actually got hurt or anything." George grimaced. "Uh-oh—incoming."

Following her gaze, I saw Alan striding toward us, with Bess at his heels. "There you are!" Alan exclaimed. "Did you hear about the fake dead body in the pool?"

"Yeah." I traded a look with Bess, who raised one eyebrow curiously. "We heard."

Luckily, Alan didn't seem interested in discussing it. "Anyway, we've been looking all over for you two," he said. "Bess wants to check out our suite, but I thought we should wait until we're all together. Should we go find it now?"

"Sure, let's go," I replied. "Anyone know how to get there?"

"I think it's this way." Alan hurried off toward the nearest set of elevators.

As it turned out, he had no idea how to find our suite. We wandered around for a while, heading down a couple of levels via elevator and then following signs pointing us down one long, windowless hallway after another. There weren't many people down there—I guessed most of the passengers were upstairs watching the ship prepare to pull out of Vancouver's busy harbor.

"Wow." George was panting slightly as we jogged up a staircase. "This ship seems even bigger on the inside than it does on the outside."

"We could be lost for days before anyone could find us." Alan wriggled his fingers in a spooky way.

I paused at the intersection of two hallways. The one we'd been following was lined with numbered cabin doors. The other was narrower and shorter, with a sign on the wall reading GALLEY—EMPLOYEES ONLY.

"Maybe we should go ask someone back there," I said, gesturing toward the sign.

"Aw, you're giving up so soon?" Alan grinned. "Where's your sense of adventure, Nancy?"

"I'm not sure. I think I lost it a few levels back," I joked weakly.

We hurried down the hallway. As we neared the corner, I heard voices ahead.

"Good, sounds like there's someone back there," Bess said.

The voices stopped abruptly as we came into sight. Three men turned to stare at us in surprise. Two of them wore Superstar Cruises uniforms. One was holding a broom and dustpan, while the other had a white kitchen apron tied on over his navy shorts. The third man appeared to be a passenger. He was in his fifties and heavyset, with a droopy mustache and prominent jowls. He was dressed in Bermuda shorts and a Hawaiian shirt.

"Excuse me," I said. "We're looking for our suite, and we're kind of lost."

"Me too," Mr. Hawaiian Shirt said, the corners of his mouth turning up beneath his mustache. "This ship is a giant maze, isn't it? It's like a floating fiefdom!" He chortled and slapped one of the employees on the back. "These fellows were just helping me find my way. Isn't that right?"

"Yes, sir," the guy with the apron said. He looked at the other employee, who smiled uncertainly and scurried off in the opposite direction. "What's your cabin number?"

Was it my imagination, or did the kitchen worker look sort of anxious? It was hard to tell in the dimly lit hallway.

"We're in the Hollywood Suite," George told him.

"Ooh la la!" Mr. Hawaiian Shirt whistled. "Sounds fancy! See you youngsters around." He nodded at us, then strolled off and disappeared around the corner.

The remaining employee gave us directions. "Enjoy your time with Superstar Cruises," he finished softly. Then he turned and hurried off.

"That was a little strange, wasn't it?" Bess said when he was gone.

"Strange? How do you mean?" Alan put an arm around her.

"Nothing," George said quickly. "Um, I mean, I didn't notice anything."

Alan shrugged. "Okay. Now come on, let's see if we can find our rooms this time!"

When we finally found it, the Hollywood Suite turned out to be pretty spectacular. We entered through a marble-floored foyer into a two-story living room with a grand piano, floor-to-ceiling windows, and a sliding door leading onto a roomy private balcony. George hurried toward the balcony, which offered a great view of Vancouver shrinking behind us as the ship chugged away. When she reached the glass doors leading out there, she gasped.

"Whoa!" she exclaimed. "We have our own hot tub!"

Just then one of the other doors opened, and Max the butler hurried out. "You found it!" he exclaimed with a bright smile. "I was just starting to worry. Nancy, your buckwheat pillow should be here any minute."

"Buckwheat pillow?" Bess echoed, shooting me a look.

I ignored her. "Thanks, Max," I said. "I really appreciate it."

"That's what I'm here for!" He hurried over to the pile of luggage stacked near the piano. "Now if you tell me who's going to be in which room, I can assist you with your unpacking if you like."

"Thanks," I said again. "But I'm sure we can . . ."

My voice trailed off. I'd just noticed something.

"Hey," I said. "Where's my suitcase?"

CHAPTER THREE

❧

Rumors and Surprises

I SHOVED GEORGE'S DUFFEL ASIDE FOR A better look at the rest of the luggage. My friends' stuff was all there, along with the big hobo bag I'd used as a carry-on for the plane. But there was no sign of my green suitcase.

"Oh, dear," Max said. "Is something missing?"

"Only the bag with most of my stuff in it," I exclaimed.

"Are you sure it's not here somewhere?" Bess

glanced around the main room. "We watched the porter label it ourselves, remember?"

"Of course I remember." My words came out clipped and short, and I took a deep breath and tried to compose myself before continuing. "Who should I call about this?" I asked Max.

"Me," he declared, patting me on the arm. "Don't fret, Ms. Drew, I'll take care of it right away. There must have been some kind of mix-up with the room tags."

That didn't seem possible, since Bess was right—I'd seen the porter label the bag myself. But I didn't get a chance to say so, since Max was already rushing out of the suite with his cell phone pressed to his ear, leaving the door standing open behind him.

"It's okay, Nancy," Alan said. "I'm sure your bag's around somewhere."

"Yeah," George said. "It's not like we're at the airport and it accidentally got on a plane headed to Timbuktu. The worst that could happen is they dropped it in the harbor." She smirked.

"Very funny," I growled.

George and Bess traded a surprised look. "Chill, Nance," George said. "It's not that big a deal. Max will track it down."

I took another deep breath, realizing she was right. What was going on with me, anyway? I wasn't normally the type to freak out over minor mishaps like this.

Maybe seeing that body shook me more than I realized, I thought. *Even if it wasn't real . . .*

That made my mind jump from my suitcase to a different kind of case. I wished I could talk to my friends about what had happened by the pool. But we couldn't talk freely with Alan around. He'd just sat down at the piano and was picking out "Jingle Bells" with one finger.

"What should we do now?" Bess asked. "Do you guys want to start unpacking, or—"

She was cut off by a sudden loud, terrified shriek from just outside the suite.

"Who was that?" Alan exclaimed.

I was already rushing toward the door. When I

burst into the hallway, a young woman was standing in front of the next door down, looking horrified. She was wearing a Superstar uniform and clutching a stack of folded towels to her chest.

"Is everyone okay?" Bess yelped, running out of the suite behind me.

My gaze had already shot from the maid to the kid crouched on the floor just across the hall. He had his back to us at first, but when he glanced back over his shoulder, my eyes widened.

"You!" I blurted out.

It was the bratty eight-year-old I'd seen earlier. What was his name again?

"Hey, it's Tobias!" George exclaimed as she skidded out into the hallway and stopped short.

"That's my name, don't wear it out," the kid snapped.

By now the maid had lowered the towels, revealing a name tag that identified her as Iris. "Oh!" she gasped. "I'm so sorry. He—he just startled me."

Tobias glared at her. "You practically broke my eardrum, screaming like that," he said. "I should sue you.

Then I could use the money to hire a helicopter to fly me out of here."

Just then a nearby door swung open. Tobias's father emerged. "What's going on out here?" he asked.

"Nothing." Tobias stood up, quickly shoving one hand deep into the pocket of his baggy cargo shorts.

"Hmm." His father leaned forward to peer at the maid's name tag. "Iris, is it? Is Tobias causing trouble?"

"No, no, no, not at all, sir." Iris took a quick step backward, clutching the towels to her again. "It's completely my fault, really. I wasn't paying enough attention to where I was going."

Tobias's father didn't look convinced as he looked over at his son. "Well, I hope he's behaving better than he was earlier today. It seems he's feeling a little, uh, cranky right now because he didn't want to come on this cruise."

"Yeah." Tobias scowled. "I wanted to go to Galaxy X. *That's* what I call a cool vacation. Not some stupid boat."

"That's enough, son." His father grabbed Tobias by the arm and pulled him into the room. "Sorry," he added once more before shutting the door.

"Wow," Bess said. "That kid's pretty obnoxious."

"Yeah, we sort of met him earlier." I glanced at the maid. "Are you okay? What'd he do to scare you?"

"Nothing." Iris shrugged. "Like I said, he just startled me. Excuse me, I'd better get back to work."

She turned and hurried off down the hall. "Excitement's over," Alan announced. "Better get back to my music." He headed back into the suite.

But I was still staring off after the maid. "She was acting kind of oddly, wasn't she?"

Bess grinned. "First your misplaced bag, and now this?" she teased. "You don't have to look for mysteries *everywhere*, Nancy."

"Yeah." George looked at the door to make sure Alan was out of earshot. "It's not like some eight-year-old is sending threatening e-mails to Brock Walker and planting fake bodies in pools."

I smiled. "I guess you're right."

We went back inside. Alan was at the piano again. Bess made a beeline for the luggage.

"I guess we might as well start unpacking," she said, picking up her cosmetics case.

I glanced at my pathetic little carry-on. There didn't seem to be much point in trying to settle in until Max found my suitcase. Besides, I had more important things to do.

"You guys go ahead," I said. "I think I'll go pick up a toothbrush in one of the onboard shops. Just in case."

"But I'm sure Max will—" George began.

"I know," I cut her off. "But I feel like taking a walk. I'll be back soon."

As soon as I was away from the suite, I pulled out my phone and texted Becca to see if she was free to talk. She texted back immediately, telling me she was in her office.

The office turned out to be a small, poorly lit, windowless cabin on one of the lower levels. It was crammed with two large desks and several filing cabinets. Becca was hunched over a laptop at one of the desks, typing frantically. When I knocked softly on the door frame, she glanced up and pushed her hair out of her eyes.

"Nancy!" she exclaimed. "Come on in. I'm just typing up the daily newsletter." She hit a button on the keyboard and grimaced. "I'm a little behind, thanks to all the commotion earlier."

"Yeah, about that." I shut the door behind me and perched on the edge of the other desk. "Did you find out anything else about what happened?"

Becca sighed. "Marcelo and the captain contacted HQ to see what to do. Verity told them to treat it as a prank and just move on."

"Verity?" I echoed.

"Verity Salinas," Becca said. "She's the CEO of Superstar Cruises."

"Oh, right. I don't think you mentioned her name before." I nodded. "So she doesn't want to involve the local police?"

Becca shook her head. "She said to let ship security handle it. They already did a little investigating and figured out that the mannequin came from one of the clothing shops on the promenade level. And that pink stuff in the water was drink mix swiped from the snack bar in the kids' playground area."

"Did they figure out who did it?"

"Not yet." Becca raked a hand through her hair, making her curls stand up wildly. "But I suppose there's no real harm done. We offered the newlyweds a free shore excursion in Ketchikan, and I think that satisfied them."

"Vince and Lacey," I said, remembering the frightened young woman and her new husband.

"Right." Becca smiled at me. "Good memory for names, Nancy. Maybe you should work in the cruise industry."

"I don't think so," I joked in return. "Bess and George could tell you I only remember details when they have to do with a case. Otherwise, I can't even find my keys most of the time!"

Becca chuckled, then glanced at her computer screen. "I don't have much time," she said. "But I guess I should fill you in on the latest trouble." She picked at a chipped spot on the corner of the desk. "I just found out today about a rumor circulating among the house-keeping staff."

"What kind of rumor?"

"That the company is already bankrupt, so nobody's going to get paid." Becca shook her head. "It's not true, obviously. The housekeeping supervisors managed to calm everybody down for now, but nobody seems to know where the rumor started. It's just one more thing going wrong. . . ."

"Yeah, that's what I wanted to talk to you about," I said. "You told me about the threat to Brock's family that made him cancel, and that some other bad stuff had happened. What's the other stuff?"

"Well, it started with an e-mail I got a couple of weeks ago."

"What did it say?"

Becca shrugged. "Just something about how I should back out of this cruise if I knew what was good for me, or something like that. But that's not all. There were a few incidents in the last couple of weeks. A shipment of supplies got lost in the mail and never turned up. Three of the ship's cooks quit a week before departure. Stuff like that."

"Okay, the e-mail sounds weird," I said. "But the other problems could just be ordinary bad luck or whatever, couldn't they?"

"Maybe. But what about the body in the pool? It takes more than bad luck to make something like that happen."

"Good point." I drummed my fingers on the desk, thinking over what she'd told me. "We should try to figure out possible motives. The e-mail makes it seem like someone's trying to scare you—maybe someone who's envious of your cool new job. Do you have any enemies onboard or any you can think of?"

"Not that I know of." Becca looked alarmed. "Do you really think someone's targeting me personally?"

"Not necessarily," I assured her. "I mean, for all we know other people could've received threatening e-mails too. Maybe someone's after your boss—Marcelo, is it?"

Becca looked dubious. "Everyone loves Marcelo. He's been in the business for years and has never had an enemy that I've heard of."

"Then maybe it's the captain," I said. "Or Verity, or

the company as a whole. Or maybe someone we haven't even thought of yet."

Becca smiled wryly. "That really narrows it down."

"Sorry." I chuckled. "I've learned it's better not to rule anything out without solid evidence. We need to keep thinking about motives and—"

I cut myself off as the door flew open. A woman stood in the doorway. She was in her early thirties, tall, blond, and attractive, dressed in a navy-blue evening gown with silver jewelry.

"There you are, Becca," the woman said in a husky, rather brusque voice tinged with an Eastern European accent. "Marcelo's wondering where you are—it's nearly dinnertime, you know."

"Oops!" Becca glanced at her watch and jumped to her feet. "Sorry, Tatjana. I lost track of time." She shot me an apologetic look. "I need to change into my evening clothes so I can greet guests at dinner. We'll have to chat later."

Tatjana glanced at me, her gray eyes curious. "Can I help with something?"

"No, I'm fine." I smiled at her. She shrugged and turned to follow Becca out of the office.

When I got back to the Hollywood Suite, I was relieved to see my suitcase standing near the piano. "You found it!" I exclaimed.

Max hurried over from the kitchenette in the corner, dusting a drinking glass and grinning at me. "Of course I did! I'm here to take care of you." He gestured to the yellow numbered tag hanging from the handle. "It got mislabeled somehow and ended up in an interior cabin at the opposite end of the ship. I'm so sorry for the inconvenience."

"It's okay," I said automatically. But I was frowning at that tag, feeling puzzled and a little uneasy. I'd watched the porter clip on the proper purple tag myself. How had it ended up being switched with this yellow one?

But I shook off the thought as quickly as it came. These things happened. It would be easy enough for one of those plastic tags to pop off while the busy porters were moving bags around.

Just then Bess hurried into the main room. She looked lovely in a dove-gray dress and heels.

"You're back!" she said. "Hurry up and get changed. And don't forget to wear something nice—Max says people usually dress up for the first night's dinner."

"Okay. Did you break the news to George?"

Bess grimaced. "I've been working on her for the past half hour. I think I finally convinced her that shorts and flip-flops are *not* proper dinner attire. But I'd better go make sure she didn't 'accidentally' spill something on the dress I loaned her."

I laughed. "I'll be ready in a few minutes," I promised.

My bedroom was beautifully designed, with a built-in bed, a large dresser, and a chair. I tossed my suitcase on the bed and clicked the latches. As my fingers brushed that yellow tag I hesitated briefly, once again wondering how the mix-up had happened. Then I shook my head and opened the suitcase.

My neatly folded clothes were still inside, held in place by a couple of nylon straps. Tucked into one of the straps was a ragged scrap of paper folded in two.

What's that? I thought. I hadn't put anything like that in there. I was positive.

I picked it up and unfolded it. When I saw the message written in handwritten block letters, I gasped.

I HOPE U GET LOST JUST LIKE UR BAG—& THAT U STAY LOST!

CHAPTER FOUR

Dinner Is Served

"I FEEL LIKE A GIANT GRAPE," GEORGE complained, tugging at the hem of her plum-colored wraparound dress. Well, technically speaking, it was *Bess's* dress. But George was wearing it. And she wasn't happy about it.

"I can't believe you didn't pack a single dressy outfit," Bess retorted. "Didn't you ever see a rerun of *The Love Boat*? Remember *Titanic*? People dress up on cruises. It's, like, a *thing*."

"Now, now, ladies," Alan put in soothingly. "You look fabulous—all three of you."

I forced a brief smile as Bess thanked him and George rolled her eyes. But I wasn't paying much attention to the conversation as we walked through the narrow halls leading from our suite to the dining room. I was still focused on that threatening note. Who could have left it in my suitcase? And why?

"It doesn't make sense," I murmured.

"What was that, Nancy?" Alan asked.

"Um, nothing," I said. "I mean, I said I hope the food's good. I'm hungry."

The others started chatting about the food, and my mind drifted again. Why would someone leave me a note like that? Before today, I'd never met a soul on board this cruise ship other than Bess, George, Alan, and Becca. Why would anyone have any reason to threaten me?

As careful as I'd been, I supposed it was possible that someone had found out why I was really there. Maybe that blogger Wendy overheard George and me talking about the case. Becca's coworker, Tatjana, could have lurked outside Becca's office long enough to eavesdrop. Someone could have hacked into Becca's e-mail account and read her messages to me last week. Far-fetched, but you never knew . . .

I shivered. Had my cover been blown? Was I trapped on a ship with someone who was out to get me?

"Wow," George said, stopping short so that I almost crashed into her. "This place is huge!"

I peered around her. We were in the entrance to the ship's main dining room, a cavernous space on one of the upper decks. It was plush and opulent, with crystal chandeliers glittering overhead and red-and-gold upholstery everywhere else. The smells of various types of food drifted toward us, along with the buzz of many conversations, the tinkle of glassware, and an occasional burst of laughter.

When we stepped inside, Alan craned his neck upward. "Check it out," he said with a grin. "Dinner beneath the stars—literally!"

Following his gaze, I saw that there were several skylights between the chandeliers. Through the closest one, we could see a large swath of the evening sky—

twilight blue washed with pink. Countless stars were just twinkling into sight, looking much closer than they did back home in River Heights.

"Gorgeous," I said, the view distracting me from my worries. At least for a moment.

A smiling hostess hurried toward us. "You're at table seventeen," she said after checking our ship IDs. "Follow me, please."

Table seventeen turned out to be a large round table set for nine located near the center of the room. When we arrived, three women in their sixties or seventies were already seated there.

"Welcome!" one of them said when she saw us. She was petite and tan, with short-cropped salt-and-pepper hair and wide-spaced blue eyes. "You young people must be some of our new dinner companions."

"Yes, we must," Alan said with a smile as he pulled out a chair for Bess. "I'm Alan, and these are my friends Bess, George, and Nancy." He pointed to each of us in turn.

"Lovely to meet you," the second woman spoke up.

She was taller and a little older than the first, with a graying blond bun and a bright smile. "I'm Alice, and these are my friends Babs and Coral."

"You can call us the ABCs," Coral spoke up with a titter. She was pleasantly plump and grandmotherly, with wire-rimmed glasses perched on her nose. "Get it? The ABCs—Alice, Babs, Coral."

"Nice to meet you," I said as I sat down between George and Babs.

"Yeah." George reached for her water glass. "I didn't realize we'd be sitting with other people."

Babs chuckled. "This must be your first cruise, then?"

"Yes, it is," Bess said. "And please don't be offended by what George said. She just meant—"

"It's all right, dear." Babs waved one wrinkled hand dismissively. "If it's your first time, a lot of things must seem rather strange."

Alice nodded. "But don't worry," she added. "The three of us are experienced cruisers. We'll show you the ropes."

"Really?" Alan said. "How many cruises have you been on?"

"Oh, dear, I'm not sure I can count that high anymore!" Coral giggled. "Let's just say it's enough that we should be able to answer any questions you may have. Right, girls?"

Alice nodded, but Babs was looking across the dining room. "I think our last two tablemates have arrived," she said.

I glanced over and saw the hostess approaching again. When I saw who was following her, I elbowed George. "Hey, it's the honeymooners!"

"Who?" Bess and Alan asked.

"Um, just someone we sort of met earlier," George told them.

By then the newcomers were at the table. Vince and Lacey both appeared to be in a much better mood than they had been the last time we'd seen them. Lacey looked lovely in a soft blue gown, and Vince was handsomer than ever in his dinner jacket and tie.

Soon more introductions had been traded. "Honey-mooners, eh?" Coral said, winking at the rest of us. "Don't worry, we won't mind if you need to kiss between courses."

Meanwhile Babs was leaning forward, peering at Lacey. "You look familiar, my dear," she said. "Doesn't she, girls?"

Alice glanced over. "Oh, yes!" she exclaimed. "You don't have a sister who works for Jubilee Cruise Lines, do you?"

Coral gasped. "You're right! Why, if Lacey had darker hair and blue eyes, she'd be the spitting image of that pretty young singer on our Caribbean cruise last year!"

Lacey looked taken aback. "Um, no, you must be mistaken. I don't have a sister."

Vince put a protective arm around her shoulders. "It's okay," he told her. Then he smiled at the ABCs. "She's a little shy. Always gets tongue-tied when someone mentions how beautiful she is, even though it happens all the time."

"Well, of course it must!" Babs exclaimed, while Coral tut-tutted pleasantly.

Lacey gave them a wan smile. "I only wish I *was* related to someone at Jubilee," she said softly. "Maybe then we'd be on one of their cruises right now, instead of taking a chance on this brand-new untested cruise line." She shivered. "I haven't felt right since Vince and I spotted that body earlier."

"Body?" Alice's eyes widened. "What body?"

"Didn't you hear what happened at the pool right before we set sail?" Vince asked.

Coral leaned forward. "No, but do tell!"

I traded a worried look with Bess and George as the honeymooners started describing what had happened. The cruise director might have smoothed things over earlier, but it seemed the gossip was still spreading.

Just then there was a clatter from the next table. I glanced over and saw that Tobias, the bratty kid from our hall, had just dropped an entire tray of rolls on the floor. His father was scolding him while his mother bent down to try to salvage the rolls. Several waiters were already making a beeline for the table.

"That kid causes a commotion everywhere he goes, doesn't he?" George said.

I nodded. I'd just noticed that Wendy the travel blogger was at the same table as Tobias. She'd traded in her casual granny dress for a pink tulle vintage prom gown and a headband with a large plastic flower on it. Her laptop sat on the table beside her plate as she chattered nonstop at the man sitting next to her. I wasn't sure she'd even noticed the roll mishap.

"Whoa!" Alan exclaimed suddenly, staring off in a different direction. "Do you see who I see?"

As I glanced that way, a flash of color caught my eye. It was Mr. Hawaiian Shirt. He was sitting at another table with half a dozen other people. The others all appeared to be chatting and having a good time, but he was slumped in his chair, playing with his fork and looking fairly miserable.

George saw him too. "Hey! That mustache guy we met earlier didn't even bother to change clothes. So why do I have to dress up?" she complained.

"Huh?" Alan glanced at the man. "No, look over there. It's Merk the Jerk!"

He was pointing toward a different table. "Merk the Jerk," I echoed. "He's a stand-up comedian, right?"

"Yeah," George said. "His real name's Lou Merk. He's had a couple of TV specials and been in a few movies and some online stuff."

"I suppose he must be part of the shipboard entertainment." Babs peered in that direction. She sighed. "I'm just so disappointed that Brock Walker had to cancel!"

Just then a pretty young waitress hurried toward us. "Good evening," she said in a lilting Jamaican accent. "I'm Daisy, and I'll be your server tonight."

"Daisy?" George grinned. "What, are all the ship's employees required to have flower names or something?"

Daisy looked confused, though she smiled politely. "Can I start you off with some drinks?"

"Iris, remember?" George glanced around at Alan, Bess, and me. "That maid we saw earlier was named Iris, remember? Get it? Flower names?"

Bess ignored her. "I'd love an iced tea with lemon," she told Daisy.

As the others gave their drink orders, I noticed several men with video cameras hoisted on their shoulders entering the dining room. "What's going on over there?" I asked the waitress when she turned toward me.

She glanced over. "Let me get the maître d' so you can ask him."

Daisy walked to the front of the dining room and moments later returned with the maître d' in tow. His name tag read MR. PHILLIPS. I repeated my question.

"The camera crew?" he said. "They're just the ad people."

"Ad people?" Bess echoed.

"Didn't you get the insert in your info packages?" Mr. Phillips looked troubled. "It should have been covered in there."

Vince glanced at his wife. "We got the insert."

"So did we," Coral put in as her friends nodded.

"That explains it," Alan said. "See, we just won this cruise last week in an online contest. We didn't have time to get any info packs in the mail or anything."

Mr. Phillips nodded and explained, "The company hired the crew to do some candid filming during this inaugural cruise—just happy guests enjoying themselves, things like that. The footage will be used for future web ads and such."

"We could be in ads?" George sounded interested. "Cool."

"I do hope you won't mind being filmed," he continued. "But of course anyone who doesn't wish to take part should inform a member of the cruise staff as soon as possible." Mr. Phillips excused himself and returned to his post.

As Daisy finished taking our order and hurried off, I glanced again at the camera crew. When had they started filming? Could they have captured any footage earlier in the day that might help with the case? I made a mental note to try to track them down later.

"That was delicious." Bess pushed her chair back from the table about half an hour later. "If you'll all excuse me, I need to go powder my nose."

Yeah, Bess actually says things like that. Without irony, even. What can I say? It works for her.

"I'll come with you," I said quickly, dropping my cloth napkin beside my plate. "Uh, for the nose powdering, that is."

"Me too." George got up and followed us.

Soon we were in the ladies' lounge. It was just as opulent as the dining room—plush carpeting, chandeliers, a wall of mirrors with delicate upholstered stools in front of them, the works. But I barely spared a glance for any of it.

"Is anyone else in here?" I asked, peeking under the stall doors.

"Doesn't look like it." Bess sat down at the mirror and pulled a compact out of her purse. "Why? Do you have any new theories?"

"Not really." I quickly told her and George my idea about talking to the camera crew. "You never know," I said. "Maybe they caught someone carrying that mannequin around or something."

"Anything's possible." George sounded dubious. She was prowling back and forth across the lounge area, tugging at her dress as if it was choking her. "I guess this means you've decided there really is a mystery, huh?"

"It's sure looking that way." I glanced around again, making doubly sure we were alone. "And that's not all—I think someone's onto us."

Bess stopped applying powder to her already flawless skin and glanced at me in the mirror. "Onto us? What do you mean?"

"Something happened right before dinner," I began. "I've been dying to tell you, but with Alan around . . ." I went on to tell them about the note in my suitcase.

By the time I finished, Bess's eyes were wide and worried. "That really sounds like someone was threatening you!"

"Don't sound so shocked," George told her. "It's not like Nancy's never been threatened before. It kind of goes with the territory."

"Maybe," I agreed. "But nobody's supposed to

know why I'm really here, remember? So who could have done it?"

Before my friends could answer, the door swung open. Two giggling preteen girls rushed in with their middle-aged moms right behind them. Bess smiled politely, then stood up.

"We should get back to the table," she said, dropping her makeup back in her purse. "We don't want Alan to worry."

I was disappointed. My friends are always good at helping me figure things out, and I really wanted to talk about possible motives and suspects. But another woman was already coming in, and I realized our private moment was over.

"Let's go," I agreed with a sigh.

The bathroom was located in a hallway between the dining room and the stairwell. As we headed toward the former, we passed a door marked EMPLOYEES ONLY. It was standing slightly ajar, and I could hear angry voices coming from inside.

I paused, a little surprised. All the ship's employees

seemed to make a point of staying polite and cheerful anywhere passengers might hear. But whatever was going on just inside that door sounded anything but polite or cheerful. Most of it was too muffled to make out, though it sounded like two men arguing. Then one of them raised his voice.

"Drop it, John!" he said sharply. "Or I'll make sure you never make it to Anchorage!"

My eyes widened. That sounded pretty ominous.

"Hey," I called to my friends, who were a few steps ahead. "Hang on, I want to—"

"Ladies!" A loud, jovial voice interrupted me. Turning, I saw Marcelo, Becca's boss, hurrying up behind me, a broad smile on his handsome face. "I hope you're not lost. Can I have the honor of accompanying you back to the dining room?"

"Sure," Bess said with a smile.

I glanced helplessly at the door. But it was too late. The voices had stopped, so I had little choice but to allow the cruise director to sweep us all back into the dining room.

CHAPTER FIVE

~

Dangerous Games

"YOU'RE UP EARLY," I SAID AS I WALKED into the main room of the suite the next morning.

Bess glanced up with a smile. She was sitting at the glass-topped coffee table, stirring milk into a steaming mug of tea.

"You too," she said. "Luckily, Max the butler gets up even earlier. He brought us these." She waved a hand at the platter of bagels, doughnuts, and other pastries on the table in front of her.

"Great." I grabbed a glazed doughnut and took a bite. Then I wandered toward the balcony. The glass doors were open, offering a spectacular view of the shoreline we were passing as the ship made its way from Vancouver to our first shore stop in Ketchikan. Low hills draped in thick forests of pine and spruce tumbled to meet the sparkling deep-blue water, while in the distance, snow-capped peaks rose to meet the sky.

"Nice scenery, huh?" Bess said. "I could stare at that view all day."

I shot her a rueful look. "Me too. Unfortunately we don't have time," I said. "Have you seen George yet?"

Bess snorted. "What do you think? She's not exactly a morning person, remember?"

I grinned. "Understatement of the year. What about Alan?"

"Haven't seen him yet either. I guess he's still asleep."

"Good. Let's get George and get out of here before he wakes up," I said. "This could be our best chance to talk freely."

Shooting one last glance at the scenery, I turned and led the way toward the bedrooms. We tiptoed past

Alan's door. The sound of loud snoring was coming from inside.

Even louder snoring was coming from George's room. We let ourselves in. She was curled up on her side, with her back to us.

Bess leaned over and poked her cousin in the shoulder. "Rise and shine," she whispered loudly.

There was no response. I grabbed George's foot and tickled it. She shot up into a sitting position.

"Hey!" she blurted out.

"Shh!" Bess and I hissed.

George blinked stupidly for a moment, then glared at us. "What time is it?" she mumbled, making a move to lie down again.

But Bess was too fast for her. Grabbing her cousin's arm, she gave a yank that almost pulled her out of bed. "Get up," she ordered. "We need to get out of here before Alan wakes up. Nancy wants to talk."

It took a little more persuading, but finally we got her up. Leaving her to get dressed, Bess and I returned to the main room. I quickly gulped down some coffee while she scribbled a note for Alan.

"I'm telling him we're checking out the spa facilities to see if we can get facials this morning," she told me. "That should sound girly enough that he won't want to join us."

"No. But he might wonder why *George* wanted to join us," I joked just as George emerged, yawning and tousled, with damp hair from the shower and dressed in shorts and a River Heights University T-shirt.

"Huh? What'd you say?" she demanded sleepily.

"Never mind. Let's get out of here." I grabbed a jelly doughnut, stuffed it in her hand, then aimed her toward the door.

When we emerged from the suite, the hallway was empty except for a maid sweeping nearby. It was Iris from the day before.

"Hi." I smiled at her as we passed. "Excuse us."

"Guess she must be assigned to Tobias's cabin, like Max is to ours," Bess whispered as we hurried around the corner.

"Yeah." I grimaced. "Poor thing."

I forgot about the maid as I led the way toward the elevators. "Where are we going?" George asked, sounding marginally more awake as she finished the last bite of doughnut and licked jelly and powdered sugar off her fingers.

"Becca's office," I replied. "I'm hoping it's still early enough to catch her there. I want to finish our talk and maybe get a look at that threatening e-mail she got before the cruise. I know it's a stretch, but I might be able to tell if it was written by the same person who left me that note yesterday."

But when we knocked on Becca's door, there was no answer. I texted her and got a reply back within a minute or two.

"Where is she?" Bess asked as I scanned the message.

"She's hosting some kind of VIP breakfast reception," I said with a sigh. "Says she'll be tied up for the next hour or two at least. Oh well."

"Does that mean I got up at the crack of dawn for nothing?" George complained.

I ignored that. "Let's go check out the pool," I

said. "Maybe we missed a clue yesterday."

But that was another dead end. When we reached the pool area, it was spotless. Any trace of "blood" was gone from the water, which sparkled like glass beneath the early morning sun. Every trash receptacle was empty and appeared to have been bleached clean. Even the pool chairs were arranged in perfect lines.

Bess glanced into the same trash bin where George and I had found that drink mix container. "If there were any clues, they've definitely been cleaned up by now," she commented. "The cleaning staff here mean business!"

"Yeah." My shoulders slumped as I considered what to do next. "Maybe we should try the kitchen. Last night I heard arguing. . . ."

I filled them in on that snippet of argument I'd overheard as we walked. George looked dubious.

"Do you really think some random squabble is part of our case?" she asked.

I shrugged. "Probably not. But you never know. We're not exactly swimming in useful clues right now, in case you haven't noticed."

The main dining room was hushed and empty as we passed. But we heard the sounds of activity coming from a door right across the hall.

"That's the café," Bess said. "It's where we're supposed to eat breakfast and lunch. Dinner, too, if we don't feel like being so formal."

"What?" George yelped. "You didn't tell me that before you forced me to dress up like I was entering some girly-girl beauty pageant."

"Give it a rest," I told her. "Wearing a dress for a couple of hours didn't kill you, did it?"

I glanced into the café, which in this case seemed to be short for cafeteria. The setting was much less formal than the dining room, with passengers choosing their food from a long buffet line, then finding seats wherever they pleased. There were quite a few early risers in there, helping themselves to eggs, Danish, or fruit salad. I even spotted Tobias's parents, though the little boy was nowhere in sight.

We continued past the door to the employees-only entrance. As soon as we pushed it open, a cacophony of sounds and smells struck us—the sizzle of butter, the smell of bacon and eggs, the shouts of a dozen or more kitchen workers asking for more pancake batter or whatever. The hustle and bustle was a stark contrast to the serene peace of most of the ship.

"Now what?" George murmured in my ear. "Someone's going to notice us and kick us out soon."

I hardly heard her. I'd just spotted a familiar face. It was Mr. Hawaiian Shirt. Today's shirt bore a different raucous pattern from yesterday's, but otherwise he looked exactly the same. He was leaning against a stainless-steel countertop, stroking his mustache with one finger as he talked to a couple of young kitchen workers washing dishes nearby.

That was kind of weird. The first time we'd encountered him, he'd acted as if he didn't know his way around the ship. And last night he'd been sitting in the dining room like just any other guest. Could he actually be some kind of supervisor or something? He didn't exactly dress like the rest of the crew, but years of amateur sleuthing had taught me to assume nothing.

"Excuse me," I said, stepping over to him. "Do you work here?"

He blinked at me. "Oh, hello again," he said. "No, I don't work here. I just came back here to thank these hardworking people for their efforts and let them know it's appreciated by someone." He waved one meaty hand to indicate the kitchen staff, though the workers nearby had turned away and seemed to be pointedly ignoring him. "Now if you'll excuse me, I need some coffee."

Pushing past us, he hurried out of the kitchen. Bess stared after him.

"That was kind of a strange answer," she said.

George shrugged. "He seems like kind of a strange guy."

I tapped the nearest worker on the shoulder. "Hi," I said. "I don't mean to bother you, but I wonder if I could ask you a few questions."

The worker, a short, swarthy man with intelligent dark eyes, shrugged. "I'm sorry, miss," he said with a shy smile. "Guests should not be back here."

"I know. This'll just take a moment." I made my

smile as ingratiating as possible. "I was just wondering if there's been any trouble around here lately. In the kitchen, I mean. Anybody not getting along?"

"I would hope not," the worker responded. "If anything is upsetting you, however, the cruise staff is always available for complaints." He picked up a stack of dripping pans. "If you'll excuse me, I have to get back to work."

He hurried off before I could respond. I frowned, glancing around for another victim. At that moment the door swung open behind us.

"This way, kids!" a cheerful voice sang out. "Next I'm going to show you where all the food on the ship is prepared! If you're good, you might even get some samples!"

"Yay, samples!" several childish voices cheered.

"Good," another kid said. "I'm starved."

That last voice sounded cranky. And familiar. Turning, I saw that a whole group of kids had just entered the kitchen, led by the youth activities coordinator Becca had pointed out to Tobias's family yesterday.

And speaking of Tobias . . .

"This is boring," Tobias went on, scowling at the coordinator. "When are you going to show us something cool?"

The coordinator's smile barely wavered. "Now, now, Tobias," he began. "The tour's barely started. Just give it a chance, and I'm sure you—" He cut himself off as he noticed my friends and me. "Oh, hello," he said, hurrying over. His name tag identified him as Hiro. "You must be lost. Are you looking for the café?"

"No, we were just looking around," I said. "Thanks."

Hiro looked uncertain. "Um, passengers really shouldn't be back here."

"Why not?" George pointed at the kids. "They're passengers, right?"

"Yes," Hiro said. "But they're only here as part of the exclusive backstage tour of the ship."

"We're going to see everything!" a little girl spoke up eagerly. "Even the engine!"

Hiro smiled at her. "That's right, Maria," he said. Then he turned back to us. "There's a similar tour for adults—I think it's the day after tomorrow. If you're interested, all you have to do is let someone from the cruise staff know."

"Okay, maybe we will," Bess said. "Come on, girls, let's move on."

George and I followed her into the hall. "Okay, smelling all that food cooking made me hungry," George said. "What say we hit up that café? I'm not much good at sleuthing on an empty stomach."

"Take it easy, George," I said. "Just because it's all-you-can-eat, that doesn't mean you have to try to eat it all."

George looked up from her fourth helping of scrambled eggs. Bess and I had finished eating a good twenty minutes ago, but George seemed to be a bottomless pit.

"I'm almost done," she mumbled through a mouthful of toast.

Bess checked her watch. "I should check in with Alan," she says. "I just realized it's been, like, an hour and a half since we left the suite. He's probably wondering where we are." She pulled out her phone. "I'm surprised he hasn't been calling or texting me."

"Maybe he's still asleep," I suggested.

"Maybe." Bess texted him. A moment later her phone buzzed. "Nope, he's up," she reported a moment later. "He just texted me back."

By the time George finished her eggs, Bess had arranged to meet Alan on the Anchorage Action deck.

When we got there, Alan was waiting for us outside an Alaskan-themed snack bar. "Good morning, ladies," he sang out, stooping to plant a kiss on Bess's cheek. "You three were out and about early today!"

"Sorry for abandoning you," Bess told him, slipping her hand into his. "I just couldn't wait to check out the spa. Did you have breakfast?"

"Yes, back at the suite," he replied, patting his belly. "I couldn't let all those pastries go to waste! But now I'm thinking I need to work some of it off before lunch. What do you say to a round of miniature golf?" He gestured to a sign nearby. "I'll buy a smoothie for anyone who can beat my score."

"Mini golf? I'm awesome at that!" George said. "You're on."

"Why don't you three go ahead?" I said. "I'm not really in the mood for mini golf. I might go check out the shops or something."

Actually, I was thinking that playing miniature golf was a waste of time when I could be investigating. If I could get away, I'd have some time to snoop around, maybe track down that camera crew and see if they'd let me look at their footage.

But Alan shook his head. "What, are you afraid I'll beat you?" he teased. "Come on, Nancy, you can't chicken out."

I forced a smile. "It's not that. . . ."

Just then a pair of small boys came charging at us from around the corner of the snack bar. "I win!" one of them shouted as both skidded to a halt.

A moment later several other kids appeared too. Finally Hiro arrived, breathless and dragging Tobias by one hand. "Wait up, kids!" he called as his charges swarmed the snack bar. "Everyone's got to sit quietly before anyone gets their snack, okay?" Finally noticing us standing there, he smiled. "Oh, hello," he said. "Can I help you folks find anything?"

"Nope, we're good, bro," Alan told him. "We're just on our way to play some mini golf."

"Wonderful!" Hiro beamed at us. "Our brand-new miniature golf course is fabulous. It features a rugged Alaska theme."

"Sounds cool, thanks." Alan glanced at me as Hiro disappeared into the snack bar. "So what do you say, Nancy? You're not seriously going to ditch us, are you?"

I shot my friends a look, then glanced back at Alan. Was that a hint of suspicion in his eyes?

"Um, okay," I said. "You talked me into it."

The mini-golf course was actually pretty cool. As Hiro had promised, it featured an Alaskan theme complete with fake glaciers, grinning totem poles, a life-size moose, and a roaring grizzly on its hind legs.

"This is awesome!" Alan exclaimed. "Who wants to go first?"

For a while we had the place to ourselves. Just as

Bess was lining up a shot at a waterfall with little fake salmon leaping out of the water, we heard voices coming our way.

"Check it out," George said. "It's that camera crew. They probably heard about my awesome swing and ran right up here to get it on film."

Two burly cameramen stepped onto the course, along with a skinny young man dressed in black jeans and a gray T-shirt. Several passengers trailed in behind them.

"This way, everyone!" the skinny guy called. "Grab some clubs and we'll get started."

"I can't believe I'm gonna be in pictures!" an old man with a ring of white hair around his bald head exclaimed with a grin. "I'm ready for my close-up!"

"Stop, Harold." The woman with him rolled her eyes, rearranging her sun hat atop her tidy red curls. "You're such a ham!"

I recognized them as part of that family reunion we'd seen at the beginning of the trip. The group had been hard to miss at dinner last night, taking up three tables all on their own.

The thin young man spotted my friends and me and hurried over. "Good morning," he said. "I'm Claude, the director of the film crew." He looked me up and down. "Did anyone ever tell you that hair of yours is totally cinematic?"

I touched my hair, feeling self-conscious. "Um, I don't think so."

Claude glanced at the cameramen, who were already filming various parts of the mini-golf course. Establishing shots, I guessed.

"Baraz, get over here!" Claude barked. "I want to get this girl on film."

One of the camera operators, a man with a buzz cut, stepped toward us. "Sure, boss," he said, pointing his camera at me.

"No, not there—we need a better background." Claude glanced around, tapping his chin. "Something to set off that hair, that all-American complexion . . ."

"How about the moose?" Alan suggested. "That might look cool."

"Perfect!" The director clapped his hands. "The strawberry blond should really pop against the dark-brown fur."

I stepped toward the moose. Everyone was staring at me. Well, almost everyone. Bess and Alan seemed to have taken the distraction as an opportunity for a romantic moment. They were standing close together by the moose's side, laughing and talking softly while holding hands. But everyone else? Staring. At me.

"Is this okay?" I asked, striking a golf stance with my club near the moose obstacle.

"Closer," the director ordered. "We need to get all of the moose in frame."

I took a step back, glancing up at the moose's head looming above me. "Okay, now what?"

"Just forget that we're here," the director said. "Pretend you're just playing golf. Laugh and toss your hair and act normally."

I didn't bother to point out that I wouldn't be acting normally if I started tossing my hair around while I was playing mini golf. I quickly lined up my shot on the green, aiming for the hole directly underneath the towering moose.

Just as I was about to swing, I sensed something—movement right above me. Acting on instinct, I dropped my club and jumped back.

A split second later, one of the fake moose's huge antlers came crashing down—right where I'd just been standing.

CHAPTER SIX

◊

Animal Instincts

"NANCY!" BESS CRIED. "ARE YOU OKAY?"

"Yes. I mean no." I glanced down at my left arm, realizing that it was hurting. There was a trickle of blood on my forearm. "I mean, um, sort of."

By now George, Claude, and various others had reached me too. "Stand back, please!" Claude ordered. "She is injured!"

"Oh, dear!" one of the older ladies watching exclaimed.

"Shall we call the medic?" the old man called out.

"Of course we should, Harold!" his wife said. "Don't be such an old fool!"

Just then a young man in a Superstar uniform elbowed his way to the front of the crowd. It was Mike, the employee who'd helped us pick out our clubs. Hiro the youth coordinator was right behind him.

"What happened?" Mike asked. "You're bleeding."

"I'll call a medic." Hiro whipped out a cell phone.

"No, I'm okay." I took a deep breath, willing my heartbeat to return to normal. Then I glanced at my arm. "It's just a scrape—see? The edge of the antler must've caught me on its way down."

George frowned and glanced at the moose. "How'd that happen, anyway?" she wondered. Grabbing the moose's nose, she swung her leg up onto its knee and started climbing.

"Miss! Get down from here!" Mike warned. "Please, the medic will be here shortly."

"I told you, I'm fine," I insisted. "I don't need a medic."

George let out a cry. "Check this out!" she exclaimed. She'd climbed higher and was straddling the moose's neck by now. "It looks like someone loosened the screws that were holding that antler in place. All it would take is for someone to touch the moose, and *bam*! Down it would come."

Bess went white. "Oh no!" she cried. "It was me! I leaned back against the moose's side to get a better view of Nancy. It's all my fault!"

"Don't be silly." I grabbed her hand and squeezed it. "You had no way of knowing those screws were loose. Anyway, I'm fine."

Mike looked troubled. "This mini-golf course is brand-new," he said. "Someone must have forgotten to tighten those screws when they were putting everything together during setup."

Hiro bit his lip and clapped his hands sharply. "Please step away from the obstacles, everyone!" he called out. "We'll have to check them all for safety before the course can reopen. This was just an unfortunate accident, but we're taking care of it."

An accident? I wasn't so sure. From what I could tell, it seemed to fit the pattern of sabotage so far.

And I'm a target again, a little voice in my head added.

I shook off the thought. Accident or not, there was

no way the saboteur could have known I'd be the one standing beneath the moose. Was there?

Suddenly nervous, I glanced around. Two more employees had appeared and were busy herding Harold, his wife, and the other onlookers over toward the snack bar. Bess still looked distraught as she stared at my arm. Alan was next to her, murmuring into her ear. Most of the others were watching George climb down from the moose, including one of the cameramen, who was filming it.

My eyes widened as I remembered the cameras. The whole incident had been caught on tape! This could be the break we needed.

I glanced around. "Where's the other camera guy—Baraz?" I asked Claude. "We should look at the footage he got and see if we can tell what happened."

Claude glanced around too. "Looks like Baraz has disappeared." He frowned and muttered, "Again."

The other cameraman heard us and stepped forward. "I might have something," he offered. "The moose was in the background of what I was filming. See?"

He held out the camera so Claude and I could see its little playback screen. George, Bess, Alan, Mike, and Hiro huddled behind me, peering over my shoulders.

The playback focused on Bess and Alan. It was obvious that the cameraman had been going for a cute, romantic human interest scene of the two of them. They were standing to one side of the moose, laughing and flirting. I was barely visible in one corner, first standing there stiffly, then shuffling closer to the moose and lining up my shot.

"No!" Bess exclaimed as she watched Alan put his arm around her on the monitor, the two of them leaning back against the moose's furry side to watch my shot. "See? It really was my fault!"

"Our fault." Alan glanced at me. "We're so sorry, Nancy."

I waved him off, focusing on the monitor. "Can you play it back again?" I asked the camera operator.

But it was no use. The accident was visible in the background, but it was a pretty awkward angle, and we couldn't see much more than we already knew. The only thing the footage confirmed was that nobody else had been close enough to tamper with the moose.

As the second playback ended, my phone buzzed. I glanced at it and saw a text from Becca: SOMETHING ELSE JUST HAPPENED, she wrote. GOING 2 CHECK IT OUT. WILL UPDATE SOON.

The medic, a brisk woman in her thirties, appeared at that moment. "Step aside, please," she ordered. "Let's have a look."

She was still examining my arm when Becca rushed in, breathless and pink-cheeked. "Nancy!" she exclaimed when she saw me.

I smiled weakly as we both realized at the same time that I was the "something else" she'd just texted me about. One of the employees must have called her.

"I'm okay," I told her. I waved a hand at the medic. "This is just a precaution."

Becca nodded, though she didn't seem to be focused on me anymore. She was staring at Hiro, who was kneeling down to examine the fallen antler. There was a strange expression on Becca's face, one I couldn't quite figure out. What did that mean?

Before I could pull her aside to ask, Marcelo arrived on the scene. "Well, now," he exclaimed in his jovial voice. "What do we have here? Attacking mooses? Or is it meeses?" He chuckled. "I can never remember which it is." He came over and put a hand on my shoulder. "How is she, doc?" he asked the medic.

"She'll be fine," the woman replied. "But I'd better take her to the clinic and clean that scrape."

"It's okay," I said. "I have a Band-Aid back in the suite."

Just then Tobias stomped in, pushing past an employee who tried to stop him. "Hey!" he shouted. "When's the stupid tour going to start again?"

Hiro looked startled, as if he'd just remembered what he was supposed to be doing. "Sorry, Tobias," he said. "I'll be right there."

Tobias snorted and turned away. "Not that I care," he announced to no one in particular. "So far it's so boring that I might as well be sitting in my room staring at the wall."

Hiro shot Becca a nervous glance, then hurried after the boy. Suddenly Becca's strange look earlier made more sense. I guessed that as assistant cruise director, she was probably Hiro's direct supervisor. He had to feel embarrassed about getting caught abandoning his young charges, even given the unusual circumstances.

"You'll like the next part, Tobias," Hiro called out. "We're going to meet Captain Peterson and see all the computers and other high-tech stuff in the control room. Won't that be cool? I heard you're a real computer whiz. . . ."

His voice faded as he disappeared around the corner. Meanwhile the medic poked me in the shoulder. "Come," she said. "We're going to the clinic. No arguing."

Ten minutes later I was sitting on a cold plastic chair in a small but well-stocked medical clinic near the center of the ship while a nurse put a Band-Aid over my scrape. The medic was at a desk nearby, scribbling notes on some paperwork.

"Can I go now?" I called to her.

She glanced up and opened her mouth to answer. At that moment the door flew open and Wendy the blogger rushed in.

"Oh my gosh!" she cried when she spotted me. "Are you okay, Nancy? I just heard what happened!"

"News travels fast around here," I said.

The nurse was already bustling forward. "I'm sorry," she said. "Patients only allowed in here."

"But I want to interview her for my blog!" Wendy protested.

"You heard her. Out," the medic said sternly. "You can visit with your friend once she's released."

I didn't bother to explain that Wendy and I weren't exactly friends. Frankly, I was surprised she'd remembered my name.

Maybe she should be a suspect, I thought. *It's odd how she keeps turning up right after bad stuff happens. And wouldn't covering a bunch of crazy cruise disasters be a big draw for her travel blog?*

I was afraid Wendy might be waiting for me when

the medic finally released me from the clinic. Instead I found my friends out in the hall.

"Oh, good," Alan joked when he saw the bandage on my arm. "We were afraid they'd have to amputate."

"Very funny," I said with a smile—and a flash of guilt for wishing he wasn't there. I really wanted to talk to Bess and George about my new Wendy theory.

But that didn't seem likely to happen anytime soon. It was lunchtime by now, and Alan dragged us off toward the café. "I've heard the buffet on this ship is spectacular," he said.

"It is," George told him. "At least breakfast was pretty amazing."

"Yeah, and George would know. She ate most of it." Bess glanced at her cousin. "I can't believe you're ready for lunch already. Do you have a tapeworm or something?"

George shrugged. "Must be the sea air."

When we entered the café, at least half the tables were already occupied. More people were in the buffet line, helping themselves to the mountains of food piled there.

I glanced around, spotting a few familiar faces in the crowd as my friends and I joined the line to grab trays. Vince and Lacey were huddled over a single plate of french fries. The ABCs were at a different table, chatting with some passengers I didn't recognize. Tobias and his parents had a table to themselves near the dessert section.

"Look, there's Merk the Jerk again!" Alan pointed toward the center of the room. "Think he'd give me an autograph?"

Without waiting for an answer, he rushed off toward the table where the comedian was sitting. Merk was talking loudly, though I couldn't make out what he was saying from that distance. Whatever it was must have been funny, though, since the crowd gathered around him was laughing. I noticed that Wendy the blogger was among that crowd. So were a couple of cameramen, who were filming the whole scene.

George was looking that way too. "There's a motive for you," she commented.

"Huh?" I glanced at her as I grabbed a tray.

"Merk," George said. "With Brock out of the picture, he's the headline entertainment on this cruise now. That's got to be a boost to his career, right? Especially if he's featured in all the ads and stuff." She gestured toward the cameramen.

Bess reached for a roll. "That's true," she said. "But what about the pool incident and the other trouble? He'd have no motive for that stuff."

"Or would he?" I said thoughtfully, jumping back again to my theory about Wendy the blogger. Could the same idea apply here? "If this cruise becomes notorious enough, everyone will want to hear about it. And one place they'll look is online video sites."

George nodded. "And voilà—there's Merk!" she said, pausing to grab a handful of potato chips off the buffet. "It kind of makes sense."

"Only kind of." Bess still looked dubious. "I mean, Merk might not be A-list. But would he really risk his whole reputation like that?"

I realized it was kind of unlikely. But there was no more time to discuss it. Alan was on his way back from Merk's table.

"I couldn't even get close enough to ask," he reported, leaning past us to pick up a sandwich, which he set on Bess's tray. "I'll have to try again later."

As we sat down and started eating, I was surprised to see the ship's captain making a beeline for our table. He was a handsome, broad-shouldered man of about fifty. I'd seen him from a distance, but hadn't met him yet.

"Good afternoon," he greeted us, his eyes flicking over the other three before settling on me. "I'm Captain Reece Peterson. I was hoping to find you here." His gaze wandered to the bandage on my forearm. "I heard about the—er—incident at the miniature golf course earlier."

"Yeah," George said. "Nancy almost got killed by that vicious moose. That's probably worth a free shore meal in Ketchikan at least, huh?"

Bess elbowed her cousin hard in the ribs. "She's just kidding," she told the captain with a smile. "Nancy's fine."

"Yeah," I added. "It's just a flesh wound."

I expected him to smile and move on. But he just

stood there for a moment, shifting his weight from one foot to the other. The expression on his tanned, chiseled face was troubled.

"Good, good," he said after an awkward delay. "Uh, Marcelo tells me there were several ship personnel on the scene assisting you when he arrived. Do you happen to recall who they were? We just want to, uh, commend them."

"Yoo-hoo! Captain Peterson!" Just then Coral hurried over, all smiles. "Are you getting acquainted with our lovely young first-time cruisers?"

The captain turned to smile and trade pleasantries with her, giving me the chance to shoot a perplexed glance at Bess and George. Why had the captain just asked me which employees had been present during my accident? Could he be worried that one of them was involved? Was it possible that he knew who I really was and why I was there? Becca claimed that she was the only one onboard who did. But what if Verity had filled him in without telling Becca?

By then Coral was moving on toward the buffet

line, saying something about testing out all the desserts. The captain turned back to me.

"About those employees, Miss Drew . . . ," he began.

I watched as Coral reached the dessert area, mostly as an excuse not to meet the captain's eye. So I was looking right at her when she reached for a pastry, let out a loud gasp—and then crumpled to the floor!

"Coral!" I blurted out, on my feet before I knew it.

Other people closer to her were exclaiming in alarm and rushing to help as well. I was halfway there when the screams started.

"What's going on?" George panted in my ear as she caught up to me. "Did Coral just faint?"

"I guess so. But what's going on there?" My gaze shot from the people kneeling beside Coral to the buffet, where several other passengers were peering at a tray piled high with pastries.

"Stop!" a man I didn't know cried as George and I came closer. "Stand back! There's a tarantula in the cream puffs!"

CHAPTER SEVEN

Unusual Suspects

I GASPED AS I SAW SOMETHING SCUTTLE over an éclair and disappear behind a pile of brownies. "Was that really . . . ," I began.

"A tarantula!" George finished. "Whoa!"

"Don't hurt her!" a voice rang out behind us, cutting through the clamor. "Please! She's friendly."

"Tobias!" Bess exclaimed. She and Alan had caught up by now. "What's he doing?"

We all watched as the kid pushed his way to the buffet. Standing on tiptoes to peer over the pastry tray, he leaned forward and scooped something up. When he turned around, we could all see a huge, hairy spider perched on his hand.

"Tobias!" His father had hurried forward by now as well. "Is that Hazel?"

"Hazel?" George echoed, raising one eyebrow.

"No wonder Coral fainted," I said, staring as the spider climbed slowly up Tobias's arm. Her black-and-orange body was thicker than his wrist. "Who wants to see something like *that* sitting on your dessert tray?"

Glancing at Coral, I saw that she was already sitting up with help from Captain Peterson and other bystanders, looking dazed but sheepish.

The captain cleared his throat and called for attention. "Let's all calm down, please," he said in a voice of authority. "Are you all right, ma'am?"

"Oh, yes, I think so." Coral was on her feet by now. "Though, silly me, I'm not entirely sure what just happened!"

"It's pretty clear what happened, I'm afraid," Tobias's father said grimly, grabbing his son by the shoulder. "Tobias must have sneaked his pet spider onboard, and then decided to cause a ruckus by dropping her in the food."

"Ow!" Tobias wriggled out of his father's grasp, the sudden motion almost causing the tarantula to lose its grip on his arm. Hazel gave a little jump, ending up clinging to Tobias's shirt. A couple of passengers nearby went pale and took a few steps backward.

"I always kind of wanted a pet tarantula," George commented to nobody in particular.

I looked at her. "Not helping," I said.

Meanwhile Tobias turned to glare at his father. "You're right, I did sneak Hazel onboard." His lower lip stuck out defiantly. "I needed *something* to keep me busy on this trip." He carefully stroked the tarantula's hairy back as she climbed up toward his shoulder. "But I *didn't* put her in the food. She could have been crushed!"

The boy's mother joined them, her face pale and angry. "Don't lie to us, Tobias," she said. "The evidence is right there on your shirt, remember?"

"I'm not lying!" Tobias glared at her, his eyes flashing

angrily. "The last time I saw Hazel she was in her cage in our stupid cabin. I told you, I'd never leave her where she could get hurt!"

"Hmm." His father didn't look convinced. "I think we'd better continue this discussion in our cabin. So sorry for the disruption, everyone." Stepping over to Coral, he put a hand on her arm. "Special apologies to you, ma'am. I hope you're okay."

"Oh, I'm just fine." Coral smiled as brightly as ever, though she still looked pale. Alice and Babs took her by the arms and led her toward their table.

Tobias was dragged off in the opposite direction by his parents, loudly proclaiming his innocence all the while. Captain Peterson watched them go, then squared his shoulders.

"All right, folks, show's over. Please go back to enjoying your meals." He glanced at several employees, who were already busy clearing away the trays where the tarantula had been. "Fresh desserts will be out shortly."

He strode off toward the exit, seeming to forget that

we hadn't finished our conversation. Good. I needed to talk to my friends about what had just happened.

"Wow, that was creepy, huh?" Alan commented, slinging an arm over Bess's shoulders.

Oops. I'd almost forgotten about him.

"Hey, Alan," I said as we walked back to our table. "Seeing that spider made me feel a little shaky. Would you mind grabbing me a soda? With extra ice?" I gestured toward the drink station at the far end of the line.

"Sure, Nancy. Be right back." He smiled at me.

"Isn't he sweet?" Bess gave a little wave as Alan loped off. "It's nice to spend time with a guy who's so nice and considerate to everyone."

"Yeah, whatever." I didn't want to waste time discussing Alan's virtues. "Listen, we need to talk."

George sat down and picked up her sandwich. "What's to talk about? This is one crazy incident that's no mystery."

"Agreed." Bess's eyes widened. "Actually, it might even solve another mystery. I bet that spider is how Tobias scared the maid yesterday! In the hallway, remember? He stuck something in his pocket—I bet it was Hazel."

"You're probably right." I sank into my chair, thinking hard. "But listen, maybe we shouldn't be so quick to assume this has nothing to do with the other incidents."

George let out a snort. "What, do you think Tobias is the one who's been sabotaging the cruise?"

"Maybe," I said. "Think about it. Hiro mentioned earlier that Tobias is good with computers."

"He did?" Bess blinked at me.

I nodded. "When he was chasing him out of the mini-golf place earlier. Anyway, if it's true—like, if Tobias is really some kind of computer genius—he could have sent those e-mails to Becca and Brock. Maybe he was trying to get the whole cruise shut down so he could go to that amusement park instead. It's obvious he wants to be anywhere else but here."

"They wouldn't shut down a cruise over a couple of e-mails," George said.

I shrugged. "Tobias is just a kid. He wouldn't necessarily realize that. Anyway, that mannequin stunt was pretty childish, if you think about it. And Becca said the drink mix came from the kids' section, remember? Plus, Tobias was nearby during the moose incident this morning."

My friends traded a glance, looking skeptical. I couldn't really blame them.

"Okay, so it's a little far-fetched," I said. "So are all our other theories so far."

"Incoming," George hissed, glancing over my shoulder.

Alan was hurrying toward us, holding my glass of soda. I sighed, then pasted on a smile. Further discussion would have to wait.

"Come on, dude." Vince the newlywed grinned as he hung at the edge of the pool, his hair slicked back. "We need one more guy for even teams."

Alan sat up straight on his lounge chair. It was an hour after lunch, and he'd insisted we all change into our bathing suits and get some sun. I was itching to get away and do some investigating, but I hadn't found the right excuse yet.

"Volleyball, huh?" Alan said, glancing from Vince to the four other guys of various ages out in the pool. "I'm not bad at that, if I do say so myself."

A few members of the film crew were nearby, getting shots of passengers enjoying the pool. One of the cameramen came closer, his lens trained on Alan and Vince. "Go on, man," he called. "This could be great stuff for the ads."

Another cameraman was filming the guys in the pool. He glanced over his shoulder at Alan. "You guys'll be Superstar superstars," he joked.

I peered at him over my sunglasses. It was Baraz, the one who'd disappeared so abruptly yesterday.

"Okay, how can I say no to that?" Alan peeled off his T-shirt and stood up, tugging up the waistband of his swim trunks.

"Have fun," Bess said, glancing up from her fashion magazine.

Alan grinned, dropped a quick kiss on top of her

head, then cannonballed into the pool to loud cheers from the other guys. I sat up, dropped the book I'd been pretending to read, and scooted my lounge chair a little closer to my friends. It was a gorgeous afternoon and the pool was busy, but none of the other sunbathers were close enough to overhear us.

"Okay, where were we?" I said briskly.

George looked up from her laptop with a smirk. "You were trying to convince us that an eight-year-old is some kind of criminal mastermind," she joked.

I smiled. "Okay, I already admitted that one's a little bit of a stretch," I reminded her. "So let's come up with some other ideas." I'd spent the past half hour stewing over the case while pretending to read my book, so I was ready. "I'm thinking we shouldn't focus too much on motives right now—it's just too random. Instead let's think about opportunity. Who could have done the things that have happened so far?"

"Just about anyone on the ship." George shrugged. "I mean, we're all stuck in this floating tin can together. Equal opportunity."

"Not really." Bess looked thoughtful. "There weren't that many people around the mini-golf place this morning. If the bolts on that antler were loose enough to let go just because Alan and I leaned back against the moose's side, it probably couldn't have been that way for long, right?"

"Good point." I thought back to the incident. "Actually, I did notice something weird right after it happened."

"What? Tobias sneaking around with a monkey wrench?" George teased.

"No. It was when Becca arrived on the scene."

Bess cocked an eyebrow. "Hang on, you're not suspecting *Becca*, are you?"

I shook my head. "It's just that I noticed her giving Hiro a really funny look when she spotted him there."

"Hiro? You mean that kiddie wrangler guy?" George tugged at the strap of her one-piece swimsuit. "Come to think of it, he totally encouraged us to check out the mini golf, remember?" She grinned. "Hey, while we're at it, playing mini golf was all Alan's idea. Maybe *he* did it!"

Bess gave her a sour look. "Very funny." Then she glanced back at me. "I do remember Hiro being nearby with the kids when we got there. I'm not sure he could've sneaked away from them long enough to loosen the bolts, but I guess you never know."

I nodded. "I'll have to ask Becca about him when I get a chance. Anybody else we should think about?"

"What about *him*?" George was staring at the action out in the pool.

I followed her gaze. The water volleyball game was in full swing. As Vince spiked the ball over the net, one of the cameramen leaned in to capture the action shot.

"Baraz," I murmured thoughtfully, watching him. "Yeah, that was kind of weird how he disappeared right after the accident."

"And that director made it sound like it wasn't the first time," George recalled. "What if he was off tossing his monkey wrench overboard?"

"Anything's possible. But why? What's his motive?" I sighed, realizing that sentiment was becoming a refrain for this case. I realized something else. "It's also possible that the moose thing was just an accident. Like someone said, it's a brand-new ship. We might have been the very first ones to test out the course. Maybe the screws didn't get tightened enough and they just let go."

"That's probably at least as likely as some eight-year-old supervillain being strong enough to loosen a bunch of bolts," George said. "Especially when he was supposed to be on a tour with a bunch of other kids and Mr. Nanny at the same time."

"True. But I'm not ready to totally cross Tobias off the list yet, given what just happened at lunch. Anyway, maybe we should move on to something we *know* wasn't an accident—namely the mannequin stunt." I glanced at a lounge chair across the pool, where Lacey was lying on her stomach, watching her new husband and the others. "I think I'll go ask Lacey a few questions about what she saw."

I hurried over to her. She squinted up at me when I arrived. "Hi," Lacey said. "It's Nancy, right?" She smiled apologetically. "Sorry, there are so many new names to remember!"

"Yeah, it's Nancy. Hi, Lacey." I perched on Vince's empty chair beside hers. "Listen, I was just thinking about what happened yesterday. It kind of gave me the creeps. Maybe we should notify the police. Were you the first person to see that mannequin in the pool?"

"I guess so." Lacey visibly shuddered. "Vince was with me, of course, but he didn't notice it at first. It was so horrible! I couldn't help screaming my head off, even though I felt like an idiot afterward."

"Nobody thinks you're an idiot," I said with a smile. "Did you notice anyone else near the pool at the time? Any kids, maybe?"

Lacey didn't seem to hear me. She was staring out at the pool toward the spot where the mannequin had been floating. "I've had the strangest feeling ever since then," she said softly, seeming to speak more to herself than to me. "It's like I'm waiting for the next terrible thing to happen." She shuddered again. "I'm really beginning to think this whole cruise is cursed!"

CHAPTER EIGHT

Following Leads

I YAWNED AS I QUIETLY PULLED THE SUITE door shut behind me. The early wake-up call I'd requested had come right on time, though Max had seemed as chipper and wide awake as ever when he'd knocked on my door. Meanwhile all I'd wanted to do was crawl back into bed, let my head sink into my special buckwheat pillow, and go back to sleep for another hour or two.

But I hadn't. The ship would be arriving in Ketchikan in a few hours, and I wanted to get some investigating done before then. Or before something else happened.

Thinking back on Lacey's gloomy prediction yesterday, I couldn't help shivering a little myself.

It's a good thing she doesn't know about the rest of the bad stuff that's happened, I thought as I hurried through the silent hallways. *If the passengers find out about all that, it could be a disaster for this ship. Not to mention Superstar Cruises.*

I quickly banished the thought. I was going to make sure that didn't happen. First on the agenda? Talking to Becca. I wanted to ask her about Hiro, and maybe take a look at that threatening e-mail.

I'd already texted Becca to check that she was awake—and alone. When I arrived at her office, she was bent over her laptop at the desk again.

"Hi, Nancy," she said, sounding tired as she glanced up. "Give me some good news. Did you figure out what's going on around here?"

"We're working on it," I said, leaning against the doorframe. "I just need to ask you . . ."

I let my voice trail off as I heard footsteps hurrying along the hallway. Glancing out, I saw a familiar figure clicking toward me on high-heeled navy pumps.

"Tatjana!" Becca said in surprise as the woman brushed past me into the office. "What's wrong?"

"Big problems," Tatjana barked out.

Becca sat up straight, weariness replaced by wariness. "Oh, no. What now?"

"We're getting tons of reports from levels five through seven," Tatjana replied. "The passengers have been calling since midnight to complain that their temperature control systems are going haywire. Half the cabins are boiling hot, and the other half are freezing."

"I'd better go deal with this." Becca sounded dismayed. She headed for the door, pausing beside me as if belatedly remembering that I was there. "Sorry, Nancy," she added. "Talk later?"

"Sure." I turned to follow her out of the room, only to find Tatjana staring at me. Again.

"May I help you?" she asked. "I report directly to Becca. I'm sure I could answer whatever questions you have for her."

"That's okay." I pasted on a bright smile. "It's nothing important."

As soon as I was safely out of sight around the corner, my smile faded and I collapsed against the wall. Unless I missed my guess, those haywire heating systems were no accident. Our saboteur had struck again—and the voyage was just getting started. I was no closer to guessing his or her identity.

Chewing my lip, I mentally ran through my suspect list. But it was pathetically short, and some of the people on it were laughable. An eight-year-old boy? Really? Was I that desperate?

I wandered up the stairs to the promenade deck, where many of the ship's shops were located. Pausing in front of a clothing store, where several expressionless mannequins posed in the window like giant creepy dolls, I flashed back to the pool incident. Unbidden, a chilling question popped into my head: *That body was fake, but what if the next one's real?*

My mind jumped to that ominous note in my suitcase, and then to the moose antler crashing down inches from me. The latter could be a random accident, maybe, but not the former. Was someone targeting *me* as well as the ship? But how had they found out about me?

The promenade deck was almost deserted at that hour, since most of the shops were still closed. I wandered past one darkened storefront after another as I thought over the suspect list. Hiro was a big question mark. Yes, he'd been around for the moose incident—and the pool one too, come to think of it. And being an employee, he'd have easy access to the mannequins and such, as well as to the heating and cooling system. But what was his motive? Could there be a clue in that weird look Becca had given him? I would have to wait until I talked to her to find out.

Then there was the disappearing cameraman, Baraz. He'd been nearby during the moose incident too. The other members of the camera crew? I had no idea. But I guessed that the crew had nearly unlimited access to the ship. Probably even the "backstage" parts, which meant he could also be involved in that heated argument I'd overheard.

And what about Wendy the blogger? I paused, noticing the ship's Internet café right across the concourse. Some of her behavior had been sort of suspicious, and she seemed pretty serious about her blog. Was that enough of a motive for her to want to ruin the cruise?

There were lights on in the Internet café, so I walked over and peered in the window, wondering if she could be in there right now, sending off her latest entry. Instead I saw an even more familiar face bent over one of the terminals.

"George!" I called, hurrying inside. "What are you doing up at this hour?"

She glanced up at me with a yawn. "Trust me, it wasn't my idea," she said, sounding cranky. "Alan woke me up with all his crashing around in the bathroom. Remind me again why we let him come?"

I ignored that. "I'm glad you're here," I said. "Feel like taking a peek at our favorite travel blogger's work?"

"You mean Wendy the weirdo? Sure." George's fingers flew over the keyboard.

Within seconds, Wendy's Wanderings was up on the screen. The blog's top entry was titled "Terror on the High Seas."

"Uh-oh," I said, shoving George aside so I could perch on the chair with her. "That doesn't sound good. . . ."

I leaned forward to read. It turned out to be a funny entry about the tarantula incident. Wendy had even done some research, discovering that Tobias and his parents lived in Vancouver, which was why Hazel hadn't been confiscated by customs agents or noticed at all until yesterday. The boy had hidden the spider's cage in his suitcase and Hazel herself in his pocket as they boarded, then kept her presence a secret from his parents until she'd appeared on the buffet, telling them he'd left her with a school friend for safekeeping. The way Wendy told it, the whole thing came across as a humorous episode.

"She's actually not a bad writer," George said as she read.

"Yeah." I scrolled down, checking out the next latest few entries. There were about half a dozen so far about the cruise, mostly short ones describing the food, entertainment, and lodgings. But there was one more that caught my attention: "Blood (Sort of) in the Water."

"Hey, she wrote about the pool thing," George said as she spotted it too. "Wow, she even got a picture of the lifeguard dragging the mannequin out of the water!" She leaned closer, peering at the photo. "The blood looks a lot more lifelike in the picture."

I nodded as I scanned through the entry. This one read more like a news report, describing what had happened and saying that ship employees claimed it was a prank. I winced when I read the last few lines: *But seeing a dead body in the pool—even a fake one—isn't the best way to start a relaxing cruise to glacier country. More like an epic fail, actually. Is it enough to sink this brand-new cruise line before it leaves the harbor? Only time will tell. . . .*

George pointed to the bottom of the entry. "She got a bunch of comments on this one," she said. "That means a lot of people read it."

"That could be our motive right there. It's pretty suspicious that she happened to be close enough to get photos before they shooed everyone away."

George scrolled back up. "Let's see if we can find out more about our happy blogger. . . ."

But the "About Me" section of the blog didn't have much information. It just gave Wendy's name and age and mentioned that she lived in Seattle when she wasn't "traveling the world in search of the next adventure."

"Should I run a web search, see if I can find out more about her?" George suggested.

I was about to tell her to go ahead when my phone buzzed. It was Bess.

"Are you with George? We're saving seats for you two at breakfast," she said. In the background, I could hear Alan chatting with someone, though I couldn't tell who. "You'd better hurry up—we don't have much time to eat before we dock in Ketchikan."

"Drat," I muttered as I hung up. "I guess more research will have to wait."

We found Bess and Alan sitting with Vince and Lacey in the café. "There you are!" Vince greeted us with a smile. "Your friends were worried that you'd fallen overboard or something."

"Nothing that drastic, just taking a walk." I sat down and smiled politely at Vince and Lacey. "So are you guys looking forward to Ketchikan?"

Lacey glanced up from buttering her toast. "Oh, we're not going ashore," she said. "We decided to skip Ketchikan and stay on the ship."

"Really? Why?" George asked.

"I'm not really in the mood for sightseeing," Lacey said softly, shooting a look at her husband.

Vince explained, "She's still a little shaken up over what happened the other day. We figured we'd just hang out on the ship, have a quiet day on our own while everyone else is away."

I was a little surprised, since this was Alaska, after all. But . . . this was their honeymoon, and it was no wonder that the brand-new husband and wife might want to spend some private time together rather than surrounded by a bunch of strangers with nowhere to really get away. I was feeling some of that myself, actually.

Maybe I should stay on the ship too, I thought as I

chewed the bagel I'd grabbed from the buffet. *That would give me a chance to investigate without having to dodge Alan or make small talk with random other passengers or whatever. I might even find a moment to sit down with Becca and really talk about the case without being interrupted every two seconds.*

It was a tempting thought. But I wasn't sure it was worth the trouble. How would I explain to Alan why I wasn't going ashore? It was probably too late to fake an illness. Besides, most of the trouble so far had been very public. If the saboteur was going to strike again, it seemed more likely to happen where the passengers *were* than where they weren't. In other words, if there was any action today. it was probably going to happen in Ketchikan, and I didn't want to miss it.

"Yo, Scott!" Alan shouted just then, jumping to his feet so fast he almost upended his orange juice. He waved his arms vigorously. "Over here, bro!"

I glanced over and saw the shore excursion specialist we'd met on the first day. He was carrying a clipboard and a stack of envelopes.

"Hi," he said when he reached our table. "Everyone ready for some big fun in Ketchikan today?" He shuffled through the envelopes. "Alan, I got your message. You four are signed up for the deluxe town tour, followed by the lumberjack show, and then a floatplane ride to the Misty Fjords."

"What?" George looked up from her french toast. "I mean, wait—what?"

I couldn't have said it better myself. "You signed us up for all that stuff?" I asked Alan. "When were you planning to fill us in?"

Alan grinned. "You're welcome," he said. "Some of these shore excursions fill up early, you know. You girls have been so busy running off getting facials and stuff that I was afraid we'd get shut out."

"Oh." I traded a look with George and Bess. Being stuck in a bunch of structured tours and activities wasn't exactly the Ketchikan experience I'd had in mind. How was I supposed to check out our suspects that way, unless they happened to have the exact same itinerary?

"It's okay," Bess said, giving Alan's shoulder a squeeze. "We appreciate it, Alan. It'll be fun. Right, girls?"

"I wanted to go kayaking," George grumbled. But seeing Bess's glare, she shrugged. "But whatever."

"Um, actually I was thinking it would be fun to just wander around town on our own," I said. "From the tour books in our suite, it looks like there's a ton to see and it's all pretty close together. But I don't mind doing that by myself if you guys want to do the other stuff."

Scott was still standing by, his hand holding a pen poised over his clipboard. "So that's down to three for the activities?" he asked.

"No!" Alan protested before I could respond. "Come on, Nancy. I put a lot of thought into these activities— I really think you'll enjoy them." He grinned. "And I won't take no for an answer!"

I hesitated, trying to figure out a way around this. But looking at Alan, I could tell it was no use. I pasted on a smile, though it felt a little weak around the edges.

"Okay," I told Scott. "Put us down for four."

CHAPTER NINE

Stalling Out

"THAT WAS COOL," BESS SAID. "I NEVER thought I'd see a bald eagle up close like that, let alone a whole bunch of them!"

"See?" Alan slipped an arm around her shoulders. "I told you guys this would be great."

I tucked my camera back in my pocket, squinting a little in the midday sunlight. It was a beautiful day with hardly a cloud in the sky, despite Ketchikan's nickname being the Rain Capital of Alaska.

"This way, people!" Scott called out. "That concludes the deluxe tour, so those of you who aren't signed up for anything else today are free to go shop, eat, or sightsee on your own. However, anyone who's signed up to see the world-famous Great Alaskan Lumberjack Show should stick around. It's just a short walk from here, so if you'll follow me . . ."

Most of us fell into step behind him, chattering about the things we'd seen over the past couple of hours. There were about a dozen people on the tour. Unfortunately, none of our suspects were among them. The only people we'd known before the tour started were the ABCs.

"I've heard this lumberjack show is a real hoot," Babs said, falling into step beside me.

I nodded and smiled, though I was feeling distracted. Yes, the tour had been fun. We'd taken a carriage ride through the picturesque town, visited a salmon hatchery, and then toured a place where people took care of injured bald eagles and other wildlife. All that had sidetracked me from the case for a while, but now I was getting restless.

When Babs turned to talk to Coral, I sidled away toward my friends. Bess and Alan were walking hand in hand, but George had slowed down to fiddle with her camera, so I was able to pull her aside.

"We're wasting time here," I whispered.

George glanced up. "What do you mean? Alan actually came through for once—that tour was cool."

"I know. But I was really hoping to get a chance to check out some of our suspects today, like Wendy or maybe Tobias."

"Okay, but how would you find those people even if we did get away?" George shrugged and glanced around. "Open your eyes. Ketchikan is a mob scene."

I saw her point. The *Arctic Star* wasn't the only cruise ship docked in Ketchikan at the moment. There were two other massive ships there, and their passengers were everywhere.

"Anyway," George went on with a grin, "I hear this lumberjack show is pretty fun. Let's check it out, and then maybe we can duck out of the fjord thing afterward, okay?"

I sighed. It would have to do. "Fine," I said. "Lumberjacks it is."

Soon we were all seated in the grandstand of the open-air arena where the lumberjack show would take place. My friends and I were at the end of a row about halfway back, with most of the seats nearby taken up by *Arctic Star* passengers. Scott was at the end of the aisle a couple of rows ahead of us.

"Relax, folks," he called out as he sat down. "The show's scheduled to start in about fifteen minutes."

"I wonder what all the other people from the ship did this morning," Alan said. "Scott said a bunch went kayaking or fishing. And some others did this tour where you go into the rain forest and do a zip-line thing. Maybe we should have tried that."

"Zip lining? No thank you." George shuddered. "We had, uh, a bad experience with a zip line once. Right, Nancy?"

I shot her a warning look. She was right—I'd had a pretty bad accident on a zip line in Costa Rica once because someone had sabotaged it to try to stop one of my investigations. Alan already knew I was an amateur detective, of course—pretty much everyone in River

Heights did. But I didn't particularly want to remind him about my little hobby. He came across as pretty goofy, but he wasn't stupid. What if he figured out what I was really doing on this cruise?

Luckily, though, Alan didn't seem to have caught the comment. "It's weird to think of a rain forest in Alaska, isn't it?" he mused. "I mean, when you think Alaska, you think snow and glaciers and stuff, not rain forest."

"Very educated comment, Mr. Environmental Studies Guy," George quipped.

Alan looked annoyed. "Hey, I may be an enviro student, but that doesn't mean I'm an expert on every environment on the planet, all right?"

"Look," Bess said, clearly trying to distract them from sniping at each other. "I think I see some other people from our ship coming in. Including our favorite arachnophile."

"Huh?" George glanced toward the entrance, then made a face. "Quick, everybody hide," she hissed. "It's Spider Boy!"

I looked too and saw Tobias entering the grandstand with his parents. For a second my instinct was the same as George's. But then I realized this might be my only chance today to do any investigating. Okay, so it involved our weakest suspect. Still . . .

"Hello!" I called to the family, standing up and waving. "There are some seats over here!"

Tobias's mother spotted me and waved back. Moments later they were making their way toward us.

George groaned softly. "Are you nuts?" she whispered. "That kid's scary enough even *without* easy access to axes and stuff."

But there wasn't time to say any more before Tobias pushed past us and flopped into an empty seat. "I hope the show starts soon," he said impatiently. "It's probably going to be the only interesting thing I get to do on this whole stupid cruise."

"Relax, son," his father said with a sigh. "It'll start soon."

"So what did you kids see in Ketchikan so far today?" his wife asked us.

The small talk continued from there. It turned out the family had spent the morning wandering around sightseeing on their own instead of joining any of the organized activities. I couldn't help wondering if that was because Tobias was being punished for the spider stunt. Had he confessed to planting Hazel on the buffet yet?

I cast around in my mind for a subtle way to ask. But Alan, of all people, beat me to it.

"Hey, buddy," he said with a grin, leaning toward Tobias. "Did you bring Hazel along to check out the show too?"

Tobias gave him a withering look. "What do *you* think, genius?" he snapped.

"Tobias! Manners!" his mother scolded. Then she smiled at Alan. "Sorry. He's a little touchy about Hazel right now."

"Yes, and he's not making it easy on himself." Tobias's father looked at his son sternly, though Tobias ignored him. "The ship is being nice about what happened, and Miss Coral has been especially gracious. But Tobias still won't admit to what he did."

His wife sighed. "It's just not like him," she murmured. "Tobias can be, er, difficult. But he's not normally a liar. I certainly hope this isn't a new phase. . . ."

"At least Hazel has been confined to her cage since yesterday," Tobias's father said, clearly trying to lighten the mood. "I'm sure everyone's glad about that—well, except maybe for Analyn."

"Analyn?" I echoed.

"She's the maid for our cabin," Tobias's mother explained with a rueful smile. "Lovely young girl from the Philippines. Poor thing—she probably wasn't expecting to see a tarantula sitting on the coffee table when she brought the clean towels in last night. Even one in a cage."

My friends chuckled, but I frowned slightly. "Wait," I said. "I thought the maid for your cabin was named Iris."

"They probably have more than one," Bess said. "Like us, remember? Our suite has Max plus the two maids."

"That's right, there are two cabin stewards for ours as well," Tobias's father said. "Analyn and a young man named John."

"Oh." Something about this was bothering me, though I wasn't sure what. "So the maid we saw, Iris—"

At that moment, Tobias leaped to his feet. "Hey! Look, there's seats right down in front!" he blurted out loudly, interrupting me. He stomped on my toes as he raced for the aisle. "Come on, let's go before someone takes them!"

"Sorry, sorry," his father said breathlessly as he and his wife followed.

"It's okay," Bess said. Then she turned and smiled sweetly at Alan. "We still have a few minutes before the show starts. Think I have time to go find a soda before that? I'm parched."

Alan jumped to his feet. "Stay here—I'll find you one."

George watched him hurry out, then turned to Bess. "How do you *do* that?"

Bess ignored her. "So what do you think?" she asked me. "Are you ready to cross our favorite spider wrangler off the suspect list?"

"I'm not sure," I said slowly. "On the one hand, it's

weird that he won't confess. It's not like he's shy about causing trouble most of the time."

"Good point," George put in. "If anything, you'd think he'd be bragging about it."

"On the other hand," I went on, "who else even knew that spider was aboard, let alone had access to her?"

"Another good point." Bess looked thoughtful. "What about the maid, Analyn? Maybe it was her, or the other cabin attendant. Either of them might have spotted Hazel while they were in there cleaning."

"Or what about the kid's parents?" George peered down toward where the family was now seated. "I mean, they seem like nice people, but so have a lot of the baddies you've busted, Nancy."

"I guess you're right. They certainly had access to the spider, since it was in their cabin." I chewed my lower lip. "But why? What's their motive?"

Just then Alan returned. "Sorry," he told Bess breathlessly. "They told me there's no time—show's about to start. Maybe we can get you a drink afterward?"

"Sure, no problem." Bess smiled and squeezed his

hand as he took his seat. "Thanks for trying."

As we waited, I thought about what George had said. Could Tobias's parents be in cahoots with their bratty son? Having a couple of adults involved made him a much more believable suspect. But why would they try to sabotage a ship? What could they possibly be trying to accomplish?

I was still pondering it when the show started. It was entertaining, but I couldn't seem to focus on it. About five or ten minutes in, I noticed that one other person didn't seem very involved in the show either. I saw Scott check his watch, then stand up and head toward the exit.

No big surprise there, I thought. *He's probably seen this show a million times.*

But his exit gave me an idea. "I'll be right back," I whispered to George, who was sitting beside me. "Bathroom break."

She just nodded, not taking her eyes off the action.

I made my way to the outside of the arena and glanced around, wondering where to start. The streets of Ketchikan were as crowded as ever, which wasn't going to make it easy to track down any of my suspects. If there was an Internet café in town, maybe I could check to see if Wendy was hanging out there. . . .

At that moment a knot of people moved aside, and I noticed Scott standing nearby. He was talking to a man I'd never seen before—his face wasn't one anyone could forget, given the large, jagged, ugly scar bisecting it. Scar Guy was maybe a few years older than Scott, dressed in ripped jeans and a grimy plaid flannel jacket. The two of them were leaning close together and appeared to be deep in conversation.

Then Scott quickly looked around, though he didn't notice me watching. He stuck one hand into the pocket of his windbreaker, pulled out something I couldn't see, and shoved it at Scar Guy. Scar Guy tucked whatever it was into his jacket, then took off without another word in the direction of the docks. Scott put both hands in his jeans pockets and started walking fast in the opposite direction.

What was that all about? I wondered. Something

about what I'd just witnessed had set all my sleuthing instincts on high alert, though I wasn't quite sure why.

I took a few steps after Scott, keeping him in sight, not certain what to do. Sure, Scar Guy looked kind of seedy. But so what? Scott could easily have friends or acquaintances in various ports, and I knew better than to judge someone on appearances. There could be a million perfectly innocent explanations for what I'd just seen. And Scott wasn't even on my radar as a suspect. Why waste time worrying about what he was doing?

But sometimes a girl just has to go with a hunch. Besides, it wasn't as if I had a better plan in mind. Putting on a burst of speed, I followed Scott as he rounded the corner and headed deeper into town.

CHAPTER TEN

Catch as Ketchikan

THIS IS A WASTE OF TIME, I THOUGHT AS I ducked into a doorway.

I'd already followed Scott for several blocks. Every so often he paused and glanced around, and I'd been careful to stay out of sight. It wasn't hard, since we were still in the touristy part of town and there were plenty of people around. Maybe if I was lucky I'd come across Wendy or one of my other suspects, and that would give me an excuse to give up this crazy idea of tailing Scott.

The crowd thinned out a little as we turned to head off the street and up a short walkway toward a low-slung wooden building. I hung back until Scott disappeared inside, then hurried forward. A sign by the door identified the place as the Totem Heritage Center.

"Cool," I murmured as I saw several intricately carved faces grinning or scowling down at me from a tall totem pole near the building.

But I wasn't here to sightsee. Pushing in through the door, I glanced around.

It took a moment for my eyes to adjust to the dim lighting. The place was small, making the collection of towering totem poles seem even taller as they loomed up in the center of the room.

There were a couple of older tourists wandering around, but I didn't see Scott anywhere. I wandered farther in, staring up at the poles. My footsteps echoed, seeming to bounce off the impassive totems. The place was cool, but a little creepy, too.

This is silly, I told myself. *I'm sure Scott's just here scoping out this place to include on future tours, or some other ship business like that. I should go, maybe try to track down Wendy or something.*

But I couldn't help remembering how Scott had acted as he walked here—stopping every few minutes to look back, as if he didn't want anyone to see where he was headed. If he was just going about his normal business, why would he act like that?

Besides, I was already here. I might as well follow through.

By now the tourists had disappeared into the adjoining gift shop. I glanced in there, but there was no sign of Scott, so I kept going, circling around the totems huddled at the center of the room.

Where'd he go? I wondered.

When I reached the back wall, I heard the sound of muffled voices. Spotting a door, I pushed it open, revealing the bright glare of daylight—and Scott's surprised face.

"You!" he blurted out harshly, freezing in place. "What are you doing here?"

My eyes darted from his face to his hand. It clutched a large wad of cash, which Scott appeared to be in the process of handing to another man. The second man was big and burly, with a wool cap pulled low over his broad, ruddy face.

"Gimme 'at," the man rumbled, grabbing the cash and then taking off, moving surprisingly quickly for someone his size.

"I—I—," I stammered, unnerved by the furious scowl on Scott's face. I looked around quickly, realizing we were alone in a small alleyway behind the building.

But when I looked back at him, his angry expression had melted away, replaced by a sheepish smile. "Sorry, Nancy," he said. "You startled me!"

"Sorry," I said, glancing in the direction where the other man had disappeared around the corner of the building.

Scott followed my gaze. "I guess you're wondering what that was all about," he said. "That guy's a poker buddy of mine—lives here in Ketchikan. I owed him some cash from the last time I was in town, and he called in the debt."

"Oh. Um, okay."

"I hope you won't say anything to the captain about

this." Scott bit his lip. "Ship employees aren't supposed to get involved with gambling while we're on duty, and I could lose my job if anyone finds out."

"Sure, don't worry. I won't breathe a word," I said, pretending to draw a zipper closed across my lips. But once I got back onboard, of course I was going to say something.

"Good." He was all smiles again. "Now, aren't you supposed to be at the lumberjack show? How'd you end up here, anyway?"

I babbled some excuse about needing air and going for a walk, which seemed to satisfy him. Then we headed out through the museum and parted ways outside.

As I hurried toward the lumberjack arena, I thought about what I'd just seen and heard. Scott's story made sense—he'd been sneaking around because he didn't want any of his coworkers to see him and possibly report him. And it wasn't as if he made a likely suspect for any of the trouble that had happened so far. I made a mental note to ask Becca what she knew about him, and maybe have George check him out online just in case. Otherwise, it seemed safe to forget the whole encounter. Well, I hoped it did anyway.

I arrived back at the arena just as the audience came pouring out onto the street. Almost everyone I saw was laughing and chattering with excitement, and I was kind of sorry I'd missed most of the show.

Then Alan spotted me and hurried over, with Bess and George trailing along behind him. "Where'd you disappear to?" he demanded. "That must've been one heck of a line at the ladies' room!"

I thought fast. "I always hate when people crawl back and forth to their seats during a show," I told him with a shrug and a smile. "So I decided to just hang out at the back and watch from there so I didn't disturb anyone."

"That makes sense," Bess said quickly, though Alan looked a bit dubious.

I couldn't really blame him. It wasn't really that kind of show.

For a moment I wondered if all this subterfuge was really worth it. Maybe I should just give in and tell Alan the truth after all. It would certainly be a lot easier than all this sneaking around, plus it would mean an extra set of eyes watching for clues.

"Anyone else hungry?" Bess asked cheerfully before I could decide.

"Starved." George checked her watch. "I vote we bag out of that fjord thing we have scheduled and find some food instead."

I glanced at Alan, expecting him to argue. But he nodded.

"I could go for that," he said. "Besides, I kind of want to get a better look at Creek Street. What do you say?"

Creek Street was one of the town attractions that we'd passed on our tour earlier. It wasn't exactly a street at all, at least not in the usual sense. Its colorful wooden buildings—shops, restaurants, historic houses, art galleries, and other attractions—lined a boardwalk-like pedestrian walkway set on tall pilings over Ketchikan Creek. We'd only caught a glimpse of it from the horse-drawn carriage, but our tour guide had recommended checking it out on foot later if we had time.

"Sure," I said. "Let's go."

Creek Street was even more crowded than the rest of town. Tons of people were crammed onto the antique wooden boardwalk, which I guessed had to hang a good fifteen or twenty feet above the water at this point.

Bess peered over the drop. "I hope these walkways are stronger than they look," she joked.

"Don't worry." Alan took her hand. "I'll keep you safe."

She fluttered her eyelashes at him. "Why, thank you, kind sir."

George groaned. "Is anyone else suddenly losing their appetite?"

"Funny." Bess stuck her tongue out at her cousin. Then she glanced around, her eyes lighting up when she spotted an Alaskan-themed gift shop just ahead. "Hey, as long as we're here, I should do some souvenir shopping. The people back home will be expecting lots of trinkets. Let's start in there!"

She made a beeline for the store's entrance without waiting for an answer. George was right behind her, but Alan paused to glance back at me.

"Coming, Nancy?" he asked.

"You guys go ahead. I'll hang here and people watch," I said. "Just tell Bess to grab me some souvenirs if she sees anything good."

I turned to gaze out over the railing as he headed after the others. Most of Creek Street was laid out on a gentle curve, following the creek's meandering course, and I had a pretty good view of the walkways farther along. I rested my elbows on the railing, enjoying the feel of the sun on my face, and idly watched for any sighting of Wendy, Tobias, or Baraz while my mind returned to the case.

Not that I had any new brainstorms. I felt as if we were going in circles, trying to match up suspects, motives, and most of all opportunity. What did anyone onboard have to gain? Sure, there was Wendy—it was possible that she was drumming up action and scandal so she could report it on her blog and attract more readers. But how did that motive fit in with the threat that had made Brock Walker cancel? She'd mentioned his absence in one of her blog entries, but only briefly.

Then there was Tobias. He definitely had a motive—he'd made no secret of the fact that he didn't want to be on the ship. And of course the tarantula incident almost had to be his doing, even if he wouldn't admit it. But I found it hard to believe he could have pulled off the pool incident so soon after arriving on the ship. And even if we threw his parents into the mix and assumed that they'd overheard me talking somehow, it seemed unlikely that any of them could have slipped that note into my suitcase. Or tampered with the heating and cooling systems on the lower decks, for that matter.

And what about Hiro? He'd been around for the mini-golf incident, and fairly close by when the "body" had been discovered in the pool. And I was pretty sure that I hadn't imagined that weird look Becca had given him. If we assumed the spider thing was a red herring, he might have been able to pull off just about everything else. But again, why?

Chewing my lower lip and squinting out at the sunlight glinting off the water, I tried to figure out if I was missing anything, overlooking any suspects. My mind flashed to Tatjana, who might have overheard me talking about the case. She was clearly several years older than Becca, but had mentioned reporting to her. Did she resent that? Could she be trying to make her up-and-coming young boss look bad, hoping to steal her job? Then I thought about Mr. Hawaiian Shirt, who always seemed to be hanging around behind the scenes and making cryptic comments. Could he have a motive we didn't know about?

But no matter how I tried to reorder everything, shuffling and reshuffling suspects, motives, and clues, I just couldn't put it all together in a way that made sense. All I knew was that *someone* was causing all sorts of trouble for the *Arctic Star*, and I needed to figure out who and why before someone really got hurt.

There was a sudden burst of activity behind me, and I glanced back just in time to see an ocean of red hair flooding my way. It was the family reunion group from the ship. The ABCs, who really did seem to know everything, had informed the table at dinner last night that the family's name was O'Malley, and that its members hailed from all over the country and even overseas and were more than two dozen strong. I smiled as I watched a four- or five-year-old girl with bright red pigtails race eagerly toward the gift shop where my friends had gone.

"Mary! Wait for me—you don't want to slip and fall in the water!" a woman shouted, hurrying after the little girl. She spotted me as she rushed past, and gave me a quick smile of recognition. "Oh, hello!"

"Hi," I said, though she was already gone. I squeezed back against the handrail, trying to stay out of the way as the rest of the group crowded past me, shouting and laughing and clearly having a ball.

Hearing a shriek from somewhere farther down the walkway, I glanced that way, hoping that little Mary hadn't gotten into trouble. I couldn't see her or her mother in the ever-shifting crowd, but just then I caught a sudden flurry of movement behind me, just at the corner of my eye.

"Hey!" I blurted out as I felt something slam into the backs of my knees. My legs buckled, my feet went out from under me, and I went flying backward. I scrabbled for a hold, but it was too late—I felt my lower back bounce off the stiff wood of the railing, and then there was nothing but air between me and the ice-cold water rushing along far below.

"Help!" I shrieked.

SPLASH!

CHAPTER ELEVEN

❦

Putting the Pieces Together

AN HOUR LATER MY TEETH FINALLY STOPPED chattering.

"Are you sure you're all right?" Bess bent closer, peering anxiously into my face.

"I'll live," I assured her, running a hand over my damp hair. I glanced at Alan and smiled. "But it's a really good thing I had our own personal lifeguard around to save me. Thanks again, Alan."

My friends and I were back on the *Arctic Star*. I was lying on a pool chair on the lido deck, letting the warm sun bake off the last of the bone-shivering chill of my unscheduled dip in the creek. Who knew water could be so cold in the middle of summer? It was a reminder that we really were in Alaska.

"You're welcome." Alan shook his head. "I couldn't believe my eyes when I came out of that gift shop just in time to see you go flying over that railing!"

"Good thing you did." George grimaced, picking at a splinter on the lounge chair where she was sitting. "Bess was ready to stay in there and shop till we all dropped, so it would've been a while before we even noticed Nancy was missing. And with all those crazy reunion redheads running amuck, who knows if anyone would've heard her yelling from way down in the water?"

I shuddered as I realized, not for the first time over the past hour, how lucky I was not to be badly hurt—or worse. Fortunately, I'd landed in a deep spot in the creek instead of on a rock or something. And I'd managed to paddle over and cling to a piling while I waited for rescue, which had come quickly thanks to Alan's shouts for help.

I glanced around the pool area. It was deserted except for us—and occasionally Max, who kept hustling back and forth to fetch me more hot tea or dry towels. Alan had texted him as soon as we'd arrived back onboard, and the butler had appeared almost instantly. And I had George text Becca, telling her not to worry, that I was safe and sound.

I felt bad for pulling Max away from what was probably supposed to be a few hours off. I felt even worse for wishing I could get rid of Alan so I could discuss the case with Bess and George before the other passengers returned from their day in Ketchikan. Once again, I wondered if I should just bring him in on the secret.

"It's weird being practically the only ones onboard, isn't it?" Bess commented.

"Yeah." Shooting a furtive look at Alan, I decided to keep the secret. It was just too complicated to explain, and he wasn't the type of guy to accept a story like that without asking tons of questions. "Um, I just realized something—I really wanted to pick up a few postcards in Ketchikan. Think I've got time to run back to shore before the rest of the passengers come back?"

"Don't even think about it, Nancy! You need to rest after what you've just been through. Let me run out and get the postcards for you," Alan insisted—just as I'd hoped he would. "How many do you want?"

Moments later he'd disappeared in the direction of the exit. George grinned at me. "Nicely done," she said.

"Was I that obvious?"

Bess rolled her eyes. "I wish we could just tell him the truth. I feel bad keeping him in the dark and sneaking around behind his back."

"Me too, especially after what just happened," I admitted. "But come on, we can sit around feeling guilty later. Right now I want to find Becca. Maybe she'll actually have more than two seconds to talk while everyone's ashore."

My friends traded a look and a smile. "Even a twenty-foot fall into ice-cold Alaskan waters can't keep our favorite sleuth down for long," George quipped.

"Did you expect anything less?" Bess replied.

"Can I borrow your phone?" I asked George. "Mine's still drying out."

Soon I was texting Becca. Her response came quickly: MEET AT PROMENADE SNACK BAR.

"Good," George said, reading the message over my shoulder. "That lady who checked us back onto the ship said that's the only place serving food until everyone reboards later. And we never did get that snack in town, thanks to the diving detective here."

"Ha-ha, very funny." I quickly texted Becca back to say we were coming, then tossed George's phone back to her. "Let's go."

When we reached the promenade deck, Becca was standing outside the snack bar, shifting her weight from one foot to the other and looking anxious. As soon as she spotted us, she rushed forward.

"Nancy, I'm so sorry. Are you *sure* you're okay?" she asked, as she looked me up and down. Then she leaned in closer and said, "Something else happened."

"Wait—you meant there was *another* incident?" I said. "Did it happen onboard or in town?"

"Onboard, about an hour ago," Becca replied. "The big central chandelier in the main theater came down."

"Came down?" Bess's eyes widened with alarm. "You mean it fell? The whole thing?"

"Kaboom." Becca looked grim. "Luckily, the theater was empty when it happened, so nobody was hurt. But you could hear the crash through half the ship. Freaked out a few of the guests who stayed behind. Plus of course it made a huge mess—broken glass and wiring everywhere. The theater will have to stay closed until it's cleaned up, which means we're scrambling to move or reschedule all the events that were supposed to happen there soon, including Merk's big performance tonight."

"Whoa." I shook my head. "So much for my theory that whoever was causing all the trouble would probably go ashore today."

"Please tell me you're getting closer to figuring out who that person is." Becca's voice shook a little. "Because things seem to be escalating, and the guests are starting to notice."

I chewed my lip. "Well, most of our suspects were in Ketchikan today as far as we know." As I said it, I realized that I didn't really know for sure that Wendy had spent the day in town. I'd spotted her briefly on the dock when we'd disembarked but hadn't seen hide nor hair of her since. But I put that aside for the moment. "What can you tell me about Scott, the shore excursions guy?"

"Scott?" Becca looked surprised. "Is he a suspect?"

"News to me," Bess put in, raising an eyebrow.

I shrugged. "I caught him acting a little oddly when I stepped out during the lumberjack show," I told Bess and George. "I didn't get a chance to fill you in before my fall."

"I don't know him that well, but I know he's worked in the industry for a while," Becca said. "Captain Peterson himself recommended him for the job, actually. He's not your best suspect, is he?"

She sounded kind of unimpressed. Unfortunately, I was afraid the rest of the list wasn't going to change that. "Um, no," I said. "Like I said, I was just curious after seeing him today. We've actually been working a few other leads."

"Yeah." George snorted. "Like our eight-year-old supervillain."

"Huh?" Becca said.

"She means that kid Tobias," I said, feeling kind of foolish. "Uh, after what happened with his pet spider yesterday, we thought maybe he or his parents could be behind some of the other trouble. We're also watching Wendy Webster, that travel blogger with the weird glasses."

"I know who you mean. Hipster chick. Talks a lot." Becca nodded. "You really think she could be our culprit?"

"Maybe," I said. "We're also keeping an eye on one of the cameramen, Baraz. He keeps disappearing at odd times, and—what?"

Becca had started laughing. "You can cross Baraz off your list," she said. "I actually just found out why he kept disappearing, and it has nothing to do with sabotage."

"Really? What?" George asked.

"He's deathly seasick!" Becca announced. "Can you

believe it? Most people on a cruise ship don't even real-ize they're on the water. But apparently he's got such a killer case of motion sickness that he's been having to run off every few minutes to barf over the side of the ship! Poor guy had no idea until it was too late, and I guess for a while he thought he could power through it. But he just fessed up and will be leaving the crew for good here in Ketchikan. Marcelo just told me about it."

"Wow," I said slowly. For a moment I wondered—could Baraz's motion sickness be a cover story? Maybe he'd guessed that we were onto him and decided to take off before he got caught. "So when did he leave the ship?"

"Way before the chandelier came down, if that's what you're thinking." Her smile faded, and she sighed. "Baraz definitely isn't our bad guy. Whoever it is is still out there."

"Don't forget to ask her about that Hiro guy," Bess said.

"Oh, right! Thanks for the reminder." I glanced at Becca. Was it my imagination, or had she visibly started at the mention of Hiro's name? "So we've noticed that youth coordinator guy, Hiro, always seems to be around when there's trouble. How well do you know him?"

"Not that well. But I doubt it's him, either." Becca glanced at her watch. "Listen, I just remembered I'm supposed to track down the captain about something important. Talk later?"

"Sure, I guess. . . ." I let my voice trail off, since she was already rushing off down the promenade deck's broad central aisle.

"Wow, she was sure in a hurry all of a sudden," George commented.

I nodded, feeling uneasy. Was there something Becca wasn't telling me?

"Come on," Bess said. "Let's go in and grab something to eat while we decide what to do next."

We headed into the snack bar. There was a counter at one end where you could order sandwiches and other light fare. A dozen or so tables were scattered around a pleasant little courtyard with a fountain at the center.

At the moment the place was nearly deserted, though one table near the fountain was occupied.

"Check it out, look who's here," George said. She raised her voice. "Yo, honeymooners! What's up?"

Vince and Lacey glanced up and waved. "Come join us!" Lacey called.

We got our food and then headed over to their table, though I really would have preferred to sit by ourselves so we could continue our discussion of the case. Then again, what was there to discuss? Our suspect list was pathetic, the saboteur was getting bolder and more dangerous with every stunt, and I was all out of ideas.

"So you three are back early," Vince commented as we sat down. "Run out of things to do in Ketchikan?"

"Something like that," I said, not really in the mood to discuss my accident. "How has your day been onboard? Pretty quiet?"

"I wish!" Lacey's hazel eyes widened. "Did you hear about the chandelier?"

"Yeah, we heard." I picked at my sandwich. "Crazy,

huh? It's a brand-new ship, after all. You guys didn't see anything or anyone suspicious around the time it happened, did you?"

George shot me a look. I could almost see the thought balloon over her head: *Real subtle, detective!*

Luckily, Vince didn't seem to think the question was weird. "We spent practically all day holed up in the gym, so we haven't seen a soul except for the attendant." He chuckled. "It's always so crowded in there— we figured today was the perfect chance to not have to wait in line for our favorite machines, or share space in the sauna. It was great! Right, honey?"

"Yeah." Lacey still looked troubled. "Now I'm thinking we're lucky the elliptical machine didn't blow up or something. It's crazy how many things are going wrong on this ship. Maybe it really *is* cursed!"

"I'm sure it's all simply a series of unfortunate coincidences," Bess said in her most soothing tone. "It's just too bad it had to happen on your honeymoon."

"Definitely." Vince checked his watch. "Hey, sweetie, we'd better roll. Iris made us an appointment to get massages before the crowds return, remember? We don't want to be late."

"Okay." Lacey stood up and smiled wanly at us. "See you at dinner."

"Yeah." Vince slung an arm around her shoulders and grinned. "Don't let the ABCs eat all the rolls before we get there, okay?"

After they left, my friends and I sat there and finished our food. We also went back to talking, going over everything that had happened and all our possible suspects. But we still couldn't come to any new conclusions.

"It just doesn't fit," I mused, picking at my last few fries. "It's like there's a puzzle piece missing—some clue or connection we're not quite getting."

George shrugged and popped a pickle slice into her mouth. "Maybe we should bring the ABCs in as junior detectives," she joked. "I mean, they know everything there is to know about cruising, right? Maybe they could figure it out."

Bess sighed. "Or maybe we should just give up and

go get a massage too," she said. "That might help us think about all this more clearly."

I stared at her for a moment, then turned to look at George. "The ABCs . . . ," I murmured, my eyes going wide as that final puzzle piece finally clicked into place in my mind. "That's it!" I exclaimed.

"That's what?" Bess blinked at me. "You don't think the ABCs are the bad guys, do you?"

"No, but I think I just figured out who is, thanks to you two." I jumped to my feet, grabbing my leftovers and flinging them in the general direction of the trash bin. "I just want to check one thing to confirm it before I tell Becca. Come on!"

CHAPTER TWELVE

Busted!

"ARE YOU GOING TO TELL US WHAT YOU'RE thinking, or what?" George panted as she raced through the halls at my heels.

"Yeah, spill it, Nancy," Bess added.

In response, I just put on another burst of speed. "There's no time to explain," I tossed back over my shoulder. "If we hurry, we should be able to get this cleared up before the rest of the passengers come back."

I could hear George grumbling under her breath, but I ignored it. Soon enough we'd all know whether my new theory was right.

"Will you at least tell us where we're going?" Bess asked.

"The gym." We rounded another corner. "And here we are."

I skidded to a stop at the glass doors leading into the ship's state-of-the-art workout facility. Pushing through, I was greeted by the mingled scents of sweat and talcum powder. The lobby was all glass, steel, and dark wood. A bored-looking young man in a silver-piped tank top was perched behind a counter, reading a muscle magazine.

"Can I help you?" he asked, glancing up as we entered.

"Yes, I have a question for you." I did my best to sound normal, like an ordinary passenger with an ordinary question. "Some friends of ours were here working out today, and I just need to know—did they stay here the whole time, or did they leave for a while and then come back?"

"Friends of yours?" The attendant wrinkled his brow. "Who do you mean? The only person who's been in here all day is that guy." He jerked a thumb toward the large, open gym area off to the left.

Glancing over, I was surprised to see Mr. Hawaiian Shirt plodding along on one of the treadmills. That was kind of weird—he didn't exactly seem like the gym rat type.

But I wasn't too interested in that just then. My heart was pounding as I leaned forward. This was even better than I'd thought!

"Are you positive about that?" I asked the attendant. "Our friends Vince and Lacey weren't here a little earlier?"

"Nope." He shrugged. "Trust me, I've been sitting here all day."

I glanced at Bess and George, who both looked confused. "Vince and Lacey?" Bess murmured.

"Thanks," I told the attendant. Then I hustled my friends toward the exit. "Come on," I told them. "We've got to get over to the spa. And let me borrow a phone—I need to text Becca again."

George handed hers over as we rushed out of

the gym and back down the hall. "What's going on, Nancy?" she asked. "Do you really think Vince and Lacey are the ones we're after?"

I sent the text, then grinned at her as I returned her phone. "Yeah. And you guys were the ones who made me realize it," I said. "When Bess talked about how we should get a massage and then you mentioned the ABCs, it made me remember a couple of things I'd forgotten about until then. Like that one of the ladies thought she recognized Lacey from a Jubilee cruise they took once."

"I remember that," Bess said. "She said Lacey must have a sister who worked there."

"Only what if it wasn't Lacey's sister, or just her doppelgänger or whatever?" I said, jogging around a corner with my friends right behind me. "What if it was Lacey herself? The ABCs said the woman on the Jubilee cruise was her spitting image except for hair and eye color. And both those things are easily changed."

George gasped. "You mean you think Lacey worked for Jubilee?"

"That's my guess," I said. "And there's our motive. Lacey—and probably Vince, too—could be working undercover for Jubilee. What better way to sabotage their greatest competition? Especially since everything on the *Arctic Star* is totally state-of-the-art."

Bess and George still looked kind of confused, but there wasn't any more time to discuss it. We'd just rounded another corner into the hall where the spa was located. Becca was already there waiting for us, along with Captain Peterson and a pair of beefy uniformed security guards.

"Nancy!" Becca rushed forward to meet me. "What's this all about?"

Captain Peterson strode forward as well. "Yes, I don't understand what's going on here." His voice was stern, but his eyes looked anxious. I guessed all the trouble on his ship must be weighing on him even more than it was on Becca.

"I'll explain everything in a minute," I promised them both. "First we need to get in there."

I led the way into the spa. The front doors opened

into a large, luxurious waiting room. There was a table at one end where I guessed the receptionist normally sat, though it was deserted at the moment. One side wall featured a large mural of a peaceful ocean scene. The other wall was lined with shelves full of various spa-type products for sale.

When we entered, Lacey was kneeling in front of the shelves, holding one of those product bottles. The cap was off, and she was watching as Vince carefully poured something into the bottle from an unmarked flask.

"Hey!" one of the security guards blurted out. "What are you two doing?"

Vince and Lacey looked up, somewhat shocked. Vince recovered quickly.

"Oh!" he said with his usual easy smile. "Sorry, you startled us. Uh, we spilled some of this lotion here and were just trying to fix it. Sorry! We'll pay for it, of course."

"Yes you will." I stepped toward them, gesturing for the security guards to come forward as well. "Better grab that from him. The police will need it as evidence."

"Police?" Lacey exclaimed, jumping to her feet as the guard stepped toward her and plucked the bottle out of her hand. She grabbed for it, but it was too late. "We just said we'd pay—we didn't do anything wrong!"

Captain Peterson cleared his throat, looking confused. "Exactly what is going on here?" he asked me. "I can't have my passengers harassing one another, or—"

"These particular passengers are onboard under false pretenses," I broke in. "I'm pretty sure they're the ones who planted that fake body on the first day, and they were also responsible for the crashing chandelier earlier today. Among other things. Like tampering with the products in here—what'd you put in that lotion bottle, guys? Itching powder, permanent dye, or maybe something more deadly?"

The captain shot the pair a glance, a relieved expression flitting over his face. "Well, innocent until proven guilty and all that, but perhaps we'd better examine the bottle and its contents and see what we can find."

Vince and Lacey traded a glance. Their expressions had gone hard and wary—they clearly realized they were busted and there was no way they were going to talk their way out of it.

"We're not saying another word until we speak to a lawyer," Lacey said, her voice steely. So much for her sweet-and-sensitive act.

"We'll sue for wrongful arrest!" Vince sounded slightly hysterical. "Our lawyers will put you and the entire company out of business!"

"Yeah, that was your motive all along, wasn't it?" I turned toward Becca and the captain. "We're pretty sure they're working for Jubilee Cruises," I explained. "They came on this cruise to sabotage it—to do everything they could to cause negative publicity and press for Superstar. One cursed voyage is all it takes, right?"

"What?" the captain exclaimed.

"So how did you figure it out?" Becca asked me. "I didn't even realize that Lacey and Vince were suspects."

"They weren't until just now," I admitted. "But once I started thinking about it, I couldn't help but be suspicious that they were the ones who just happened to 'discover' that fake body in the pool, remember?

Lacey's scream was what attracted the attention of everyone within earshot, so lots of people would be sure to see it."

"That's right!" Bess exclaimed. "Then she stuck around to cry and shudder and tell everyone who'd listen how terrible it was."

Lacey glared at her, then at me. "You can't prove anything," she snapped.

I ignored her and explained to the captain and the others about the ABCs' comment at dinner the first night. "And there was one other clue that helped me put things together," I went on. "Something Bess said reminded me of it. See, when we ran into Vince and Lacey a little while ago, they said something about Iris scheduling a massage for them. That made me realize that Iris must be the maid assigned to their cabin."

"Iris?" George frowned. "You mean the same Iris we keep seeing in the hall outside our suite? I thought she was the maid for Tobias's cabin."

"No—Tobias's parents said she wasn't, remember?" Bess's eyes went wide. "Oh, now I get it!"

I smiled at her. "Yeah. That bugged me when they said it, but I forgot about it until the massage thing came up. Iris didn't have any reason to spend so much time in our hall—unless she was just snooping around the ship looking for trouble. When I found out she was Vince and Lacey's maid, I started to consider that maybe, just maybe, she was working undercover with them."

Captain Peterson turned to one of the guards. "Go find Iris and bring her to me," he ordered.

As the guard hurried off, I continued explaining. "I'm guessing Iris spotted that tarantula by chance the first time."

"Well, probably not chance exactly," George put in with a grimace. "I bet Tobias scared her with it on purpose."

"Whatever." I shrugged. "The point is, she must have told Vince and Lacey about it, and the three of them cooked up the idea to freak everyone out by planting it on the buffet. I'm guessing Iris sneaked into the cabin and stole the spider, and then one of the other two slipped it onto the buffet and just waited for the fireworks to start."

"Poor Hazel." Bess shook her head. "She could've been hurt or killed!"

George shot her a disbelieving look. "Are you seriously feeling sorry for a spider?"

"What can I say?" Bess shrugged. "I'm an animal lover."

I ignored them. "Once I figured out the first two big pranks—the spider one and the body in the pool—it wasn't hard to guess how they might have pulled off some of the other stuff. Iris could probably get access to the temperature controls, so that explains all the hot and cold cabins last night. Any of them could have started the rumors about the crew not getting paid, or sent Brock Walker that e-mail threat. And of course the happy honeymooners stayed onboard while almost everyone else was gone, so it would have been relatively easy for them to mess with the chandelier. Especially since we just confirmed that they weren't anywhere near the gym, where they claimed to be all day."

"Bad cover story, guys." George smirked at Vince and Lacey. "You should've just said you were in your cabin all day, or smooching on some deserted deck somewhere. You're supposed to be honeymooners—we would've believed it."

"Anyway," I continued, "we didn't see them near the mini-golf course, but it wasn't that crowded up there. Any of the three of them could've easily sneaked in there at some point and rigged that moose's antler to fall on someone."

"Yeah. Good thing Nancy has quick reflexes." Bess shuddered. "She could've been killed!"

"Wait a minute!" Vince blurted out, sounding panicky. "What moose? We didn't do that! And we weren't trying to *kill* anyone!"

"Shut up!" Lacey glared daggers at him.

But Vince didn't even seem to hear her. He shoved forward past the security guards. "No, seriously!" he told the captain. "I mean, okay, you caught us. I confess and all that—we're working for the vice president of Jubilee." He turned to look at Becca. "He hates your friend Verity, by the way. Says she's a traitor to the company. But he still likes your grandfather. That's why we sent you that message."

"Yeah," Lacey spat out. "Too bad you didn't listen."

"Wait, back up," I broke in. "What message? You mean that threatening e-mail Becca got before the cruise started?"

"What threatening e-mail?" Captain Peterson put in, sounding confused.

"It wasn't supposed to be a threat," Vince protested. "It was supposed to be a warning! We didn't want Becca to get mixed up in all this."

"More like you didn't want her to work for the competition at all," I said.

"Whatever." Vince shrugged. "My point is, yeah, we did most of that stuff, okay? But we never tried to actually hurt anyone, so whatever this moose thing is you're talking about, we had nothing to do with that! I swear!"

"Would you shut your big fat mouth?" Lacey snapped. "Or I'll shut it for you!"

"All right, I think I've heard enough." The captain gestured to the guards. "Take them into custody, and let's contact the local police."

A few minutes of chaos followed. Vince pleaded for mercy, while Lacey called him every bad name in the book. My friends and I stepped back and watched as the security guards hustled them both out of the spa. The captain followed, his cell phone pressed to his ear and Becca at his side.

"Think Vince was lying about the moose thing?" George wondered.

"Probably," Bess said. "I bet he panicked when he realized that could be seen as, like, attempted murder or something."

I shrugged, feeling troubled. "Maybe. On the other hand, those loose bolts might have been an oversight like we originally speculated." I bit my lip. "Anyway, I just realized something else. There's no way those two could've planted that note in my suitcase."

"But Iris probably could have," Bess pointed out.

"I guess. But why? She had no way of knowing I was

there to investigate, and otherwise it's just too random."

"Whatever," George said. "You solved the case, right? I mean, Vince just confessed right in front of us. So yay us—now we can relax and enjoy the rest of the cruise."

Just then Becca stuck her head back in through the spa door. "Are you three coming?" she asked. "The captain just called the Ketchikan police to let them know we're on our way. He wants you to come along and give your statements at the station."

"Coming," I said, doing my best to shake off the loose ends tickling my mind. George was right—we'd solved the case.

Yay us.

Later that afternoon I took back my ship ID as the check-in woman smiled and waved me through. "Welcome back aboard, Miss Drew," she said. "Just in the nick of time!"

I thanked her, though my words were lost in the blare of the ship's air horn announcing our imminent departure from Ketchikan. Bess and George had stopped to wait for me just past the check-in, though Becca and the captain had hurried on ahead.

"Well, that was fun," George said when I joined her and Bess. "When I heard we'd be going ashore at Ketchikan, I never thought I'd be spending so much time in the local police station."

"You and me both." I smiled. We'd spent the past two hours at the precinct, giving our statements and answering questions from the captain and the cops. Vince and Lacey had been arrested, along with Iris—it turned out my guess was right and she was a Jubilee plant too.

Bess stretched her arms over her head, looking happy. "So now that we're officially on vacation, what do you want to do first?" she asked. "Should we go get our nails done? Or maybe check out some of the shops?"

"Ugh." George made a face. "With all the activities they've got on this ship, *that's* what you want to do? Shopping and primping? You can do that stuff at home!"

"Before we do anything else, can we please get a snack?" I suggested. "Suddenly, I'm starving."

My friends agreed, and we headed for the stairwell. Halfway to the next floor, we heard the sound of voices somewhere just above us.

"Is that Becca I hear?" George commented. "She didn't get far."

When we reached the landing, Becca and the captain were standing there with Marcelo, Becca's boss. All three of them looked grim and anxious.

"What's wrong?" Bess asked.

Becca spun to face us. "I thought the trouble was over!" she cried. "But something else just happened— the ship's jewelry store just got robbed!"

"What?" George exclaimed.

"Are you sure that wasn't Vince and Lacey too?" I put in.

"Definitely not." Captain Peterson shook his head. "Marcelo says it happened within the past half hour or so—someone must have taken advantage of the usual pandemonium of the passengers reboarding."

By the way he was talking to me, I guessed that Becca must have filled him in on who I was and why I was onboard, though Marcelo looked confused. "We'd appreciate it if you didn't mention this to anyone until we've had a chance to look into it," he said, obviously still taking us for ordinary passengers.

"Of course," Bess told him.

"I'd better go look into this," the captain said, rubbing a hand over his face and looking weary. He glanced at Becca and Marcelo. "As you just said, we don't want this to get out to the passengers. So you two had better go do your thing and keep everyone happy—and distracted."

Becca and Marcelo nodded and dashed up the stairs to the lido deck, with the captain right behind them. My friends and I followed more slowly.

"Wow," Bess said. "What do you think of that?"

George shrugged. "It might not mean anything much," she pointed out. "I mean, jewelry stores get robbed all the time, right? Maybe someone sneaked onboard from the town or something."

I bit my lip as those nagging loose ends crowded back into my mind—that note in my suitcase. The moose incident. The heated argument I'd overheard in the kitchen. And even some of the pre-cruise mischief, which none of the culprits had fessed up to at the police station. Were those things just random red herrings?

"Maybe," I said slowly. "Or . . ."

I didn't finish. We'd just reached the deck, and I spotted Alan rushing toward us.

"There you are!" he exclaimed. "I was afraid you'd missed the departure." He shook his head mock sternly at me. "I still don't know why you all decided to come ashore to try to catch up with me. I told you I'd get your postcards, didn't I?"

Bess linked an arm through his. "We know," she told him sweetly. "But we remembered some other shopping we wanted to do. That's why I texted you to say we were coming back to town. It's just too bad we never found each other."

It was a pretty lame cover story for where we'd really been, but Alan didn't question it. As he started chattering eagerly about trying the ship's climbing wall or something, I traded a look with Bess and George, wishing we were free to continue our conversation.

But it didn't really matter, because I knew we were all thinking the same thing. There was no way that Vince, Lacey, and Iris had robbed the jewelry store—not if the timing was what Marcelo said it was.

Those loose ends started flapping away in my mind again as I realized that maybe we weren't going to be able to relax and enjoy this cruise just yet. . . .

Dear Diary,

OKAY, SO WE DIDN'T SOLVE *EVERY* mystery. But maybe on the next part of the tour— the train ride to Denali—I'll have time to think everything through, clue by clue, and help Becca.

Then I'll be able to pan for that gold!

READ WHAT HAPPENS IN THE NEXT MYSTERY

IN THE NANCY DREW DIARIES,

Strangers on a Train

"NANCY! DOWN HERE!"

I hurried down the last few steps to the landing and saw Becca Wright waving as she rushed up the next set of steps toward me. The cruise ship's atrium stairwell was deserted except for the two of us, just as she'd predicted. Almost everyone aboard the *Arctic Star* was gathered along the open-air decks watching the view as the ship chugged into the picturesque port of Skagway, Alaska.

"I don't have much time," I told Becca. "Alan thinks I'm in the ladies' room. He wants to get a photo of all of us at the rail when we dock."

"I don't have much time either." Becca checked her watch. As the *Arctic Star*'s assistant cruise director, she was always busy. "I'm supposed to be getting ready for disembarkation right now. But I just found out something I thought you'd want to know right away. The police caught the robber!"

I gasped, flashing back to the events of the day before yesterday. While the ship was docked in a town called Ketchikan, someone had robbed the shipboard jewelry store.

"Really, they caught someone already? That's amazing!" I exclaimed. "Who was it?"

"A guy named Troy Anderson," Becca replied, leaning down to pluck a stray bit of lint off the carpet. "I guess he's well known to the local authorities as a petty thief and general troublemaker type. They caught him over in Juneau trying to fence the stuff he stole."

I blinked, taking that in. It wasn't exactly the answer I'd been expecting. "So he wasn't a passenger or crew member on the *Arctic Star*?"

Becca raked a hand through her dark curls. "Nope.

Which is weird, right? I have no idea how he got onboard." She smiled weakly. "Maybe it's a good thing you're still here, Nancy. I hope you're in the mood for another mystery?"

The *Arctic Star* was the flagship of the brand-new Superstar Cruises, and this was its maiden voyage. However, things had gone wrong from the start. *Before* the start, actually. That was why Becca had called me. We'd known each other for years, and she knew I liked nothing better than investigating a tough mystery. She'd called me in—along with my two best friends, Bess Marvin and George Fayne—because she was worried that someone was trying to sabotage the new ship.

And she'd been right. Just a few days into the cruise, I'd nabbed the saboteurs, Vince and Lacey. They were working for a rival cruise line, trying to put Superstar out of business.

Then the jewelry store robbery happened—*after* Vince and Lacey were in custody. And I'd realized that maybe the mystery wasn't over after all.

"Do you think this Anderson guy had an accomplice on the ship?" I asked. "If so, maybe that person was also responsible for some of the other stuff that's been going wrong."

Becca bit her lip, looking anxious. "I hope not. Because I was really hoping all the trouble would be over after you busted Vince and Lacey."

I knew what she meant. I'd been trying to convince myself that the case was solved. That a few dangling loose ends didn't matter. That those loose ends were just red herrings, easily explained by bad luck, coincidence, whatever.

What kind of loose ends? Well, for instance, there was the threatening note I'd found in my suitcase the first day onboard. Vince and Lacey claimed to know nothing about that. They also denied being involved in most of the problems that had happened before the ship set sail. And they claimed to know nothing about the fake moose antler from the mini-golf course that had missed crushing me by inches. They also seemed clueless about the angry argument I'd overheard from the ship's kitchen that had ended in what sounded like a threat: *Drop it, John! Or I'll make sure you never make it to Anchorage.* And they insisted that neither of them was the person who'd pushed me off a raised walkway in Ketchikan, sending me tumbling twenty feet down into icy water.

I shivered, thinking back over the list. It didn't take an expert detective to realize that the most serious of those incidents seemed to be directed at yours truly.

"We have to accept that the case might not be over quite yet," I told Becca. "If the robber does have an accomplice on this ship, he or she might still try to cause more trouble. We'll have to keep our eyes open for clues."

"Do you think—," Becca began.

At that moment I heard a clang from the stairwell. I spun around and saw Alan standing on the top step of the flight coming up from below. He was staring up at Becca and me with a strange expression on his face.

"Alan!" I blurted out, cutting off the rest of Becca's comment. "I—uh—didn't hear you coming."

I hadn't seen Alan Thomas coming the first time I'd met him either. Had that really happened only a few short weeks ago? I'd been having lunch with Bess and George at one of our favorite cafés near River Heights University. Suddenly Alan had appeared beside our table, drooling over Bess and begging her to go out with him.

It wasn't the first time that type of thing had happened. But it was the first time Bess had said yes. She said it was because she saw something different in Alan. He was different, all right. He was outgoing and cheerful and kind of excitable—nerdy, as George liked to call it. I guess that worked for Bess, because the two of them had been together ever since.

Then Becca had called, begging me and my friends to come solve her mystery. Our cover story was that we'd won the cruise in a contest. When Alan found out we would be staying in a luxury four-bedroom cabin, he'd practically begged to come along. He was an environmental studies major at the university, and this trip was supposed to give him a head start on his sophomore year research project. That was nice for him, but it made things kind of complicated for the rest of us. See, Becca had sworn us to secrecy—we weren't supposed to tell a soul why we were really onboard the *Arctic Star*. Not even Alan. Had I just blown our cover?

"Nancy! I've been looking all over for you!" Alan exclaimed, hurrying toward me. "Did you get lost on the way to the bathroom or something? You're missing some amazing views."

"Nope, I was just chatting with Becca, that's all." I forced a smile, studying Alan's face. Had he overheard what Becca and I were talking about? His gray eyes looked as guileless as ever. Or did they? Something about the way they were peering into mine made me wonder just how much he'd heard while coming up the stairs. . . .

FOR ACTIVITIES, STICKERS, AND MORE, JOIN THE ACADEMY AT GODDESSGIRLSBOOKS.COM!

Strangers on a Train

Nancy Drew DIARIES™

Strangers on a Train

#2

CAROLYN KEENE

Aladdin
NEW YORK LONDON TORONTO SYDNEY NEW DELHI

ALADDIN

An imprint of Simon & Schuster Children's Publishing Division

1230 Avenue of the Americas, New York, NY 10020

First Aladdin paperback edition February 2013

Copyright © 2013 by Simon & Schuster

All rights reserved, including the right of reproduction in whole or in part in any form.

ALADDIN is a trademark of Simon & Schuster, Inc., and related logo is a registered trademark of Simon & Schuster, Inc.

NANCY DREW, NANCY DREW DIARIES, and related logo are trademarks of Simon & Schuster, Inc.

Also available in an Aladdin hardcover edition.

For information about special discounts for bulk purchases, please contact Simon & Schuster Special Sales at 1-866-506-1949 or business@simonandschuster.com.

The Simon & Schuster Speakers Bureau can bring authors to your live event. For more information or to book an event contact the Simon & Schuster Speakers Bureau at 1-866-248-3049 or visit our website at www.simonspeakers.com.

Designed by Karina Granda

The text of this book was set in Adobe Caslon Pro.

Manufactured in the United States of America 0316 OFF

10 9

Library of Congress Control Number 2012949339

ISBN 978-1-4169-9073-4 (pbk)

ISBN 978-1-4424-6611-1 (hc)

ISBN 978-1-4424-6571-8 (eBook)

Contents

Dear Diary,

HOW DID IT HAPPEN?

How did someone ever figure out I was a detective, working undercover?

Bess, George, and I have been posing as contest-winning passengers aboard the *Arctic Star*, and I thought I had pretty much solved the mystery on this amazing cruise ship.

But now it seems as though *I'm* being targeted. My luggage and laundry have been ransacked, and when we were traveling to Denali, I was almost cut to shreds by jagged glass.

I always cover my every move. . . .

Don't I?

CHAPTER ONE

Going Ashore

"NANCY! DOWN HERE!"

I hurried down the last few steps to the landing and saw Becca Wright waving as she rushed up the next set of steps toward me. The cruise ship's atrium stairwell was deserted except for the two of us, just as she'd predicted. Almost everyone aboard the *Arctic Star* was gathered along the open-air decks watching the view as the ship chugged into the picturesque port of Skagway, Alaska.

"I don't have much time," I told Becca. "Alan thinks I'm in the ladies' room. He wants to get a photo of all of us at the rail when we dock."

"I don't have much time either." Becca checked her watch. As the *Arctic Star*'s assistant cruise director, she was always busy. "I'm supposed to be getting ready for disembarkation right now. But I just found out something I thought you'd want to know right away. The police caught the robber!"

I gasped, flashing back to the events of the day before yesterday. While the ship was docked in a town called Ketchikan, someone had robbed the shipboard jewelry store.

"Really, they caught someone already? That's amazing!" I exclaimed. "Who was it?"

"A guy named Troy Anderson," Becca replied, leaning down to pluck a stray bit of lint off the carpet. "I guess he's well known to the local authorities as a petty thief and general troublemaker type. They caught him over in Juneau trying to fence the stuff he stole."

I blinked, taking that in. It wasn't exactly the answer I'd been expecting. "So he wasn't a passenger or crew member on the *Arctic Star*?"

Becca raked a hand through her dark curls. "Nope.

Which is weird, right? I have no idea how he got onboard." She smiled weakly. "Maybe it's a good thing you're still here, Nancy. I hope you're in the mood for another mystery?"

The *Arctic Star* was the flagship of the brand-new Superstar Cruises, and this was its maiden voyage. However, things had gone wrong from the start. *Before* the start, actually. That was why Becca had called me. We'd known each other for years, and she knew I liked nothing better than investigating a tough mystery. She'd called me in—along with my two best friends, Bess Marvin and George Fayne—because she was worried that someone was trying to sabotage the new ship.

And she'd been right. Just a few days into the cruise, I'd nabbed the saboteurs, Vince and Lacey. They were working for a rival cruise line, trying to put Superstar out of business.

Then the jewelry store robbery happened—*after* Vince and Lacey were in custody. And I'd realized that maybe the mystery wasn't over after all.

"Do you think this Anderson guy had an accomplice on the ship?" I asked. "If so, maybe that person was also responsible for some of the other stuff that's been going wrong."

Becca bit her lip, looking anxious. "I hope not. Because I was really hoping all the trouble would be over after you busted Vince and Lacey."

I knew what she meant. I'd been trying to convince myself that the case was solved. That a few dangling loose ends didn't matter. That those loose ends were just red herrings, easily explained by bad luck, coincidence, whatever.

What kind of loose ends? Well, for instance, there was the threatening note I'd found in my suitcase the first day onboard. Vince and Lacey claimed to know nothing about that. They also denied being involved in most of the problems that had happened before the ship set sail. And they claimed to know nothing about the fake moose antler from the mini-golf course that had missed crushing me by inches. They also seemed clueless about the angry argument I'd overheard from the ship's kitchen that had ended in what sounded like a threat: *Drop it, John! Or I'll make sure you never make it to Anchorage.* And they insisted that neither of them was the person who'd pushed me off a raised walkway in Ketchikan, sending me tumbling twenty feet down into icy water.

I shivered, thinking back over the list. It didn't take an expert detective to realize that the most serious of those incidents seemed to be directed at yours truly.

"We have to accept that the case might not be over quite yet," I told Becca. "If the robber does have an accomplice on this ship, he or she might still try to cause more trouble. We'll have to keep our eyes open for clues."

"Do you think—," Becca began.

At that moment I heard a clang from the stairwell. I spun around and saw Alan standing on the top step of the flight coming up from below. He was staring up at Becca and me with a strange expression on his face.

"Alan!" I blurted out, cutting off the rest of Becca's comment. "I—uh—didn't hear you coming."

I hadn't seen Alan Thomas coming the first time I'd met him either. Had that really happened only a few short weeks ago? I'd been having lunch with Bess and George at one of our favorite cafés near River Heights University. Suddenly Alan had appeared beside our table, drooling over Bess and begging her to go out with him.

It wasn't the first time that type of thing had happened. But it was the first time Bess had said yes. She said it was because she saw something different in Alan. He was different, all right. He was outgoing and cheerful and kind of excitable—nerdy, as George liked to call it. I guess that worked for Bess, because the two of them had been together ever since.

Then Becca had called, begging me and my friends to come solve her mystery. Our cover story was that we'd won the cruise in a contest. When Alan found out we would be staying in a luxury four-bedroom suite, he'd practically begged to come along. He was an environmental studies major at the university, and this trip was supposed to give him a head start on his sophomore year research project. That was nice for him, but it made things kind of complicated for the rest of us. See, Becca had sworn us to secrecy—we weren't supposed to tell a soul why we were really onboard the *Arctic Star*. Not even Alan. Had I just blown our cover?

"Nancy! I've been looking all over for you!" Alan exclaimed, hurrying toward me. "Did you get lost on the way to the bathroom or something? You're missing some amazing views."

"Nope, I was just chatting with Becca, that's all." I forced a smile, studying Alan's face. Had he overheard what Becca and I were talking about? His gray eyes looked as guileless as ever. Or did they? Something about the way they were peering into mine made me wonder just how much he'd heard while coming up the stairs. . . .

I dismissed the thought as quickly as it came. Alan was pretty much an open book. Like I said, he'd declared his adoration of Bess the first time they'd met. In fact, he seemed to blurt out pretty much every thought that entered his head. If he'd heard anything important, I'd know it.

"We'd better get back out there," I told him, still smiling. "I don't want to miss any more scenery."

"Smile and say Alaska!" Alan sang out.

Bess giggled, tossing back her blond hair as the sea breeze whipped it across her face. "No way," she said. "If I say that, my face will look funny. I'll stick with the traditional." She struck a pose leaning against the gleaming brass railing, with the Skagway shoreline behind her. "Cheese!"

Alan snapped the photo. "Gorgeous!" he exclaimed, hurrying over to let Bess check out the screen on his digital camera.

George rolled her eyes. "Are we going to stand around here taking pictures all day, or are we actually going to get off this ship and *do* something?" she grumbled.

I grabbed her arm and pulled her aside, dodging a few excited passengers who were rushing toward the gangplank leading to the dock below. "Leave Alan alone for a sec," I said quietly. "I've been dying to tell you what Becca just told me."

"What?" George immediately looked interested. Shooting a quick glance at Alan to make sure he wasn't close enough to hear us, she lowered her voice. "Was it about Vince and Lacey? Did they finally fess up to leaving that nasty note in your luggage?"

Right. That was another unexplained occurrence from earlier in the cruise. The note had read, *I HOPE U GET LOST JUST LIKE UR BAG—& THAT U STAY LOST!*

"No. But the cops caught the jewelry thief." I quickly filled her in.

When I was finished, George let out a low whistle. "So it wasn't anyone from the ship? That's weird."

"I know, right? There's no way he got through security on his own." I glanced over at the exit station set up near the gangplank. Several crew members were there, dressed in Superstar's crisp navy-and-silver uniforms, running ship IDs through a scanner as passengers disembarked for the day's shore stop. Even though the area around the exit was chaotic, with dozens of excited passengers shouting and laughing and eager to start their day in Skagway, the ship's staff maintained perfect order, channeling each person through the scanner station before ushering him or her down the gangplank. Watching the well-organized procedure made it seem impossible that anyone could board unscanned or undetected.

"So who helped him get aboard?" George wondered. "He must have an accomplice, right? A crew member, or maybe another passenger?"

Instead of answering, I cleared my throat loudly. "Get any good shots?" I asked Alan, who was coming toward us with Bess on his heels.

"Of course." Alan winked. "It's easy to get good shots when you have such a beautiful model."

George smirked. She doesn't have much patience for gooey romantic talk. Especially when it came from Alan. "Enough with the photo session," she said. "Let's get off this boat and have some fun."

"Speaking of fun," Bess said as we all wandered

toward the exit station, "what's on the agenda for today?"

"You girls weren't there when Scott came around at lunch yesterday, so I signed us up for a few things," Alan said. He glanced around. "Where is Scott, anyway? He said I should check in with him about the exact schedule."

"I don't see him." I scanned the exit area, which was growing more crowded by the second. Half a dozen raucous redheads—members of a large family reunion—had just entered. I also spotted a few other familiar faces. But I didn't see the lean, tanned form of Scott, the shore excursion specialist, anywhere.

A statuesque blond woman in a Superstar uniform saw me looking around and stepped toward me. "May I help you, Ms. Drew?" she asked in a husky voice heavily shaded with an eastern European accent.

"Oh, hi, Tatjana." I smiled at her, though I couldn't help a flash of unease. Tatjana worked for Becca, and she'd almost caught the two of us discussing the case a couple of times. "Um, we were just looking for Scott so we could check about today's trips."

"He is already onshore," Tatjana replied. "You should be able to find him on the dock once you've disembarked."

"Okay, thanks," Bess said with a smile. "Come on, guys. We'd better get in line."

We headed across the lobby. "Look, it's the ABCs," Alan said, nodding toward three gray-haired women at the back of the line. Alice, Babs, and Coral were experienced cruisers who were seated at our table at dinner.

"And Tobias," George added with considerably less enthusiasm.

I couldn't help a slight grimace myself when I saw the eight-year-old boy. He was pulling at his mother's hand as she and her husband chatted with the three older women.

"Looks like Coral has forgiven him for scaring her half to death with that pet tarantula of his," Bess whispered with a smirk.

"I guess so." I'm not scared of spiders, but I still shuddered a little as I recalled the incident. Tobias had smuggled his tarantula onto the ship, and the hairy eight-legged critter had ended up crawling over the pastries one day at lunch. "That's only fair, though," I added. "Vince and Lacey stole Hazel and put her on the buffet, remember? Tobias didn't have anything to do with it." I shrugged. "Well, unless you count sneaking the spider onboard in the first place . . ."

I let my voice trail off, since we'd reached the group by now. The ABCs and Tobias's parents greeted us cheerfully. Tobias himself ignored us. That was typical. He'd made it clear from the start that he didn't want to be on the cruise, and his attitude generally varied from sullen to downright obnoxious.

"Do you young people have some exciting shore activities planned for today?" Babs inquired.

"I guess so." George shot a look at Alan. "You'll have to ask our own personal event planner."

Alan grinned and swept into a goofy bow. "At your service."

"Are you taking that scenic train trip through the mountains?" Tobias's mother asked. "We're really looking forward to that, aren't we, Tobias?"

"I guess." Tobias shrugged, looking less than

enthusiastic. "Hey, here comes Hiro. He probably wants me to go on some boring tour with him or something."

Sure enough, the youth activities coordinator, a young man in navy shorts and a silver-piped polo shirt, was wandering toward us. He spotted Tobias and waved.

"Have fun onshore, Tobias!" he called. "I'll see you for movie night tonight, right?"

"Whatever." Tobias waved back, then turned to peer at the line in front of us. "When are we getting off this stupid ship, anyway?"

"Patience, Tobias," his mother said. "We have to wait our turn."

Luckily, that didn't take long. A few minutes later we were all making our way down the long gangplank together.

Bess shaded her eyes against the bright morning sun. "This place looks pretty cool."

"Oh, it's supposed to be wonderful," Coral assured her. "Skagway was an important site during the Klondike gold rush in the late 1800s. The main street is supposed to look like a postcard straight out of that time. We can't wait to see it!"

"Sounds like fun, eh, son?" Tobias's father clapped the boy on the back. "Well, have a nice day, everyone. We'll see you back on—"

"Sir! Excuse me, sir!"

We all turned. A young man in a tidy navy-and-silver uniform was running down the gangplank, apologizing profusely as he pushed past other passengers. He looked familiar, and when he got closer, I realized he was one of the busboys from the main dining room.

He skidded to a stop in front of Tobias's father. "I'm so glad I caught you," he said breathlessly, holding up a camera. "You left this in the café after breakfast. I'm sure you'll want it with you today."

Tobias's father's eyes widened. "I hadn't even noticed!" he exclaimed, taking the camera. "Thank you so much, young man. You're right, I'm sure I'll want to take lots of pictures today." He fished a couple of bills out of his pocket. "Thank you for tracking me down."

"Thank *you*, sir." The busboy blushed slightly, then

pocketed the money. He glanced around at the rest of us. "I hope you all enjoy your day in Skagway."

As he turned toward the gangplank, another man rushed down. "Sanchez! There you are," he barked out, grabbing the busboy by the arm. "Come with me. *Now*."

My friends were already moving down the dock, chatting with the ABCs. But something about the second man's behavior made me curious. I took a step after him as he dragged the busboy to a quiet spot behind a trash bin.

"What is it, boss?" the busboy asked, sounding confused and a little scared.

No wonder. The second man's face was livid. It was obvious he was trying to keep his temper under control, but he wasn't having much luck.

"I'll tell you what it is," he exclaimed, jabbing a finger at the busboy's chest. "You're fired, that's what!"

CHAPTER TWO

In the Line of Fire

"WHAT?" THE BUSBOY'S FACE WENT PALE. "Why? What did I do, boss?"

"You know what you did. You just thought we'd never find out." The boss glared at him.

I winced, feeling sorry for the busboy. He started to protest, looking confused and terrified, and his boss responded, though their voices were too low for me to hear what they were saying anymore. I glanced around for my friends, wondering if they'd noticed what was going on.

Instead I saw a heavyset man with a droopy mustache

hurrying over. I didn't know his name, but I'd seen him a few times on the ship. I assumed he was another passenger, since he always wore a Hawaiian shirt and shorts rather than a navy-and-silver uniform. But he seemed to spend a lot of time hanging around with the staff.

Right now he was zeroing in on the busboy and his boss. "What's going on over here?" he demanded as he rushed up to them. "Is there a problem?"

The boss dropped his hold on the younger man's arm. "It's nothing to worry about, sir," he said smoothly, though his brow was still creased in anger. "Please enjoy your day in Skagway."

Mr. Hawaiian Shirt ignored him, peering at the busboy's anxious face. "You okay, son?" he said. "Because if there's some sort of trouble, you've got to speak up for yourself."

The busboy's face went red. He glanced from his boss to the other man. "It's nothing," he muttered.

"That's right," his boss put in. "Thanks for your concern, sir. Now if you'll excuse us—"

I guess I was staring as all this went on. Because just then, the busboy turned and met my eye. He spun toward his boss.

"It's not right!" he said suddenly, his fists clutched at his sides. "I don't know anything about any illegal drugs! Whoever said they found them in my locker is lying."

"Drugs?" Mr. Hawaiian Shirt barked out. "What's this all about?"

By now the raised voices were attracting attention, even on the busy Skagway dock. Some of the passengers who were disembarking nearby were looking over, and a moment later I saw the tall, broad-shouldered form of the *Arctic Star*'s captain striding in our direction.

"What's going on over here?" Captain Peterson asked. Glancing from the red-faced busboy to Mr. Hawaiian Shirt, he frowned. "Never mind, don't tell me. Let's take this back to the ship. Now." He grabbed the boss by the elbow and the busboy by the shoulder, steering both men toward the gangplank.

"Wait!" Mr. Hawaiian Shirt hurried after them. But he was cut off by a group of laughing redheaded children from the family reunion. By the time he dodged around them, the captain and the two employees had disappeared into the ship.

I caught up to him by the foot of the gangplank. "Wow, what was that all about?" I asked in what I hoped was a friendly, casually curious tone. I stuck my hand out. "By the way, I'm Nancy. Nancy Drew. I've seen you around the ship, remember?"

"Uh, sure." The man glanced at me and shook my hand, though he looked distracted. "Nice to meet you. Fred Smith."

"So what do you think was going on with those two?" I said. "Can you believe that guy fired the busboy in front of everyone? Crazy, right?"

"Just business as usual, I suppose. Excuse me." Fred Smith pulled a cell phone out of his pocket. He hit a button and pressed the phone to his ear, turning away and disappearing into the crowd.

Okay, so much for that. I looked around for my friends. They were a few yards down the dock, gathered around Scott, the shore excursion specialist.

"Where'd you disappear to?" George asked when I joined them.

"Nowhere. Remember that nice busboy with the dimples who cleaned up the drink Coral spilled last night?" I said. "I think he just got fired."

Scott glanced at me. "You talking about Sanchez?" he asked. "Yeah, just heard about that. Something about finding drugs in his locker."

"Really? Wow, crazy," Alan commented.

Scott shrugged. "It happens. Just an unfortunate side effect of dealing with a large crew of workers from all different backgrounds." He grimaced slightly. "Some of them less, um, savory than others. Like Sanchez, for instance." He cleared his throat and pasted a pleasant smile on his face, as if realizing he'd said too much. "In any case, I hope you won't let this incident spoil your day here in Skagway."

"Don't worry about that." George glanced toward the town's main street, which was lined with old-timey buildings. "This place looks pretty cool so far. Now, about that train ride . . ."

The others went back to discussing the day's activities. I was only half listening, though. Could the incident I'd just witnessed have anything to do with our case? That man, Fred Smith, had been one of our suspects the last time around. It was strange how he always seemed to be nearby whenever there was trouble. Did he need to go back on the list? Or could the busboy himself be the jewelry thief's accomplice? Scott had all but come out and said the guy might have a questionable past.

I chewed my lower lip, trying to figure out how all the clues might fit together. I wished I could question Scott about the busboy, since he seemed to know him. But I couldn't, not with Alan standing right there. I didn't want to raise his suspicions by seeming too interested in something like that—especially if he'd heard any of what Becca and I had been talking about earlier.

Come to think of it, I wasn't sure I wanted to raise Scott's suspicions either. Becca and Captain Peterson were still the only two people on the ship who knew why my friends and I were really there. And I wanted to keep it that way. I'd already come close to blowing my cover with Scott back in Ketchikan. I'd seen him sneak out of a tourist show to meet with a seedy-looking guy with a big scar on his face. That had made me suspicious enough to tail him through town, but he'd caught me following him—right as he'd met up with another tough-looking man and handed over a wad of cash. He hadn't been happy about seeing me, since he'd explained he was paying off some gambling debts, which could get him in trouble if the captain found out about them.

I sighed, rubbing my face and stifling a yawn. I hadn't had enough sleep last night, and it was making it hard to focus. Besides, there wasn't much I could do to find out more about the firing right now. I'd just have to ask Becca about it later.

"Smile!" Alan sang out, snapping another picture.

I forced a smile. Bess, George, and I were posing in front of a big black-and-red train car on display in a little park. A sign explained that it was a rotary snowplow, built in 1899 to clear Alaska's heavy snows off the tracks.

After Alan took a couple of more photos, Bess checked her watch. "Hey, does anyone remember what time we need to be at the station for the scenic train ride?" she said. "Was it twelve or twelve thirty?"

George gave her a strange look. No wonder. Bess has a memory like an elephant. She rarely forgets a name, a face, or anything else.

But Alan lowered his camera. "I don't know," he said. "Maybe we'd better double-check."

"Thanks, sweetie." Bess tilted her head and smiled up at him. "We'll wait for you right here while you run over there."

Alan blinked. "Oh. Okay, I'll be right back."

As he hurried off, Bess turned to me. "All right, Nancy," she said briskly. "You've been walking around in a fog for the past hour. What are you thinking about?"

I grinned weakly. "I'm that obvious?"

"Oh, yeah." George leaned back against the snowplow sign, watching as Tobias and his mother posed for a photo his father was taking. "So spill."

I glanced around to make sure nobody was close enough to hear us. The area was crowded with visitors, mostly passengers from our ship and the two others currently docked in Skagway. I wasn't surprised that my friends had noticed I was a little distracted. My mind wouldn't stop buzzing around the incident on the dock. Did it mean something? I couldn't decide.

"I was thinking about that busboy," I said. "It's probably not related to the case, but you never know, right?"

"I guess." Bess looked dubious.

"How would something like that be related?" George asked, sounding even more doubtful.

I frowned. "I don't know, okay? I just want to make sure we don't miss any clues, or—" I cut myself off with a yawn.

"Sorry, are we keeping you up?" George said with a smirk.

I almost snapped back at her, but I swallowed the retort. "Sorry. Guess I'm pretty tired. My wake-up call got messed up this morning, remember?"

The suite where we were staying had its own butler, an enthusiastic, outgoing young man named Max. One of his duties was handling our daily wake-up calls, and that morning he'd entered my room at five a.m. on the dot.

"I *know* I requested a seven thirty wake-up call," I murmured, stifling another yawn.

"Whatever, everyone makes mistakes." George shrugged. "Max said it was just a text mix-up or something, right? And he apologized like crazy for, like, the entire morning."

Bess nodded. "I don't know why you didn't just go back to sleep, Nancy."

"I tried. But your boyfriend was snoring so loudly next door that I couldn't."

"So *that's* why you're so cranky today," George muttered.

I shot her a look. "That, and I still can't believe you knocked my bagel on the floor yesterday at breakfast."

George protested. "I told you that wasn't my fault. Alan totally bumped into my arm!"

"Yeah, yeah," Bess put in. "It's always Alan's fault with you, isn't it, George?"

"Shh," I said as I saw Alan hurrying toward them. "Speak of the devil . . ."

That was the end of any private talk for the moment. We wandered around town, sightseeing and shopping for souvenirs and snacks, until it was time to head back to the station for our scenic train excursion.

"Wow, this is cool," Bess said as we entered the old-fashioned train car. "It's like stepping back in time."

I nodded, though I wasn't paying much attention. I'd spotted a couple of our fellow passengers from the *Arctic Star* in the car. One of them was young travel blogger Wendy Webster. As usual, she stood out in the crowd in her plaid skirt, tank top, and long scarf. She looked up from her laptop computer and spotted us.

"Hey, guys!" she called, shoving her oversize black-framed glasses up her nose and waving. "Is this place epic or what?"

"Sure, if you say so," George said. "Totally epic."

Hearing shouts of laughter from the other end of

the car, I glanced that way. Hiro was seated there, surrounded by about half a dozen kids from the *Arctic Star*, though I noticed Tobias wasn't among them.

"Dibs on the window seat." George pushed past me and flopped into the seat. I sat down next to her, while Bess and Alan sat down in front of us.

Soon the train was winding its way into the mountains. The scenery was so incredible that it actually woke me up a little. The train chugged along the tracks, which wound their way up steep inclines and across rusty iron bridges, all the while revealing stunning views of foothills blanketed with dense evergreen forests, rivers cutting through mountain passes, and distant peaks still dusted in snow even though it was summer.

Eventually, though, my mind started to wander. I glanced ahead at Wendy, who was snapping photos and oohing and aahing along with everyone else. She'd been one of our original suspects too. That had made sense at the time. We'd thought she might be drumming up readers for her blog by creating weird happenings to write about.

But now? Was she still a viable suspect? What would she have to gain by smuggling a jewelry thief onboard? Money, I supposed. Everyone liked money, right? Then again, by that logic, *everyone* could be a suspect. . . .

I shook my head, which was feeling fuzzy and sleepy again. "Be right back," I told George. "I want to go get some fresh air."

"Uh-huh." George was peering at the little screen on her camera and didn't even glance over as I stood up.

I made my way down the aisle, swaying side to side with the motion of the train. At the end of the car, a door led on to the little open-air platform between our car and the next. I stepped out there and took a deep breath of the cool, clean mountain air. I had the platform to myself for the moment, so I stepped over to the railing and looked out. It was kind of a scary view. The train was hugging the side of the mountain on a ledge so narrow I couldn't see the edge of it when I looked down. I'm not normally afraid of heights, but I gulped when I saw the dizzying drop-off to the valley floor far, far below.

Suddenly the door to the next car burst open, and someone stomped out onto the platform. It was Scott, the shore excursions guy. He had a cell phone pressed to his ear.

". . . and you'd better figure out a way to fix things before I get to Anchorage," he hissed into the phone, his voice practically seething with fury. "Because if you don't, I'm going to—"

He cut himself off abruptly as he noticed me standing there, staring at him. Clicking the phone off, he glared at me. His face was twisted with anger, making him look like a completely different person than usual.

He took a quick step toward me. I clutched the railing behind me—the only thing between me and a two-hundred-foot drop to my certain death.

"You!" Scott growled. "What are *you* doing out here?"

CHAPTER THREE

~

Rebuilding the List

I SUCKED IN A DEEP BREATH, READY TO scream for help. At that moment the door to my train car flew open.

"Nancy!" Bess exclaimed. "There you are." She rushed out, with Alan and George right behind her.

"I told you she went outside," George said.

Alan grinned. "Okay, but you weren't too sure," he teased. "All we knew was that we turned around and she was gone!"

I looked at Scott. His face had relaxed into its usual

calm, jovial expression. He caught me looking and smiled sheepishly.

"Sorry if I startled you, Nancy," he said. "You startled me, too. I guess that's what I get for trying to do two things at once, huh?" Dropping his phone into his shirt pocket, he reached for the door. "Enjoy the scenery, folks."

As he left, Alan tugged at my arm. "Check it out. I want to get a shot of you guys standing here when we pass that waterfall up ahead," he said. "Hurry, Nancy— get over there between Bess and George."

I obeyed, though I wasn't focused on the scenery. I'm not the type of person who gets rattled easily, but Scott had really scared me for a second. The depth of anger in his eyes had been terrifying. Could there be a dark side to him? Maybe a *criminal* side? I'd asked Becca about his background after the incident in Ketchikan, and she'd assured me he was an industry veteran who'd been recommended by Captain Peterson himself. That had been enough to make me cross him off the suspect list then. Was it time to investigate him a little further now?

I wished I could talk to both my friends about it. As it was, the best I could hope for was talking to one of them. As we wandered back toward our seats, I poked Bess in the shoulder.

"This train ride is really romantic, isn't it?" I said meaningfully. "It's nice that you and Alan are getting to enjoy it together."

Bess got the hint right away. "Come to think of it, it's a little crowded around here to call it romantic." She linked her arm through Alan's and peered up at him with a smile. "Should we go find the caboose and take some pictures there? Just the two of us?"

"Sure, Bess. Your wish is my command."

Soon they were heading out the door toward the back of the train. I grabbed George and pulled her in the opposite direction, stopping when we reached a block of empty seats a couple of cars up.

"Very smooth," George said. "Good thing Alan's so clueless. He obviously doesn't even realize we keep trying to ditch him."

"Yeah." I glanced around, double-checking to

make sure we wouldn't be overheard. It seemed pretty safe. Our closest neighbors were a pair of senior citizens snoozing in their seats several rows away. There were also a few members of that family reunion huddled at the windows up near the front of the car, but the clanking, chugging sounds of the train drowned out their conversation. "So listen," I told George, "something happened right before you found me just now. . . ."

I filled her in on the incident with Scott. George looked surprised.

"Shore Excursion Scott?" she said. "You really think *he* could be our bad guy?"

"I don't know." I sighed, leaning back in my seat and staring out the window at the looming mountains. "But he was obviously angry with whoever he was talking to on the phone. What if it had something to do with that robbery?"

"What if it didn't?" George countered. "You said he mentioned fixing something before he got to Anchorage. That's the ship's next stop, remember? He was probably just doing business, organizing the buses to take us from the ship to the city, something like that."

"Maybe." I flashed back to the moment he'd lunged toward me. "But if you could've seen his face when he realized I'd heard him . . ."

"Okay, there's that." George leaned past me to snap a photo of a picturesque mountain pass. "But Becca said he has a good rep, right?"

"Uh-huh. She said the captain recommended him for this job. And he's worked in the cruise industry for quite a while."

George nodded. "Okay. The other thing is, you admitted yourself that you're sleep deprived today. You're probably a little on edge from that. Totally understandable, right? But isn't it possible it's making you freak out over something that's not really freak-out-worthy?"

I couldn't help smiling at her choice of words. "Maybe," I admitted, stifling yet another yawn. "Still, we both know from experience that you can't always tell who's a criminal based on their public reputation. Or even who their friends are." I flashed momentarily to that hulking tough guy Scott had met in Ketchikan, and the man with the scarred face he'd talked to briefly before that. He'd claimed they were poker buddies. Was he telling the truth? "It might be worth checking him out a little more," I added. "Just in case."

"Agreed." George frowned. "Although I'm starting to wonder whether this jewelry robbery business is even worth stressing over. I mean, the cops are already on the case, right? They're way better equipped to handle this kind of investigation—you know, the kind with real criminals. Possibly *dangerous* criminals."

"Yeah, I guess," I said. "But if there's someone on the ship involved—"

"Then the cops will figure it out." George shrugged. "That's their job. Besides, it was probably that busboy we saw get fired earlier. So we could be doing all this investigating and sneaking around for nothing."

"Maybe." I wasn't quite as convinced as she seemed to be. After all, neither the busboy nor his boss had mentioned anything about the robbery—just the illegal drugs. "But even if that busboy *is* the robber's accomplice, we still don't know who left me that threatening note. That couldn't have been the busboy—he'd never even laid eyes on me at that point."

"How do you know the busboy didn't leave the note?" George countered, tapping her foot against the seat in front of us. "You're famous, you know. Sort of, anyway."

I cocked an eyebrow at her. "How do you figure?"

"How many times have you been written up in the papers back home in River Heights for solving mysteries big and small?" George said. "All those stories end up on the newspapers' websites, you know. For all the world to see with a quick web search. So maybe your rep as the Sherlockina Holmes of the Midwest preceded you, and that busboy thought you were coming to Alaska to investigate him. He might have been trying to scare you off before you got started."

"Sounds a little far-fetched, but I suppose anything's possible." I shook my head. "Until we know for sure, we've got to keep our eyes open. I mean, I know we thought the case was closed when we caught Vince and Lacey."

"But they swore they didn't do some of the bad stuff," George said with a nod. "Like pushing you off that walkway in Ketchikan, and the moose antler thing, and some of the problems Becca told us about from before the cruise started."

"Yeah. A few of those incidents could've been accidents or red herrings," I said. "Maybe somebody just bumped me innocently on that narrow walkway, and I lost my balance. And maybe there was an oversight and the screws on that moose antler never got tightened properly, so it fell when Bess and Alan leaned on it."

"And maybe the pre-cruise problems were just bad luck or human error or whatever," George went on.

"Right. But *someone* left that note in my suitcase. And if that same someone might possibly have been the one who pushed me over the railing back in Ketchikan, I need to figure out who it is before something even worse happens. If it turns out that busboy was behind it all like you said, cool. All we've lost is some time and energy we could've used for sightseeing today." I shrugged. "If not? Then we'd better not waste an entire day looking at pretty scenery and shopping for souvenirs while the real culprit could be planning his or her next move."

George didn't answer for a moment, instead clearing her throat loudly. Glancing up, I saw Hiro hurrying down the aisle. He spotted us, too, and smiled.

"Having a nice time?" he asked, pausing and leaning a hand on the back of our seat. "The scenery is spectacular out here, isn't it? I thought I'd miss the warm blue waters of the Caribbean when I left Jubilee to take this job. But it's been great to see a new part of the world."

"You worked for Jubilee before?" I was surprised, though I wasn't sure why. The cruise industry was really pretty small, and Jubilee Cruise Lines was one of its largest players. A lot of the *Arctic Star*'s crew, including Becca, had worked for Jubilee before being lured away by Superstar Cruises.

Hiro nodded. "I was assistant cruise director on one of the ships," he said. "It was a great job, but when I heard Superstar had a spot open for kiddie coordinator, I jumped at it. I love working with kids." He checked his watch. "Speaking of which, I'd better scoot. Got a bunch of the little rascals waiting for me right now. Enjoy the rest of the ride, ladies."

"Thanks," George and I chorused as he hurried off.

"That's weird," George said once he was gone.

"What?" I asked.

She shrugged. "Becca's the assistant cruise director on our ship, right? And I thought you said she was Hiro's boss. So it sounds like he took a demotion to take this job. Why would someone do that? Especially since it sounds like he was skeptical about leaving the Caribbean to come to Alaska?"

"Good question. But I'm not totally sure Becca is actually his boss," I said. "I'll text her right now and ask."

I pulled out my phone and started tapping out a quick text. "Cool, your phone's working again," George said, peering over my shoulder.

"Uh-huh." My phone had gone dead—or at least temporarily unconscious—after my unplanned dip in the cold waters beneath that walkway in Ketchikan. "After it dried out, it was fine."

"So are you going to ask Becca about Scott, too?" George asked.

"I think I'll wait and ask her about that in person." I tucked the phone away. "Seems too complicated to do via text. Anyway, I guess this means Hiro's still on the suspect list?"

"Definitely," George said. "He was around when the moose antler crashed. And you said Becca acted weird when you asked about him that time—maybe she's suspicious of him too."

"Maybe." I thought about that conversation. As soon as I'd mentioned Hiro's name, Becca had rushed off, claiming she needed to be somewhere. "But if she thinks we should investigate him, why wouldn't she just say so?"

"Got me." George shrugged. "Anyway, we already know Scott's on the list now too. Who else?"

I thought about our previous suspect list. "Well, there's Wendy."

"Wendy the Wacko?" George nodded. "Yeah, she's too weird *not* to keep on the list, I guess. But actually,

I'm thinking it's more likely to be a crew member than a passenger. Like Scott or Hiro. Or maybe Tatjana—we were suspicious of her before, right? I mean, how would someone like Wendy sneak around the ship causing trouble? She doesn't exactly blend into the background."

"True. But Wendy still has a decent motive," I said. "She really wants her blog to be a success. What better way than making sure this cruise is one everybody wants to read about, even if it's a crime she's writing about?" I remembered one more suspect we hadn't discussed yet. "And let's not forget Fred."

"Fred? Who's Fred?"

"Mr. Hawaiian Shirt," I said. "I forgot to tell you, he turned up right after the busboy got fired and started trying to get involved."

"Weird. The guy acts like he'd rather be working on the ship than traveling on it," George said. "Pretty sure I've seen him in the kitchen more often than I've seen him at the pool."

"Yeah." I didn't say anything else, mostly because about a dozen redheads were pouring into the train car. They were all chatting and laughing, and several of them were clutching cameras. They rushed over to the other family reunion members, overflowing into the seats near ours.

One of them, a twentyish young woman with an auburn ponytail, glanced at George and me with a smile. "Hi! You're from our ship, right?" she said. "Isn't this fun?"

"Yeah, it's great," George said.

Obviously we'd lost our quiet conversation spot. Probably just as well—if George and I stayed away too long, Alan might get suspicious. Especially if he'd heard even a little of my conversation with Becca earlier. He might be clueless, but he wasn't stupid. I didn't want to give him any excuse to figure out what was going on behind his back. I sure didn't want to risk blowing my cover—for Becca's sake and the safety of the ship's passengers.

I stood up, returning the redhead's smile. "Sorry, I think we took your seats," I told her. "We'd better go find our friends now. See you back on the ship."

"Wait up a sec, guys," George said. "I have to tie my shoe."

"Hurry up," Alan told her as he, Bess, and I stopped. "Scott said we're running late, and I don't want to miss my chance to make my fortune."

Bess grinned, squeezing his hand. "Don't get your hopes up, sweetie," she said. "This gold-panning place is just a tourist spot right here in town. It's not exactly breaking new ground in the next gold rush."

George glanced up from fiddling with the laces of her sneakers. "Still, gold's gold," she said. "Scott said this place guarantees we'll each get to find some real gold in our pans."

"Yeah. Like three granules of gold dust, probably," Bess said.

As they continued squabbling amiably, I glanced forward. We were at the tail end of the large group of *Arctic Star* passengers making its way from the train station to the next activity in Skagway. Scott was at the front, leading the way.

My gaze lingered on him. He was back in professional mode, smiling and helpful, with no hint of the terrifying anger I'd seen. Could George be right? Had my exhaustion—not to mention my obsession with this case—made me see something that wasn't there?

I forgot about that as the crowd shifted and I spotted another familiar figure. It was Fred. He wasn't part of the group heading to the gold-panning place—instead he was scurrying along the sidewalk across the way with his hands in his pockets and his head tucked down between his shoulders. Almost as if he didn't want to be seen. Interesting.

George finally finished tying her shoe. "Come on, let's hurry," she said. "I want to make sure I get the best gold-panning spot."

"You guys go ahead," I said. "I, um, need to find a restroom. I'll meet up with you in a minute."

"You sure?" Alan said teasingly. "Don't expect us not to steal your gold if you take too long, Nancy!"

I forced a smile, trying to keep Fred in view out of the corner of my eye. "I'll have to take my chances. See you in a bit."

By the time I pushed my way through the eager, gold-crazed crowd around me, Fred had disappeared. I hurried off in the direction I'd last seen him going. Whew! I spotted him again as soon as I rounded the next corner. He was just a few yards ahead of me, moving fast.

I fell into step behind him, doing my best to keep a few people between us. Good thing. Halfway down the block, Fred stopped abruptly, then turned and peered behind him. Oops.

Luckily, he didn't seem to see me. But it reminded me to be careful.

I continued to tail him. It wasn't easy. He stopped and stared around suspiciously every few moments. What was he doing?

Finally he ducked into a large souvenir shop. I waited a moment, allowing a few other people to pass before stepping inside myself.

The place was cavernous and crowded, packed with tourists pawing through tables overflowing with

T-shirts, key chains, stuffed animals, and every other imaginable form of souvenir knickknack.

But where was Fred? I glanced around but couldn't see him anywhere. Outside, his brightly colored Hawaiian shirt had made him easy to spot. In here, surrounded by every flavor of colorful tchotchke? Not so much.

I moved deeper into the store, dodging a sticky-looking little girl cooing at a stuffed arctic fox and several loud, excited women with Boston accents exclaiming over some salmon jerky. Still no sign of my quarry.

Then I spotted a flash of orange and red toward the back of the store near an oversize stuffed grizzly bear wearing a Skagway souvenir hat and an apron emblazoned with the Alaskan flag. Hurrying closer, I finally spotted Fred.

He was huddled behind the bear, deep in conversation with Sanchez, the fired busboy!

CHAPTER FOUR

Unpleasant Surprises

MY HEART POUNDED AS I CREPT CLOSER
to the stuffed bear. Fred appeared to be doing most of
the talking. But he was keeping his voice too low for
me to hear what he was saying.

"Nancy! Hey, Nancy! Over here!" a voice yelled
loudly, cutting through the din of the souvenir shop.

I glanced back over my shoulder, wincing. It was
Wendy the blogger. She was rushing toward me,
clutching her laptop under one arm as she used the
other to wave vigorously at me.

Biting back a groan of dismay, I quickly turned

toward Fred and the busboy. But they were gone.

By then Wendy had reached me. "Hey, girl," she said breathlessly. "What's up? Shopping for some new shades?" She grinned.

"Huh?" Glancing down at the nearest table, I realized it was filled with garish novelty sunglasses. "No, just looking around." I sneaked another glance around the store, but Fred was nowhere in sight. Had he skedaddled when he'd heard Wendy's bellowing and realized I was watching him? If so, what did that mean? Did he know I was investigating, or was he just trying not to let anyone see him talking to the fired busboy?

"Cool." Wendy grabbed a pair of moose-print socks off another table. "Wow, some of this stuff is tacky."

I wasn't sure she had much room to talk, given her usual crazy thrift-shop style. But I was less concerned with her fashion choices than with her position on my suspect list. Deciding to try to salvage the situation with a little subtle interrogation, I gave her a friendly smile.

"So what are you doing here?" I asked. "I thought

everyone was still down the street learning to be gold panners."

"Oh." Wendy tossed the socks back on the table. "Nah, I did a gold-panning thing like that in California once and it was kind of lame, so I decided to save my pennies this time."

"Oh?" Was it my imagination, or had she briefly grimaced when she'd said the part about saving her pennies?

"Yeah. Figured I'd skip it and see if I could find something a little more interesting to share with my readers."

"So have you found anything yet?" I asked.

She grinned, waggling a finger in my face. "Nuh-uh, not telling!" she singsonged. "You'll just have to check out my blog to find out."

"Guess I'll have to do that," I said politely.

"Really?" she said eagerly. "Cool! Tell all your friends to go there too, okay? Because so far, this trip isn't exactly driving zillions of hits to the blog. I knew I should've done the Elvis pilgrimage to Graceland this time instead."

Interesting. So her blog, Wendy's Wanderings, wasn't exactly setting the Internet on fire these days. Was that suspicious? I wasn't sure, though I supposed it did make Wendy's theoretical motive even stronger.

Before I could come up with any more questions, Wendy's eyes lit up. "Whoa, check that out!" she exclaimed, racing toward a nearby table full of earrings. I didn't understand why she was so excited until I read the sign, which explained that the earrings were made of moose droppings. Wendy pulled a camera out of her pocket and snapped a few photos. "That's so going on the blog," she murmured gleefully.

As she started digging through the earrings, I decided to take the opportunity to exit stage right. "See you later," I said, hurrying off before she could answer.

Once I was back out on the street, I texted Becca to see if she was available to meet with me. She texted back almost immediately, saying she was free for a few minutes if I could meet her back on the ship.

Soon I was hurrying into a snack bar on one of the *Arctic Star*'s middle decks. Becca was sitting at a table with her laptop open in front of her. She glanced up when I came in and waved me over. A handsome young man was bustling around behind the counter, but otherwise the place was a ghost town. Actually, the whole ship was all but deserted. Other than the employees who'd swiped my ID and checked me in, the only person I'd seen since boarding was a maid vacuuming one of the hallways.

"Hi," I said, sitting down across from Becca. "You know, this ship is kind of creepy when it's empty." My words echoed in the almost deserted snack bar.

"I know what you mean. The ship feels different without passengers. Kind of peaceful, and yes, maybe a little creepy." Becca snapped her laptop shut.

Meanwhile, the young bartender had just come around from behind the counter. He was carrying a pair of tall, frosty glasses of iced tea.

"There you go, ladies," he said, setting the drinks down in front of us. "Anything else?"

"Thanks, Omar." Becca smiled at him. "And yes,

actually, could you do me a favor? Marcelo's up in his office, and I know he'd love a cup of coffee. Would you mind bringing him one?"

"Sure thing."

As the young man hurried out, coffee cup in hand, Becca winked at me. "Okay, now we can talk freely. At least until he gets back."

I grinned. "Nicely done. I didn't realize you had such a talent for misdirection and deception. Have you ever considered leaving the cruise industry and going into undercover work?"

Becca chuckled, but soon her face went serious again. "So what did you want to talk about, Nancy? Are we any closer to figuring out who helped that robber get onboard?"

"I don't know." I took a sip of my iced tea. "But I have a question for you. What do you know about the busboy who got fired this morning?"

"John Sanchez?" Becca nodded. "How did you know about that?"

I explained about the scene I'd witnessed on the dock. "So now I'm wondering if there's a connection," I finished.

Becca shook her head. "That wasn't very professional," she said with a sigh. "Chuck must have been too upset to wait until they were back onboard. I know he thinks of his entire staff as family."

"Chuck?" I echoed.

"Sanchez's boss," Becca explained. "He got an anonymous tip this morning advising him to check the guy's locker. When he did, he found the drugs hidden under a spare apron."

"An anonymous tip?"

"Yeah, apparently someone e-mailed him from one of the public computers in the ship's Internet café," Becca said. "The message wasn't signed. Why? Do you think any of this is connected with the case?"

"I'm not sure yet." I tucked the info away to think about later. I knew we might not have much time before the bartender came back, and I wanted to ask her all my questions. "I also wanted to talk to you about Scott again. You know—the shore excursions guy. You said he's got a good rep in the industry, but how well do you really know him?"

Becca shrugged. "Not that well. I never met him before he got hired here. All I know is he used to work for Happy Seas Cruises, and his old boss put in a good word for him with Captain Peterson. Why? Has Scott done something suspicious? You asked about him before, right?"

"Maybe. I don't know. Sort of." The more time passed after the incident on the train, the more I doubted my own reaction. Was I grasping at straws by treating Scott as a viable suspect?

"Okay." Becca checked her watch, then glanced toward the door. "But listen, Omar will be back any second, and I want to talk to you about something."

"What is it?" I asked, a little distracted by my own thoughts.

"It's Tatjana. She's been acting, well, kind of strange lately."

Instantly I snapped back to attention. Even though

Tatjana had been on the original suspect list, I hadn't been thinking much about her lately, mostly because my suspicions of her were based on the way she seemed to keep turning up whenever I was discussing the case with Becca. Which really wasn't all that suspicious, given that Becca was her boss.

"What do mean, acting strange?" I asked.

Becca twirled her straw in her iced tea, her expression troubled. "It's probably nothing. It's just that she hasn't been answering calls or texts right away lately. And a couple of times I haven't been able to find her where she was supposed to be—it's like she just disappears now and then. It's not quite enough to put my finger on, but . . ."

"Okay. I'll look into it," I said. "As a matter of fact, Tatjana is—"

I cut myself off as I heard rushing footsteps. Glancing at the door, I expected to see Omar returning. Instead I saw that Hiro had just burst in, red-faced and breathless.

"Hi," he said, looking startled to see us there. "That is, um . . ."

"What are you doing here?" Becca blurted out.

I was surprised to see him too. "I thought you were herding kids at the gold-panning place," I said with a smile.

"That wrapped up a few minutes ago." Hiro returned my smile, though it looked a bit forced. "The passengers are on their own for the rest of the afternoon. Even the little kids."

Becca stood up. "Excuse me," she said, looking strangely uncomfortable. "I just remembered I'm supposed to take care of something before the passengers get back. I'd better go. Talk to you later, Nancy."

"Wait," I said. "I—"

It was too late. She was gone. And Becca had never answered my text about Hiro.

I glanced at Hiro, who was shifting his weight from foot to foot, looking as agitated as one of the hyper little kids he was paid to entertain. Maybe this was another opportunity for some impromptu interrogation.

"Were you looking for Omar or something?" I asked. "He should be right back, if you want to sit down and wait."

"Oh!" Hiro glanced at me with that same forced smile. "That's okay. I was just looking for, um, someone else. Thanks, though."

With that, he darted out the door. I shrugged. Oh well, so much for that. But what was up with Becca? Her behavior reminded me that this wasn't the first time she'd reacted oddly to seeing Hiro. What was that all about?

My phone buzzed, interrupting my thoughts. It was George calling.

"Where are you? Never mind, don't tell me—just get over to the ice cream parlor near the gold-panning place pronto," she hissed. "Alan's driving us crazy asking where you are, and we're running out of excuses. Bess can only distract him for so long by fluttering her eyelashes and laughing at his lame jokes."

I sighed, all thoughts of snooping around the nearly empty ship fleeing my mind. "Be right there," I promised.

"Do we really have to change for dinner?" George complained as we walked down the carpeted hallway toward our suite a few hours later. "I'm starved. And if we don't get there soon, Babs will snarf all the rolls."

"Yes, we do," Bess told her. "We've been walking around all day in summer weather, and we all could use a shower and some fresh clothes." She wrinkled her nose. "Plus I think you spilled half the gold dust you panned down your shirt."

"Really?" George plucked at her T-shirt, trying to get a look at it.

I, for one, was looking forward to showering and changing. After I'd rejoined my friends at the ice cream parlor, we'd spent an hour or so wandering around seeing the sights. Then we'd returned to the ship, where Alan had insisted on finding a spot on one of the upper decks so we could watch the ship pull away from Skagway. By now we were all sunburned and hungry.

Bess reached for the door, but it opened before she could touch the knob. Our butler, Max, stood in the doorway, grinning at us. He was short and wiry, with thick blond hair, dancing blue eyes, and seemingly boundless energy. Upon first meeting him, he'd reminded me of a golden retriever in human form, and my impression hadn't changed since.

"Welcome home!" he exclaimed. "How was Skagway?"

"Great," Alan said. He started telling the butler all about our day as we entered the suite.

I didn't hear much of what he said as I headed for my bedroom. My stomach grumbled as I yanked open a dresser drawer. I was so busy puzzling over everything that had happened that day that it took a moment for me to register that the drawer was empty.

"Huh?" I mumbled, blinking at the sight. Hadn't I folded and put away some shirts in there just that morning?

I opened another drawer above the first one, wondering if I'd stuck the shirts in with my underwear by mistake. Stranger things had been known to happen when I was distracted by a case.

But that drawer was empty too. I checked the other drawers—nothing in any of them. In fact, the only clothes in my room were the ones I'd left in the little built-in hamper near the door.

I stepped outside. The others had disappeared into their own rooms by then, and Max was whistling a cheery tune as he swept the floor.

"Hey, Max," I said. "Do you know what happened to my clean clothes?"

"You mean the ones I sent out for laundering this morning?" he asked brightly. "They should be back first thing tomorrow."

I glanced over my shoulder at the dirty clothes spilling out of my open hamper. "Which ones did you send out?" I asked. "Because my hamper's still full."

"I know." Max shrugged and grinned. "You left me a note right on the hamper, remember?"

"A note?" It had been a very long day since that early wake-up call, and my mind felt sluggish, unable to deal with this new wrinkle. "What note?"

"The one where you said you'd stuck your clean clothes in the hamper and the dirty ones in the drawers, so I should be sure to send out the right ones." Max grinned and winked. "Most guests do it the other way around, but I don't like to judge."

I put a hand to my forehead. "You sent all the clothes in the drawers out to be washed?"

"Yes." Max's smile faded slightly. "Isn't that what you meant by the note?"

"What note?" I said again. "Can I see it?"

"I threw it away." He shrugged. "Why? Is there a problem? I'm sorry if I misunderstood. . . ."

My mind spun, still refusing to take this in. I'd been pretty tired that morning, but I knew I hadn't left Max any notes about my laundry. That meant that one of two things was happening here. One of the possibilities was that Max was lying to me—that there *was* no note. So he'd either sent out the wrong laundry by mistake, or worse yet, on purpose. Was this just another innocent error along with that messed-up wake-up call? Or should he be a suspect? My mind shot from the laundry to the wake-up call to the note in my luggage, trying to work out whether Max could be the accomplice I was looking for.

The other possibility was even more disturbing. Maybe the note was real—which would mean someone had sneaked into our suite and planted it on my laundry hamper. Who would do something so petty and weird? Somehow it didn't fit in with the other incidents we were investigating.

"I'm so sorry, Miss Drew." Max looked stricken now as he realized how upset I was. "Did I do something wrong?"

His voice had risen, both in pitch and volume. Bess stuck her head out of her room. "Is everything okay?" she asked.

"Not exactly . . ." I quickly outlined the problem, with Max interrupting every few lines to apologize. He also offered to run down to the shipboard shops and pick me up something to wear at his expense.

But Bess shook her head. "It's okay," she told both of us. "I've got plenty of clothes. Come on in, Nancy— you can borrow something of mine."

I smiled weakly. "Thanks," I said, following her into her room. "Sometimes it's nice having a friend who's a fashion plate."

The following day I awoke feeling rested and ready for anything thanks to a nice dinner (in one of Bess's dresses) and a full night's sleep (in a T-shirt and sweatpants borrowed from George). My doubly clean laundry was back by the time I got up, plus Max had whisked off the stuff from the hamper, promising to get it washed quickly.

The butler was acting so apologetic about the laundry mix-up that I was starting to doubt my suspicions of him from the night before. I'd had a few minutes to discuss those suspicions with Bess in hurried whispers while she was finding me something to wear, and she'd seemed pretty dubious too. Still, we'd agreed that it was worth adding Max to the suspect list. Why not? It wasn't as if we were any closer to solving this thing.

After a leisurely breakfast, we joined most of the rest of the passengers on the upper decks. The ship was cruising through Glacier Bay today, and we were all expecting some spectacular views.

The scenery didn't disappoint. Soon everyone was oohing and aahing over the jagged icy-blue-and-white glaciers surrounding us, framed by the majestic snow-capped mountains rising in the distance. I even forgot about the case for a while. Then I noticed Wendy wandering past, clutching her camera and her laptop, and it all came crashing back. I bit my lip, wishing I could steal a few minutes to discuss my latest thoughts with my friends. But I couldn't; not with Alan right there.

"Should we try the next deck down?" he asked, leaning over the rail to snap another photo. "There might be better views down there."

"Doubtful," George said. "If you're bored, just say so, dude."

"I'm not bored," Alan answered quickly. He shifted his weight from one foot to the other. "I just don't want to miss anything."

"Tobias!" an irritated voice called out from nearby, distracting me from whatever George said next. "Settle down, son. Let's not bother the other passengers."

Glancing that way, I saw Tobias swinging on a railing. His mother was snapping pictures nearby, while his father glared irritably at the boy.

George was looking that way too. "Looks like you're not the only one with a short attention span, Alan," she said with a laugh.

"Ha-ha, very funny," Alan answered.

Suddenly I had an idea. "Looks like Tobias's poor parents are at the end of their rope," I said, keeping my voice casual. "Too bad Hiro isn't around to take him to get his energy out on the climbing wall. Especially since there's probably nobody else there right now—he could go crazy on that thing."

"Good point, Nancy." Bess turned her big, innocent blue eyes toward Alan. "Maybe you should offer to take him, sweetie. I know you've been dying to try the climbing wall."

That was exactly what I was counting on. Alan had mentioned wanting to try the ship's state-of-the-art rock-climbing wall several times, but as far as I knew, he hadn't done it yet. Probably because Bess had no interest in such things.

"Oh," Alan said, glancing from Bess to the scenery and back again. "Um, I guess that's not a bad idea.

We could just go for a little while—give Tobias's folks a break."

"What a nice idea." Bess squeezed his arm, turning on that million-watt smile of hers that never fails to turn guys into jelly. "Why don't you go suggest it to them? I'm sure they'd really appreciate it."

Moments later Alan and Tobias were disappearing into the nearest stairwell. "Come on," I told Bess and George, heading away from the crowds at the rail. "We need to talk."

Soon the three of us were huddled behind a stack of lounge chairs. I started by filling them in on the previous day's chat with Becca and subsequent encounter with Hiro, since this was my first chance to talk freely to them since then. We discussed all that for a few minutes, though we didn't reach any new conclusions.

"Did you tell George about your newest suspect?" Bess asked.

"You mean Max?" I said.

"Max?" George said. "You're kidding, right? The guy doesn't exactly seem like a hardened criminal."

"I know," I said. "But it's weird how he keeps messing things up lately—and how it always affects me."

"Paranoid much?" George rolled her eyes. "I mean, seriously, Nancy—a botched wake-up call? Sending out the wrong laundry? This is your evidence that he's up to no good?"

"I know, I know." I glanced around to make sure nobody had wandered close enough to hear us. "But what if he's been in cahoots with that jewelry thief all along? He definitely had access to our luggage, which means he could have left that nasty note in my suitcase on the first day. And maybe now he's just trying to distract me however he can, hoping it'll throw me off the case." The argument sounded weak even to my own ears.

"Okay, there's that," Bess said diplomatically. "What about the rest of the suspect list?"

We went on to discuss our other suspects, including Wendy, Scott, Fred, and Tatjana. Could any of them be the thief's accomplice? None of us could come up with any compelling evidence for or against.

"It just doesn't quite add up, does it?" I said at last, leaning against the stack of chairs and squinting up into the cloudless blue sky. "We have a whole bunch of suspects, but not much solid evidence. Just vague clues that could mean anything. We've been investigating for days, and it feels like we're no closer to figuring out who could be the thief's accomplice."

George opened her mouth to respond. Before she could say a word, another voice spoke up from behind us.

"Thief's accomplice?" Alan said. "What the heck are you guys talking about?"

CHAPTER FIVE

Comic Relief

"ALAN!" BESS BLURTED OUT.

Alan looked over the stack of chairs. His forehead was creased in a puzzled frown. "What's going on?" he asked, looking at each of us in turn.

"Um . . ." George gulped. "We were just, ah, role-playing. That's it—we're actually super geeks, and we're really into, um, acting out famous true crimes from history. Now you know our secret—oh well, we're pathetic nerds."

Alan shook his head. "Nice try." He glanced at me. "I thought I was going crazy when I heard you talking to the assistant cruise director about clues and stuff. And now here you are again, discussing suspects and evidence and accomplices. . . ."

Uh-oh. Apparently Alan had overheard more than I'd thought yesterday morning. Added to his accidental eavesdropping just now? Well, it seemed the cat was out of the bag.

I took a deep breath, glancing at my friends. "I guess our secret's out. We'd better fill him in."

"Fill him in?" George echoed cautiously. "Um, you mean . . ."

"The truth," I finished for her. I was annoyed at myself for being so careless, letting him find out more than he should. But besides that? I was mostly, well, relieved. Now we wouldn't have to sneak around behind Alan's back anymore, which should make our lives— and the investigation—much easier. Maybe he'd even be some help.

"Okay, if you say so," Bess said. She turned and took Alan's hands in hers. "I'm sorry we haven't been honest with you. It's only because Becca swore us to absolute secrecy. We didn't win this cruise in a contest. We were called in to look into some mysterious happenings. See, Becca knows Nancy from way back, and when she suspected someone was out to sabotage the *Arctic Star* . . ."

From there, the three of us took turns telling him the whole story. Alan's eyes got wider and wider as we talked. When we finished, he let out a loud puff of breath.

"Wow," he said. "This is insane!" He turned to stare at me. "And you're some big-time girl detective? I had no idea!"

"Yes, you did," Bess said. "I know I mentioned it a couple of times. Remember? When we saw that mystery movie on our third date, I told you Nancy would've had the case solved in half the time."

"Oh, okay, right, I guess you did say something like that." Alan shrugged. "But I didn't think she was so, you know, *serious* about it. I mean, I figured her dad's a hotshot lawyer, so she was probably just goofing around, pretending to investigate his big cases or whatever. . . ."

"Shh," I hissed, noticing Wendy wandering closer, staring down at the screen on her camera. "Incoming."

"Huh?" Alan said, his voice sounding way too loud. "Hang on, I have a question—is this the real reason why Nancy is always running off to the bathroom and stuff?"

Bess pinched him on the arm. "Quiet, then," she murmured. "We have to keep this on the down-low, okay?"

"Oh!" His eyes widened again, and he nodded, shooting a suspicious look around. "I gotcha. Top secret stuff, right?"

I cringed. This was what I'd been afraid of. Alan was so excitable—what if he blurted something out at the wrong time?

Oh well. Whatever happened, we were just going to have to deal with it. Might as well look on the bright side. Four heads were better than three, right? With Alan helping to keep an eye on our suspects, maybe we'd actually crack this case before the end of the trip.

"Come on," I said once Wendy had passed by, luckily without noticing us. "We can talk more back at the suite later. This could be our once-in-a-lifetime chance to check out this awesome scenery."

"Are you sure you want to go to the show?" Alan asked, straightening his tie and glancing into the mirrored wall in the suite's entryway. "Wouldn't you rather take this chance to, you know, sleuth around or whatever while the rest of the passengers are busy?" He waggled his eyebrows meaningfully.

I bit back a sigh. "No, it's fine," I said, double-checking to make sure Max was safely out of earshot in one of the bedrooms. "I'm sure most of our suspects will be there tonight. Two birds with one stone and all that."

"Right." Bess reached up to flick a speck of lint off Alan's sleeve. "Besides, I know you've been looking forward to seeing Merk's show, sweetie."

The idea behind Superstar Cruises was that passengers would get the chance to spend time with the celebrity talent hired as the ship's entertainment. Unfortunately, the *Arctic Star*'s main attraction, A-list action star Brock Walker, had canceled at the last minute due to Vince and Lacey's shenanigans. That had left C-list comedian Merk the Jerk as the ship's headliner. Tonight was his first performance—his original show had been postponed when Vince and Lacey had sabotaged the chandelier in the ship's main theater. Now the place was cleaned up and the show was back on.

"We'd better get moving if we want decent seats," George said, heading for the door. "It's first come, first served."

The theater was already crowded when we arrived, but we still managed to find good seats near the front.

"This is going to be awesome!" Alan rubbed his hands together, leaning forward to peer at the stage. "I heard Merk does a really funny bit about cruise fashions."

"Hmm." I wasn't too interested in speculating about the comedian's set. Instead I was glancing around for our suspects. But I hadn't spotted any of them by the time the lights dimmed.

"Here we go," George whispered.

Becca's boss, Marcelo, stepped out onstage, looking dapper in a dark suit. A smattering of applause greeted his appearance, and he raised both hands and smiled.

"Thank you, thank you," the cruise director said. "I know we're all looking forward to having our funny bone tickled by our wonderful celebrity guest, Merk the Jerk. First, though, the captain would like to say a few words. Sir?"

He turned and swept into a gallant bow. Captain Peterson strode out onstage and shook Marcelo's hand, then took his place at the microphone.

"Good evening, everyone," he said. "Before we get started with tonight's entertainment, I want to fill you in on the schedule for the next few days. As you know, the *Arctic Star* departed Glacier Bay just before dinnertime tonight and is now cruising toward Seward, where we'll dock for a few days while most of you travel by comfortable motor coach to Anchorage to begin the land tour portion of your trip."

He went on to explain that some of the ship's personnel—Scott, Hiro, Tatjana, and several others— would be accompanying us as we visited Anchorage and then traveled north from there to Denali National

Park. The rest of the staff, including Becca, Max, and the captain himself, would stay behind to ready the ship for the return voyage down the coast to Vancouver.

"Yikes," George breathed in my ear. "Sounds like our suspects are splitting up."

I nodded, feeling a pang of concern. At least Max was the only staff member on our list who wouldn't be traveling with the passengers. Still, if he was our culprit, that would mean he'd have plenty of free time to plan more trouble before we returned. And the captain had said "most of" the passengers would be going on the land tour. What if Wendy was planning to save money by skipping it and staying behind on the ship? Or what if Fred decided he'd rather hang out with his pals in the kitchen than go with the rest of us? I wondered whether one of us should stay behind on the ship just in case.

Reaching into my pocket, I touched my phone. Maybe I should text Becca and get her advice about what to do. Before I could decide, the lights dimmed again and raucous music poured out of the speakers. I realized the captain had left the stage, and it was time for Merk's show to start.

The comedian strode out with a cocky grin on his face. "Welcome, ladies and grunts!" he shouted. "I hope you're enjoying your stay on the *Arctic Star*, where the drinks are cold and the passengers are old."

"Ba-*dum*-bum," George said with a grin, while people all around us laughed, booed, or cheered.

The show continued from there. My friends seemed to be enjoying themselves, laughing and clapping and letting out hoots of approval. But I couldn't seem to focus on the comedian's act.

"Be right back," I hissed at George.

Luckily, we were near the end of our row, so I only had to climb over her and a few other people to get out. Soon I was in the hushed, carpeted hallway outside the theater. An older man was out there, fiddling with his hearing aid.

"Funny show, eh?" he said conversationally. "Just wish I could hear it a bit better."

"Yeah, it's great. Excuse me, I need to find the

ladies' room." I smiled at the man, then hurried off around the nearest corner. Pulling out my phone, I started tapping out a message to Becca as I walked.

A moment later, the sound of muffled but excited-sounding voices pulled my attention away from my text. Where was that coming from?

There was a door standing ajar just ahead; the voices were coming from that direction. Curious, I hurried forward and peered in.

The door opened into what looked like some kind of meeting room. About a dozen people were inside, gathered around a large, polished wooden table. Most of them were dressed in ship uniforms, but the person standing at the head of the table was wearing a loud Hawaiian shirt.

Fred looked up and saw me staring in at him. His face twisted into a scowl.

"Why do you keep turning up everywhere I look?" he exclaimed, jabbing a finger in my direction. "If you're spying on me, you'll be sorry!"

CHAPTER SIX

Sharp Questions

"WH-WHAT?" I STAMMERED, TAKEN ABACK. "Spying? Uh, no, sorry, I just . . ." My voice trailed off. The other people in the room had turned to stare at me, and I recognized one of them as Daisy, our usual dinner waitress. "Hi, Daisy," I said, taking a step toward her. "It's me, Nancy."

Daisy was popular with all of us for her bright smile and friendly attitude. But she wasn't displaying either at the moment. "H-hello, Nancy," she said quietly.

"So what's going on in here?" I asked her, and glanced around. "Is everything all right?"

Daisy shot a look at Fred. "Er, nothing," she said quickly. "It's nothing. Everything's fine. We're just listening."

There was a low murmur of assent. None of the other employees were meeting my eye. Then a young man stood up. I was pretty sure he worked as a lifeguard at the pool.

"Nobody here has agreed to anything," he said, his voice quavering. "There's no need to tell our bosses about any of this."

"That's enough," Fred said sharply. "You don't have to tell her anything." He glared at me. "Your cover is blown, young lady," he said, his words dripping with sarcasm.

I froze. Was Fred on to me? "I—I don't know what you—," I began.

He didn't give me a chance to continue. "I've seen you talking with the assistant cruise director more than once. You two looked pretty chummy." He crossed his arms over his chest. "You're working for Superstar, aren't you? Keeping the little people in line? I hope you're proud of yourself!"

My heart rate slowed slightly. "Huh?" I said. "The little people? What are you talking about?"

Fred rolled his eyes dramatically. "You can drop the act. We both know why you're here. But you might as well give up. Unionization is coming—it's right, and you can't stop it."

I blinked, taking that in. "Unionization?" Glancing around at the worried faces staring back at me, I finally realized what was going on here. "You're trying to form a union?"

"Like we said, we're just listening to what he has to say," someone spoke up. "Please don't tell management, or we could lose our jobs."

"Don't worry, I'm not trying to get anyone fired." I turned to Fred. "So you're a union organizer?"

He still looked hostile. "Yeah. As if you didn't know that already."

"I didn't." I shrugged. "I had no idea, actually. And you can all relax—I'm not here to turn you in to management. I had no idea any of this was going on, and as far as I'm concerned, it's none of my business."

"So you're not going to tell?" Daisy asked.

I shook my head. "As long as there's nothing illegal going on here—and it sounds like there's not—your secret's safe with me."

Murmurs of relief came from around the room. Daisy's sunny smile reappeared. "Thanks, Nancy," she said.

"No need to thank me." I smiled back, then returned my attention to Fred. "So this whole time, you've been trying to organize a union?" I said. "That explains why you spend so much time in the kitchen and places like that."

Fred still looked suspicious and a little confused. "Hang tight, people," he told the employees. "I'll be back in a minute." Then he steered me out into the hallway. "So you're really not a management spy?" he asked when we were alone. "Then why are you always talking with Becca Wright? And why do I keep running into you everywhere I turn?"

"Becca's an old family friend," I told him. "As for running into each other, that's bound to happen. This ship is big, but not *that* big."

"Hmm." Fred still didn't look entirely convinced. But he shrugged. "All right, then. You don't really fit the mold, anyway. But when you turned up on the dock in Skagway after John Sanchez got fired, I really started to wonder."

"Yeah, that was weird, wasn't it?" I realized that just because Fred was a union organizer, it didn't necessarily mean he couldn't also be my culprit. I might as well take this opportunity for a little snooping. "But I heard they really did find drugs in his locker."

Fred frowned. "That's what they say. I find it pretty hard to believe."

"Oh? How so?"

"That kid was a model employee. Hardworking, well-liked, no history of any kind of trouble. Definitely no history of being mixed up with drugs." Fred squared his shoulders. "This is exactly why I'm here—to help workers." He looked back into the room. "At least maybe seeing him get axed with no real evidence got some of the others to wake up and listen."

Personally, I wasn't sure that finding illegal drugs

among someone's possessions counted as "no real evidence." But it was pretty obvious that Fred had latched on to the incident and was planning to milk it for all it was worth and then some.

"You could be right," I said. "Then again, there have been some odd things happening on this cruise. Maybe this Sanchez guy had something to do with all that."

"Huh?" Fred looked confused. "What odd things?"

"You know—like the jewelry store getting robbed, and the chandelier falling in the theater," I prompted. Okay, so I already knew that Vince and Lacey had sabotaged the chandelier. I figured it would still be interesting to see his reaction.

"I thought they caught the robber, didn't they? And I heard the chandelier thing was some kind of accident." He chuckled. "Actually, I'm not convinced the thing actually fell at all. Figured Merk the Jerk just felt like lounging by the pool for a few more days instead of doing an honest night's work."

He was already glancing back toward the room behind him. But I wasn't ready to let him go just yet.

"There was an accident on the mini-golf course, too," I said. "An antler came off that big fake moose."

"Really? Wow, didn't hear about that one. Were any employees hurt?"

"No, no employees were nearby." I didn't bother to tell him that *I* was the one the antler had almost landed on. Unless he was a better actor than I thought, I was pretty sure this was the first he was hearing about the incident.

"Crazy." He rubbed his chin. "Guess being friends with the assistant cruise director gets you all the gossip, huh? But listen, you can tell your friend Becca that John Sanchez wasn't involved in any of that stuff. He's a good kid." He glanced over his shoulder again. "Now if you'll excuse me . . ."

"Sure." I watched as he hurried back into the meeting room. I wasn't ready to take Fred's word that the busboy couldn't be our culprit. He had too much to gain by insisting that Sanchez had been wrongly terminated.

As for Fred himself? Now that I knew why he was

really on the ship, his suspicious behavior didn't seem so suspicious anymore. I was pretty sure I could cross him off the suspect list.

"Now this is traveling in style!" George exclaimed, settling back against her comfortable seat. "Where else can you sit on your rear end and get views like this?"

"No argument there," I said. "But you're going to give me a shot at the window seat sometime, right?"

George grinned. "Maybe. If you're nice to me."

We were aboard the train that was carrying us from Anchorage to Denali National Park. It was definitely a different experience from the train ride in Skagway. This train was a sleek, modern double-decker. We were on the top level, which featured two double rows of seats and enormous windows that offered an uninterrupted panoramic view of the scenery we were passing. The bottom level held the dining cars.

Alan leaned over from his seat beside Bess across the aisle. "Aren't you glad I talked you into coming, Nancy?" he whispered. "You wouldn't have wanted to miss this just to stay on the boat and keep an eye on you-know-who."

I glanced around to make sure nobody was listening. Luckily, all the nearby passengers were glued to their windows and paying no attention to our conversation.

"Yeah, you were right, Alan," I said. "I'm glad we're all here."

It was true. As it turned out, all my suspects except Max were going to be on the land tour. Well, and Fred—he'd stayed behind on the ship too. But when I'd told the others about my encounter with him, they'd agreed with my decision to cross him off the list. Becca had said she'd keep an eye on Max while we were gone, so I'd decided it wasn't worth leaving someone behind, especially for such a weak suspect.

Thinking about that reminded me that we'd been on the train for at least an hour, and I hadn't done a thing except admire the scenery. "Think I'll stretch my legs for a bit," I said, standing up.

"Good plan," George said, snapping a photo as the train rumbled over a bridge crossing a scenic river. "We've still got a long way to go."

I nodded. The trip to Denali would take about eight hours. That should give me plenty of time to check out all the suspects onboard. I'd already seen that Wendy and Hiro were in our car, and I figured Scott and Tatjana couldn't be too far away—most of the *Arctic Star* people seemed to be seated in the same section of the train.

Heading up the aisle, I came to Wendy first. Good. The blogger still wasn't my favorite suspect, and I was hoping I could cross her off my list with a few key questions. I mean, sure, maybe writing about odd happenings on the cruise could drive more viewers to her blog. At least, it had seemed like a decent motive when we were only talking about falling moose antlers and similar incidents. But it just didn't seem like a good enough reason to aid and abet a jewelry store robbery.

"Hey," I said, pausing beside her seat. "Enjoying the scenery?"

"Sure. What's not to like?" Wendy grinned up at me and patted the empty seat beside her. "Want to hang for a bit? Tobias's dad is sitting here, but he just left to take Tobias for a walk to see the rest of the train. Guess the kid was getting restless."

"Thanks." I sat down and glanced across the aisle, where Tobias's mother was staring out the window with her camera in hand. "So you're sitting with Tobias and his family, huh?"

"Yeah, we were talking last night at dinner, and they invited me to hang with them today," she replied. "They had an extra seat, and I didn't want to get stuck with some stranger." She barked out a laugh. "Anyway, they're cool, even if Tobias is kind of a pain. He's been freaking out about Hazel."

"The spider?" I couldn't help a slight shudder.

"Uh-huh. Their room steward is taking care of the thing back on the ship while they're gone, and Tobias is afraid she'll get squashed or something." She grinned. "Maybe Hazel should've tagged along. She could have had my seat. Now *that* would be a photo worth posting on my blog!"

I smiled. "Speaking of your blog, I bet all your readers will love reading about your adventures in Denali."

"Yeah, I hope so." A shadow passed across Wendy's face. "They're not exactly flocking to read about the trip so far."

"Really?" Apparently things hadn't picked up since I'd last talked to her, a couple of days earlier.

"Uh-huh." She picked at the back of the seat in front of her. "I was really hoping that blogging this trip would grab me some attention out there. You know— get some buzz going, maybe attract some advertisers or get me some paying gigs, whatever. Make this writing thing happen, you know?"

"Actually, I don't know that much about how blogs work," I said. "Do you mean you're hoping someone will want to pay you to turn your blog into a book or magazine article or something?"

"That would work." She cracked a rueful smile. "But really, I was just hoping maybe one of my posts might go viral. If it's big enough, something like that can lead to TV interviews or whatever, and then from there, who knows?"

"Oh." I wasn't sure what to think. It sounded as

if Wendy was doing everything she could to succeed at this blogging thing. Would that include helping a thief?

"Yeah, so here I am in this supercool place—" She sighed and glanced out the window. "And I still can't get anybody to pay attention. I'm starting to think this trip was a big, fat, expensive mistake."

"My friends and I won the cruise in a contest," I said. "I guess I didn't really think about how much it must cost."

"Let's put it this way," Wendy said. "My cousin works for one of the big travel websites and got me a serious discount. And I *still* had to sell my car to pay for it."

"Ouch." So much for crossing Wendy off the list. In my experience, desperate people sometimes did desperate things. And based on what she was saying, Wendy was as desperate as they came.

"Wah, wah, let me play the world's tiniest violin, right?" Then she wiggled her shoulders, as if shaking off her gloomy thoughts. "What will be will be, as they say. Anyway, look at me, spilling my guts to someone I just met, like, a week ago!" She laughed. "Sorry about that."

"It's okay," I said. "I understand how money troubles can get you down."

"Yeah. But when you get right down to it, I'm lucky I get the chance to, like, follow my bliss. That's enough reason to stay optimistic, right?" She grinned. "And hey, the trip's not over yet. Who knows, maybe somebody'll get eaten by a grizzly bear and I'll be there to document it!"

I noticed Tobias and his father making their way down the aisle. "Looks like your seatmate's back," I told Wendy. "I should go."

"Okay. But hey, thanks for listening."

"Anytime." I got up, exchanging greetings with Tobias and his father as I passed them.

Then I wandered up toward Hiro's seat. I'd been just about ready to cross Wendy off the suspect list, but this changed everything. Was it time to move her to the top?

Hiro was deep in conversation with another passenger. Not wanting to interrupt, I kept moving past his seat, planning to check the next car for Tatjana and Scott.

Before I reached the door, Alan caught up with me. "Hey," he said. "Glad I caught you. We heard we're about to pass through an area where you can sometimes see moose grazing in a field right along the train tracks! Come check it out."

"Oh. Um . . ." That did sound cool. But I wasn't really in the mood for wildlife watching.

But I should have known better than to protest. Alan wouldn't take no for an answer. Before I knew it, I was heading back toward our scats.

When I got there, I saw that George had moved across the aisle to sit with Bess. "What are you doing over there?" I asked.

George shrugged. "Bess had better snacks," she said. "Anyway, this is your chance to snag that window seat for a while."

"Good point." I glanced at Alan. "You don't mind, do you?"

"Go for it." He waved a hand toward the seats.

I sat down by the window, and he took the seat

beside me. For the next few minutes we watched for moose, but there was no sign of them.

"So where are the meese?" George asked, sounding impatient.

"Guess they're not out today," Alan said.

"Don't worry," Bess put in. "Even if we don't see any now, everyone says we'll see tons of them on our tour through Denali tomorrow. The wildlife viewing is supposed to be spectacular there."

"Cool." George grinned. "Think I'll get to pet one?"

"I don't think that's such a good idea," Bess said. "Moose actually injure more people in Alaska every year than grizzly bears."

"Really?" George sounded skeptical. "Where'd you hear that?"

"It's one of the fun facts in the brochure about this land tour," Bess said. "Didn't you read it?"

After a bit more bickering, the cousins went back to peering out their window, while Alan and I did the same. The two of us chitchatted about the scenery we were passing. But soon I was feeling restless again. The clock was ticking, and I didn't want to miss my chance to check out our suspects while we were all trapped on the train together.

"Excuse me," I said. "Think I'll go explore the train a little."

"No way, you can't leave now," Alan said with a grin. "We might still spot those moose!"

"No, seriously." I lowered my voice. "I want to go have a look around, if you know what I mean."

His eyes widened. "Oh!" he exclaimed. "Wait—do you have a new lead or something? Did one of the suspects do something suspicious?"

He was whispering, sort of. But his voice still seemed way too loud. "Shh," I cautioned, hoping the people in the seats nearby weren't paying attention.

"Oops. Sorry." He pressed a couple of fingers to his mouth, pretending to lock his lips shut. "But seriously," he whispered. "If you need help . . ."

"No, it's okay." I sighed and leaned back in my seat. "Actually, it can probably wait."

We still hadn't seen any moose—and I hadn't done any more investigating—by the time Hiro stood up and said it was time for our section of the car to head downstairs for lunch. George hopped to her feet immediately.

"Finally!" she exclaimed. "I'm starved!"

"Really?" Bess raised one perfectly groomed eyebrow. "Even after eating all my pretzels *and* my granola bar?"

George ignored that and stepped into the aisle. "Come on, let's get down there."

Alan stood and moved into the aisle behind her. "After you, ladies," he said, sweeping a hand forward in a little mock bow.

Bess smiled. "So gallant!" she cooed.

I crawled out of my seat and straightened up. "Thanks," I told Alan. As he leaned down to grab his knapsack off the floor beneath the seat, I caught up with Bess and George. When we started down the stairs, we saw Tobias and his family ahead of us. The little boy turned and spotted us.

"Hey, where's Alan?" he demanded.

"Right behind us." Bess glanced over her shoulder. "At least I thought he was."

"Here I am," Alan exclaimed, bursting into the stairwell. "Hey, Tobias. What's up? How's my girl Hazel?"

Bess, George, and I traded a glance as Alan and Tobias started chattering away, mostly about Tobias's pet spider. "I guess they must have bonded at the climbing wall yesterday," Bess murmured with a smile.

We all continued downstairs together. There were plenty of windows in the dining car, so we were able to enjoy more scenic views as we ate. Tobias was at the next table, along with his parents and Wendy. The little boy kept turning around in his seat to talk to Alan.

"What can I say?" Alan said with a grin. "I have a way with kids."

Tobias's mother heard him and turned with a smile. "Sorry if he's being a pest," she said. "He was so excited when he found out you were an environmental studies major. He wants to be a zookeeper when he grows up."

After the meal, we all headed back upstairs. Tobias went past his seat, following Alan down the aisle. "So do you get to study tarantulas in your college classes?" he asked.

"Dude, we study *every* kind of spider," Alan said with a laugh. "It's awesome!"

I glanced around the car to see if Hiro was free. He was nowhere in sight, so I decided maybe it was time to look for Scott and Tatjana. Bess and George had already taken their seats together, but I hovered beside my row, realizing I couldn't tell them what I was really doing. Not with Tobias hanging around and several other passengers close enough to hear.

"I'll be back in a bit," I said, patting my purse. "I'm going to the restroom to brush my teeth."

"Are you kidding?" Alan exclaimed. "Didn't you hear what our waiter told us just now? He said we'll be coming up on a great view of Mount McKinley soon. You don't want to miss that!"

His voice was loud and enthusiastic, as usual. I cringed as several nearby passengers turned to stare at us. So far, letting Alan in on our real purpose hadn't helped much with the undercover stuff.

"Um, okay," I said, figuring I could whisper my real plans to him once we sat down. "Want the window seat this time?"

"Nah, you can have it. I'm taller—I can see past you just fine." Alan stood back to let me by.

Stepping past him, I dropped into my seat. "Ow!" I cried as I felt something jab into my skin. I leaped up again, almost hitting my head on the curved glass of the window.

"What's wrong, Nancy?" Bess exclaimed.

I stared down in horror. "Glass! Shards of broken glass all over my seat!"

CHAPTER SEVEN

❧

Narrowing the Field

"GLASS?" BESS CRIED. "WHAT DO YOU MEAN?"

I was bending down, examining the gleaming shards on my seat. They were silver, almost invisible against the upholstery. But they were definitely there.

Alan leaned closer. "Glass?" he exclaimed. "Are you sure?"

"Yes, I'm sure." I rubbed my backside. "Trust me."

The commotion from our seats was attracting attention. Tobias was still hanging around, and he pushed past Alan to peer at me.

"Hey, did the glass poke you in the *behind*?" he asked loudly.

I ignored him, carefully cleaning up the seat. Meanwhile Wendy appeared by our seats as well.

"Nancy?" she said. "What's going on? I heard you yell."

She sounded a little too eager. I glanced up and saw a camera in her hand. Could she have done this? Maybe set up a situation she thought could win her that breakthrough blog post she wanted?

"Someone dropped smashed glass on Nancy's seat," Bess told Wendy.

"What? You're kidding, right?" Wendy asked.

"I don't know." I forced a laugh. "But don't worry, everyone. I think I'll recover."

"Let me see those." Alan grabbed my hand for a closer look at the shards. "It looks like a glass was smashed—maybe from the dining car."

I squeezed my eyes shut. This situation was spinning out of control. The last thing I needed was to become some kind of mini-celebrity on this train. If everyone was watching me, it would be that much harder to do any investigating.

When I opened my eyes, Hiro was making his way toward us. "What's going on back here?" he asked.

"Nothing. I'm fine," I assured him.

"Nothing," Alan said quickly. "Except that someone put slivers of glass all over Nancy's seat. Anyone who would do that must be a sick person. Who knows what he or she might do?"

Hiro looked confused and concerned. "Okay, somebody had better fill me in here."

When he heard the story, Hiro insisted on contacting the train's security team. Several officers arrived moments later, shooing everyone in our car back down to the dining car while they searched the entire upper level. Finally we got the all clear and returned to our seats.

"Thanks for taking that glass for me, Nancy," George said, clearly trying to lighten the mood. "That was technically my seat, you know."

"I know. And you're welcome." I stuck out my tongue at her. "You want it back?"

"No way," Alan spoke up. "Go ahead and sit down, Nancy. After what you've just been through, you deserve the window seat. I'll sit right here with you and keep an eye out for any more trouble."

"Um, thanks." I sat down.

Across the aisle, I could see Bess and George with their heads bent close together, talking in whispers. I wished I could be over there with them, discussing this latest twist in the case. Because it had to be related, didn't it? There was no way it was a coincidence that broken glass had turned up on my seat.

A moment later my phone buzzed. I pulled it out and found a text from George.

BESS & I THINK U SHOULD GET CHECKED OUT BY A MEDIC WHEN WE GET TO DENALI, JUST IN CASE.

I didn't bother to text back; I just leaned forward so I could see past Alan to their seat. Both Bess and George were staring back at me. I rolled my eyes and shook my head.

A moment later, another text came:

SRSLY, NANCY. WHAT IF A. IS RIGHT AND SOMEONE

PUT SOMETHING ON THE SHARDS? COULD BE THE SAME
PERSON WHO PUSHED U OFF THE WALKWAY IN K.

This time I typed a return text: LIKE U SAID, G,
THE GLASS WASN'T ON MY SEAT. IT WAS ON YOURS.

George texted back again: HM, GOOD POINT. MAYBE
THE BAD GUY IS AFTER ALL OF US NOW.

I realized I hadn't thought of that. Just then Alan
glanced over.

"Who are you texting?" His voice sounded impos-
sibly loud.

"Um, nobody," I said. "I mean, I'm just sending a
note to Ned. My boyfriend."

"Oh, right." Alan nodded. "I met him that time we
all went out to dinner together, remember? Nice dude."

I smiled weakly until he turned his attention back
to the scenery. Then my fingers flew over the tiny keyboard. WHY WOULD SOMEONE BE AFTER U GUYS NOW?

The response came quickly: MAYBE WE R GETTING
TOO CLOSE TO THE TRUTH.

I leaned back, feeling troubled. Could my friends
be right? Were we all in danger now?

After a moment I texted them again: SO WHAT SHOULD WE DO?

The response: U SHOULD STAY PUT. B & I ARE GOING TO INVESTIGATE.

I frowned and texted: NO! IF SOMEONE IS AFTER U TOO, IT'S TOO DANGEROUS. WE NEED TO COME UP W/A PLAN.

I sent the text and waited for the response. Instead I heard the sounds of activity across the aisle. Glancing over, I saw Bess and George getting up.

"Where are you two going?" Alan asked before I could.

"Just taking a walk," Bess said sweetly. "Keep an eye on Nancy while we're gone, okay? She needs to relax and recover."

"Absolutely." Alan reached up and squeezed her arm as she went past.

"Hey!" I called as my friends hurried up the aisle. But neither of them responded. "Let me out," I told Alan. "I'm going with them."

"Ah, ah, ah!" He shook a playful finger in my face.

"You heard the lady. Relax and recover time."

I gritted my teeth, tempted to kick him in the kneecap and make my escape. But I held myself back. He was only trying to help. Besides, how much trouble could my friends get into on this train? I decided to let them go. Maybe I could convince Alan to lower his voice enough for the two of us to discuss the case. A fresh perspective might be just what I needed.

"Okay," I said, turning to glance out the window. "If anything can help me relax, it's looking at all this."

"I know, right? Beautiful."

We spent the next few minutes chatting about the scenery we were passing. At some point I realized it was probably the first time I'd ever had a real conversation with him, just the two of us. It was kind of weird. But kind of nice, too.

After a while Tobias appeared. Seeing my friends' empty seats across from us, he flopped into the aisle seat. "Hey, Alan," he said. "My dad says Mount McKinley is the tallest mountain on the whole continent. Is that true?"

Alan grinned at him. "Hey there, little man," he said. "I bet your dad is right."

"Oh." Tobias looked impressed. "Do you study mountains and stuff in your classes, or just animals?"

"We study it all," Alan replied. "The whole shebang."

I looked at him. For a while, I'd almost forgotten that he wasn't on this trip only because of Bess. He was also supposed to be getting a head start on his college research project for the next year.

"That reminds me," I said. "Have you had any ideas for your big sophomore project yet?"

"Not really," he said. "But it'll come. I'm just taking it all in, letting it simmer."

"Need any help brainstorming?" I offered. "I'm usually pretty good at coming up with ideas for stuff like that. What are the parameters of the project?"

Tobias sat up and perched on the edge of the seat. "Do you have to write a report for school?" he asked Alan. "You should write about spiders! I got an A on the report I did about Hazel."

"Cool," Alan told him. Then he glanced at me.

"And thanks. Maybe sometime, I guess."

"Wait! I have a better idea." Tobias swung his leg around, kicking the seat in front of him. "You could write about the bone smugglers!"

"The what?" Alan asked.

"My mom read about it in the newspaper when we were getting ready for this trip." The kid sounded excited. "She said the police arrested some guy for stealing tusks and bones and stuff from rare Alaskan animals." He poked Alan on the arm. "Which Alaskan animals are the rarest? Think we'll see any when we tour the park tomorrow?"

"I don't know, little buddy. What do you mean by rare?" Alan said.

"He probably means endangered species," I put in. I wasn't too interested in their conversation, though I couldn't help being a little surprised that Alan didn't seem to know much about Alaskan wildlife. Still, I guessed an environmental studies degree covered a lot of ground. He couldn't be expected to know everything about every ecosystem in the world, especially after only a year of study.

"Right." Alan shrugged. "Maybe you can ask the tour guide at Denali about it, Tobias." He grinned. "You can also ask him if there are any tarantulas there!"

I shot him a look, pretty sure he had to be kidding this time. Even I was pretty sure that tarantulas were mostly found in warmer parts of the world.

"Yeah, right," I said. "Tarantulas in Alaska?"

"Hey, there are spiders everywhere, right?" Alan shrugged again. Then his face lit up. "Here come Bess and George."

I glanced up and saw my friends hurrying toward us. Tobias saw them too and jumped out of their seats.

"Switch places back?" Alan said, standing up quickly as they reached us. "No offense, Nancy. But I miss my best girl."

"Sure, whatevs." George flopped down beside me. "Yo."

"Yo yourself. Find out anything interesting?" I asked quietly.

She took a quick look around. Tobias was hanging on the back of Alan's seat across the way, still chattering away at him about grizzly bear skulls or something.

"We tracked down Scott and chatted with him for a while," George told me. "We realized there's no way he's our guy."

"Really? How come?"

"Because he was in full view of a number of people up on the main deck from the time we arrived to the time you found that note in your luggage." She added, "In the detective biz, we call that lack of opportunity."

"Thanks for the lesson, detective." I rolled my eyes. "But I see your point. And I guess his weird behavior on the train could be explained away by the gambling stuff he told me about when I saw him meeting with those tough guys in Ketchikan. If he's still in debt, he's probably stressed, especially if that sort of thing could get him fired if anyone finds out." I thought back to that scary encounter. "No wonder he wasn't thrilled to catch me listening in on his phone conversation, even by accident, since he knows I know about his problem."

George nodded. "Next we went looking for Tatjana.

We found her, but didn't get to talk to her much. She blew us off after, like, three minutes. Said something about needing to go downstairs to take care of some paperwork."

"Hmm. Think she was telling the truth?"

"Who knows? Everything she says sounds mysterious in that crazy Russian-sounding accent of hers. But that's probably because I've watched too many old *Rocky and Bullwinkle* cartoons." George grinned. "Anyway, we looked for Hiro on our way back here, but we couldn't find him."

"No mystery there. He's probably still with the security people or something." I was still thinking about Tatjana. She'd been on the list for a while, but we hadn't really investigated her very much. "Anyway, we can talk to him later. For now, I'm thinking maybe we should focus on finding out more about Tatjana."

"Wow, that was a long train ride." George stretched as we all climbed off the bus that had carried us from the train to the lodge where we would be staying that night, a pleasantly rustic place on the outskirts of Denali National Park. "I can't believe it's only four in the afternoon."

"Yeah, well, we left Anchorage pretty early," I pointed out.

"After all that sitting, I'm ready to go out and stretch my legs," Alan put in, slinging Bess's carry-on bag over his shoulder. "Good thing I booked us on that horseback-riding excursion this afternoon. It should be a nice long ride, since it stays light so late here this time of year. Come on, we'd better get checked in and changed or we'll be late."

I traded a look with my friends. As usual, Alan had signed us all up for an activity without checking in first. Not that I had anything against horseback riding. But I'd been hoping to have some free time to investigate this afternoon, since from what Scott had told us, we'd be on our Denali bus tour for most of the following day.

As we entered the lodge's impressive wood-and-stone lobby, I noticed Tatjana standing off to one side of the check-in desk. She was chatting with the ABCs and a couple of other passengers. Okay, maybe this was my chance.

"Can you guys check us in?" I asked Bess and George. "I just want to, um, look around the lobby."

Bess followed my gaze and nodded. "Of course."

"Thanks." As they headed for the check-in desk, I eased closer to Tatjana. The other passengers were talking excitedly about the scenery they'd seen that day. As Babs described her impressions of a particularly scenic gulch, I hovered on the edge of the group, waiting for an opportunity to join the conversation.

Before I got the chance, I was distracted by the sound of George's voice. Her very *loud* voice.

"What are you talking about?" she exclaimed. "What do you mean, our reservation was canceled?"

CHAPTER EIGHT

Reservations

THE NEXT FEW MINUTES WERE PRETTY chaotic. I rushed over to find the lodge staff apologizing profusely, saying that someone had called the day before to cancel the reservation for the cabin Bess, George, and I were supposed to be sharing. The interesting thing? Nobody seemed to know exactly who the caller had been. He or she—nobody seemed sure about that, either—hadn't left a name.

Soon Tatjana and Hiro appeared and got involved, and they were still trying to work things out when the buses arrived to take people off to the various afternoon excursions, including the horseback ride Alan had booked for the four of us. Deciding to look for the silver lining in the situation, I offered to stay behind and straighten out the room mix-up while my friends went on the excursion. Maybe I would have my chance to investigate today after all.

Alan still didn't seem to catch on to the whole silver-lining angle, since he tried to change my mind, insisting that Tatjana and Hiro could take care of it for us. Luckily, Bess and George were a little more savvy. They dragged him off toward their bus.

The lobby cleared out quickly as most of my fellow passengers headed off on their activities. Within minutes the place was all but deserted, though I noticed Wendy paging through some brochures over near the entrance. It looked as if she'd decided to skip today's optional trips. No wonder, after what she'd told me earlier. Becca had arranged for Superstar to comp all the activities my friends and I did, but I'd caught a glimpse of the prices when Scott had passed out some information earlier. Most of the activities weren't exactly cheap, especially for someone in Wendy's financial situation.

Thinking of Scott reminded me of what my friends had figured out. Thinking back, it *did* seem unlikely that he could have planted that threatening note. Unless he'd had help from someone else—like Max, for instance. This whole time we'd been focusing on *one* person who could be the jewelry thief's accomplice. What if there was more than one person involved? If so, maybe we shouldn't be so quick to cross someone like Scott off the list. True, he probably couldn't have left me that note. And it seemed unlikely he could have been the one to push me off that Ketchikan walkway, either, since I'd seen him heading in the opposite direction shortly beforehand. But what about the other stuff—the moose antler, the loud argument I'd overheard in the ship's kitchen, the pre-cruise problems, and of course sneaking the robber aboard? There was no reason he couldn't have been involved in any of those incidents.

It was an interesting thought. But Scott had disappeared, presumably to accompany the excursion groups, so I turned my attention to two handier suspects, Hiro and Tatjana. They were still having a stern discussion with the front desk staff. I stepped back and watched the pair. What if one of them had canceled that reservation? It certainly would have been easy for either of them to do it. But why? Was it just another way to throw me off balance, warn me not to mess with them?

I looked around for Wendy again, but she'd disappeared. There were only a few other passengers still lingering in the lobby. An elderly couple sitting by the fireplace. A cluster of women heading into the dining room. A woman with an active young toddler from the redheaded reunion group.

I watched as the redheaded mother led her child around by one chubby hand. The redheads had been around when I'd been pushed off that walkway. And the whole extended family seemed kind of excitable. What if one of them had bumped me by accident? That would mean the whole Ketchikan incident was a red herring—no pun intended.

But if one of the redheads had bumped me,

wouldn't he or she have noticed and fessed up? And wouldn't that person have been the one to call for help instead of Alan?

Thinking about the incident in Ketchikan brought my mind back around to Scott again—and the rough-looking guys he'd met with there. Okay, so he had a reasonable explanation for meeting them, and I had enough sleuthing experience to know I shouldn't jump to conclusions based on appearance. That didn't change the fact that both those guys would be totally believable as robbers or thugs in the movies. What if my new theory was right, and I needed to be looking for more than one culprit? What if Scott was one of them, and had helped one of his "poker buddies" onto the ship?

Pulling out my phone, I sent a quick text to Becca, asking for a description of the thief the police had arrested.

My phone rang almost immediately. It was Becca.

"Got your text," she said. "I don't know what the guy looks like, but I can try to find out."

"Cool, thanks," I said. "Anything interesting happening on the ship?"

"Not really," she replied. "But I've been asking around about John."

"John?" For a moment I couldn't place the name. "Oh! You mean the fired busboy?"

"Yeah." I heard her sigh. "The more I talk to people who know him, the weirder that whole situation seems. Everyone swears he's the nicest, most honest guy around. Nobody I've talked to can imagine him getting mixed up with drugs." She paused. "Do you think that could mean something? Is it connected to our case somehow?"

"I don't know. But I'll keep it in mind. Call or text as soon as you find out about the jewelry thief, okay?"

"Will do."

Wandering closer to the desk, I found that Tatjana and Hiro were still working arrangements out with the lodge staff. "Don't worry, Nancy," Hiro told me. "We'll have this sorted out shortly."

"Thanks," I said.

As I watched them, my mind returned to my new theory. If we really were looking for two culprits instead of one, which pairings made the most sense? I'd already thought of Scott and Max—Scott could have smuggled the robber aboard, Max could have planted the note, and either of them could have fiddled with the moose antler, though neither of them made sense as the walkway pusher. Besides, what connection did they have to each other? Did some other pairing make more sense? Maybe Max and Hiro, or Scott and Tatjana?

I was about to text Becca again to see if she knew of any connections among our suspects. But at that moment I spotted Wendy wandering toward me.

"Hey, Nancy," she said. "Why aren't you off white-water rafting or whatever?"

I quickly explained the room situation, watching her closely for any sign that she already knew about it. But she barely seemed to pay attention. In fact, she seemed distracted and a little jittery.

"Bummer," she said. "But listen, epic news. I was

just hanging outside chatting with some peeps and surfing the net, and I think I came up with a fab new idea to promote the blog!"

"That's great," I said. "What is it?"

She grinned, tapping her laptop, which was tucked under one arm as usual. "Top secret for now," she said with a coy smile. "You'll have to wait and see after my investigation is complete!"

With that, she hurried off, humming under her breath. I stared after her, feeling troubled. What kind of "investigation" was she talking about?

I started to follow her, but Tatjana intercepted me. "Good news, Nancy," she said. "I can show you to your room now. The porters are already fetching your luggage."

"Thanks." I followed her out of the main lodge building. Most of the guest rooms were located in small separate cabins out back.

Tatjana led me to a cabin at the edge of the complex. It overlooked a small meadow dotted with wildflowers. Beyond that began a thick tangle of forest.

"Very nice, yes?" Tatjana said as we stepped inside. "They gave you an upgrade due to the misunderstanding."

The place *was* very nice. There was a small sitting room, a full bath, and three bedrooms. Our luggage was already piled near the door.

"It looks great," I said. "Thanks for straightening this out."

I glanced at her, trying to figure out a way to question her about the case. But she was already on her way out the door. "Have a lovely evening, Miss Drew," she called over her shoulder.

"You too," I said, though she was already gone.

With a shrug, I walked over to the coffee table and dropped my purse on it. I could unpack later. Right now I wanted to get back out there.

First, though, I headed into the bathroom to wash my hands. As I reached for the towel hanging under the window, I caught a glimpse of movement outside.

I took a better look, guessing it might be some of

the area's well-known wildlife. Instead I saw Tatjana tiptoeing past, heading for the woods!

"What?" I murmured, all my detective instincts suddenly on alert.

Dropping the towel, I raced outside and around to the back of the cabin. By the time I got there, Tatjana was just disappearing into the woods.

I sprinted across the meadow, hoping she didn't look back—and also hoping that nobody else was looking out the windows of the nearby cabins. Luckily, Tatjana didn't seem to realize she was being followed. As I ducked into the shade of the thick evergreens, I could hear her footsteps up ahead, crunching on the dried pine needles that carpeted the forest floor.

My heart pounded as I followed, trying to keep a little quieter myself. Was I about to solve the case?

I trailed her for about five minutes. Finally she stopped short in a pretty little sun-dappled clearing. Huddling behind a broad tree trunk at the edge, I watched as she glanced around, then pulled a compact out of her pocket and applied a fresh coat of lipstick. Weird. What was she doing out here?

I was so focused on watching Tatjana that it took me a moment to notice the hurried footsteps coming up behind me. By the time I tuned in, it was too late. I spun around.

"Hey!" Hiro blurted out, looking as startled as I was. "What are you doing here?"

CHAPTER NINE

~

Strange Discoveries

"HIRO!" MY HEART POUNDED AS I RECOGNIZED the danger I was in. We were pretty far from the lodge out here—definitely too far for anyone to hear me scream if Tatjana and Hiro were up to no good.

I glanced back at Tatjana, who was coming toward us. "Nancy!" she cried, her eyes flashing with anger. "Did you follow me?"

"Obviously she did," Hiro snapped, frowning at her. "I told you to be careful!"

I cringed back against the tree trunk as he spun to face me. My eyes darted around, looking for anything I could grab to use as a weapon—a rock, a fallen branch . . .

"Nancy, please don't tell anyone you saw us out here," Hiro begged.

I blinked, focusing back on his face. All the anger had disappeared from his expression. Now he just looked anxious and kind of freaked-out.

"Yes, please, Nancy," Tatjana put in. "If anyone knows we are together, especially Becca—"

"Wait," I said, confused. "What's going on here?"

Hiro reached for Tatjana's hand. "Don't worry," he told her, his voice thick with emotion. "Even if they fire us, it was worth it." He planted a kiss on her lips.

I blinked. Okay, I'm no Bess, but I recognize romance when I see it. "So you two are—a couple?" I asked. "That's why you're sneaking around out here?"

"Yes." Tatjana squared her shoulders. "But you cannot tell Becca. She wouldn't understand."

Hiro nodded. "I know you're friendly with Becca," he told me. "So I suppose you already know that she and I used to date when we both worked for Jubilee."

"Actually, I didn't know that." But now that I did, some things were starting to make a lot more sense.

"We broke up when we both got hired by Superstar." He shrugged. "She's technically my boss now, so we didn't think it would be appropriate to keep seeing each other. Then Tatjana came along. . . ." He glanced over at Tatjana and squeezed her hand, which he was still clutching. "Anyway, we weren't sure at first how serious things were between us, so we kept our relationship a secret."

Tatjana added, "It seemed a good idea at the time."

"Yes. But now that things are more serious, we're worried that Becca won't understand." Hiro sighed, running his free hand through his spiky dark hair. "In fact, I'd planned to talk to her about it before now, but I can't seem to catch her alone."

"That's why you burst in on us," I realized. "At the snack bar the other day. You were looking for Becca, right?"

He nodded. "I ran into Omar—the kid who works at that snack bar—and he said she was up there." He smiled ruefully. "I didn't even stop to think that she might not be alone."

"Sorry about that." My mind was clicking along, adding this piece to my puzzle of clues and incidents. This explained why Becca and Hiro always seemed so awkward together. And why Becca never had much to say when I questioned her about him. And also why Tatjana had been harder for her to reach lately.

"You won't tell her, will you?" Hiro asked anxiously. "I plan to talk to her as soon as we get back to the ship."

"I won't say a word."

Leaving them together, I headed back through the woods toward the lodge. Halfway there another thought occurred to me. Could this new information also explain the busboy's firing? Maybe he'd caught the two of them together, and they'd been afraid he'd tell Becca. . . .

"Doubtful," I muttered before I'd even finished the thought. It was worth keeping the possibility in the back of my mind, but now that I knew their secret, Hiro and Tatjana just didn't seem like the type of people who could have made that anonymous tip against an innocent man.

When I reached the meadow, I saw a flash of movement. It was Tobias. He was crouched near the edge of the woods with a digital camera.

I walked over to him. "What are you doing out here?" I asked. "I thought you'd be off on a day trip."

"Nope." Tobias straightened up. "My mom had a headache, so we stayed here." He grinned. "Good thing, too! Wendy wants me to take pictures of all the birds and animals and stuff I can find. She says she'll pay me if she decides to use any of them on her website!"

"Really? Are you sure she said that?"

"Uh-huh." Tobias turned and snapped a photo of a bird flying past. "She knows I like exotic animals and stuff, so she figures I can get some good ones."

"And she said she'd pay you for them?" That seemed odd, given that Wendy was supposed to be broke. Could this have something to do with her mysterious new plan?

Tobias stared at me as if I had two heads. "Didn't I just *say* that?"

"Where is Wendy right now?" I asked.

Tobias shrugged, fiddling with his camera. "She was in the lobby when I saw her."

I headed for the lobby, but Wendy wasn't there. She wasn't in her room or the restaurant, either. I wandered around the grounds for a while, but there was still no sign of her.

"Oh well," I murmured, pausing on the lodge's unoccupied back deck.

The lounge chairs out there looked comfortable, so I sank onto one. It had been another long day. I leaned back, staring up at the still-bright early evening sky and thinking about the case. I realized I'd just crossed two more suspects off my list. The more I thought about it, the more certain I was that Hiro and Tatjana didn't have anything to do with the case. That only left me with a few live suspects: Wendy, Max, maybe Scott. Was it time to start looking for some new ideas?

Pulling out my phone, I checked to see if Becca

had texted back yet about my questions. She hadn't, and I was about to stick the phone back in my pocket when I realized I hadn't checked in with Ned in a couple of days.

I tapped out a quick message to him, mostly saying hi and updating him on the case. It was pretty late in River Heights due to the time difference, so I wasn't expecting an answer until the next day.

Hearing a noise, I looked up and saw Tobias creeping along in the distance near the woods. He was too far away for me to see whatever bird or other local critter he was focused on, but seeing him reminded me of what he'd just told me.

Why would Wendy pay him for photos? It had to have something to do with her new plan. But what kind of money-making scheme could involve amateur photos of Alaskan animals? I wondered if Alan might have any guesses. After all, he was the expert on wildlife and such.

At least he was *supposed* to be. Suddenly I remembered the odd answers he'd given Tobias on the train earlier. It had almost sounded as if he didn't know much about the native creatures of Alaska. But wouldn't an environmental studies major know about things like that, especially if he was planning to make this trip the basis of a yearlong school project?

That brought another question to mind. What if Alan wasn't what he claimed to be? I sat up straight, disturbed by the idea. But I couldn't quite shake it. After all, Bess had just met Alan a few weeks ago—she really didn't know him that well yet. Could he be pulling some kind of scam on her or something?

"You're letting this mystery go to your head, Drew," I said to myself with a half smile. I glanced down at the message on my phone screen, hesitating for only a moment before adding a few quick lines, asking Ned to check up on Alan when he got the chance. That shouldn't be hard, since they were both students at the university.

I hit send and leaned back in the lounge chair again. There. With that taken care of, I could go back to working on the case—beginning with tracking down Wendy. Still, the lounge chair was comfortable, and the evening temperature was perfect. Maybe I could just sit here and rest for a few minutes first. . . .

My eyes drifted shut, and moments later I was asleep.

Unfortunately, my unplanned siesta made it hard to fall asleep that night. It didn't help that it never really seemed to get dark in Alaska at that time of year. When Bess, George, and Alan returned from their ride at almost nine o'clock, it was still as bright as midday. And when we all headed into our separate rooms a couple of hours later, the sun was just sinking toward the horizon. I tossed and turned and finally drifted off after a while, but awoke suddenly at around two a.m.

Yawning widely, I got up and tiptoed toward the bathroom, trying to be quiet so I wouldn't wake Bess and George. After using the facilities, I wandered over to the sink to wash my hands. I glanced out the window at the moonlit landscape.

I blinked. Was the near darkness playing tricks on my eyes? Or was that a hooded figure sneaking off toward the woods?

My sleepy mind struggled to figure out what this meant. I pressed my nose to the window, trying to get a better look. Was that Hiro sneaking off to meet Tatjana?

I blinked again, trying to focus my fuzzy mind. Maybe it was Hiro, or Tatjana for that matter. But what if it wasn't?

That thought woke me up a little more. Hurrying out to the main room, I slipped on the shoes I'd left near the door and pulled a jacket over the shorts and tee I was sleeping in. Then I let myself out of the cabin as quietly as I could.

The figure had disappeared by the time I rounded the cabin and crossed the meadow. But he or she had been heading toward the same trail into the woods that Tatjana had used earlier, so I hurried that way too.

The woods were a lot darker and spookier at this time of night. Animal calls and rustling noises came from every direction. I did my best to ignore them, listening for any sound of human footsteps.

Enough moonlight filtered through the treetops for me to follow the narrow trail through the woods.

I hurried along until the trail split, then hesitated. Tatjana had gone right earlier. Should I go that way now?

Then I heard the crack of a branch somewhere off to the left. I turned and went that way.

After walking for a few more minutes, I started to doubt my decision. I hadn't heard another sound from up ahead. What if that cracking branch had been caused by an animal? My quarry could be a long way down the other fork by now.

Then I froze as I heard a sudden loud sound up ahead. It was muffled by the trees surrounding me, and I wasn't sure what had caused it. It didn't sound like footsteps—more like a loud but muffled grunt or squeal. What if it was an animal?

My heart pounded as I suddenly flashed back to all those wildlife warnings they'd given us on this cruise. Not to mention Bess's comments about dangerous moose, and Tobias's excited talk about grizzly bears and other native wildlife. What if I was about to stumble across a bear, a wolf, an irritated moose?

I stayed rooted in place, waiting for the sound to come again. But all I heard were the normal noises of the forest. Finally I crept forward again, moving slowly and carefully, wondering if I was being foolish. Maybe it would be smarter to go back to the lodge, get some backup. . . .

Then I saw the trees open up into a clearing just ahead. It was larger than the one where Hiro and Tatjana had met earlier. But that wasn't the only difference. This clearing had a ramshackle corrugated shed in the middle of it.

I crouched behind a tree and scanned the clearing for the hooded figure. When nothing moved, I stepped carefully into the clearing.

The shed's door was standing ajar. I realized that could explain what I'd heard—a rusty metal door scraping over the earth might make just that sort of weird sound. Scurrying over, I peered inside. It was dark in there, of course, and at first I couldn't see a thing.

Then my eyes adjusted a little, and I saw something large and square shoved into the darkest corner. A box?

What was it doing way out here? And what was inside?

I carefully dragged it out. It was fairly large and surprisingly heavy. When I peeled back the packing tape holding it shut, a strange musty odor tickled my nose, and I let out a sneeze.

BANG!

Suddenly a shot rang out. I gasped and jumped back as a bullet pinged off the metal shed wall—inches from my head!

CHAPTER TEN

New Connections

ACTING ON INSTINCT, I LUNGED FOR COVER behind the shed as another gunshot exploded out of the woods. Leaping across the clearing and into the trees, I ran for my life.

My breath came in ragged gasps, making it hard to hear whether anyone was following me. But no more shots came. Finally I dared to slow to a jog and glanced up at the moon, trying to gauge which direction I needed to go to return to the lodge. I made my best guess and circled around that way, hoping I wasn't too far off. If I went the wrong way, I could end up hopelessly lost in countless acres of Alaskan wilderness.

It wasn't a comforting thought. I ran as fast as I dared, trying not to make too much noise. After a while I found myself on a trail. Was it the same one I'd taken in? I had no idea. The trees all looked the same, and I couldn't see the moon anymore through the thick canopy overhead.

Just as I was starting to fear I'd gone the wrong way, that I was racing ever deeper into the forest, I caught a glimmer of light through the trees ahead. Could it be the lodge? I ran faster, glancing back over my shoulder for pursuers. . . .

CRASH!

I let out a shrill scream as I smashed into something.

Make that some*one*. "Nancy?" a familiar voice said.

Glancing up, I blinked in surprise. "S-scott," I stammered.

Panic grabbed me for a second. Was Scott the person I'd followed? Had that light come from the flashlight he was using to track me? Was he about to finish the job he'd started back in the clearing?

Then I blinked as I realized we were standing at the edge of the woods. The lodge was right there on the other side of the meadow, and there was a light on in one of the cabins—that was the glimmer I'd seen through the trees. Scott wasn't holding a flashlight. He wasn't wearing a dark hoodie, either—just jeans and a T-shirt.

I slumped with relief, gulping in deep breaths of air to try to catch my breath. "Sorry I crashed into you," I said as soon as I could talk again.

"It's okay." Scott looked concerned. "What are you doing out here this time of night? I saw you wandering into the woods a little while ago."

"Y-you did?" I glanced at those nearby cabins. Several had windows facing onto this meadow, just like mine. More lights were blinking on in some of them now. Obviously my scream had awakened people. Oops.

Scott nodded. "I got dressed and came out to see if I could catch up to you," he said. "I was afraid you might not realize how dangerous the Alaskan wilderness can be, especially at night."

"Yeah, no kidding." I took a deep breath, looking

back at the dark forest. "Um, did you hear gunshots a few minutes ago?"

"Gunshots? Come to think of it, I guess I did. Probably some locals hunting or something. Why? Is that what scared you?"

I hesitated, not sure whether to trust him with what had really happened. By then I could see several people hurrying across the meadow toward us. In the lead was a big, beefy guy in a security guard's uniform.

"What's going on out here?" he asked in a deep voice.

I glanced at his name tag, which identified him as Hank. "Sorry," I said with an apologetic smile. "I couldn't sleep, so I went for a walk."

Bess and George arrived moments later. George was rubbing her eyes, looking less than half awake, but Bess pushed her way forward. "Nancy, are you okay?" she exclaimed. "We heard a scream, then realized you were gone. What happened?"

"I went walking in the woods and stumbled across a shed out in a clearing." I waved a hand in the general direction of the forest. "There was a box inside, and I

was about to open it to see what was inside when someone shot at me."

Gasps came from all around. "Shot at you?" Hank
the security guard said. "Are you sure?"

"Absolutely. The bullet landed close enough for me
to see it."

Hank looked grim. "I'd better go out and have a
look around," he said, patting the holster at his waist.

"I'll come with you," Scott offered. "I want to know
what's going on out there."

A couple of other men also volunteered to go along.
Soon the group was tramping off into the woods, following my vague directions to the clearing.

"Come on, Nancy." Bess put an arm around my
shoulders. "Let's get you inside."

We went into the main building, where one of the
hotel's night staff rustled up some hot tea. Some of the
other people I'd awakened were there too, so I couldn't
tell Bess and George the rest of the story, though they
kept giving me curious looks. Half an hour later, the
men finally returned.

I jumped to my feet and hurried over. "Well?" I asked Hank.

"We found your shed," he said. "But there was no box there. And no sign of the shooter." He shrugged. "Did see a coupla fresh bullet holes in the wall, though."

"The box was gone?" My heart sank, though I supposed I shouldn't be surprised. Instead of chasing me, the shooter must have grabbed the box.

"We'll notify the police just in case," Hank said. "But chances are it was a hunter who mistook you for a hare or something."

"Okay," I said. "But that doesn't explain the box."

"Hmm." Hank didn't quite meet my eye. "Maybe it was a cooler of beer or something."

"It definitely wasn't any kind of cooler," I insisted. "It was a cardboard box, about this big." I made a shape with my hands. "It smelled really weird, like whatever was inside had been stored in a moldy basement or something."

"Well, I'll let the cops know about that. Now you'd better get to bed, miss."

I frowned, annoyed, as I realized he didn't care about the box or what may have been in it. Why would I make up something like that?

Still, it wasn't as if I could prove anything. So I let it go. Maybe my friends and I could hike back out there in the morning and look around.

"I still can't believe someone actually shot at you last night," Bess said as she slathered butter on a piece of toast.

"You're not the only one." I glanced around the lodge's homey restaurant. It was early, but lots of people from our group were there having breakfast. Scott was among them; he was sitting at a large table with the ABCs and a couple of people I didn't know. As I scanned the room, I caught several people watching me. Was one of them the hooded figure I'd followed into the woods? It was a creepy thought.

George noticed the glances too. "You're the talk of the lodge, Nancy," she commented. "Everyone's buzzing about what happened last night."

"Yeah. I can't believe nobody woke me up." Alan speared a sausage with his fork. "I missed the whole thing."

"It's okay, sweetie." Bess patted his hand. "Nancy's fine, and that's what matters."

The other tables were too close to risk talking about the case, so we spent the next few minutes chatting about the day's plans while we ate. We were scheduled to catch a bus over to the visitor center of Denali National Park in a couple of hours. There, we would split up into several smaller buses for an all-day guided tour.

Finally Bess took one last sip of her grapefruit juice. "I'm stuffed," she said. "Think I'll take a walk. Want to come?" She smiled at Alan.

He jumped up, dabbing some syrup off his face with a napkin. "Sounds good."

"Have fun," George said, reaching for another slice of bacon.

As Bess and Alan made their way out of the crowded restaurant, Wendy hurried in past them. She glanced around, then made a beeline for our table.

"Uh-oh," I told George under my breath. "Bet I'm about to be interviewed for the next big blog post."

George smirked, but didn't have time to say anything before Wendy reached us. "Nancy!" the blogger exclaimed breathlessly. "I heard you were in here. Everyone's all atwitter about you, you know. What really happened last night, anyway? I tried to talk to that security guard afterward, but the dude wouldn't tell me a thing."

"There wasn't much to tell," I said. "I just wandered into the woods, and I guess someone out there wasn't happy to see me."

"Oh." To my surprise, Wendy didn't seem too interested. Shooting a look around, she set her laptop on the table and sank into the seat Bess had just vacated. "But listen, I just figured out who you really are."

I blinked. "Um, what?"

"You're the big-time amateur detective from the Midwest, right? Don't tell me there's another Nancy Drew out there who looks just like you."

I exchanged a slightly panicky look with George. "Uh . . ."

"Don't worry. If you're here, like, investigating a case or something, I won't blow your cover." Wendy waved a hand. "But this totally changes things. I might be willing to share my thing—*if* you promise to give me the scoop for my blog, that is."

"Your thing?" I echoed.

"Wait," George broke in. "How'd you figure out that Nancy's a detective?"

Wendy shrugged and reached for piece of bacon. "It wasn't that hard." She popped the bacon into her mouth, continuing to talk as she chewed. "I've noticed how Nancy always seems to be around when weird things happen. So when I found out about the mysterious stuff going on around here, I wondered if . . . Well, you know."

Her smile looked a little sheepish. I realized what that meant. *I'd* been one of *her* suspects!

"So anyway, I did a little research after all the excitement last night. Made me miss some beauty sleep, but I didn't want to wait." She grimaced. "I heard there's not much in the way of wireless access once we're out in the park. We might not even have cell phone coverage."

"Go figure," George said innocently.

"Yeah." Wendy shrugged. "Anyway, it didn't take me long to find tons of info on you, Nancy."

"Really?" I said. "Like what?"

Wendy opened her laptop and slid it over in front of me. "Here you go."

My eyes widened. She'd opened up some kind of search engine. There on the screen was a whole page's worth of stories about me! There were articles from the River Heights paper about various cases I'd solved. A write-up of a local service award I'd received last year. Even a link to a video of me standing beside my father while he was interviewed on TV after winning a big case.

"Wow," I said. "I mean, I know you can find just about everything online. But this is kind of creepy!"

George reached for her coffee cup. "I'm always telling you this stuff is out there, Nancy." She glanced at Wendy and rolled her eyes. "I swear, sometimes you'd think Nancy was older than my grandma."

I just stared at the screen. This whole time, I'd been wondering why someone would target me and my friends when we were supposed to be here undercover. But when you came right down to it, we weren't really undercover at all. We were using our real names. Anyone with Internet access could find out who we were with the click of a mouse.

The realization was so overwhelming that it took me a moment to realize Wendy was still talking. "Anyway," she was saying, "I figured it made sense for us to team up to solve the case, you know?"

"The case?" I gulped. "Um, how did you find out about it?"

Wendy shrugged. "The news is out there—all you have to do is look for it," she said. "But actually, it was Tobias who clued me in."

"Tobias?" I shot a confused look at George, who shook her head. "Wait, how did Tobias know about it?"

"I don't know. I guess he saw it online too," Wendy said. "The kid's really into weird animal stuff, in case you haven't noticed."

"Weird animal stuff?" George said. "Wait—what case are you talking about?"

"Duh—*my* case." Wendy sounded a little impatient. "And yours too, maybe, I guess. Are you here to investigate the Alaskan smuggling ring?"

"Smuggling ring?" I echoed. "Um, no. What smuggling ring?"

"Seriously? That's not why you're here?" Wendy looked suspicious. Then she shrugged. "Look, I'll show you."

She grabbed the laptop and started typing. A moment later she shoved it over to me again.

Another search result was up on the screen. This time, all the links had to do with smuggling. Specifically, smuggling animal parts, like tusks, teeth, and bones of rare or endangered species.

"Wow," I said. "Check this out, George."

We skimmed a few of the articles, many of which talked about the latest international smuggling ring, which the authorities had so far been unable to bust. I felt a growing sense of excitement as I read. Was this the puzzle piece I'd been looking for?

"Well, here's a motive for us," George said, clearly

thinking the same thing. "What if someone's been smuggling rare Alaskan animal parts into Vancouver on cruise ships? It says right here that Vancouver's a big hub for that sort of thing."

"Wait," Wendy broke in. "You think whoever's doing this is someone from our ship? Crazy!"

"Maybe. And this would explain the weird, musty smell coming from that box last night." I couldn't help shuddering at the thought that the box might have been full of animal bones and such. "The trouble is, how do we prove it? We don't know who that figure in the hoodie was. And we don't even have the box as evidence."

Just then I noticed a security guard hurrying toward us. He was a different guy from the one last night.

"Nancy Drew?" he said. "Hi. Hank filled me in on your situation during shift change this morning. I just wanted to let you know that the local police are on the case. We'll keep you posted. In the meantime, just holler if you need anything. My name's John." He pointed to his name tag.

"Thanks, John." I stared at his name tag, and suddenly the final puzzle piece clicked into place in my head. A grin spread over my face. "Thank you very, very much!"

"What are you looking so happy about all of a sudden?" George asked as the guard hurried away.

"I think I know how to find out who I followed into the woods last night," I said. "Maybe even how to solve the entire case—*if* it's not too late."

"Really?" Wendy exclaimed. "How can I help?"

"Can you go online and find out someone's cell phone number?" I asked. "Even if it's a super-common name—like Fred Smith?"

CHAPTER ELEVEN

Final Surprise

"AMAZING, NANCY," GEORGE SAID. "I CAN'T believe you figured things out just from some security guy's name tag."

We were sitting in the lobby of the lodge with Bess, Alan, and Wendy. The police were still there. They were dragging Scott toward the door, though he wasn't going easily. He was sputtering with anger and calling the cops every name in the book. It was getting close to time for the buses to leave for the park, and a lot of our fellow *Arctic Star* passengers were in the lobby, watching the show.

"Well, *I* can't believe Scott was our culprit all along," Bess said. "I figured he was off the hook, since we knew he couldn't have planted that note in Nancy's bag."

"I still don't understand exactly what happened," Alan complained. "Anyone care to fill me in?"

"Scott was the hooded person I followed into the woods last night," I told him. "He was going to meet his contact at that shed. He needed to confirm that the contact had brought the box of illegal stuff—and probably also needed to pay him for it, of course. Then Scott could smuggle the box onto the *Arctic Star* and pass it off to someone else when he got back to Vancouver."

"So was Scott the one who shot at you?" George asked.

"I don't think so," I replied. "That was the contact. It seems Scott had already left the shed area by the time I got there. See, he was planning to leave the box in the shed until we were all off touring Denali today. Then he'd have plenty of time to go get it and hide it somewhere." I shrugged. "He was already back at the lodge—and had removed that hoodie—by the time he heard the shots. He was doubling back to see what was going on when I stumbled into him."

"Then what happened to the box?" Alan wondered.

"Like I said, Scott's contact took those shots at me. I guess he heard me crashing around in the woods and hid to see what was going on." I grimaced. "Once he scared me off, he must've moved the box to a different hiding place, which is why the security guard didn't see it. But the police found it when they searched Scott's room just now."

"Wow." Bess shook her head. "Wait—but you still haven't told us how you figured out it was Scott."

"That's where Fred Smith came in." I traded a smile with Wendy. "See, the security guard who came to update me this morning was named John. That reminded me that I've been hearing that name a lot lately."

"So?" Alan looked confused. "John's a pretty common name."

I smiled. "Right. That's why it took so long for me to put two and two together. John Sanchez is the name of the busboy who got fired—and framed, according to

Fred Smith." I shrugged. "John is also the name of one of the people I overheard arguing in the kitchen our first night on the ship."

"I almost forgot about that," George said. "I always figured that was just a red herring, since it seemed so random."

"Yeah, I wasn't too sure myself," I said. "But I realized that the John from that argument could've been John the busboy. And that maybe someone was threatening him because he'd stumbled on to something incriminating."

Bess's eyes widened. "I get it!" she exclaimed. "Everyone says John the busboy is super honest, right? He found out about what Scott was doing, so Scott framed him to get him fired."

"Not at first," I said. "I guess Scott thought his threats were enough to keep John quiet for a while. But when Vince and Lacey got arrested and security was tightened—and especially after the jewelry store got robbed—he decided it was safer to just get him out of the picture."

"So Scott was involved in the jewelry store thing, too?" Wendy asked.

"Uh-huh. The police already got him to fess us to that. He loaned his ship ID to one of his sleazy friends—probably one of the guys I saw him meeting with in Ketchikan. The guy was only supposed to pick up something from Scott's cabin, but on his way out I guess he decided the jewelry store looked like easy pickings."

"Wow," George said. "But wait. I still don't get how you knew Scott was behind all this."

"I didn't," I admitted. "Like I was saying, that's where Fred Smith came in. He was trying to help John the busboy, so I figured he was our best bet to get John to tell us who threatened him in the kitchen that day."

"Scott?" Alan guessed.

I nodded. "Scott was the one who framed him. He also threatened his friends and family, so John was too scared to go to the police even after he got fired. But Fred talked him into telling him the truth."

"Cool." Wendy looked impressed. "So the case is

closed." She leaned over and poked me. "Don't forget, you promised I could break the news on my blog. Exclusive interview, right?"

I hesitated. I wasn't thrilled about having this story splashed all over Wendy's travel blog, especially after seeing all the information about me out there on the Internet already. Still, Wendy had provided a key clue in solving the case. Maybe I owed her that scoop.

"Um, sure," I said uncertainly. "But can we do it later? It looks like the bus is here." I pointed to the large bus pulling to a stop outside.

George jumped to her feet. "Come on, let's go get in line."

We were waiting to board the bus when Tatjana found us. "I just finished talking with the police," she told me. "I thought you'd like to know that Scott is agreeing to make a full confession about the smuggling business." She pursed her lips and shook her head disapprovingly. "I still can't believe he's a criminal!"

"But he confessed to everything?" I asked.

She shrugged. "Almost everything. He realized he'd

get off easier if he ratted out the rest of the smuggling ring. He also confessed to planting those drugs to get John Sanchez fired. And to giving that Troy Anderson fellow his security card to get him on the ship." She smirked. "He was pretty angry that the guy robbed the jewelry store on his way out, since he blames that for getting him busted."

"He didn't know that Nancy was on the case." George clapped me on the back. "She always gets her man!"

"Hmm." Tatjana didn't look too impressed by that. "Anyway, it seems he was also responsible for some funny business Becca was worried about before the cruise. Probably to distract her from his real mission."

I nodded, thinking back over the various troubling little incidents Becca had told me about, checking those off my mental list. "What about the falling moose antler, and the glass on my seat?" I asked. "Oh, and the note in my suitcase—we know he couldn't have done that himself, but if he got someone else to do it . . ."

I trailed off. Tatjana was shaking her head. "I don't know anything about any of that. Scott claims he had no idea you were investigating him. He had no reason to try to hurt you." She glanced at her watch. "Excuse me. I need to start getting things organized."

She hurried off. "Never mind, Nancy," Bess said. "I know you like to tie up all the loose ends, but those things are no big deal."

"She's right," George added. "We knew all along that the fallen moose could've been an accident."

"On my seat? By the window?" That didn't seem super likely to me. "And what about the note in my suitcase?"

George glanced over at Tobias, who was waiting with his parents a few yards away. "Maybe that was a prank," she said, nodding toward him. "You-know-who's cabin is right next to ours, and we all know he's a bit, uh, exuberant."

There was no more time to discuss it as Tatjana, Hiro, and the bus driver starting herding us all onto the bus. I realized there were a few other loose ends we hadn't discussed—like my fall into the creek in Ketchikan, our canceled reservation, even the crazy laundry mix-up. I couldn't help wondering if there was yet another culprit still out there—maybe Max? But no, he probably couldn't have pushed me off that walkway, and he definitely couldn't have planted the glass. . . .

My phone buzzed, interrupting my thoughts. It was Becca texting me with a description of the jewelry thief. "Too bad I didn't think to ask that question earlier," I murmured as I scanned the message.

"Huh?" George glanced over at me. She'd snagged the window seat yet again.

"I asked Becca to find out what the jewelry thief looks like," I said, showing her the text. "She just heard back from the cops, who described him as an average-size white male in his mid-thirties with a large scar bisecting his face. Just like one of the guys I saw with Scott in Ketchikan."

"Whoa. If we'd known that earlier . . . ," George began.

I nodded, staring at the phone's little screen. "I know."

Hiro was walking up the aisle, checking names off a list. He paused by our seats and grinned. "Better get all your calls and texts in now," he said, gesturing toward my phone. "Won't be much cell coverage out in the park."

"So I've heard." I smiled back, then tucked my phone away. "But that's okay. I'm sure we'll have better things to do than chat on the phone."

As the bus pulled away from the lodge, I did my best to shake off those last few doubts. Maybe my friends were right. We'd solved two separate cases already. What were a few minor loose ends, anyway?

It wasn't too hard to put the case out of my mind as we entered Denali National Park. Three smaller buses were lined up, waiting for us. They looked like school buses that had been painted green. Tatjana had already divided our group into three, and we all headed for our assigned buses. My friends and I ended up on the first to depart.

As we trundled off down the road, I glanced around at my fellow passengers. The ABCs and a few other acquaintances from the ship were onboard, along with Tatjana. However, Hiro, Wendy, Tobias and his family, and others were on the other two buses.

Within minutes, the visitor center had disappeared

behind us, and we were surrounded by wilderness as far as the eye could see. A great greenish-yellow plain stretched out on either side of the road, and we almost immediately spotted a herd of caribou grazing in the distance. Farther off were gorgeous snowcapped mountains, including Mount McKinley, which our guide, a chipper young woman, told us most Alaskans referred to by its original native name, Denali. She also told us that the park covered around six million acres, and that the road we were on was the only one in the entire place.

We were kept busy for the next couple of hours admiring the scenery and spotting wildlife. The bus stopped a few times so we could get out and take pictures—of Dall sheep high up on a cliff, a family of grizzly bears in the valley below the road, and a particularly scenic overpass.

The bus had paused to let a moose cross the road when my phone rang. George was taking pictures through the front windscreen, but she looked over at me in surprise. "Hey, you still have a signal! Who is it?" she asked.

"Don't know." I checked the readout. "Oh, it's Ned! Wonder why he's calling instead of texting?"

Bess smiled. "Duh. He probably misses hearing your voice."

I stuck out my tongue at her as I picked up the call. "Ned!" I exclaimed. "I miss you. How are you? What time is it there?"

"Nancy?" His voice sounded fuzzy and very far away. Glancing at the readout, I saw that I barely had one bar's worth of reception.

"Ned? I can hardly hear you. I'm in the middle of Denali National Park, and—"

"Nancy, listen," he cut me off. "I checked into this Alan guy like you asked, and I—"

BZZZ. The line went dead.

"Ned?" I said.

"Dropped?" George asked.

"Yeah. No surprise, I guess." I shrugged, not wanting to mention what he'd said, since Alan and Bess were in the seat right behind us. "Guess I'll call him back when we get back to the lodge."

I couldn't help wondering what Ned had found out about Alan. Was it good news or bad news?

George was still taking pictures of the moose, which seemed to be taking its time ambling across the road. "Good thing Tobias isn't on our bus," she said. "He'd probably want to get out and say hello."

"Be nice," Bess said, leaning forward from her seat. "That kid knows a lot about animals. He probably knows moose can be dangerous."

I glanced back to see if the other buses had caught up to ours yet. But there was no sign of them. "Looks like Mr. Moose is moving on," I said. "He might be gone before Tobias's bus gets here."

The tour continued. Our guide used the moose's appearance to warn us once more about keeping a safe distance from the animals, especially the larger and more dangerous ones. Alan raised his hand.

"My girlfriend claims moose are more dangerous than grizzly bears," he said with a grin. "True or false?"

"Depends how you look at it," the guide responded. "It's true that people have been hurt and killed by both species. Moose aren't normally as aggressive as bears, though females with young can be quite protective. But due to their numbers and large size . . ."

I barely heard the rest of the guide's answer, distracted by wondering once again about Alan. Was he just joking around by asking a question like that? Or was it a clue that he might not be what he seemed? I wished Ned had been able to finish whatever he was trying to tell me.

But there was no point in fretting about it now. Even if Ned had found out something bad—like that Alan was only posing as a university student to impress Bess—there wasn't much I could do about it at the moment. If there was another mystery there, it could wait until we got home to River Heights.

Oohs and aahs were rising around me, and I realized we'd just come into view of a gorgeous lake. I didn't waste another thought on anything but soaking up the scenery until we stopped at a picnic grounds for lunch.

The lunch spot was just as scenic as the rest of the park. It overlooked part of the valley, with rocky foothills behind it. We all ate quickly, talking about everything we'd seen so far. Then people scattered in different directions, snapping photos of scenery, wildflowers, and some Dall sheep visible on a ridge nearby. I pulled out my own camera to get a shot of a curious ptarmigan, but as the bird waddled away, I once again found myself feeling a little distracted. I just couldn't seem to totally forget about those loose ends—especially that note in my suitcase and the smashed glass on my seat. It was hard to believe either of those things was an accident or even a prank. But who could have done them? And why?

I wandered off by myself around a pile of boulders, not wanting Bess and George to notice my expression. They both know me pretty well, and I wasn't in the mood for their teasing. Leaning against one of the rocks, I stared at the mountains in the distance and tried to puzzle out some answers.

"Nancy!" Alan burst into view, breathless and giddy. "You have to come check this out. I just spotted a litter of adorable baby foxes!"

"Really?" The guide had mentioned that we would

probably encounter some foxes in the park, though we hadn't seen any yet. "Where are they? Did you tell Bess and George?"

He tugged on my sleeve. "Hurry, before they wander off," he urged. "I'll find Bess and George and bring them over."

I tried to shake off my distraction. "Okay. Where are they?"

He pointed to an outcropping nearby. "That way. Just climb over those rocks and down the other side and you'll see them."

"Cool." As he rushed off in the other direction, I headed for the outcropping. I was still deep in thought as I carefully picked my way over the rocky ground and clambered down the steep far side. That put me in a little valley near a creek sheltered on three sides by rocky slopes.

I glanced around, but there were no foxes in sight. Hearing a noise behind me, I turned around—and found myself face-to-face with an irritated-looking moose and her calf!

CHAPTER TWELVE

~

Final Answers at Last

"OH!" I BLURTED OUT BEFORE I COULD STOP myself. My mind raced; what had that guide told us about mother moose being dangerously protective of their babies? I wished I'd paid more attention. "Easy does it."

The moose lowered her head, her ears back and her hackles raised. She grunted, moving her huge body between me and the calf.

I glanced over my shoulder, ready to scramble back up the slope. But it was steep and pretty high. Would I have time to make it to safety before the moose charged?

Or was it better to stand still and hope she'd realize I wasn't a threat? Those seemed to be my only two choices, since the moose were blocking any other escape.

Then I heard footsteps at the top of the rocky slope. Glancing up, I saw Alan peering down at me.

"Thank goodness!" I cried. "Alan, quick—toss a stone or something behind the moose to distract it, then help me up!"

Alan bent and picked up a rock. He wound up and threw it—right at the baby moose!

The calf bleated in surprise and pain as the rock bounced off its head. That riled up the mother moose even more. She took a step toward me.

"What are you doing?" I cried. "I said throw it *behind* them, not *at* them!"

Alan smirked. "I was hoping for a grizzly bear," he said. "But thanks to Encyclopedia Bess, I figured Mama Moose here would do just as well."

I gaped up at him, my brain not quite processing what he was saying. But he wasn't quite finished.

"Maybe this will teach your father not to meddle

in other people's lives," he growled, throwing another stone at the baby moose.

Luckily, that one missed. But the mother moose was pawing now, looking really angry. Alan picked up a large rock, tossing it from hand to hand.

"D-don't do this, Alan," I said, my voice shaky. "Bess and George will be along soon."

"Don't count on it," Alan sneered. "I just sent them off looking for those imaginary fox kits—in the other direction."

Despite the danger, my mind couldn't help fitting this piece into the puzzle. "It was *you*!" I said as realization dawned. "You're the one who was responsible for all those loose ends!"

"Ding-ding-ding! Give that lady a prize," he said sarcastically. "Took you long enough to figure it out." He hefted the rock. "You know—for such a fabulous detective."

I gulped, glancing at the moose. If Alan threw one more rock at her baby, I was pretty sure it would be the last straw. I had to distract him.

"So you were the one who left that note in my suit-case?" I asked, trying to keep my voice from shaking.

"That was an easy one," he said with a mirthless laugh. "I pretended I'd left my passport in my suitcase. Nobody even gave me a second look when I was paw-ing through our bags. I switched the tags on your suit-case and slipped that note inside."

He actually sounded proud of himself. "Okay, good one," I said, pressing back against the rock wall and trying to keep my voice calm. The moose eyed me sus-piciously and let out a snort, but stayed where she was. "Um, so what about the mini-golf moose thing? Was that you too?"

"Of course. I was just bummed that the antler mostly missed you." Alan looked at the real moose, seeming amused. "Who knew it was the real version that would finish you off?"

"And you pushed me off the walkway in Ketchikan, didn't you?" Now that I thought back, I couldn't believe I hadn't seen it sooner. "I could have been killed!"

"Bingo!" His mouth twisted with amusement. "Not

that it wasn't fun to mess with you in smaller ways too. Like changing your wake-up call, and bumping George so she'd knock your bagel on the floor, and getting all your clean laundry sent out. Oh, and canceling your reservations yesterday too."

"And the glass all over my seat?" I waited for the answer, though I already knew it.

"That too." Alan sounded impatient. "But enough chitchat. I know you're stalling. Or are you just trying to get me to confess?" He barked out a laugh as he hoisted the rock again. "Because if that's your game, you might as well give it up. You can't prove anything, even if Mama Moose doesn't trample you."

"She won't have to," a confident but rather high-pitched voice rang out behind him. "We just heard you confess to everything!"

Alan dropped his rock and spun around in surprise. Tobias stepped into view, with Wendy right behind him.

"The kid's right," Wendy said. "We heard it all."

Tobias glared at Alan. "I came to look for you when our bus got here," he said. "I wanted to ask you if there were any interesting spiders around this place."

Alan didn't respond. Casting a desperate look around, he shoved past Wendy and took off running. "Guys?" I called up as gently as I could, keeping one eye on the mother moose. "A little help here?"

"Right." Tobias grabbed the rock Alan had dropped. He hurled it a few yards behind the moose, where it landed in some weeds with a thud.

The mother moose heard it and spun around, shoving her calf aside and snorting suspiciously at the spot where the rock had landed.

Meanwhile Wendy bent and stretched a hand down, then grabbed my arm and helped to pull me up as I scrambled for safety. Whew!

"Where'd he go?" I asked as soon as I caught my breath. "Hurry—we have to find him! Who knows what he's capable of?"

"I still can't believe Alan was after you this whole time," Bess said. "How stupid am I?"

I glanced at her. She and George and I were on the

lodge's back deck, relaxing in lounge chairs and enjoying the bright Alaska evening.

"Don't beat yourself up," I said. "He had us all fooled."

"Not me," George put in with a frown. "I never liked the jerk."

"You never like any of the guys Bess dates," I reminded her with a half smile.

The smile faded as I sighed, thinking back on the events of the day. Everything was kind of a blur for the few minutes after I'd climbed out of that moose pit. Wendy, Tobias, and I ran back and told Hiro and Tatjana what had happened. A search was mounted, and Alan was found quickly. There weren't many places to hide in the sparse landscape, and Alan wasn't much of an outdoorsman.

Soon the bus driver was radioing for help, and we were waiting for the police to come and take Alan away. In the meantime, he'd had quite a bit to say. Apparently my father had been the prosecuting attorney who'd helped get Alan's father put away for life for fraud and embezzlement. Alan had vowed revenge, but he'd decided that just going after my dad wasn't enough. He wanted to hurt him by hurting his family—which meant me. And that must have been what Ned was calling to tell me before the call was dropped.

That was the whole reason he'd pursued Bess. He'd figured it would be an easy way to get close to me, figure out my weaknesses. The Alaska trip was a lucky break for him. It had given him lots of opportunities to mess with me.

Then he'd found out that I really was a pretty accomplished sleuth. That had made him realize he needed to up the ante. He'd started watching for a chance to *really* hurt me. His original plan had involved causing an accident during that horseback excursion I'd ended up skipping, but spotting that mother moose had provided him with a second chance.

"I couldn't believe the way he kept threatening you, even when the police were dragging him away." Bess shivered, wrapping her arms around herself. "Swearing he'd never rest until you and your dad paid . . . What a nut!"

"Good thing Wendy recorded his whole rant on her smartphone." George grinned. "I loved the way she waved the phone in his face and told him she was going to forward it to the police." She leaned back in her chair. "You know, I thought that chick was a real weirdo at first. But she's okay."

"Tobias, too," Bess put in. "I'm glad he finally started to enjoy this vacation. He's actually kind of a cool kid."

I glanced at her with a wry smile. "It just goes to show that people aren't always what they seem."

"No kidding," Bess said with feeling. "I still can't believe I fell for a jerk like Alan."

We heard the door swing open behind us. Sitting up, I saw Wendy hurrying over.

"There you are!" she said. "Listen, I know you've had a tough day, Nance. But I'd love to get a post about this whole dealio up before the story hits the wires." She winked. "Nothing like an exclusive for a little free publicity, right? So how about it? Can we do that interview now? Maybe get some photos of the day's hero?" She formed her hands into a mock camera lens, framing me inside it.

Once again, I hesitated. I *really* owed her now. But I still didn't like the thought of losing even more of my anonymity if she got her wish and the story went viral.

"I've got an even better idea," I told her. "You should focus your story on the *real* hero of today."

"Who, the moose?" George put in. "You're right, she showed great restraint in not stomping you. But I doubt she's in any mood for interviews."

I ignored her, standing up and smiling at Wendy. "Let's go find Tobias," I said. "I'm thinking maybe you could focus your story around him. Isn't that the kind of thing that's more likely to go viral? Kid hero saves the day?"

Wendy's eyebrows shot up. "Oh my gosh, you're so right!" she exclaimed. "I know I can get some serious attention with that story. Nancy, you're a total genius!"

"You don't know the half of it," George said with a smirk.

But Wendy was already heading for the lobby, shouting for us to hurry up and follow. "Come on," I told my friends with a smile. "Let's go help her track down her new victim—er, I mean star."

"And maybe *then* we'll be able to relax and enjoy the rest of the trip?" Bess said.

I grinned. "Definitely."

Dear Diary,

WOW! THAT'S ABOUT ALL I CAN SAY.

I would never have believed that the bones of endangered animals were valuable enough to be smuggled.

But almost more incredible was that Alan posed as Bess's boyfriend just to get revenge on me.

As spectacular as Alaska was—Mount McKinley did take my breath away—I can't wait to get back to River Heights.

'Cause in the end, there's no place like home.

READ WHAT HAPPENS IN THE NEXT MYSTERY

IN THE NANCY DREW DIARIES,

Mystery of the Midnight Rider

"IS THAT HER?" I ASKED, SHADING MY EYES against the glare of the afternoon sun. "The one in the beige breeches and tall boots?"

Ned grinned. "You'll have to be more specific, Nancy. Just about everyone out there is wearing beige breeches and tall boots."

The two of us were leaning on the rail of a large riding ring at the local fairgrounds. At the moment it was crowded with horses and riders warming up for their next class. All of them—male and female, teenagers and adults—were dressed almost exactly alike.

"You have a point," I said with a laugh. "So how are we supposed to know who to cheer for once the class starts?"

Just then one of the horses separated from the others and trotted toward us. "Ned Nickerson? Is that you?" the rider called.

Ned waved. "Hi, Payton! It's good to see you again."

"You too." Payton halted her horse in front of us and smiled shyly. She was about sixteen, with a slender build and delicate features that made her look tiny atop her horse, an enormous bay with a splash of white on its forehead.

"Payton, this is my girlfriend, Nancy Drew," Ned said. "Nancy, this is Payton Evans."

"Nice to meet you," I said. "Your horse is beautiful."

"Thanks." Payton leaned forward to give the horse a pat on its gleaming neck. "He's actually not mine, though. I'm riding him for my trainer—he's one of her sale horses. He's still a little green, but he's coming along."

"Green?" Ned raised an eyebrow. "Looks kind of reddish-brown to me."

I rolled my eyes at the lame joke. "Green just means he's not fully trained yet," I explained.

"That's right." Payton smiled at me. "Are you a rider, Nancy?"

"Not really." I shrugged. "But I took some lessons when I was a kid. And I never miss coming out to watch this show." I returned her smile. "Even when I'm *not* acquainted with one of the star riders."

I glanced around, taking in the hustle and bustle surrounding me. The annual River Heights Horse Show was a prestigious competition, attracting top hunter-jumper riders from all over the country.

Payton's smile faded slightly. "I'm not the star," she said, her voice so soft I could barely hear it over the thud of hoofbeats and chatter of riders and spectators. "The horses are the stars. I'm just along for the ride."

"You don't have to be modest," I told her with a chuckle. "Ned's told me all about you. He says you've been riding since you were practically in diapers, you've had all kinds of success on the A circuit, and that you're supertalented and hard working."

Payton shrugged, playing with the tiny braids in her mount's mane. When she responded her voice was even quieter. "It's easy to work hard at something you love."

As an experienced amateur detective, I'm pretty good at picking up clues. But it didn't take a super-sleuth to tell that Payton wasn't comfortable with our current line of conversation. Time for a change of subject.

"Anyway," I said, "Ned also tells me your mom and his mom were college roommates."

"That's right." Payton stroked her mount as he snorted at a leaf blowing past. "When Mrs. Nickerson heard I was coming to this show, she was nice enough to offer to let me stay with them so I don't have to stay in a hotel."

"She's thrilled to have you here, and she can't wait to see you tonight," Ned assured Payton. "I'm supposed to tell you not to eat too much today, since she and Dad are planning a big welcome barbecue for you tonight."

I chuckled. "That sounds like your parents," I told

Ned. "So are Payton's parents going to be staying with you too?"

"No," Payton answered before Ned could say anything. A sad look flitted across her face. "They have to stay in New York for work today and tomorrow, and then they've got a family obligation that will keep them busy for most of Saturday. But they promised they'll be here in time to watch me ride in the Grand Prix on Saturday."

"The Grand Prix? What's that?" Ned asked.

I rolled my eyes at him. "Weren't you paying attention when I dragged you to this show last year?" I joked. "The Grand Prix is the big jumping competition on Saturday night. It's sort of like the equestrian competitions you see in the Olympics. Huge, colorful fences that are, like, ten feet high."

Payton laughed. "Not quite," she said. "Even the best Olympic horse couldn't jump a ten-foot fence! The heights are more like five feet."

"Close enough," I said with a shrug. "Anything I can't step over myself looks high to me."

Ned poked me on the shoulder. "Here come Bess and George," he said. "I was wondering where they'd disappeared to."

"Bess said she wanted to grab a soda." I noticed that Payton looked slightly confused as she watched my two best friends approach. "George is short for Georgia," I explained with a wink. "But nobody calls her that unless they're trying to get under her skin."

Payton nodded. "Got it."

By then Bess and George had reached us. Both had sodas, and George was also holding a paper cup of French fries smothered in ketchup. The scent of grease wafted toward me, temporarily overwhelming the pleasant horsey smell of Payton's mount.

"Payton Evans, George Fayne, Bess Marvin," Ned said, pointing at each girl in turn as he made the introductions. "Bess and George are cousins, believe it or not," he added with a grin.

"What do you mean 'believe it or not'?" Payton asked.

I laughed. Bess and George may share the same

family, but that's about all they have in common. Bess is blond, blue-eyed, and as girly as they come. George is, well, pretty much the opposite of that. For instance, Bess had dressed up to come to today's show in a pretty dress, stylish flats, even a matching bow holding back her shoulder-length hair. George? She was wearing what she wore just about every day. Jeans, T-shirt, and sneakers.

"Don't pay any attention to him," Bess said. "It's nice to meet you, Payton."

"So you're the superstar rider Ned keeps talking about," George added, popping a fry into her mouth. "He's been totally geeking out about how you're probably going to be in the next Olympics. Is that true, or is he just pulling our legs?"

Payton shrugged, playing with the reins resting on her mount's withers. "Actually my trainer tells me the Chef d'Equipe of the US team is supposed to come watch the Grand Prix at this show."

"The chef de what?" Bess asked as she reached over and snagged one of George's fries.

"That's the person in charge of the Olympic team," Ned explained. "Mom and Dad were talking about it last night after Payton's dad called to make final arrangements."

"Wow," I said. "So this big-time Olympics guy is coming to watch you ride? Maybe so he can decide if you should try out for the US team?"

"I guess so." Payton shrugged again. "I mean, we don't know for sure that he's coming to see me in particular. But my trainer and my parents seem to think so."

"Awesome." George reached out and tentatively patted Payton's horse on the nose. "So is this the horse you'll be riding when he's watching?"

"No. I'll be riding my own horse—my most experienced jumper. His name is Midnight." Payton smiled as she said the horse's name. "He's really cool. Maybe you guys can meet him later."

"We'd love to," Bess said. "As long as it's not *too* much later. Because I'm sure Nancy and Ned have other plans this evening." She waggled her eyebrows at me.

"Sure we do," Ned said. "My parents are throwing that barbecue tonight, remember? You're both invited."

"Oh, right." Bess pursed her lips. "Okay, but that's not what I'm talking about." She waggled a playful finger in Ned's face. "I certainly hope you're planning to take Nancy somewhere more romantic than a family barbecue—or a horse show—this weekend. It's your anniversary, remember?"

"How could he forget? You've only been reminding him twice a day for the past month." I was exaggerating, but only a little. Bess is nothing if not a romantic.

"Yeah. Give it a rest already," George told her cousin. "I'm sure Ned has it all under control."

"Of course I do. I mean, what could be more romantic than this?" Ned slipped one arm around my shoulders, helping himself to a couple of George's fries with the other hand. "Fried food, horse manure—what more could any girl want?"

"Heads up!" a voice barked out, cutting through our laughter. It was another rider—a sharp-chinned teenage girl on a lanky gray horse. The horse was cantering straight at Payton and her mount!

Payton glanced over her shoulder, then shifted her horse aside just in time to avoid a collision. "Um, sorry," she called to the other rider, even though from where I stood it looked as if the gray horse was the one at fault.

The gray horse's rider pulled him to a halt and glared back over her shoulder. "Is this your first horse show, Payton?" she snapped. "This is supposed to be a warm-up ring. If you want to stand around and gossip, do it somewhere else."

"Sorry," Payton said again, though the other rider was already spurring her horse back into a canter.

"Nice girl," George commented with a snort. "Friend of yours?"

Payton sighed. "That's Jessica. I don't even know her that well—she rides at a barn a few miles from mine, and we end up at most of the same shows. I have no idea why she doesn't like me, but she's never exactly made a secret of it." She grimaced and gathered up her reins. "But she's right about one thing—I shouldn't be standing around. I'd better get back to my warm-up. I'll see you guys later, right?"

"Sure. Good luck," Bess said.

We watched her ride off. "She seems nice," I said to Ned.

"Yeah, she is." Ned reached for another fry despite George's grumbles. "Our moms try to get together as often as they can, so I've known Payton for a long time. Haven't seen her in two or three years though." He licked the salt off his fingers. "Her parents both have pretty intense jobs. Mr. Evans is some kind of high-powered financier, and Payton's mom is a medical researcher at one of the top hospitals in New York City."

"Wow." George whistled. "Impressive."

"Yeah. And I guess what they say is true—the apple doesn't fall far from the tree. Because Payton's kind of intense herself." Ned glanced out toward the ring. "Her parents say she started begging for riding lessons when she was about three or four, and she's spent every possible minute in the saddle since. I guess it's no wonder people are starting to talk about the Olympics."

Turning to follow his gaze, I saw Payton cantering the big bay horse near the center of the ring, where several jumps were set up. Her face was scrunched up with concentration as she steered around the other riders going every which way. As I watched, she aimed her mount at the highest of the jumps. I held my breath as the horse sailed over easily.

"Nice," Bess said.

"Yeah," I agreed. "I can't wait to see her compete. How long until it's her turn?"

"I'm not sure." Ned glanced at the gate a short distance away. A steady stream of riders had been going in and out the whole time we'd been standing there.

"I guess you'll have to follow the clues to figure it out, Nancy," George joked.

I grinned. My friends like to tease me about my recreational sleuthing. But the truth is, they seem to like it just as much as I do. At least, they never complain when I drag them into yet another case. Not much, anyway.

We all watched Payton and her horse glide easily over another jump. As she landed, I caught a flurry of activity immediately behind where my friends and I were standing. Glancing over my shoulder, I saw a woman striding in our direction. She was petite and deeply tanned with close-cropped reddish-blond hair a few shades darker than my own. As she rushed past us to the rail, the woman was so focused on the activity in the ring that she almost knocked Bess's soda out of her hand.

"Payton!" she hollered. Her voice was surprisingly loud for such a small person, cutting easily through the clamor of the warm-up ring. "Over here—now!"

Soon Payton was riding over again. "Dana!" she said breathlessly. "I thought you were going to meet me at the in-gate." She glanced at us. "So did you meet Ned and his friends? Guys, this is my trainer, Dana Kinney."

"Huh?" Dana barely spared us a glance and a curt nod. "Listen, Payton, we need to talk—now."

"What is it?" Payton checked her watch. "I was

about to leave for the ring. I'm on deck, I think."

"Then I'll make this quick." Dana clenched her fists at her sides, staring up at Payton. "One of the show stewards just received an anonymous tip about you."

"About me?" Payton looked confused. "What do you mean? What kind of tip?"

Dana scowled. "Whoever-it-is is claiming that you drug all of your horses!"

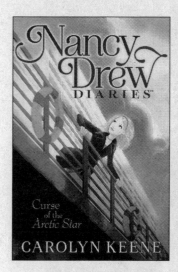

FOR ACTIVITIES, STICKERS, AND
MORE, JOIN THE ACADEMY AT
GODDESSGIRLSBOOKS.COM!

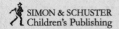

Mystery of the Midnight Rider

Nancy Drew DIARIES™

Mystery of the Midnight Rider

#3

CAROLYN KEENE

Aladdin
NEW YORK   LONDON   TORONTO   SYDNEY   NEW DELHI

ALADDIN

An imprint of Simon & Schuster Children's Publishing Division

1230 Avenue of the Americas, New York, NY 10020

First Aladdin paperback edition May 2013

Copyright © 2013 by Simon & Schuster

All rights reserved, including the right of reproduction in whole or in part in any form.

ALADDIN is a trademark of Simon & Schuster, Inc., and related logo
is a registered trademark of Simon & Schuster, Inc.

NANCY DREW, NANCY DREW DIARIES, and related logo
are trademarks of Simon & Schuster, Inc.

Also available in an Aladdin hardcover edition.

For information about special discounts for bulk purchases, please contact
Simon & Schuster Special Sales at 1-866-506-1949 or business@simonandschuster.com.

The Simon & Schuster Speakers Bureau can bring authors to your live event.

For more information or to book an event contact the Simon & Schuster Speakers Bureau
at 1-866-248-3049 or visit our website at www.simonspeakers.com.

Designed by Karina Granda

The text of this book was set in Adobe Caslon Pro.

Manufactured in the United States of America 0316 OFF

10 9

Library of Congress Control Number 2013933925

ISBN 978-1-4424-7860-2 (pbk)

ISBN 978-1-4424-7861-9 (hc)

ISBN 978-1-4424-7864-0 (eBook)

Contents

Dear Diary

PAYTON EVANS HAD NAMED HER HORSE after the exact time he was born: Midnight.

I had never seen such a magnificent horse before. His coat gleamed in the sunlight. His mane and tail both looked like there had never been one sleek hair out of place.

And when Payton rode him, she looked just as perfect.

Ned told me Payton had been riding horses forever, and that she and Midnight were first-class champions.

She was so lucky to have figured out what she wanted to do with the rest of her life.

CHAPTER ONE

Riding High

"IS THAT HER?" I ASKED, SHADING MY EYES against the glare of the afternoon sun. "The one in the beige breeches and tall boots?"

Ned grinned. "You'll have to be more specific, Nancy. Just about everyone out there is wearing beige breeches and tall boots."

The two of us were leaning on the rail of a large riding ring at the local fairgrounds. At the moment it was crowded with horses and riders warming up for their next class. All of them—male and female, teenagers and adults—were dressed almost exactly alike.

"You have a point," I said with a laugh. "So how are we supposed to know who to cheer for once the class starts?"

Just then one of the horses separated from the others and trotted toward us. "Ned Nickerson? Is that you?" the rider called.

Ned waved. "Hi, Payton! It's good to see you again."

"You too." Payton halted her horse in front of us and smiled shyly. She was about sixteen, with a slender build and delicate features that made her look tiny atop her horse, an enormous bay with a splash of white on its forehead.

"Payton, this is my girlfriend, Nancy Drew," Ned said. "Nancy, this is Payton Evans."

"Nice to meet you," I said. "Your horse is beautiful."

"Thanks." Payton leaned forward to give the horse a pat on its gleaming neck. "He's actually not mine, though. I'm riding him for my trainer—he's one of her sale horses. He's still a little green, but he's coming along."

"Green?" Ned raised an eyebrow. "Looks kind of reddish brown to me."

I rolled my eyes at the lame joke. "Green just means he's not fully trained yet," I explained.

"That's right." Payton smiled at me. "Are you a rider, Nancy?"

"Not really," I replied. "But I took some lessons when I was a kid. And I never miss coming out to watch this show." I returned her smile. "Even when I'm *not* acquainted with one of the star riders."

I glanced around, taking in the hustle and bustle surrounding me. The annual River Heights Horse Show was a prestigious competition, attracting top hunter-jumper riders from all over the country.

Payton's smile faded slightly. "I'm not the star," she said, her voice so soft I could barely hear it over the thud of hoofbeats and chatter of riders and spectators. "The horses are the stars. I'm just along for the ride."

"You don't have to be modest," I told her with a chuckle. "Ned's told me all about you. He says you've been riding since you were practically in diapers, you've had all kinds of success on the A circuit, and you're super talented and hardworking."

Payton shrugged, playing with the tiny braids of her mount's mane. When she responded, her voice was even quieter. "It's easy to work hard at something you love."

As an experienced amateur detective, I'm pretty good at picking up clues. But it didn't take a super-sleuth to tell that Payton wasn't comfortable with our current line of conversation. Time for a change of subject.

"Anyway," I said, "Ned also tells me your mom and his mom were college roommates."

"That's right." Payton stroked her mount as he snorted at a leaf blowing past. "When Mrs. Nickerson heard I was coming to this show, she was nice enough to offer to let me stay with them so I don't have to stay in a hotel."

"She's thrilled to have you here, and she can't wait to see you tonight," Ned assured Payton. "I'm supposed to tell you not to eat too much today, since she and Dad are planning a big welcome barbecue for you tonight."

I chuckled. "That sounds like your parents," I told

Ned. "So are Payton's parents going to be staying with you too?"

"No," Payton answered before Ned could say anything. A sad look flitted across her face. "They have to stay in Chicago for work today and tomorrow, and then they've got a family obligation that will keep them busy for most of Saturday. But they promised they'll be here in time to watch me ride in the Grand Prix on Saturday."

"The Grand Prix? What's that?" Ned asked.

I rolled my eyes at him. "Weren't you paying attention when I dragged you to this show last year?" I joked. "The Grand Prix is the big jumping competition on Saturday night. It's sort of like the equestrian competitions you see in the Olympics. Huge, colorful fences that are, like, ten feet high."

Payton laughed. "Not quite," she said. "Even the best Olympic horse couldn't jump a ten-foot fence! The heights are more like five feet."

"Close enough," I said with a shrug. "Anything I can't step over myself looks high to me."

Ned poked me on the shoulder. "Here come Bess and George," he said. "I was wondering where they'd disappeared to."

"Bess said she wanted to grab a soda." I noticed that Payton looked slightly confused as she watched my two best friends approach. "George is short for Georgia," I explained with a wink. "But nobody calls her that unless they're trying to get under her skin."

Payton nodded. "Got it."

By then Bess and George had reached us. Both had sodas, and George was also holding a paper cup of French fries smothered in ketchup. The scent of grease wafted toward me, temporarily overwhelming the pleasant horsey smell of Payton's mount.

"Payton Evans, George Fayne, Bess Marvin," Ned said, pointing at each girl in turn as he made the introductions. "Bess and George are cousins, believe it or not," he added with a grin.

"What do you mean, believe it or not?" Payton asked.

I laughed. Bess and George may share the same

family, but that's about all they have in common. Bess is blond, blue-eyed, and as girly as they come. George is, well, pretty much the opposite of that. For instance, Bess had dressed up to come to today's show in a pretty dress, stylish flats, even a matching bow holding back her shoulder-length hair. George? She was wearing what she wore just about every day. Jeans, T-shirt, and sneakers.

"Don't pay any attention to him," Bess said. "It's nice to meet you, Payton."

"So you're the superstar rider Ned keeps talking about," George added, popping a fry into her mouth. "He's been totally geeking out about how you're probably going to be in the next Olympics. Is that true, or is he just pulling our legs?"

Payton played with the reins resting on her mount's withers. "Actually, my trainer tells me the chef d'équipe of the US team is supposed to come watch the Grand Prix at this show."

"The chef de what?" Bess asked as she reached over and snagged one of George's fries.

"That's the person in charge of the Olympic team," Ned explained. "Mom and Dad were talking about it last night after Payton's dad called to make final arrangements."

"Wow," I said. "So this big-time Olympics head guy is coming to watch you ride? Maybe so he can decide if you should try out for the US team?"

"I guess so." Payton shrugged again. "I mean, we don't know for sure that he's coming to see me in particular. But my trainer and my parents seem to think so."

"Awesome." George reached out and tentatively patted Payton's horse on the nose. "So is this the horse you'll be riding when he's watching?"

"No. I'll be riding my own horse—my most experienced jumper. His name is Midnight." Payton smiled as she said the horse's name. "He's really cool. Maybe you guys can meet him later."

"We'd love to," Bess said. "As long as it's not *too* much later. Because I'm sure Nancy and Ned have other plans this evening." She waggled her eyebrows at me.

"Sure we do," Ned said. "My parents are throwing

that barbecue tonight, remember? You're both invited."

"Oh, right." Bess pursed her lips. "Okay, but that's not what I'm talking about." She wagged a playful finger in Ned's face. "I certainly hope you're planning to take Nancy somewhere more romantic than a family barbecue—or a horse show—this weekend. It's your anniversary, remember?"

"How could he forget? You've only been reminding him twice a day for the past month." I was exaggerating, but only a little. Bess is nothing if not a romantic.

"Yeah. Give it a rest already," George told her cousin. "I'm sure Ned has it all under control."

"Of course I do. I mean, what could be more romantic than this?" Ned slipped one arm around my shoulders, helping himself to a couple of George's fries with the other hand. "Fried food, horse manure—what more could any girl want?"

"Heads up!" a voice barked out, cutting through our laughter. It was another rider—a sharp-chinned teenage girl on a lanky gray horse. The horse was cantering straight at Payton and her mount!

Payton glanced over her shoulder, then shifted her horse aside just in time to avoid a collision. "Um, sorry," she called to the other rider, even though from where I stood it looked as if the gray horse was the one at fault.

The gray horse's rider pulled him to a halt and glared back over her shoulder. "Is this your first horse show, Payton?" she snapped. "This is supposed to be a warm-up ring. If you want to stand around and gossip, do it somewhere else."

"Sorry," Payton said again, though the other rider was already spurring her horse back into a canter.

"Nice girl," George commented with a snort. "Friend of yours?"

Payton sighed. "That's Jessica. I don't even know her that well—she rides at a barn a few miles from mine, and we end up at most of the same shows. I have no idea why she doesn't like me, but she's never exactly made a secret of it." She grimaced and gathered up her reins. "But she's right about one thing—I shouldn't be standing around. I'd better get back to my warm-up. I'll see you guys later, right?"

"Sure. Good luck," Bess said.

We watched her ride off. "She seems nice," I said to Ned.

"Yeah, she is." Ned reached for another fry despite George's grumbles. "Our moms try to get together as often as they can, so I've known Payton for a long time. Haven't seen her in two or three years, though." He licked the salt off his fingers. "Her parents both have pretty intense jobs. Mr. Evans is some kind of high-powered financier, and Payton's mom is a medical researcher at one of the top hospitals in Chicago."

"Wow." George whistled. "Impressive."

"Yeah. And I guess what they say is true—the apple doesn't fall far from the tree. Because Payton's kind of intense herself." Ned glanced out toward the ring. "Her parents say she started begging for riding lessons when she was about three or four, and she's spent every possible minute in the saddle since. I guess it's no wonder people are starting to talk about the Olympics."

Turning to follow his gaze, I saw Payton cantering the big bay horse near the center of the ring, where several jumps were set up. Her face was scrunched up with concentration as she steered around the other riders going every which way. As I watched, she aimed her mount at the highest of the jumps. I held my breath as the horse sailed over easily.

"Nice," Bess said.

"Yeah," I agreed. "I can't wait to see her compete. How long until it's her turn?"

"I'm not sure." Ned glanced at the gate a short distance away. A steady stream of riders had been going in and out the whole time we'd been standing there.

"I guess you'll have to follow the clues to figure it out, Nancy," George joked.

I grinned. My friends like to tease me about my recreational sleuthing. But the truth is, they seem to like it just as much as I do. At least they never complain when I drag them into yet another case. Not much, anyway.

We all watched Payton and her horse glide easily over another jump. As she landed, I caught a flurry of activity immediately behind where my friends and

I were standing. Glancing over my shoulder, I saw a woman striding in our direction. She was petite and deeply tanned, with close-cropped reddish-blond hair a few shades darker than my own. As she rushed past us to the rail, the woman was so focused on the activity in the ring that she almost knocked Bess's soda out of her hand.

"Payton!" she hollered. Her voice was surprisingly loud for such a small person, cutting easily through the clamor of the warm-up ring. "Over here—now!"

Soon Payton was riding over again. "Dana!" she said breathlessly. "I thought you were going to meet me at the in-gate." She glanced at us. "So did you meet Ned and his friends? Guys, this is my trainer, Dana Kinney."

"Huh?" Dana barely spared us a glance and a curt nod. "Listen, Payton, we need to talk—now."

"What is it?" Payton checked her watch. "I was about to leave for the ring—I'm on deck, I think."

"Then I'll make this quick." Dana clenched her fists at her sides, staring up at Payton. "One of the show stewards just received an anonymous tip about you."

"About me?" Payton looked confused. "What do you mean? What kind of tip?"

Dana scowled. "Whoever it is, they're claiming that you drug all your horses!"

CHAPTER TWO

~

Rules and Rumors

PAYTON GASPED. "WHAT?" SHE CRIED.

"Drugging horses?" Bess whispered to me. "That's bad, right?"

"I'm guessing that's a big yes," I whispered back, my gaze skipping from Dana to Payton and back again. Both of them looked upset.

"How could someone say that?" Payton exclaimed. "It's not true!"

"*I* know that, and *you* know that," Dana said evenly. "So who's trying to convince the stewards otherwise?"

"Who or what are the stewards?" George put in.

Dana blinked and glanced at her, looking impatient and a little confused. I had a feeling the trainer hadn't even taken in Payton's quick introduction. "The stewards are in charge of enforcing the rules of this competition," Dana snapped. "Including the ones about not using illegal substances on the horses. Which *somebody* seems to think Payton is breaking. Just exactly what I need right now to add drama to my already busy day." She scowled at Payton.

Just then I heard Payton's name coming over the loudspeaker. Payton heard it too.

"They're calling me to the ring," she said, her expression still tight and anxious. "I'd better go. We can figure this out after my round."

"Whatever." Dana hurried over to open the gate so Payton could ride out. Then the trainer strode off alongside the horse, letting loose with a rapid-fire barrage of instructions for Payton's coming round. My friends and I trailed along at a safe distance behind the horse.

"Wow," I said. "What do you think that's all about?"

Ned shook his head. "I don't know. But I can tell you one thing—Payton's not a cheater. She wouldn't dope her horses."

"How do you know?" George shot him a sidelong look. "You already said you haven't seen her in a couple of years. What if she's decided to do whatever it takes to get to the Olympics?"

"No. Payton's just not like that," Ned replied. "I told you, I've known her pretty much forever. She's never even cheated at checkers." One corner of his mouth turned up in a half smile. "In fact, once when we were kids our families were spending the weekend together at the beach. We were digging in the sand and found this fancy engraved pocketknife. I figured it counted as buried treasure and wanted to keep it."

"Yeah, sounds like you," George put in.

"Very funny," I said, knowing she was kidding. Everyone knows Ned is pretty much the most honest guy in the Midwest.

He shrugged sheepishly. "I was young and the thing was cool, okay? But Payton wouldn't rest until she tracked down the rightful owner."

"Okay." George didn't seem convinced. "But that was then, and this is the *Olympics*."

"Doesn't matter." Ned is usually pretty easygoing. But when he gets that stubborn look in his eye, there's no changing his mind. "I know she's not a cheater."

We'd reached the main ring by then. Payton was already riding in, her horse's ears pricked toward the colorful jumps.

"Come on, let's go watch," George said, hurrying toward a free row in the bleachers.

A buzzer sounded, and Payton sent her horse into a canter. "I hope she's not so freaked out by what just happened that she gets distracted and messes up," Bess fretted. "Those jumps look awfully big!"

"I wonder if that's exactly why someone started the rumor about her drugging her horses," I said. "Maybe one of her competitors is trying to get an edge any way they can."

"Would somebody really do that?" George said dubiously. "For a horse show?"

"Some of these shows can pay pretty decent prize money," Ned said. "Payton's father used to grumble about all the money he spent on Payton's riding until she started winning jumper classes. That shut him up pronto."

"Really? Then maybe it really was—ooh! That was close!" I interrupted myself as one of Payton's horse's hooves clunked against the fence he was jumping.

"It's okay," Bess said. "The rail didn't come down. I'm pretty sure that means no penalties."

We all stayed silent as we watched the rest of the round. None of the other rails came down either. When Payton brought her horse down to a trot after the last fence, I heard a loud whoop. Glancing toward the gate, I saw Dana at the rail pumping her fist.

"Maybe that'll put Payton's trainer in a better mood," I quipped.

"I know, right?" George made a face. "I thought *Payton* seemed a little intense until Trainer Frowny Face came along."

The crackle of the loudspeaker prevented any further comment from the rest of us. "That was Payton Evans with a clear round," the announcer said. "Which puts her in first place."

A loud curse came from nearby. Glancing that way, I saw a short, lean man in his thirties kicking at a fence post with a scowl on his face. He was dressed in breeches and a polo shirt and had a riding crop tucked into the top of one tall boot.

My friends saw him too. "Looks like somebody's not happy that Payton did so well," George murmured.

"Yeah," Bess added quietly. "I'm guessing he's one of the ones who *didn't* have a clear round."

"He's not the only one who doesn't look thrilled." I'd just spotted Jessica, the girl who'd almost run her horse into Payton's earlier. She was riding toward the in-gate to start her round. But instead of focusing on her horse or the jumps, she was glaring at Payton.

"Come on, let's go congratulate Payton." Ned got up and hurried to meet Payton as she rode out of the gate.

The rest of us followed, arriving just as Payton slid

down from the saddle beside Dana. "That was great!" I said. "We had a lot of fun watching you own that course."

"Thanks." Payton gave the horse a pat, then ran up her left stirrup. "He was really amazing, wasn't he?"

Dana grabbed the reins and pulled them over the horse's head, leading him off almost before Payton could finish with the other stirrup. "Listen, you almost ate it at that yellow oxer," she told Payton. "Looked like you took your leg off. I told you a million times you can't do that, especially with this horse."

"Yeah, sorry about that." Payton didn't argue. "I'll remember from now on."

"You got away with it this time, but you won't at Grand Prix heights." Dana frowned. "You have to stay focused!"

I couldn't help wincing. The trainer's voice was awfully loud, and people were turning to stare curiously at her and Payton. But Payton didn't seem to notice. She was nodding thoughtfully as Dana went on to detail every mistake Payton had made during the round.

"Wow," George whispered in my ear. "And here I thought she just put herself into first place! You'd never know it listening to the Dana of Doom."

Finally Dana's cell phone chimed, interrupting her monologue. "I've got to go," she said abruptly, glancing at the screen. "They need me over at the pony ring. I'll meet you later to talk about your next class." She tossed the horse's reins at Payton and rushed off without waiting for a reply.

My friends and I caught up to Payton. "So when do you find out if you won?" Ned asked her.

"Will there be a jump-off if someone else goes clear?" George added. "Those are fun to watch on TV."

"There's no jump-off in this particular class." Payton unbuckled the chin strap of her riding helmet as she led the horse along the path leading to the barns. "So I just have to wait until everyone goes to find out the final placings."

George looked disappointed. "No jump-off?"

"Nope, sorry." Payton smiled. "But don't worry, there will probably be one in the Grand Prix if you come to watch that. And some of the other jumper classes too."

"Cool." George immediately looked happier.

"Anyway, like I was saying before, we're all really impressed with how you did just now." I gave George a sidelong look. "Jump-off or no jump-off."

"Yeah," Bess said. "Especially considering that upsetting news you got right before you started."

Payton shrugged. "I learned back when I was still riding ponies that I can't let anything distract me when I'm in the ring. I just need to focus and get the job done, no matter what." She cracked a wry smile. "My dad calls it the Evans Edge."

"The Evans Edge?" George grinned. "Love it! But now I need a motto like that of my own." She thought for a second. "How about the Fayne Fierceness?" She struck a pose like an action hero.

"More like the Fayne Fail," Bess said.

Ned and I laughed while George shot her cousin a disgruntled look. "That's still better than the Marvin Misery."

We spent the rest of the walk inventing insulting names for one another. As soon as we arrived at the barn, though, we forgot all about that. There was too much to see. Horses were hanging their heads out over their stalls doors. Riders hurried here and there. Farther down the aisle, a farrier was tapping nails into the shoe of a patient horse.

As we headed down the aisle the opposite way, a young woman appeared. She was dressed in jeans and short boots, with a rag tucked into one back pocket and a hoof pick sticking out of the other. Her hair was a mess, and there was a big greenish smudge on the front of her T-shirt.

"Sorry I didn't get up to the ring to meet you, Payton," she said breathlessly. "I'll take him now."

"Thanks, Jen." Payton handed the reins to the woman, who cooed at the horse as she led him away.

"Who's that?" George asked as Jen and the horse disappeared around a corner. "Your personal servant? Must be nice."

Payton laughed. "Not mine—the horse's," she said.

"Jen is a groom. It's her job to help take care of the horses. A big, busy barn like Dana's couldn't survive without a team of great grooms." She patted a horse that was sticking its nose out over the nearest stall. "So would you guys like to meet my horses?"

"Sure, we'd love to!" Bess said. "How many do you have?"

"Nine, but only four are at this show." Payton headed down the aisle, with the rest of us following. "The rest are either youngsters or taking a break."

"Nine horses? Wow." George whistled. "And here I thought it was hard work taking care of my family's dog!"

Payton laughed. "Luckily, I don't have to take care of them all myself. Most of my horses live at Dana's barn, where her amazing staff does all the hard work. All I need to do is show up and ride." She stopped in front of a stall where a copper-colored chestnut with a blaze was nosing at a pile of hay. "Here's one of my guys now. . . ."

She went on to show us a couple of more horses.

"So which one are you riding in the Grand Prix?" Bess asked as she patted a pretty gray mare.

Payton smiled. "I was just about to introduce you to that one. Come on, let's go see Midnight."

We followed her to yet another stall. Inside stood a tall, impressive-looking dark bay without a speck of white on him anywhere. A weather-beaten man with slicked-back dark hair was running a brush down the horse's long legs.

"This is Mickey," Payton said, gesturing toward the man. "He's Midnight's groom." She introduced us, though Mickey hardly looked up from his task.

"Midnight is gorgeous," Bess said, reaching out to touch the horse's velvety nose. The horse sniffed her hand, then snorted loudly, blowing horse snot all over Bess's face and dress.

"Yeah, and he knows it!" Payton laughed. "He's quite a character. Hope he didn't get you too gross."

"No biggie," Bess said with a smile, reaching into her purse for a tissue. That's one of the good things about Bess. She might look all girly and delicate, but it takes more than a little horse snot to faze her!

Payton turned to Mickey. "I was thinking of taking him out for some hand grazing, if that's okay."

Mickey just nodded, reaching for the halter hanging just outside the stall door and quickly buckling it onto the horse's big head. Then Payton clipped a lead line to Midnight's halter and led him out.

"Wow, he looks even bigger out here," George commented.

"I guess a bigger horse must make those Grand Prix jumps look smaller, huh?" I joked.

Payton chuckled. "It doesn't hurt," she agreed. "Do you guys want to tag along while I graze him?" She reached into her pocket and held her hand up to the horse's muzzle. I wasn't close enough to see what she'd pulled out, but whatever it was, the horse slurped it up eagerly and then nuzzled her for more.

"What do you feed a horse like Midnight?" I asked. "Treats, I mean—like you just gave him."

"My horses love all kinds of treats." Payton gave a light tug on the lead to get Midnight moving. "Most of them aren't too picky—they'll eat carrots, apples, mints, whatever. One or two are more particular, but most horses have at least one or two favorite snacks."

"Just like people, huh?" Ned said.

We left the barn and headed over to a grassy area near the fence separating the fairgrounds from the parking lot. The bright sunlight bounced off the bumpers and mirrors of the many cars parked out there, and Midnight snorted and danced in place at first as he took it all in. But he settled quickly, lowering his head and nibbling at the grass.

I glanced at Payton. She was watching her horse, a contented expression on her face. I hated to ruin her mood, but I was curious about what had happened earlier.

"So that drugging thing was weird," I said. "What do you think that's all about?"

Payton's expression darkened. "I don't know. But it's not true."

"Nancy knows that," Ned put in quickly. "I already explained that you're not that kind of person."

Before Payton could say anything else, there was a buzz from the pocket of her breeches. "That's my phone," she said, fishing it out. "Dad's right on schedule. . . . Hi, Dad."

My friends and I drifted away to give her some privacy. "What's with the questioning, Detective Drew?" George joked. "You think Payton has some kind of deep, dark mystery that needs solving?"

I grinned. Like I said, my friends like to rib me about my interest in mysteries. "You never know," I said. "Maybe it's like we were saying before—someone could be trying to knock out the competition to improve their odds of winning the big-money classes."

"Or maybe it's a mistake," Ned said. "I doubt Payton would be mixed up in anything nefarious, even secondhand." He shrugged. "Sorry, Nancy. You might be stuck just watching a horse show this weekend instead of solving another mystery."

"Yeah," Bess put in. "And she might be stuck just watching a horse show instead of doing something romantic for her anniversary, too."

We were all still laughing about that when Payton wandered over to us, tucking away her phone with one hand while hanging on to Midnight's lead with the other.

"That was my dad," she said. "He likes to check in after each of my rounds to see how it went."

"Really?" George looked impressed. "He keeps that close tabs on your show schedule? I mean, you only finished riding, like, twenty minutes ago. How'd he know he wasn't going to call while you were in the air over a big fence?"

Payton laughed. "Don't worry, I turn off my phone while I'm in the ring. But to answer your question, Dad has an app on his phone with a timer that keeps track for him." She tugged on Midnight's lead to keep him from wandering too close to the fence. "His job is so busy that that's probably the only way he could keep track short of hiring an extra employee just to keep track of my show schedule."

"You sound like you're only half joking about that extra employee thing," Ned said.

"You know Dad," Payton said. "He's pretty serious about results—he doesn't like to miss a detail."

Between her father, her trainer, and herself, I couldn't help thinking that Payton was under a lot of pressure to perform well at these shows. Still, she seemed to be handling it awfully well, especially for someone her age.

Midnight took a couple of bites of grass, then lifted his head and stepped toward the parking lot fence again. Payton didn't let him get too close, once again pulling him back with the lead.

"Looks like Midnight must believe that old line," I said. "You know, the one about the grass being greener on the other side?"

"He wouldn't actually try to escape out into the parking lot or anything, would he?" George eyed the horse nervously. "I mean, I know there's a fence, but . . ."

Payton laughed. "Are you kidding? Midnight could clear that tiny fence in his sleep." Her eyes twinkled. "But don't worry—there's no grass out in the parking lot. He definitely wouldn't be interested in going out there when he—"

She cut herself off with a gasp as something suddenly flew at the horse out of nowhere. *SPLAT!* Whatever it was hit Midnight, leaving a huge red mark on his side.

With a terrified cry, the horse yanked the lead out of Payton's hand, reared up, and spun away.

CHAPTER THREE

~

Food for Thought

"MIDNIGHT!" PAYTON CRIED.

"Loose horse!" Bess shrieked.

Midnight stopped, his hooves splayed out and his big brown eyes rolling. He snorted, then spun around as a shout came from out in the parking lot.

Ignoring the shout, I focused on the horse. "Easy, boy," I crooned, trying desperately to remember what to do about a loose horse. Had we even learned that in those childhood lessons? Doubtful. Most of the ponies I'd ridden wouldn't move out of a slow walk for anything short of a meteor landing behind them.

Luckily, Payton recovered quickly from her surprise. "Just stay where you are, everybody," she said in a calm but commanding voice. Then she stepped toward the horse. "Settle down, Midnight. It's okay."

Midnight snorted again, tossing his head and prancing in place. I held my breath as Payton took another step. "What if he jumps the fence like she was saying?" George whispered. "He could be halfway across River Heights before we could take three steps after him!"

"Shh," I hushed her. "He's not running amok yet. Let's see what happens."

"Good boy, good boy," Payton singsonged as she sidled closer. "Easy now . . ."

She took another step. The horse tensed, but then he lowered his head and blew out a sigh. Payton caught hold of the lead rope dangling from Midnight's halter and gave him a pat.

"Is he hurt?" Ned asked. "What hit him, anyway?"

Good question. I glanced out at the parking lot, wondering about the source of that shout. Several people were milling around over near the entrance. A couple of them were holding signs, though I couldn't read them from where I was standing.

Meanwhile Payton stepped around to examine the bloody-looking mark on the horse's side. She almost immediately heaved a big sigh of relief.

"It's okay—he's not hurt. It was just a tomato," she reported. "An overripe one, from the smell of it."

"Yuck," Bess said. "Who would throw something like that at a horse?"

"I think I know." One of the people out in the parking lot had turned, giving me a better view of her sign. "Check it out—some animal rights activists are protesting out there."

George turned to look. "Ugh, PAN? I've heard about them," she said. "They let some goats and sheep loose at the state fair last summer. Caused all kinds of problems."

"Yeah, I heard about that." Bess shook her head. "I love animals as much as the next girl, and I hate to think of them being mistreated. But PAN definitely takes things too far."

I knew what she meant. PAN—short for Pet-Free Animal Nation—was a national group that advocated an end to "animal slavery," which they interpreted as everything from using animals for scientific testing to "forcing" cats and dogs to serve as family pets. They were notorious for showing up at events like livestock auctions or dog shows and causing trouble. As a local attorney, my father had helped prosecute them the last time they'd passed through our part of the country. Now it seemed they were back for more.

"Wait," I said as I glanced out at the protesters again and spotted a familiar face. "I think I recognize one of them. Isn't that the lady who got all that publicity last year when she tried to save that half-rotted old tree behind the elementary school? What's her name again?" I searched my memory. "Annie something, right?"

"Annie Molina," Ned supplied. "I remember her. She was in the paper last month for stopping traffic to protest the new housing development out by the river."

Payton wasn't paying attention to our conversation.

She was busy talking soothingly to Midnight, who still seemed tense and jumpy. "I'd better get Midnight back to the barn," she said. "If anyone throws something else our way right now, he just might lose it."

"We'll come with you," Bess said.

George glanced out at the group in the parking lot. "Shouldn't someone report what happened to show security or something?"

"Good idea," I said. "There were some security guards hanging out near the entrance where we came in, remember?"

Ned nodded. "I'm on it. I'll meet you back at Payton's barn."

As he headed off toward the main gate, the rest of us accompanied Payton and Midnight toward the barn. When we got there, Dana was waiting.

"Payton!" the trainer exclaimed, rushing over. "Where were you? You're supposed to be warming up right now—a bunch of people scratched from your next class, so they want us up there stat. Didn't you get my text?"

"Sorry, I was a little distracted," Payton said. I expected her to tell Dana what had happened, but instead she glanced around with an anxious look on her face. "Has anyone seen Mickey?" she called out.

Jen, the groom we'd encountered earlier, stepped out of a nearby stall. "He ran to the trailers to get something," she said. "Do you need me to take Midnight?"

"Yes," Dana snapped before Payton could answer. "Come on, Payton. We should have been up at the ring five minutes ago."

As Jen took Midnight's lead, Payton shot Bess, George, and me an apologetic look. "Talk to you guys later," she said, hurrying after her trainer, who was already rushing off down the aisle.

"Wow," George said. "That woman is intense."

"Yeah." I stared after Payton, but I wasn't really thinking about Dana. "It's kind of weird, isn't it?"

"What?" Bess shot me a look. "You mean that Payton doesn't seem to mind Dana yelling at her all the time?"

"No—that Payton's best horse got attacked so soon after she found out about that anonymous drug rumor."

George rolled her eyes. "That's our Nancy," she joked. "Always looking for a mystery wherever she goes."

"And usually finding one." Bess turned to me. "What are you saying? Do you really think there's a connection?"

"Think about it, Nancy," George said. "How would those nutty protesters even know Payton's horse would be hanging out near the parking lot fence? It's too coincidental to think they were targeting her. They probably just tossed that tomato at the first horse that wandered close enough."

"You're probably right," I admitted. "Still, you have to admit it's kind of strange."

"Kind of," George agreed. "But everything about the big-time horse show world seems a little strange to me."

"Me too," Bess said. "For all we know, people at these shows might make anonymous complaints against the competition all the time. Maybe George is right and we shouldn't jump to conclusions."

"Maybe." I shrugged. "Let's find Ned so we can all watch Payton ride again."

"Here she comes," Bess said as Payton trotted into the ring. This time she was riding a dapple gray horse.

"She's looking good," George said. "Isn't that one of the horses she introduced us to?"

"Yeah, I think it's one of hers," Ned said. "What was its name again? Rain Cloud, maybe?"

A pair of teenage girls were sitting on the bleacher bench in front of us. They were maybe a year or two younger than Payton, dressed in breeches and flip-flops. One of them turned around with a smile.

"It's Rain Dance," she supplied. "She's one of Payton's younger jumpers, but they've been doing great all season."

"Oh! Thanks." I returned the girl's smile. She nodded, then turned back to watch as Payton sent the horse into a canter.

Payton rode a big circle around several of the jumps at a brisk trot. Then a buzzer sounded, and she picked up speed and aimed her mount at the first jump, an airy arrangement of blue-and-white rails suspended between a pair of standards painted with the name of the show. The horse sailed over with half a foot to spare.

"Nice," I said.

"Did you see that?" a loud voice came from a few yards down the bleachers. "She really messed up the approach. Not a good way to start."

I glanced that way. The speaker was a middle-aged man with salt-and-pepper hair, prominent jowls, and beefy shoulders. He was surrounded by teen and pre-teen girls in riding attire. All the girls tittered loudly at his comment.

"Typical Payton," one of the girls said. "She's always getting her fancy horses to cover for her."

"Uh-huh." The man smirked. "Just watch her gun that poor mare to the next one."

Glancing back at the ring, I saw Payton and her horse approaching the next jump. Once again, the pair cleared the obstacle effortlessly before executing a tight turn to the next one.

"She's lucky that mare is so forgiving," the jowly man said, his voice just as loud as before. "If she tried to ride most horses that way, she'd be off at the first fence." He smirked. "At least she can serve as an example of how *not* to ride."

Beside me, I could tell that Ned was gritting his teeth. A second later he stood up.

"Excuse me," he called to the man. "Payton Evans is a friend of ours, and we don't appreciate your remarks. Keep it down, okay?"

The man stared at Ned. "Sorry, buddy," he said, though he didn't sound very sorry to me. "I just call 'em as I see 'em."

Ned frowned. Like I said, he's pretty easygoing. But he has a temper under there somewhere, and the best way to bring it out is to insult his friends or family.

"Listen . . . ," he began.

Just then another girl rushed over to the group around Mr. Jowly. "Hey, Lenny, that new black pony won't let Tina do up his girth," she said breathlessly. "You'd better come before she starts crying again."

The man quickly stood up. "I'm coming," he said. "There's nothing much to see here anyway." Shooting one last glance toward the ring, he stomped down the bleachers after the girl. The other girls followed, with some of them casting curious or annoyed glances in our direction.

"Nice going, Nickerson," George said with a laugh. "It takes some real attitude to almost start a rumble at a horse show."

I heard the two teens in front of us snicker at George's comment. Then they both turned around. "Are you guys really friends of Payton's?" the girl who'd spoken up earlier asked.

"Yeah. Why?" George asked.

"I'm just surprised you don't know about Lenny Hood, that's all," she said. "He never has anything nice to say about Payton."

"Why not?" I asked at the same time as George asked, "Who's Lenny Hood?"

"Lenny's, like, one of the winningest trainers on the A circuit," the second girl spoke up. "Rumor has it he asked Payton to come ride with him when she started getting really good."

The first girl nodded. "But Payton turned him down flat. Now every time she beats one of his students, he totally holds a grudge."

Interesting! My mind immediately flashed again to that anonymous tip. Could Lenny Hood be behind that? Was he trying to get revenge, or maybe just looking to throw Payton off her game so his students could beat her?

"You said that's a rumor, right?" I said, leaning closer to the girls. "That he wanted Payton to train with him? Do you think there's any truth to it?"

The two girls exchanged a look, then shrugged in unison. "You know how it is on the circuit," one of them said. "Everybody talks, and usually there's at least some little bit of truth or whatever. . . ."

A snippet of a popular song came from her friend's lap. "Oops, Maria just texted me," the friend said. "We'd better go."

"Okay." The other girl stood up. "Tell Payton good

luck in the Grand Prix," she told us. "We're all pulling for her." Shooting a glance toward the spot where Lenny and his groupies had been sitting, she added, "Well, most of us, anyway."

She followed her friend, who was already making her way down the bleachers. Soon they'd both disappeared into the crowd.

"That was interesting," I said, wishing I'd had more time to talk to the girls. "Think it could mean something?"

"Something like a new mystery?" Bess patted my hand. "Give it up, Nancy. You know you're just looking for something to take your poor disappointed mind off the fact that your boyfriend is totally ignoring your anniversary."

I sighed and traded a look with Ned. He merely smiled. I might be *slightly* obsessed with mysteries. But Bess was just as dogged when it came to romance.

"Should I start with hot dogs or burgers?" Mr. Nickerson asked as he hauled a cooler out through the sliding glass doors leading onto his family's back deck. "Or maybe we can dig those chicken tenders out of the freezer if anybody wants 'em."

Ned grinned. "I'd say you should start by firing up the grill, Dad," he said. "That thing's so old it'll be a miracle if we don't end up calling out for pizza."

"Very funny." His father pretended to pout. "Don't pay any attention to him, Bertha. He just doesn't understand you like I do." He patted the ancient grill on the hood. "Now, where'd I put the charcoal?"

"Your dad is living it up old-school, huh?" George said to Ned as Mr. Nickerson headed toward the shed at the back of the lawn. "When's he going to join the modern era and get a gas grill like everyone else?"

"Probably never," Ned replied. "Mom already knows that Bertha comes first in Dad's heart."

"That's right." Mrs. Nickerson looked up from setting out a stack of paper plates on the picnic table. "If that man could marry a grill, I'd still be single."

I laughed along with the others. There were about a dozen people in the Nickersons' spacious, shady backyard. George had been lounging on a wicker chair since we'd arrived twenty minutes earlier, drinking a soda and trading jokes with Mr. Nickerson. Ned was helping his mother carry stuff out from the kitchen, and Bess was stirring sugar into a pitcher of freshly squeezed lemonade. Various friends and neighbors of the Nickersons were there too, helping or chatting or just enjoying the beautiful evening.

"Ah, here's the guest of honor now!" Mrs. Nickerson said.

Payton stepped out of the house, her hair still damp from the shower and a bashful smile on her face. "Hi, everyone," she said with a little wave. "Nice to meet you all."

There was a flurry of introductions. I wandered over to Bess and George, who were watching from nearby. "I hope Ned's dad finds the charcoal soon," I said. "I bet Payton's starving after her busy day."

"She did really great today, didn't she?" Bess said. "I can see why everyone thinks she's a shoo-in for the Olympics."

George glanced out into the yard. "Here comes Mr. N. with the charcoal."

"Payton!" Mr. Nickerson said when he spotted her. "You're here."

"Yeah, she's here, Dad." Ned grinned. "And I seem to recall you promising her you'd have a burger ready for her by the time she got out of the shower."

"Oops." Mr. Nickerson set the bag of charcoal beside the grill. "Well, what can I say—creating food with fire is an art, and that can't be rushed." The grill's lid let out a loud creaking sound as he opened it.

"Ol' Bertha's really singing," one of the adults joked.

Ned's father didn't respond. "What's this?" he said, reaching into the grill and pulling out a folded piece of paper.

"Probably ol' Bertha's 'I quit' note," George called out.

Most of the group shouted with laughter. But I just smiled and stepped closer, curious. If this was one of the pranks Ned and his father were always playing on each other, I wanted a front-row seat.

Mr. Nickerson unfolded the paper. There were just a few lines on there, typed in a large, bold font:

PAYTON: IS RIDING FOR THE GOLD WORTH YOUR LIFE?
QUIT WHILE YOU AND YOUR HORSES ARE AHEAD.
AND ALIVE.

CHAPTER FOUR

Taking Note

"WHAT IS THIS?" MR. NICKERSON FROWNED and glanced around at the group. "Is this someone's idea of a joke? Because it's not very funny."

"What is it, dear?" His wife hurried over.

I stepped toward my friends. "You know how you were teasing me about trying to find a mystery earlier?" I said quietly. "Well, I think one just found me. Or us. Or Payton, to be exact."

Payton wandered toward us just in time to hear her name. "What are you talking about, Nancy?" She sounded confused. "What's going on?"

I didn't get a chance to answer. Mrs. Nickerson swept over and dragged Payton off toward the house, while Mr. Nickerson called for attention.

"Something just came up," he told his friends and neighbors. "We need to talk privately with Payton for a few minutes." He handed the tongs he was holding to one of the men. "Rick, can you see about getting Bertha started?"

"Well, I can't make any promises, but I'll try," the man replied with a smile.

Mr. Nickerson thanked him and headed for the door. He paused and glanced at me. "Nancy, maybe you should join us."

"Right behind you," I said, following him into the house.

Ned, Bess, and George came too. "Is everything all right?" Bess asked. "What happened?"

"Mr. Nickerson found a threatening note in the grill," I said. "It's addressed to Payton."

Mr. Nickerson nodded. He handed the note to Ned, who read it with Bess and George looking over his shoulder.

"Whoa," George said.

Mr. Nickerson grabbed the note back. "I think we'd better call Payton's parents."

"And the police, as well," Mrs. Nickerson added.

"No, wait!" Payton's face had gone pale. "Please don't call my parents. I don't want them to worry."

"That's sweet, dear," Mrs. Nickerson said. "But they'll want to know their only daughter could be in danger."

"You don't understand." Payton bit her lip. "My parents are always pushing me to be the best. They wouldn't want me to get scared off by some random jerk trying to steal my focus." She smiled, though it looked forced. "They'd probably trot out that old line about how sticks and stones might break my bones, but words can never hurt me."

Mrs. Nickerson frowned. "Nonsense," she said. "I know your parents always encourage you to do your best, but your safety is more important than anything, and I'm sure they'd agree. Hand me that phone," she ordered her husband.

"But what if this is just some kind of prank?" George spoke up. "Like one of Payton's fellow riders trying to psych her out or something?"

I guessed she was thinking about that girl from the schooling ring earlier. "It's possible," I mused aloud. "Someone from the show grounds could've followed Payton here and planted that note."

Mrs. Nickerson's eyes widened in alarm. "All the more reason to notify the police!" she exclaimed.

"Or maybe you just need to notify someone who might actually be able to figure out what's going on." George pointed at me. "Done."

Mr. Nickerson raised an eyebrow. "She has a point," he said to his wife.

"Yeah," Ned agreed. "There's no point getting Mr. and Mrs. Evans all riled up over nothing. Let's let Nancy look into it first. If it's just some prankster or crazy competitor, she'll figure it out."

His mother glanced at me, seeming uncertain. "Well . . ."

Meanwhile, Payton just looked confused. "Let

Nancy look into it?" she said. "What do you mean?"

"Oh, right." Bess smiled. "Payton doesn't know about our local sleuthing prodigy."

She and the others took turns explaining. Payton listened, nodding along but still looking skeptical.

"Nancy Drew, girl detective—I know it sounds weird, right?" Ned finished with a chuckle. "But trust me, Payton. If anyone can help you, it's Nancy."

"I suppose it wouldn't hurt to give her a chance to look into it a bit," Mrs. Nickerson said slowly. She glanced at her husband, who nodded.

"It's worth a try," Mr. Nickerson said. "But if you can't clear things up quickly, Nancy—or if you sense any real danger—we'll definitely be calling in the troops." He put a hand on Payton's shoulder. "And I want you to be careful until we know what's going on, all right? We'll keep an eye on you while you're here, of course. But you might want to mention this to your trainer, so she can keep an extra-close watch while you're at the show."

"Ned and I were planning to spend the day at the

show tomorrow anyway," I said. "We can help keep a lookout."

"And we can come help," Bess said, and George nodded.

"Thanks, you guys." Payton sounded grateful. "I'm sure this is nothing. Really."

"All right." Mrs. Nickerson still didn't sound completely convinced. "We'll give this a chance. But please let us know if you uncover anything worrisome, Nancy." She stood up. "Now we'd better get back out there before our other guests think we've abandoned them."

She hurried outside with her husband right behind her. Bess, George, and Payton headed out too. I started to follow, but Ned stopped me with a hand on the arm.

"I have a confession to make," he said once we were alone. "I, um, wasn't planning on taking you to the horse show tomorrow."

"You weren't? But I thought—"

"I know I told you that was the plan." He shrugged, looking sheepish. "But I was actually going to whisk you off for a romantic picnic at Cliff View Park instead. You know—for our anniversary."

"You were?" I was touched. "That sounds amazing. Even Bess would be impressed."

He laughed. "Yeah, it was killing me today not to just tell her so she'd get off my back," he said. "But I wanted it to be a surprise."

"I'm surprised." I smiled and stood on tiptoes to kiss him on the cheek. "Thank you."

"But that's what I'm saying." Ned sounded troubled. "I don't think we can go. Not with this Payton business hanging over our heads. I'm worried about her. Plus, you just pretty much promised my folks we'd be at that horse show all day tomorrow."

I cocked an eyebrow. "Or at least all day until we solve the mystery. What if we get there early and wrap it up before lunchtime? Then we could still have our picnic in the afternoon."

That made Ned look happier. "True. Do you think you can figure it out that quickly?"

"So far the most obvious theory is that this might

be a straightforward case of envy-based petty sabotage." I shrugged. "How tricky could it be?"

I yawned as I pulled my car into the show's parking lot. It was early—so early that I found a parking spot pretty close to the gate. Spotting a familiar car a few spots down, I pulled out my cell phone and called Ned.

"Are you here?" his cheerful voice asked after just a couple of rings. He's definitely a morning person.

"Just got here," I replied as I climbed out of my car. "Where are you?"

"At the barn with Payton. Mom and Dad insisted I drive her over and not let her out of my sight. They're still pretty freaked out about the whole situation."

"I know." I pocketed my keys. "That's another good reason to solve this mystery as quickly as possible."

"Yeah. Are Bess and George with you?"

"They're meeting us here later. They didn't see the point of getting up quite this early." I glanced around again at the nearly empty parking lot. "They figured nobody would be around to question at the crack of dawn. And I didn't want to tell them why I was in such a hurry."

He chuckled. "Got it. So what's the plan?"

"You stick with Payton," I said. "I talk to some other people, start figuring out a suspect list. I'll call or text if I find anything interesting."

After we hung up, I headed for the entrance gate. Halfway there, I heard someone calling my name. It was Annie Molina, the local activist. She was rushing toward me, her full, flowing skirt billowing out around her legs and her round face cracked into a broad smile. Her PAN cohorts from yesterday were nowhere in sight. Maybe they were sleeping in, just like Bess and George.

"Nancy Drew!" she exclaimed. "It is Nancy Drew, right? Carson Drew's daughter, the one who's always getting written up in the papers for solving crimes and such?" She tittered, pushing aside a lock of curly brown hair as the breeze tossed it into her face.

"Yes, that's me. It's Annie, right?"

"Yes!" Annie looked thrilled that I'd recognized

her. "I just wanted to say hello, and to tell you a few things you might not know about horse shows like this one."

Uh-oh. Here it came.

"I'm sorry," I said quickly. "I really need to—"

"These horses are nothing but slaves!" Annie exclaimed dramatically. She paused and waited for my reaction.

"I see," I answered quickly and dodged around her, heading for the entrance. "Well, thanks for the info. We'll catch up later."

"Wait!" she cried.

But I didn't. I made a break for the gate, easily leaving her behind.

Once inside, I headed toward the barn where Payton's horses were stabled. Halfway there, I spotted Dana. She was riding a large chestnut gelding with four white stockings. I leaned on the rail to watch.

This was the first time I'd seen Dana on a horse, and I was impressed. She might come across as tense and abrupt on the ground. But all that disappeared in the saddle. She looked like a fluid part of her mount. There was a jump set up in the middle of the ring, consisting of some bright-yellow-striped rails with a planter full of flowers underneath. The horse was eyeing the obstacle nervously. Every time he got near it he spooked, jumping to the side and speeding up.

Dana didn't react except to bring the horse back around. Again and again, until the horse was barely flicking an ear at the jump. Finally she turned him and trotted directly toward the obstacle. The horse's ears pricked forward with alarm, and I held my breath, certain that he was going to put on the brakes.

"Get up," Dana urged, her voice stern but calm. At the same time, she gave the horse a tap behind her leg with the crop she was holding.

The horse lurched forward, speeding up and zigzagging a bit. But Dana kept him straight with her legs and the reins. With one last kick, she sent him leaping over the jump. He cleared it by about two feet and landed snorting and with his head straight up in the air. But Dana calmly circled around and came again. By the fifth or sixth time, the horse was jumping calmly.

As she brought the gelding to a walk and gave him a pat, Dana noticed me standing there. "Hello," she said, riding over. "You're Payton's friend. Uh, Lucy, right?"

"Nancy," I corrected. I smiled and nodded at the horse. "Looks like you were making him face his fears."

Dana chuckled and stroked the gelding's sweaty neck. "He's a good jumper, but a huge chicken about certain types of things. All he needs is a little patience and he gets over it. I just wanted to make sure it was now, with me, and not in the show ring with his twelve-year-old owner."

I nodded, a little surprised. The Dana sitting in front of me right now seemed like a whole different kind of person from the one I'd seen with Payton yesterday. But I pushed the thought aside.

"Listen, I know you're probably really busy," I said, "but I was hoping to talk to you about something. Do you have a second?"

"Just barely." Dana checked her watch. Then she

dismounted and led the horse out through the gate nearby. "I need to get this guy back to the barn, then meet a student at a different ring for a lesson. What did you want to talk about?"

I hesitated, not sure what to say. My usual method was to treat everyone as a suspect until the evidence indicated I should do otherwise. Dana was Payton's longtime trusted trainer. But did that mean she was innocent?

"It's about Payton," I said, deciding to keep it vague—just in case. "I'm, um, worried about her."

Dana stopped fiddling with the horse's stirrups and turned to face me. "Oh?" She peered into my face. "That's funny. I'm pretty worried about Payton myself."

"Really? How so?"

Dana unsnapped her riding helmet and pulled it off, running a hand through her short hair. "She's not herself lately. I'm afraid she's losing her competitive edge."

"You mean because of what happened yesterday?" I asked. "The accusation that she drugs her horses?"

Dana blinked. "Actually, I almost forgot about that. No, this has been going on since way before yesterday. At least a month, maybe longer. It's like somewhere along the way, she just lost it."

"What do you mean?"

Dana shrugged, some of that impatience I'd seen yesterday creeping back into her expression. "Hard to describe. Just that these past few shows, it's like she's not that into it anymore." The horse shifted his weight, and Dana glanced over at him.

"Okay." I could tell the trainer was getting antsy. "So is there any chance this drug thing isn't the first time someone tried to psych her out, started a rumor or whatever? Could there be other incidents she didn't tell you about?"

"I suppose it's possible. Payton's a teenager, after all, and everyone knows they aren't always super forthcoming." Dana glanced at me, then grimaced as she belatedly remembered—or noticed—my age. "No offense."

"None taken. Do you know if Payton has any

enemies? Like competitors who might want to throw her off her game or something?"

"Funny you should ask." Dana frowned. "For such a sweet, hardworking girl, Payton *has* managed to make a couple of enemies."

I held my breath. Now we were getting somewhere! I wondered if one of the enemies Dana was alluding to could be Lenny Hood. The more I thought about the comments he'd made yesterday, the more troubling they seemed.

"Who are—," I began.

The shrill buzz of Dana's phone cut me off. She whipped the phone to her ear. "Dana here," she said.

She listened to whoever was on the other end for a moment. Her expression went grim. When she hung up, she didn't keep me in suspense about why.

"Well, that does it," she said. "Midnight just flunked his drug test!"

CHAPTER FIVE

Test Case

"WHAT?" I EXCLAIMED. "WHAT DO YOU MEAN, he flunked?"

Dana dropped her phone into her pocket. "What do you think I mean?" she snapped. "They found a forbidden substance when they tested his urine. Theobromine, to be specific."

"Theobromine? What's that?"

"What do I look like, a chemist?" Dana said. "All I know is it's an ingredient in chocolate, and tea, and maybe some other stuff like that."

I wrinkled my nose in confusion. "I don't get it.

Who would give chocolate or tea to a horse, and why? And even if they did, who would even know something like that was against the rules?"

Dana's frown deepened. "Anyone who shows seriously on the A circuit, that's who. Or they *should*, anyway. I know for a fact that Payton knew. Someone she knows at another barn got in big trouble for letting her horse drink cola at shows. Similar kind of thing."

I almost smiled at the image of a horse drinking cola. But this wasn't the time.

"How does the testing work?" I asked. "I mean, did someone just go grab Midnight out of his stall just now and—"

"Not just now." Dana stared at me as if I were the stupidest person on the face of the earth. Or at least at this horse show. "He was chosen for testing at a show a few weeks back. Takes a while to get the results, and if it's negative you never hear anything. But if it's positive . . ."

"I see." This put a new spin on the case. If Payton was being framed or psyched out, it clearly hadn't started at this particular show. "Could someone have slipped him something with theobromine in it, then set him up to be tested that day?" I asked. "Like the same person who gave the stewards that anonymous tip, for instance?"

"It doesn't work that way." Dana shook her head. "The testing is totally random. There's no way to tell which horses will be pulled at any given show."

I could feel my theories deflating in the face of the facts Dana was telling me. "All right, then who does the actual testing? Any chance there was some hanky-panky there?"

"No," Dana replied flatly. "The testers are mostly vets or other outside people, and they send the samples to an independent lab. Everything's carefully monitored by the USEF—that's the national governing body of these shows. There's about a one in a zillion chance of hanky-panky in the process."

"So you're saying it's got to be true," I said. "Midnight really did have theobromine in his system. How did it get there?"

"That's what *I'd* like to know." Dana sounded

testy. "Apparently the level of theobromine they found is borderline, so there's going to have to be some kind of official ruling made about whether a suspension is warranted. Luckily, our records are clean, but . . ."

"You mean yours and Payton's?"

"And Midnight's, too." Dana yanked her phone out of her pocket. "I need to talk to Payton about this. *Now*. Here, take him back to the barn."

She tossed the chestnut gelding's reins at me. I gulped. "Wait, I—"

It was too late. Dana was already stomping away, madly texting as she went. A moment later she disappeared around the corner of the nearest building.

I stared up at the horse, who suddenly seemed a lot taller than he had a second ago. Definitely a *lot* taller than those ponies from my long-ago lessons.

"Nice horsie?" I said uncertainly. "Um, good boy?"

I gave an experimental tug on the reins. The horse yanked his head up, almost ripping the reins out of my hands. He regarded me suspiciously, then took a step backward.

"Wait," I said. "Don't do that. Um . . ."

"Hi," a friendly voice said behind me. "You're Payton's friend, right? Are you okay?"

It was one of the teens who had filled us in about Lenny Hood the day before. "Oh, hi," I greeted her with relief. "Listen, Dana just left me with this horse, and I'm not sure what to do with it."

The girl reached out to take the reins from me. "That's Dana," she said with a touch of fondness in her voice. "When she gets hyped up about something, she tends to forget that not everyone is there to be her servant." She giggled. "One time my grandma came to one of my shows, and Dana wanted her to jog a horse so Dana could see if it was lame. My grandma's seventy-six, uses a cane, and never touched an animal bigger than her Pekingese!"

I smiled. "So is Dana your trainer too?" That explained how the girl knew so much about Payton.

"Uh-huh. I'm Rachel, by the way."

"Nancy. Thanks for rescuing me." I gestured at the horse, who now stood placidly at the other end of the reins. "I think he was about to take off for the hills."

Rachel giggled again. "No problem. See you later."

She headed off with the horse in tow. My smile faded as my mind returned to what Dana had just told me. As if Ned's parents and my anniversary plans weren't enough, now I had an even more important reason to want to solve this case quickly. If I didn't, and the horse show officials decided against Midnight, Payton could lose her chance to ride in front of the Olympic chef d'équipe tomorrow!

I pulled out my phone and called Ned. "Sorry, it looks like I might need a rain check on those anniversary plans after all." I filled him in on the news about the drug test.

"Wow," Ned said. "That's serious business."

"I know. So did Dana find Payton and tell her? What does she think?"

"I don't know." Ned sounded worried. "I was actually about to call you for two reasons. The first is that I lost track of Payton a few minutes ago."

"What? But you promised your parents you'd stick

with her." I wasn't really that worried about Payton's physical safety while she was on the busy horse show grounds. But still, we'd promised.

"I know, but it's really their fault," Ned said. "My mom called me a little while ago, and I guess Payton must have wandered off while I was on the phone."

I leaned against a handy fence post. "Okay. What's the second reason you were going to call me?"

"Like I said, my mom called." Ned sounded grim. "I guess she was feeling guilty about keeping all this from Payton's parents. So she called them a little while ago."

"Oh." I couldn't say I was surprised. Mrs. Nickerson wasn't the type of person to be comfortable keeping secrets. Especially from one of her best friends. "How'd they take it? Were they freaked out?"

"Not exactly. They said it wasn't the first time something like this has happened."

"What?" I pressed the phone closer to my ear as several preteens wandered past me, chatting and laughing loudly. "What do you mean?"

"A similar note turned up at a show Payton rode in a couple of weeks ago," Ned said. "It was tucked under the windshield wiper of her parents' car after the show. Sounds like Payton's dad was convinced it was just sour grapes from some competitor. He insisted everyone ignore it. Wouldn't even let Payton tell Dana or anyone else at the barn."

"Wow." I took that in, adding it to the growing case file taking shape in my head. "So whoever's trying to scare Payton either knows her well enough to know which car belongs to her family . . ."

"Or is a stalker type who follows her around so he or she can leave those notes in weird locations," Ned finished. "Creepy."

"Definitely. Which means this case just got a lot more serious." I bit my lip. "We'd better get back to work. I want to find Dana again—she was about to tell me about Payton's enemies when she rushed off."

"Sounds like a plan. I'll try to find Payton and let her know what's going on."

As I hung up the phone, it buzzed again. Checking

the readout, I saw a text from Bess reading WE'RE HERE.

I texted back, and soon we met up near the entrance. "Those PAN freaks are back again today," George said before I could say a word. "They practically accosted us on our way past."

"Uh-huh." I wasn't interested in the protesters just then. "But listen, you guys will never believe what's been happening around here. . . ."

Their eyes widened as I filled them in. When I finished, George let out a low whistle. "Do you really think someone could be stalking Payton?" she said. "But why?"

"And is it connected with Midnight's drug results?" Bess added.

"That's what we need to find out. I'm hoping Dana can help." I sighed. "She started to tell me about how Payton has a few enemies, but that phone call interrupted and then she rushed off."

"I can tell you one enemy," George said. "That girl Jessica. If looks could kill, we would've witnessed a murder at least twice over just yesterday."

"Yeah." I agreed. "Jessica really seemed to have it out for Payton. But she's even younger than Payton herself. I could see her leaving nasty notes, maybe. But would she really follow Payton back to Ned's house to do it? And what about that drug test?"

"I don't know," Bess said. "But I know who else should be on the suspect list—that rude trainer we heard insulting Payton yesterday."

"Lenny Hood." I nodded. "I was thinking about him too. I definitely want to ask Dana about him."

"So let's find her and ask," George said. "Where do you think she could be?"

"Last time I saw her, she was looking for Payton." I shrugged. "Guess we should start by checking at the barn."

We hurried across the show grounds, pausing at each riding ring we passed just long enough to ascertain that Payton wasn't in any of them. She wasn't at any of her horse's stalls, either, or hanging out on the benches out front with the other kids from her barn.

The day before, Payton had shown us around the

stabling area and pointed out the tack stall where all the saddles and other equipment were kept. When I glanced in, the place was deserted except for Rachel and a younger girl in riding clothes. They were huddled around one of the saddle racks in the corner, their voices loud and excited.

"Hi," I said as my friends and I stepped in. "Have either of you guys seen Dana lately? Or Payton?"

The girls spun around. "Nancy!" Rachel exclaimed. "Oh my gosh, I can't believe it!"

"Can't believe what?" I asked.

"Come look!" She grabbed my sleeve, dragging me to the saddle rack. "Can you believe someone did this to Payton's saddle?"

I gasped. The saddle's seat had been slashed to ribbons!

CHAPTER SIX

Vandal Scandal

"ARE YOU SURE THIS IS PAYTON'S SADDLE?"
I asked the girls.

"Definitely," the younger one spoke up. "It's practically brand-new, too. Her dad bought it for her after she won a big class at Devon."

"I already texted Dana to tell her," Rachel put in. "She's on her way."

"Good." I leaned closer to the saddle for a better look, but didn't touch it. If Dana called the cops, I didn't want to mess up any potential evidence.

"Pretty thorough job," Bess said over my shoulder.

"Yeah." The leather seat was a total loss. Every inch of it was sliced all the way down to the padding underneath.

"Who would do something like this?" the younger girl wondered, her voice shaking a little.

I turned to face her. "I was just going to ask you two the same thing," I said. "Do you know of anyone who dislikes Payton?"

Rachel and the younger girl traded a look. Then they both shrugged.

"Out of the junior riders on the circuit, it's mostly just Jessica," Rachel said. "Jessica Watts. She's this rider from another barn near ours. She's always super rude to Payton when they compete against each other."

"Or even *see* each other," the second girl added.

"Yeah, I'm pretty sure we've seen her in action." George grimaced.

"She's around Payton's age, right?" I said. "Brown hair, narrow chin, rides a tall gray horse?"

"That's her," Rachel confirmed.

"Why doesn't she like Payton?" Bess asked.

"We don't know," Rachel said, as the other girl nodded. "Probably just because Payton usually beats her, I guess."

"Does Jessica hate Payton enough to do something like this?" George waved a hand at the ruined saddle.

Rachel glanced at it, looking dubious. "I don't know. I always thought she was just kind of snotty. But you never know, I guess."

A thought occurred to me. "That big jumper class Payton won—the one you mentioned just now—did Jessica ride in that class, too?"

"You mean the one that got Payton's dad to buy her the saddle?" the younger girl asked. "That wasn't a jumper class, it was an eq class."

"A what class?" George asked.

"Eq—that's short for equitation," Rachel explained. "That's where the rider is judged instead of the horse. You know—for having the proper riding position and stuff."

"Okay," I said. "But was Jessica in it too?"

"Jessica doesn't do eq," Rachel said. "She only rides jumpers."

"And hunters, sometimes," the other girl put in. "At least she used to, before she sold her pony."

My head was spinning with all the horse show jargon. But the one fact I needed seemed clear enough regardless of the details. "So Payton didn't beat Jessica out for some big prize in that particular class?"

"Not *that* one." The younger girl giggled. "Just, like, every *other* class Jessica's ever been in."

So the saddle probably wasn't some kind of symbol of a particularly heinous defeat. That didn't necessarily mean Jessica couldn't still be the culprit. But I didn't want to jump to conclusions.

"Anyone else you can think of who might have it out for Payton?" I asked, waiting for Rachel to mention Lenny Hood. After all, she was one of the ones who'd told us about his history with Payton.

Instead it was the younger girl who spoke up. "Um, maybe," she said hesitantly. She paused, shooting a look at Rachel. "What about Cal?"

At that moment Dana burst into the room like a small tornado. "This is the absolute last straw!" she exclaimed breathlessly. "I'm serious. Payton has to stop messing up my life, or I won't be around to live it! Then where will you all be? Who will be there to fix all your disasters and help pick up the pieces, huh? I ask you!" She glared at the two girls, who didn't answer. In fact, both of them were inching backward toward the door.

"Did you find Payton?" I asked, stepping forward. "What did she say about—"

"No, I didn't find Payton!" the trainer cut me off irritably. "You'd think at a small-town show like this, she wouldn't be so hard to track down. Just one more way she's making my life difficult."

She pushed past Bess and snatched the ruined saddle off the rack. Then she stomped toward the door.

"Wait!" I said. "I need to ask you—"

"Sorry," she cut me off again. "I need to find Payton. Like, seriously, *now*."

"Wow," Rachel said once the trainer was gone. "She seemed really mad."

"Yeah." The younger girl grabbed Rachel's arm to

check her watch. "We better go start tacking up, or she'll be mad at us next."

The two of them rushed out of the room without another word. "Leave it to Nancy," George said.

"Leave it to Nancy what?" I asked, distracted by my thoughts.

George smirked. "To show up at an innocent, fun-filled day at the horse show, and have everything go down the drain."

Bess rolled her eyes. "You're blaming Nancy just because a mystery happened to show up where she happened to be?" she said. "That makes about as much sense as Dana blaming Payton because someone vandalized her saddle."

"Right." I was kind of disturbed by the trainer's reaction myself. "It's like Dana can't wait to criticize everything Payton does."

"Think she should be a suspect?" George asked.

"You never know," I said. "But there are a few better ones I want to check out first. Like Jessica Watts, and Lenny Hood, and maybe this Cal that girl just mentioned, whoever that might be."

Bess nodded. "And what about the animal rights group from the parking lot? They're the ones who tossed that tomato."

"True, though I haven't seen any sign that any of them has actually been inside the show grounds, which would make it hard for them to slash the saddle." I paused. "Besides, I can't imagine why they'd be targeting Payton in particular."

"Maybe because she wins a lot?" George suggested. "They might figure it'll make more of a splash for their cause or whatever."

"I don't know. Sounds a little far-fetched. Still, you're right—let's not cross anyone off the list just yet." Spotting Midnight's groom hurrying past outside, I stepped into the aisle. "Hey, Mickey!" I called.

The groom stopped and glanced at me. "Yes?" he said politely, no hint of recognition on his weathered face. "Can I help you?"

"I'm Payton's friend," I prompted him. "Nancy. We met yesterday."

"Oh." Mickey didn't seem interested. But that didn't matter—I wasn't looking for small talk. Just information.

"You've probably seen the animal rights people protesting outside, right?" I said. "I was wondering if you've noticed them at any other shows in the past couple of months. Especially the recent one where Midnight got drug tested?"

For the first time, the groom showed a glimmer of emotion. Namely, confusion. "I don't know. I don't usually leave the grounds much during a show." He shrugged. "Didn't hear anything about any protesters the past few shows, though."

"Did you hear about the ones at *this* show?" George asked.

"Yeah." The groom shot her a look. "I heard. Had to clean their mess off Midnight's coat yesterday, didn't I?"

"Okay, one more question," I said. "Do you know of anyone around here named Cal?"

"Cal?" Mickey blinked. "The only Cal I know of is Cal Kidd. He's a jumper rider—and he's the one who sold Midnight to Payton."

CHAPTER SEVEN

Research and Gossip

BEFORE I COULD QUESTION MICKEY FUR-
ther, his cell phone buzzed. "Excuse me," he said after
glancing at the screen. "I have to go."

He hurried off. "He's not exactly Mr. Chatty, is
he?" Bess said.

"It's okay. At least now we have a name." I glanced
at George. "Feel like looking up Cal Kidd on your
smartphone?"

"On it." George pulled out her fancy phone, a gift
from her parents for her last birthday. Her fingers flew
over the keypad.

"So this Cal is Midnight's former owner," Bess mused, leaning against the door frame of the tack room as we waited. "If he sold the horse to Payton, why would he be mad at her now? I don't get it."

"I don't either," I said. "Maybe he thinks she cheated him on the price somehow? Although that wouldn't make much sense either, since her parents would have been the ones actually paying, right?"

"Got it," George spoke up. "There are quite a few articles about Cal Kidd on the web." She held the phone's tiny screen closer to her face, scanning whatever was on there. "Whoa. Looks like he's had some gambling problems. Got in a bunch of debt, even went to prison for a bit. Was out of the whole horse show scene for a couple of years and is just now getting back into it."

"Really?" That sounded interesting. I leaned closer. "Anything about Midnight on there?"

"Hold on, I'm reading. . . ." George went silent.

Bess glanced down the aisle. "Someone's coming," she said. "Maybe we should find a more private spot to talk about this."

I nodded, following her gaze. A gaggle of tweens in riding clothes were coming our way, chattering excitedly at one another.

"Let's go," I said, grabbing George's elbow and steering her down the aisle in the opposite direction. She didn't say a word—just kept reading, occasionally hitting a key with her thumb.

The show grounds were getting busy by now, and it wasn't easy to find a spot where we wouldn't be overheard. Finally we happened upon a small courtyard behind the show office. Nobody was out there, and it was hidden from the main path by a line of shrubs and a large Dumpster.

"Yuck, not exactly my favorite," Bess said, glancing at the flies buzzing around the Dumpster.

"Never mind, we won't be here long." I turned to George. "What've you got?"

George looked up from her phone. "Okay, here's the gist of this Cal Kidd guy's history." She started pacing back and forth like an overcaffeinated university lecturer. "He was some big-time jumper rider for years—started winning big classes when he was almost as young as Payton. Everyone thought he was destined for the Olympic show-jumping team."

"Sounds familiar," Bess put in.

"Yeah. He had lots of sponsors buying him horses and riders wanting him to be their trainer. Only then, like I said, he got mixed up in gambling. Ended up in serious debt, lost all his supporters and clients, and had to sell off his horses."

"Including Midnight?" Bess asked.

"Yeah. That's the weird thing, though." George stopped pacing and glanced down at the phone in her hand. "It sounds like Midnight wasn't even one of his better horses. In fact, it sounds like he didn't have much success with him at all, even though he won everything there was to win on every other horse he rode." She shrugged. "Midnight didn't start winning anything important until after Payton bought him."

"Interesting." I stared at the brick wall of the office building, trying to fit this into what we knew about the case so far. "Could Cal be trying to get Midnight back now that the horse is a superstar—a potential Olympic horse?"

"Could be," George agreed. "That would be a good way to jump-start his return to the sport." She grinned. "Did you see what I did there? *Jump*-start?"

"Yeah, you're a comic genius," Bess said dryly. She turned to me. "But would he really want Midnight back? George just said Cal didn't have much luck with him the first time. Maybe they didn't get along."

"Maybe. I don't know. But it's worth checking out." I chewed on my lower lip, trying to figure out how to proceed. "I should've asked Mickey if Cal is at this show."

"One way to find out." Bess pointed at the building in front of us. "Let's go ask at the office."

Within minutes, we had the information we needed. The pleasant woman manning the show secretary's desk told us that Cal Kidd had reserved a block of three stalls at the show. She even pointed us in the right direction.

My friends and I headed that way. "So what are you going to say to Cal Kidd?" Bess asked me.

"I'm not sure yet," I said. "I guess I'll just mention Midnight and then—hold on, is that my phone?"

I dug my cell phone out of my pocket. A text had just arrived from Ned:

FOUND P. SHE & D ARE TALKING PRIVATELY IN THE TACK RM.

George peered at the screen. "Yikes," she said. "I'm surprised we can't hear Dana yelling from here."

I grimaced, then sent a quick response:

KEEP US POSTED. B, G, & I ARE CHECKING OUT A LEAD.

"I wonder how Payton is taking the news about Midnight's drug-test results," Bess said. "She seemed pretty broken up by that drugging accusation yesterday—this is much worse."

"Yeah." I squinted at the number on the barn we were approaching. "Look, I think we're almost to Cal Kidd's stalls."

It took another few minutes of wandering around and asking people for help before we found our way to the very back of the barn, where Cal Kidd's three stalls were tucked into a corner. Unlike Dana's section in her barn, which was spotless and fully decked out in her barn colors, Cal's area here seemed a bit shabby and bare. However, the horses looking out of the three stalls appeared healthy and well groomed.

"Hello?" I called as Bess patted a curious chestnut mare. "Mr. Kidd?"

There was no response. A woman sweeping the aisle in front of the next block of stalls looked our way. "You looking for Cal?" she called in a friendly tone. "He's not here."

I stepped closer. "Do you know when he'll be back?"

"Not sure. Haven't seen him all day, actually," the woman said. "I talked to him a bit yesterday, and I don't think he has any classes today, so I guess he might not be back until feeding time tonight. Want me to let him know you were looking for him if I see him then?"

I was disappointed, but tried not to let it show. "Um, that's okay. We'll just check back later. Thanks."

Returning to my friends, I told them what the woman had said. "Guess there's no point hanging around here, then." Bess gave the chestnut one last pat, then stepped back. "Maybe we should head back and see what's going on with Payton."

"Hey, did you guys see this?" George was peering up at a cork bulletin board hanging between two of the stalls. It was the only bit of decoration in Cal's area, containing several ribbons and photos, though I'd barely glanced at it before. "This must be Cal Kidd. Look familiar?"

I stepped closer. "Yeah," I said. "That looks like the same guy we saw yesterday. The one who seemed so angry when Payton beat him in that first class we watched."

George nodded. "I think you guys are right. The photos on my phone were so small that I didn't recognize him before."

"So that's interesting," Bess said. "First Payton turns Cal's old horse into a big success, then she starts beating him during his big comeback."

"That can't be easy to take, especially since she's, like, half his age," George added. "Think it's enough of a motive to mess with her?"

"Maybe." I stared at the photo for a moment, then turned away. "Come on, let's go find Ned."

As we walked out of the barn, George started fiddling with her cell phone again. "What are you doing?" Bess asked.

"Looking up our other suspects," George replied. "Lenny Hood and Jessica Watts."

"Finding anything interesting?" I asked.

"Not yet—just regular stuff about their show results or whatever." George tapped a few more keys. "I'll let you know."

She was still searching when we neared the building where Dana's block of stalls was located. Just outside, half a dozen teenage riders were gathered by the benches outside the barn entrance. As we neared them, I was pretty sure I heard Payton's name.

"Hold up," I whispered, stopping my friends.

George looked up from her phone screen. "Huh?"

I shushed her, trying to hear what the teens were saying. A pretty brunette was talking. ". . . and if she gets suspended, there's no way they'll even consider giving her a chance at the team this year."

Another girl pursed her lips. "I bet she did it. She's so intense—like she'd do anything to win."

"Yeah," a third rider put in. "Plus, if you ask me, there's no way someone her age could win all those big jumper classes without a little, you know, extra help." She smirked as several of the others giggled.

"Come on, you guys," a petite blond girl spoke up. "I think Payton's really sweet, and she seems super honest, too. Maybe it wasn't her fault."

That was all I needed to hear. I strode forward to confront them. "Are you guys talking about Payton Evans?" I asked.

The girls all looked startled. One of them, a tall redhead with freckles all over her face, met my eye.

"Who wants to know?" she asked.

"I do," I responded evenly. "I'm a friend of Payton's. If there's something going on, I'd like to know about it."

The redhead considered that for a moment, then glanced at the others. "Whatever," she said at last.

"Everyone is going to know soon anyway. Payton's Grand Prix horse just flunked a drug test."

"Yeah," the brunette put in, her eyes flashing with excitement at the gossip. "And Payton's supposed to ride him tomorrow night!"

"If Midnight ends up on the suspended list, that'll be the end of that," another girl said.

"But I heard the test result was actually sort of inconclusive or whatever," the blonde said. "The committee gets to decide whether they're going to suspend or just give a warning."

"Do you think they'll decide before tomorrow?" George asked. "That's when the Grand Prix is, right? The one the Olympic guy is coming to watch?"

"Yeah," the redhead said. "And I bet they'll decide before then. Otherwise it'll look bad if the news gets out."

"And it will." The brunette giggled. "I bet the entire show grounds knows by the end of today!"

"You know that's got to be killing Dana," one of the others put in. "I'd pay to see that freak-out!"

The girls already seemed to have forgotten that my friends and I were there. Or maybe they were just too caught up in their gossip to care. I was about to move on when something occurred to me. The last I'd heard, even Payton hadn't found out about the test results yet. I supposed that was what she and Dana were discussing when Ned texted me, but that was only about twenty minutes ago. How had the gossip spread so fast?

I cleared my throat to remind the girls I was still there. "Where did you first hear about this?" I asked, focusing on the redhead, who seemed to be the ringleader.

"News travels fast around here," she said breezily.

Not good enough. "No, seriously," I pressed her. "Who told you about the drug-test results?"

The girl seemed taken aback that I was pressing the point. For the first time her bravado wavered, and she shot a quick, uncertain look at the pretty brunette. Aha.

"Well?" I asked, turning my attention to the brunette. "How'd you hear? Did someone tell you, or were you skulking around in the barns eavesdropping on people?"

The brunette frowned. "I wasn't eavesdropping," she said, sounding insulted. "Someone told me, okay?"

"Okay. So who was it?"

She looked stubborn. "Who are you, anyway?" she asked, crossing her arms over her chest. "I've never seen you guys at the shows before."

"She told you, we're friends of Payton's," George said. "Now spill it. Who told you?"

"Just tell them already, Val." The redhead sounded bored now. "It's not like Jessica was even being sneaky about it. I'm sure she's told lots of people already."

"Jessica?" I said quickly. "Do you mean Jessica Watts?"

"Yeah." The brunette sounded surly. "Whatever, it might've been her. But you didn't hear that from me, okay?"

I traded a quick look with Bess and George. How in the world had Jessica found out about the test result so quickly? It wasn't as if she and Payton were friends—far from it. Then again, if she was the one who'd slipped something to the horse, she might have some kind of insider knowledge. . . .

I opened my mouth to ask how long ago Jessica had started spreading the news. Before I could get a word out, a loud shout cut me off:

"Look out—loose horses!"

CHAPTER EIGHT

Fast and Loose

MORE VOICES CAME FROM VARIOUS DIREC-
tions, picking up the shout: *"Loose horses! Loose horses!"*

"Oh my gosh," one of the teen girls said. "I hope
my pony didn't duck out under his stall guard again!"

She and the other girls rushed off around the corner of the barn. My friends and I followed, swept up by
the general excitement.

"Uh-oh," George said as we rounded the corner
and skidded to a stop.

Three horses were running around wildly in the
grassy area between barns. Two of them were big

bays, and the third was a rangy liver chestnut.

"That's not Midnight, is it?" Bess said, pointing at one of the bays.

George gasped. "It *does* look like him! And check it out, there's Dana trying to grab him."

I saw that George was right. Payton's trainer was among those trying to catch the loose horses. She was moving slowly toward the excited bay, her arms out as she spoke soothingly to him.

"Hold up. Actually, I don't think it's Midnight." I peered at the horse. It was hard to get a good look, since he was currently dodging back and forth trying to avoid Dana. But then he lifted his head so I had a clear view of his face. "Nope, it's not him," I said with relief. "See? That horse has a white star on his face, and Midnight doesn't."

"Oh, you're right," Bess said. "Look, I think Dana's got him."

We watched as several people, including some of the teenage girls we'd just been talking to, helped catch the other two horses. Soon all three escapees were heading back into the barn.

"Whew, that was kind of crazy," George said. "The action never stops around here!"

Bess laughed, but I just rubbed my chin. "Yeah," I agreed. "It's kind of suspicious, isn't it?"

George looked surprised. "What do you mean? Do you think someone let the horses out on purpose? Why?"

"Yeah," Bess put in. "Especially since none of them belonged to Payton."

"I know. But doesn't it seem awfully coincidental that one of them was a big bay gelding from Dana's barn? One that looks a lot like Midnight?" I shrugged. "I mean, we all mistook him for Midnight for a second there. Maybe someone else did too."

"Oh!" Bess's eyes widened. "I didn't think of that. So you think this really could be connected to the case?"

"I don't know. But we can't rule it out. Let's go find Payton. I think we need to talk to her about all this."

We headed into the barn. A couple of grooms and a middle-aged woman were fussing over the recently recaptured bay gelding, who was now standing quietly cross-tied in the aisle.

"Excuse me, do you know where Dana went?" I asked one of the grooms.

"I'm not sure." The groom seemed distracted as he ran a rag down the horse's legs. "Tack room, maybe? She was talking to Payton in there when the horses got loose."

"Thanks." I led the way down the aisle.

As my friends and I neared the tack room, we could hear the sound of a raised voice. "Uh-oh," Bess whispered. "Sounds like Dana's not happy."

"Sounds like Payton's not either," I said as another angry voice joined in.

I wasn't sure we should be listening to their argument. But it wasn't as if they were making any attempt to be quiet—half the barn could probably hear them. My friends and I took a few steps closer, stopping just short of the doorway.

". . . and it's like you don't even care about your own reputation anymore, let alone mine!" Dana was yelling.

"That's not fair!" Payton exclaimed, sounding upset. "If it was up to me, I wouldn't even be at this show!"

"Huh?" George murmured, raising an eyebrow at Bess and me.

"Shh," I hushed her, leaning closer to the door.

"Look, I know you're upset about missing your friend's party or whatever—," Dana began.

"It's my cousin," Payton snapped, cutting her off. "My favorite cousin, who's been like an older sister to me my whole life. And it's not just some party—it's her *wedding*!"

"Okay, whatever, I'm sorry," Dana said. "But in this industry, you need to be willing to make sacrifices. And it's not every day that the chef d'équipe wants to show up and watch you ride. . . ."

Unfortunately, she lowered her voice just enough so it was impossible to make out whatever she said next. I backed up a few yards, and my friends followed.

"This adds a new wrinkle," I said quietly. "It sounds like Payton wanted to skip this show to go to her cousin's wedding."

"I wonder if that's the family obligation that's keeping her parents away until tomorrow night," Bess said.

"Probably," I agreed, remembering Payton's comment the day before. "In any case, Dana must've insisted she skip the wedding so she could ride in front of the Olympics guy."

"Maybe Payton's parents, too," George said. "It sounds like they're pretty competitive and ambitious."

"Yeah. Even if it wasn't their idea, they must've agreed with Dana. Because if they thought Payton should go to the wedding instead, they could've overruled her." I shook my head. "You know, I'm starting to feel really sorry for Payton. On the one hand, she's living out her dream—riding at these big shows, super successful, aimed for Olympic glory."

Bess nodded, clearly seeing where I was going with my thought. "But there's a dark side too," she said. "Her life isn't really her own. She has to make sacrifices to be the best." She sighed. "It's just too bad Dana seems to be so, you know, *mean* about it."

"Yeah." George glanced in the direction of the tack

room. "She really doesn't sound too sympathetic, does she?"

Her comment made another thought pop into my head. It was one that had been dancing around at the edges of my thoughts all day.

"You're right," I said slowly. "If Dana's the one who forced Payton to come to this show, could that be a clue in itself?"

"What do you mean?" Bess asked. "Do you think Dana should be a suspect?"

"I'm not sure," I said. "I mean, this isn't the first time we've witnessed her being kind of hard on Payton. But if she's the culprit, what's her motive?"

"Good question." George pursed her lips thoughtfully. "She's Payton's trainer. So if Payton looks good, she looks good, right? Why would she want to mess that up?"

"And would she really slash up that saddle?" Bess wondered. "I mean, she seems kind of hot-tempered, but not *crazy*."

"Yeah, I can't quite picture her going at the saddle

with a knife either," I admitted. "Still, we'd better put her on the list. Just in case." Something else occurred to me. "And actually, even if she's not the best suspect for some of the stuff that's happened, there's one thing that fits perfectly. She's the one in charge of Midnight's care, right? Including everything he eats. So she was in the best position to toss some chocolate or whatever into his bucket to make him flunk that test, right?"

"I guess so." Bess looked uncertain. "But if that's true, wouldn't she get in trouble too?"

"I don't know." I realized I still wasn't clear on how the whole suspension system worked. "Let's see if we can find someone to ask."

George glanced toward the tack room. "Good idea. We probably shouldn't be here when they come out."

I had to agree with that. If Dana might be our culprit, it probably wasn't a good thing for her to catch us eavesdropping.

My friends and I tiptoed away around the corner, then started looking around for someone to ask about the drug rules. The first familiar face we saw belonged to Mickey. He was outside Midnight's stall, stuffing hay into a hay net. The big bay gelding was watching the man's work with interest.

"Hi." I walked over and gave Midnight a rub on the nose, then smiled at the groom. "Do you have a second?"

This time I was pretty sure he recognized me, though he seemed less than thrilled to see me. "Uh, I guess," he mumbled without enthusiasm.

"We were just talking about Midnight's drug results, and we realized we don't understand how the system works," I said. "Who gets suspended when something like that happens?"

"The horse does, of course. Plus whoever signs on the entry form as that horse's primary caretaker," Mickey replied, yanking the cords to tie the hay net shut. "Normally that's the trainer, unless the owner signs as trainer for some reason."

"Oh." I shot a look at my friends. What Mickey was saying seemed to rule out our latest theory, since Dana would be the one who got suspended rather than Payton.

Mickey hung the hay net just outside the stall door, patting Midnight as the big bay horse eagerly yanked a few strands out and chewed. "Wouldn't be the worst thing for this guy to get suspended," the groom murmured, running one calloused hand up and down the gelding's neck. His voice was so low that I wasn't sure he'd meant to be overheard.

"What was that?" I asked. "Did you say it would be *good* for Midnight to get suspended?"

"'Course not," he said gruffly. "It's just that Midnight could use a break, that's all. He's been campaigned pretty hard this year. Too many weeks standing in a tiny stall, riding in trailers . . . Ah, never mind. Stupid thought."

"No, I understand." Bess shot the man her most winning and sympathetic smile. "You're just worried about Midnight. I think that's sweet."

Mickey merely grunted in response. But his expression lightened a little bit. Bess has that effect on people. I don't know how she does it.

"Yeah, you must be really worried about what

happened," I said, trying to sound casual. A lot of people are more likely to talk if they don't realize they're being interrogated. I had a feeling Mickey was one of those people. "Especially since someone obviously tried to hurt Midnight by dosing him with theobromine." I reached out to stroke the gelding's velvety nose. "That can't be good for him, right?"

"Not likely to hurt him," Mickey responded. "Especially not in such a small amount."

"Oh. That's good," I said. "Still, who would want to give him something they knew would test? And how would they even do it?" I eyed the hay net as Midnight took another bite. "Do you think someone sneaked in and slipped something into his food?"

"Not likely." Mickey sounded certain. "We've got a foolproof system here."

"You do? What is it?"

The groom shrugged. "Really want to know? I'll show you." He headed off down the aisle without another word.

Trading a look with my friends, I shrugged and

then followed. Soon we were all crowding into a stall at the end of the row. Like the tack stall, it wasn't set up for horses. Instead it contained at least a dozen large feed sacks, piles of empty buckets, a folding table with a bunch of small plastic bags on it, and a bunch of other stuff I didn't take in right away. Tacked to one wall was a poster-board list of horses' names written in different colors. Beside each name was some additional writing in black ink, though it was too small to read from where I was standing.

"Feed room," Mickey said, and I hid a smile. I knew where we were.

"So all the horses' grain comes from here?" George asked, peering into a large bag labeled as alfalfa pellets.

"Uh-huh." Mickey pointed to a neat row of buckets along one wall. "One color for each horse. Feed gets measured out there." Next he indicated the plastic bags on the table. "Supplements there."

"Supplements?" I echoed.

"Vitamins. Joint aids. Stuff like that," Mickey said. "When it's time to feed, grab the bag and dump it in the matching bucket. No way to mix things up."

Bess stepped closer to the poster and peered up at the list of names. "Midnight's color is purple," she said. She moved over to the line of buckets. "Hey, wait a minute. It looks like someone already added some supplements to this purple bucket."

"Can't be." George picked up a plastic bag filled with powder. A purple sticker was on it. "His bag's right here."

Mickey frowned. "What are you talking about?" He glanced at the bag in George's hand, then stepped over and peered into the purple bucket. His face went pale, and he grabbed the bucket with one hand, reaching into it with the other. "There *is* some kind of powder in here!" he exclaimed. Lifting his fingers to his nose, he gave them a sniff. "Smells like bute. But that can't be! Midnight isn't supposed to get that!"

CHAPTER NINE

~

Mixed Messages

"BUTE? WHAT'S THAT?" GEORGE ASKED.

Mickey didn't answer. He was already sprinting toward the door, calling out for the other grooms. "Nobody feed anything!" he shouted. "I've got to tell Dana about this. We'll have to figure out if any of the other feed was tampered with."

A couple of the other grooms rushed in. They seemed surprised to see us in there.

"What's going on?" asked Jen.

"We're not sure," I told her. "Um, Mickey just noticed there was some extra stuff in one of the buckets."

"Yeah, he called it bute," George added. "What is that?"

"It's a medication," Jen replied. "It's very common—sort of like aspirin for horses. Some of ours get it after a tough day of showing. Which bucket was it in?"

"Midnight's," Bess replied.

"What?" Jen exclaimed. "But that's not right—Midnight isn't allowed to have bute today!"

"Why not?" I asked. "I thought you said it was common."

The groom looked distraught. "It is, but you're not allowed to give it at the same time as certain other drugs," she explained. "And Midnight is scheduled to get one of those other drugs tonight. If he ended up with both in his system and then got tested . . ."

She let her voice trail off. I could guess what she was thinking. Midnight was in enough trouble with the drug testers already, without another positive result to add to the mess.

"Anyway," Jen went on after a moment, "I know there was nothing extra in that bucket an hour ago—

I mixed all of this afternoon's feed myself!"

She and the other groom started checking all the buckets. My friends and I took the opportunity to slip out of the feed room.

"So what do you think?" George asked as we wandered down the aisle. "Does this make Mickey a suspect?"

"Maybe," I said. "It sounds like he wouldn't mind one bit if Midnight got a vacation. And a drug suspension would be a sure way to do it."

Bess nodded. "Especially since he was so quick to tell us that the theo-whatever stuff the test found wouldn't hurt Midnight any. That makes it a likely choice for someone who's worried about the horse's welfare, right?"

"Good point." I couldn't help feeling dubious. "But if he's the culprit, why would he just blurt all that info out to us? I mean, he pretty much handed us his motive on a silver platter."

"Guilty conscience?" George suggested.

We'd reached the barn exit by then. Bess paused in

the doorway, squinting against the sunlight streaming in from outside. "No, maybe Nancy's right," she said. "Mickey seemed genuinely surprised and upset when he saw that powder in Midnight's bucket just now. Either he's a really good actor . . ."

"Or he's not the one who put it there," I finished for her. "Besides, I just thought of something else. Mickey said it's the *trainer* who gets suspended when a horse fails a drug test. Not the owner or rider. So Dana would be the one going down. Would Mickey really want to get his boss suspended from showing? Seems like that could be bad for his own income."

"I don't know," George said. "But I just remembered something else. Mickey was hanging around when Payton took Midnight out to graze yesterday. But then when we came back after the tomato incident, he was nowhere in sight. Remember? Payton handed Midnight off to another groom."

"So what?" Bess said.

"So what if Mickey was out in the parking lot convincing those PAN loonies to tomato-bomb a certain big bay horse?" George said. "It could've all been part of his plan to scare Payton into quitting so Midnight would get a chance to go lounge in a field or whatever."

I sighed. "The more we talk about Mickey as a suspect, the more far-fetched it seems," I said. "I mean, I could maybe see him slipping something into Midnight's feed or whatever, thinking he's doing the horse a favor. But would he really follow Payton around leaving nasty notes, or convince someone to toss tomatoes, or slash up a saddle, or let a bunch of other horses loose?"

"Who knows?" George shrugged. "We don't know the guy. Maybe he's a secret psycho."

I didn't respond. I'd just noticed someone hurrying past outside. "Hey," I said, lowering my voice. "Isn't that Jessica Watts?"

"Where?" George turned to look. "Yeah, that's her. What's she doing hanging around this barn?"

"Good question." I watched as Jessica disappeared around the corner. "I mean, it's a public place, so it's probably a coincidence. Maybe her horses are in this barn too. Maybe she has friends in this barn. Maybe she's looking for the bathroom."

"Or maybe she's sneaking out after tampering with Midnight's feed bucket," George said. "Let's follow her and see where she goes."

I didn't have any better plan to suggest, so I nodded. "Stay back so she doesn't see us," I warned as we hurried off in the direction the girl had gone.

George tossed me an amused look. "What, do you think this is our first stakeout?" she joked.

"Shh!" Bess warned as we rounded the corner. "There she is."

We tailed Jessica halfway across the show grounds. She didn't seem to be in any hurry. Every so often she would wave to someone passing by or even pause to say hello. Finally she entered a snack bar.

"Looks like she's just looking for something to eat," Bess said.

"Maybe not." George had darted forward to peer inside through a window. "Look who she's talking to now!"

Bess and I joined her at the window. "Oh!" Bess exclaimed softly. "It's that nasty trainer—what's his name again?"

"Lenny Hood." I gripped the edge of the window as I stared inside. Payton and Lenny Hood were standing at the back of the small restaurant, heads bent together as they talked. I couldn't see Jessica's face, but Lenny's expression was focused and intense.

"I wish we could hear what they're saying," Bess murmured.

"Me too," I said. "What if they're in cahoots, working together to frame Payton for that drug violation?"

"Exactly what I was thinking," George said. "With Payton out of the picture, Jessica would have a better shot at some of those ribbons. And the prize money that goes with them."

"Lenny Hood's students, too," Bess agreed. "Think we can get any closer?"

"Not without them seeing us," I said. "Let's just wait and see what they do next."

We didn't have long to wait. Within minutes,

Jessica and Lenny were leaving the snack bar. My friends and I stayed hidden around the corner, though it probably wasn't necessary, since neither of our culprits so much as glanced our way before hurrying off in opposite directions.

"Now what?" Bess asked. "Should we split up and follow them?"

I didn't answer for a second. I'd just spotted another familiar face wandering into view across the way. "Look," I said. "Isn't that Cal Kidd?"

Bess gasped. "What's he doing here? I thought he wasn't at the show today."

"That's what his neighbor told me," I said. "Looks like she was wrong."

"So what do you want to do?" George glanced after Lenny, who was almost out of sight already. "If we don't hurry, we'll lose track of all of them."

"I'll follow Cal," I decided quickly. "You guys take the other two, okay?"

I rushed off, leaving it to them to work out the details. Cal was strolling along with his hands in his pockets, not seeming in any particular hurry. It was easy to keep him in sight as he wandered along the paths, pausing once to watch a pony trotting around in one of the schooling rings and again to pat a free-ranging dog.

Finally I realized he was heading toward the big old-fashioned wooden barn, where his show stalls were located. I waited until he'd disappeared inside, then cautiously entered myself. It was busier in there than it had been earlier in the day, and I had no trouble making my way to the back section without Cal noticing me.

I hid in the hayloft with a view of Cal's area and waited to see what he did next. For a while, that wasn't much. He puttered around for a good twenty minutes—first checking on each of his horses, then sweeping the aisle by his stalls. Finally he grabbed a magazine with a horse on the cover, sat down on a tack trunk, and started flipping through the pages.

Sneaking a peek at my watch, I wondered what to do. By the looks of things, I could stand here all day and see nothing important. Why waste time when every second counted? Still, Cal was on the suspect list. I had to figure out whether he needed to stay there.

That meant it was time to stop spying and take some action. I climbed down from my hiding place and walked right over to Cal.

"Hello," I said. "You're Cal Kidd, right?"

He glanced up from his magazine. "That's me. And you are?"

"My name's Nancy," I said. "I'm, uh, a journalism student. I'm here interviewing people at this horse show as part of a class project."

"Cool." Cal's smile was polite but a little distant. "So lay it on me. What do you want to know?"

I scanned my mind for a good opening question that wouldn't make him suspicious. "Um, you're a jumper rider, right? What made you get into that?"

"It's kind of a family thing." Cal tossed aside the magazine and stood, stepping over to pat the nearest of his horses. He had only a couple of inches on me, though he was so lean that he seemed taller. "My mom rode when my sister and I were kids, and we just kind of followed along in her footsteps. Or boot steps. Whatever." He grinned.

I had to admit he was kind of charming. No wonder he'd had so many clients and admirers before his fall from grace. Then again, I'd learned long ago that appearances could be deceiving. Some of the worst criminals I'd nabbed—or that Dad had helped convict—could seem like the most agreeable people in the world.

"Okay," I said. "What's your favorite thing about the sport?"

"The horses, of course. Though the speed and thrill aren't bad, either." Cal glanced at me. "Hey, don't you need to, like, write this down or record it or something? I'm feeding you pearls of wisdom here!" His grin faded slightly as he studied my face. "Wait a minute, you look kind of familiar—didn't I see you hanging around with Payton Evans yesterday?"

Oops. I hadn't realized he'd even seen us by the ring after Payton's round. "Um, yeah," I said. "I was interviewing her, too."

"Hmm." Suddenly Cal looked a lot less friendly.

"Well, here's some more info for your class project. The big-time show-jumping world is a tough business, not a game of My Little Pony, okay?"

"I'm not sure what you mean." I backed away, feeling nervous all of a sudden.

His eyes narrowed. "I mean it's no place for little girls," he growled. "You can tell your friend Payton Evans that the next time you interview her. Now if you'll excuse me, I have business to attend to."

He stalked off, glowering, and disappeared around the corner. I collapsed against the wall, my heart pounding. I knew I should probably follow him to see where he was going. But after the threat he'd just made, I was none too eager to face him again.

"If it *was* a threat," I murmured to myself, still not quite sure what had just happened. Either way, his reaction was weird enough to keep his name on the suspect list for sure.

"Here she comes," George said.

Following her gaze, I saw Bess jogging toward us.

We were behind the show office again. I'd texted both my friends after leaving Cal's barn, telling them to meet me there whenever they were finished.

"I hope you guys found out something interesting." Bess was huffing and puffing as she reached us. "Because my detective work was a total bust."

"Really? What happened?" I asked.

Bess leaned against the wall to catch her breath. "Nothing, pretty much," she said. "Lenny went back to his barn and talked on his cell phone for a while. Not about anything interesting, as far as I could hear. Then he went over to one of the rings to watch some of his students ride. He was still there when I left."

"Okay." I turned to George. She'd arrived just moments before Bess, so we hadn't had a chance to compare notes yet. "What about you?" I asked.

"I followed Jessica back to her barn," George said. "She sat down on a tack trunk and started texting, so I got bored and took a look around."

Bess snorted. "Some detective you are, Ms. Short Attention Span."

George ignored her. "Anyway, I ended up chatting with Jessica's trainer. And guess what I found out?"

"What?" I asked.

"It turns out Jessica might be a jerk, but she's not our culprit." George looked pleased with herself. "Because she wasn't even *at* the show where Midnight got tested."

"Are you sure?" I asked.

"Positive. The trainer lady knew exactly which show I was talking about. I guess she's friends with Dana—she'd just heard the gossip and seemed pretty bummed out that Midnight might get suspended. She said the rest of the barn was at the show in question, but Jessica had the flu or something that week."

"Interesting." I twirled a lock of hair around my finger as I tried to fit this piece into the puzzle.

Bess was frowning. "So this means Jessica couldn't be our culprit, right?" she said. "She wasn't around to slip something into Midnight's food at that show."

"Right," I said. "Unless she really is in cahoots with Lenny Hood, of course."

"Oh, right." George's face fell. "I forgot about that."

"Actually, with all the weird stuff that's happening, it's seeming more and more likely that there could be more than one culprit at work," I said. "That would certainly make it easier to make all the pieces fit."

"Okay," Bess said. "So what do we do now?"

"I'm not sure." I glanced at the sky, which was showing streaks of red. "It's getting late, and the show will be winding down for the night pretty soon. Maybe we should find Payton and see what she wants to do."

My phone buzzed before my friends could respond. It was a text from Ned, asking where we were. Oops. In all the excitement, I'd forgotten to update him in a while.

I let him know where we were, and he was there within minutes. "What have you been up to all day?" Bess asked him. "Planning some romantic getaway for your anniversary?"

"Actually, yes." Ned grinned and winked, then turned to take my hand. "I'm officially sweeping you away with me."

"Huh?" I said.

"Since we had to cancel our picnic, I want to make it up to you," Ned said. "I'm taking you out to dinner. What do you say?"

"Picnic? What picnic?" Bess asked.

Ned ignored her. "So how's Italian sound?" he asked, squeezing my hand.

My stomach grumbled, and I realized I'd forgotten to eat lunch. "It sounds fantastic." I glanced at my friends. "Can you guys finish up here without me? We should probably check in with Payton, and—"

"Go." Bess gave me a little shove. "Have a nice time." She pulled me back toward her, gave a sniff, and wrinkled her nose. "But for Pete's sake, stop off at home and take a shower first. You smell like a horse!"

"This is nice," I said, reaching for my water glass. The ice cubes clinked against the crystal as I took a sip. I glanced around. We were seated in the crowded dining room of the most popular Italian restaurant in River

Heights. "I can't believe you actually got us a table here on a Friday night."

Across from me, Ned looked happy and handsome as he lifted his own water glass in a toast. "Only the best for you," he said with a wink. Then he chuckled. "But seriously, it's only because my mom plays tennis with the owner. Don't tell Bess that, though."

"Your secret's safe with me." My smile faded as I returned my attention to my pasta. It was delicious, even though I could barely remember ordering it. In fact, I'd spent most of the two-plus hours since leaving the show grounds only half-focused on what I was doing. The rest of my mind kept returning to the case. The Grand Prix was tomorrow night, and I had no idea when the powers that be would make their decision about whether Payton and Midnight could still enter. If I didn't figure something out fast, there was a chance Payton could miss her chance to impress the Olympic chef d'équipe. And I didn't want that to happen if I could help it.

It took me a moment to realize that Ned had said

something. Blinking, I shot him a sheepish smile. "What? Um, sorry. Guess I'm a little distracted."

He looked sympathetic. "I hear you. I'm worried about Payton too."

I reached over and squeezed his hand, grateful as always that he was so understanding about my sleuthing. "Thanks. It's just that we don't have much time, and—"

"I know." Ned speared a meatball with his fork. "I called Mom and Dad to tell them Dana would be dropping Payton off when they finished for the day. They asked how everything went, but I didn't mention that slashed-up saddle. Now I'm wondering it it's a mistake to keep it from them. Whoever did that has some serious anger issues."

"Maybe Payton will tell them when she gets home," I said.

"Maybe." Ned sounded dubious. "But she's the one who didn't even want to tell her parents about that note." He sighed, setting down his fork. "I'm thinking it might be almost time to bring in the police."

I didn't answer. I couldn't really disagree with his point.

"Things just aren't coming together," I mused, staring at my plate. "There are a lot of people on our suspect list, but none of them quite fits all the evidence."

"I know. Like that girl Jessica—she's got a motive, but she wasn't at the show where Midnight got drugged," Ned said. "Plus, could she really sneak into Dana's barn in broad daylight to slash that saddle or tamper with Midnight's feed without anyone seeing her?"

"I'm not sure. We did see her outside right after those horses were let loose. But what about those threatening notes? I'm not even sure she's old enough to drive—how would she follow Payton all the way back to your house?"

"Unless she's teaming up with that other trainer like you said," Ned said.

I nodded. I'd filled Ned in on our latest theories on the ride over. "These big-time trainers all seem to attend most of the same shows, so I'm guessing Lenny was probably at the one in question," I said. "But everyone says he's super successful in the show world. Would he really risk his whole reputation on this kind of garbage, just to take out a teenager?"

Ned shrugged. "Okay, change of pace—how about those animal protester people?"

"You mean PAN?" We'd passed the protesters on our way out of the show, though I'd noticed that Annie Molina wasn't with them. "I don't know. I'm not sure they'd be likely to target any particular person, and so far everything seems to be aimed at Payton."

"Good point." Ned reached for the salt. "They did throw that tomato, though, right?"

"Yeah, but we're wondering if someone put them up to it." That made me realize we'd never followed up on that particular angle. I made a mental note to try to talk to Annie or one of her cohorts the next day.

"Okay," Ned said. "So other than Lenny and Jessica, who else have you got? What about that Cal Kidd guy? Or Dana? Or the groom?"

"All still on the list." I sighed. "It's just that none of

them quite . . . hold on." My phone was buzzing from my purse. Fishing it out, I saw that I'd just received a text. It was from Payton:

NANCY, SORRY 2 BOTHER U—I'M STILL AT THE SHOW, EVERYONE ELSE WENT HOME, & NOW I THINK SOMEONE IS STALKING ME!

CHAPTER TEN

Signing Statement

"CAN'T YOU DRIVE ANY FASTER?" I COM-plained, gripping the armrest of Ned's car.

"Not without breaking the sound barrier." Ned spun the steering wheel, sending his car screeching into the fairgrounds' parking lot. It was a much different sight from the one we'd left a couple of hours earlier. Only a few cars were still parked there, along with several large horse trailers hulking in the pale floodlights positioned here and there throughout the lot.

Ned screeched to a stop near the gate, not bothering to park between the lines. "Let's go," I said, hopping out of the car.

We sprinted in through the gate, the guard barely looking up as we passed. "Where did she say she was?" Ned asked.

"She didn't." I put on a burst of speed. "Let's check Dana's barn. If Payton's not there, I'll text her again."

We burst into the barn. It was dim and quiet in there, the only light coming from a few safety bulbs in the aisle.

"Payton!" Ned hollered. "Where are you? It's Ned and Nancy! Payton!"

I held my breath, listening for a response. "There," I said, spinning and pointing toward the tack stall. "I heard footsteps."

"Payton?" Ned hurried that way. Halfway there, he skidded to a stop as Mickey emerged, rubbing his eyes.

"Hello?" the groom said, sounding sleepy. "What's all the shouting about?"

"Mickey!" I rushed over to him. "Have you seen Payton?"

"Payton?" Mickey blinked at me. "What do you mean? I thought she left with Dana and the others an hour ago."

I pulled out my cell phone and sent Payton a text: WHERE ARE U?

"If everyone else left an hour ago, what are you still doing here?" Ned asked Mickey, sounding suspicious.

Mickey was looking more awake by the second. "I stay here every night," he said. "Extra security. Dana doesn't want to take the chance of anyone messing with the horses overnight."

I couldn't help thinking he wasn't doing such a hot job as an amateur security guard. He hadn't even known Payton was still here.

Unless he's the one who was stalking her, I thought with a shiver.

"Any response yet?" Ned asked, glancing at the phone in my hand.

I shook my head. "Let's check her horses' stalls. Maybe she's in with one of them."

Leaving a confused-looking Mickey behind, we

jogged down the aisle. The first stall we checked contained only a sleepy-looking gray mare.

"Midnight's stall is right over there." I hurried across the aisle and peered inside. "Payton!"

"Nancy!" Payton was leaning against Midnight's side. She straightened up and came to the door. "Thanks for coming. I'm really sorry to bother you guys—Bess told me you were out on a date."

"It's no problem." Ned unclipped the stall guard to let her out. "What happened?"

Payton bit her lip. "I kind of lost track of time and never told Dana I needed a ride," she admitted. "By the time I realized it, everyone was gone."

"You could have called my parents," Ned said. "They'd come get you. Or I would have."

"I know. I was planning to call your dad." Payton glanced at Midnight, who was hanging his head out over the door as if listening to the conversation. "I was just going to say good night to the horses first. I was coming out of Midnight's stall when I saw someone in the aisle."

"Was it Mickey?" I asked.

Payton shook her head. "That's what I thought at first, but it wasn't him. I called out, and instead of answering, the person ran away."

"What did he look like?" I said. "Was it definitely a man?"

"I think so—I'm not sure." Payton bit her lip again. "I really didn't get a good look. It was pretty dark. But it looked like a big guy with broad shoulders. Maybe bald?" She shrugged. "Like I said, it was hard to see, and I guess I wasn't thinking too clearly. . . ."

"It's okay." I put an arm around her shoulders. "Are you sure it wasn't show security or something?"

"I don't think so. Why would a security guard run away as soon as I said something to him?" Payton sounded shaken. "Anyway, I wasn't sure what to do. I was still standing here in the aisle when I heard a weird whistle."

"A whistle?" Ned echoed. "What do you mean?"

"It's hard to describe. It sounded like some kind of—of signal or something, you know? Like in the movies?" Payton let out a low two-note whistle, then shook her head. "I know that sounds crazy."

"Not really," I said. "Not after everything else that's happened around here lately."

She nodded. "Anyway, I was kind of spooked. So I ducked back into Midnight's stall and hid behind him while I texted you."

"I'm glad you did." I glanced at Ned. "Speaking of show security, maybe we should let them know about this. They can keep a lookout for this guy. They might've noticed him entering or leaving the grounds."

"I'll run over to the gate and talk to the guard there," Ned offered. "You guys should probably stay with Mickey until I get back."

"Okay." As he hurried away, Payton and I headed toward the tack room. Mickey was still in the aisle where we'd left him.

"What's going on?" he asked, sounding totally awake by now. "Payton? I didn't know you were here."

"I know, I'm sorry." Payton smiled weakly. "I should have remembered you'd be around and come to find you. Then I wouldn't have had to bother Nancy and Ned."

"It's okay, we really don't mind." I steered her into the tack room and over to a chair. "You should sit down for a minute."

Mickey followed us in, perching on the edge of a cot that was now sitting in the middle of the small room. "Is someone going to tell me what this is all about?"

I filled him in on what Payton had just told me. "Have you seen or heard anything unusual tonight?" I asked.

"Not a thing, sorry." Mickey shot Payton a worried look. "Are you sure it wasn't me you saw?" he asked. "I was pretty tired when I made my rounds last time. Might not have heard you."

"It definitely wasn't you," Payton told the groom with a shaky smile. "This guy was a lot bigger than you. Plus, he definitely reacted when he realized I'd seen him." She glanced at me. "Still, I'm starting to wonder if I panicked for no reason. Maybe it was just some local guy poking around after hours out of curiosity. He might've been as scared as I was."

"What about that weird whistle?" I asked.

"Maybe it was a bird?" She stifled a yawn. "Like I said, I was kind of panicked, so I didn't know what I was hearing at that point."

Just then Ned rushed into the tack room. "Alerted the guards," he said breathlessly. "They'll be on the lookout. Also, Dana just called."

"She called *you*?" Payton asked in surprise.

"Yeah. I guess she's been trying to reach you, but couldn't get an answer."

"Oops." Payton reached into her pocket. "I forgot, I turned off my phone when I hid in Midnight's stall." She looked sheepish. "I was afraid it would ring and give away where I was hiding. So what did Dana want?" She looked apprehensive, and I couldn't blame her. In her current condition, the last thing Payton needed was another scolding from her trainer.

But I felt better when I noticed that Ned was grinning. "She was calling with good news," he said. "She just heard from the show officials or whoever. You guys are in for the Grand Prix tomorrow!"

"What?" Payton looked startled.

"That's great news!" I exclaimed. "So they decided not to suspend?"

"That's right." Ned flopped into another chair. "You guys know how fast Dana talks—I couldn't keep up with all of what she was saying. But I guess the fact that the levels were so low, plus your good reps, made them decide in your favor."

I shot a look at Mickey. The groom looked thoughtful, but his weathered face was difficult to read beyond that. Was he thinking that his plan had failed? I just couldn't tell.

"Wow," Payton said. "I can't believe this."

My attention shifted back to her. "You don't look as thrilled as I thought you'd be," I said. "Aren't you happy that you'll get to ride in the Grand Prix?"

"Sure, of course," Payton said quickly. "It's just that this has all been so crazy, you know?"

"What do you mean?" Ned asked.

Payton sighed. "I feel bad for putting Dana through so much trouble. She likes a drama-free barn—that's why she won't take on just anyone as a client, no matter how talented they are. Like, have you guys ever heard of Cal Kidd?"

"As a matter of fact, we have." I was surprised that she even had to ask. Then I realized I hadn't yet had a chance to mention my suspicions to her. "Um, what about him?"

"I heard he wanted to train with Dana for his big comeback," Payton said. "I guess they've known each other for a long time or something—at least that's what I heard." She added, "But he has kind of a bad rep from his gambling days—too much drama and gossip—so Dana turned him down."

"She did?" This added yet another new wrinkle to things. Could we be looking at this all wrong? Could Cal be our culprit—but trying to punish *Dana* rather than Payton?

"Interesting you should mention Kidd," Mickey spoke up, breaking me out of my thoughts. "I caught him skulking around here last night after hours."

"You did?" I spun to face him. "What happened?"

"Just what I said." The groom shrugged. "I was making the rounds right after everyone left, and saw him hanging around near the feed room. When I asked what he was doing there, Kidd refused to answer and took off."

"Interesting." I shot Ned a meaningful look. "Um, come on, Payton. We'd better get you home."

"Right." Ned clapped Mickey on the shoulder. "Thanks for your help."

"Sure," Mickey murmured, stifling a yawn.

Leaving him to his cot, Ned and Payton and I headed out. Soon we were outside in the cool evening air. Nobody was in sight out there; the only activity was a cat stalking something in the shadow of the next barn.

"That's it, then!" I blurted out. "I bet Cal Kidd is our culprit!"

"Exactly what I was thinking," Ned agreed.

Payton wrinkled her brow. "What are you guys talking about?"

"It all makes sense!" I was feeling excited now. "All

this time we've been thinking the mischief around here has been aimed at you. But it's really been aimed at *Dana*! Cal must be mad at Dana for turning him down, so he's trying to get back at her."

"I don't understand," Payton said, shaking her head. "Most of the stuff hasn't had anything to do with Dana."

"Sure it has. Any sabotage of her star rider could be considered sabotage of her as well." My mind raced as I tried to fit all the pieces together. "And what about those loose horses? We thought whoever let them out was targeting you, because one of them was from Dana's barn and looked a little like Midnight. But maybe the Midnight thing was a coincidence. Maybe the only important thing was that the horse came from Dana's barn."

"But about Midnight . . . ," Ned began.

"I was just getting to that," I said. "The suspension thing works too. Because as Midnight's trainer, Dana was the one who'd pay the price if the horse got suspended. It all makes perfect sense!"

"Okay, I see what you're getting at," Payton said. "And it *would* make perfect sense. Except that everyone on the circuit knows I always sign the entry forms as my own trainer."

That brought me up short. "What?"

Payton nodded. "I sign my own entry forms. There was even an article about it in one of the industry magazines just last month. So I'm sure someone like Cal probably knows about it."

I was struggling to catch up to this new twist. "Wait, but someone told us it's always the trainer who signs," I said.

"Yeah, that's the normal way." Payton glanced at Ned with the ghost of a smile. "But you know my parents don't believe in doing things the normal way. They've always insisted I sign for myself. Dana wasn't thrilled about that at first. In fact, I was afraid that drama might get me kicked out before my first show with Dana."

"I still don't get it," I said. "Why would your parents even care who signs some horse show entry form?"

"I don't know. I guess it's supposed to teach me to be responsible for myself, or more independent, or something," Payton replied. "Just another part of the Evans Edge."

"Can you even do that, though?" Ned wondered. "I mean, you're still a minor."

"You're right, actually my parents have to sign too because of my age," Payton amended. "But in their eyes, *I'm* the one who's ultimately responsible." She glanced at me. "So anyway, this means that even if Midnight had ended up suspended, Dana would have been in the clear. I'm the only one who would've been in trouble."

"Oh." I thought about that for a second. "And you're sure Cal would know about that? You said he's been away from the show scene for a while."

"That doesn't matter," Payton said. "The gambling stuff was only part of the reason Dana didn't want Cal in her barn. The other reason is that he's supposed to be some huge gossip. Trust me, he's got to know."

My shoulders slumped. "Okay, so much for that theory," I muttered. Come to think of it, maybe I'd been too quick to latch onto it anyway. After all, those threatening notes didn't really fit either. Why would someone targeting Dana leave them in such obscure spots, knowing that Payton might not even tell her trainer about them?

Ned stifled a yawn. "Okay, back to the drawing board, I guess," he said. "Maybe we should all head home and sleep on it."

"But what about your date?" Payton sounded worried as we headed toward the parking lot. "I didn't mean to ruin it."

"It's okay, we were almost finished anyway," I said.

"Yeah." Ned grinned at Payton. "Although I was kind of looking forward to dessert. You can make it up to me by giving me half of yours next time our families go out together."

That actually made Payton laugh. "It's a deal."

The next morning I arrived at the show bright and early. Bess and George were with me, though George wasn't particularly happy about it.

"I can't believe people voluntarily wake up this early," she mumbled, stifling a yawn as the three of us walked along the path leading toward Dana's barn.

"Get over it," Bess told her cousin. "The Grand Prix is tonight, and we need to figure out before then who's trying to sabotage Payton."

"That's right," I agreed. "We don't want this hanging over Payton's head on the biggest night of her riding life. Otherwise she might not ride her best in front of the Olympics guy."

"Okay, okay, you're right," George admitted. "So what's the plan?"

"Good question. I can't stop thinking about Cal Kidd," I said.

Bess and George traded a look. I'd filled them in on last night's events on the ride over.

"I thought you ruled that out when you found out Payton signs her own entries," Bess said.

"Right. But here's the thing. What if Cal actually doesn't know she does that?" I kicked at a stone on the path. "Payton seemed convinced that everybody knows, but I'm not sure we should assume anything."

"I suppose it's worth checking into," George said. "So you still think Cal might be getting revenge on Dana?"

"Maybe. I can't stop thinking about what Mickey said about seeing Cal sneaking around the barn the other night. Why would he be there if he's not our culprit?"

"Unless Mickey is lying about that to throw suspicion off himself," Bess suggested.

"Even if it's true, how do you know it's Dana Cal is after?" George put in. "I still think he could be after Payton because of the Midnight connection."

I glanced at her. "You know, I almost forgot about that. Probably because while we were talking about Cal last night, Payton never even mentioned that he used to own Midnight."

"Why would she?" George shrugged. "It's old news, at least to her. But what if it's Cal's real motive? What if he's targeting Payton because he wants his star horse back, and he figures scaring her out of the saddle is the best way to do it?"

"Except that Midnight wasn't his star horse," Bess reminded us. "He wasn't anything special until Payton bought him."

"I still think we should go question Cal," George said. "He's looking like our best suspect either way."

"I've got a better idea." I pointed toward the ring we were passing. "Isn't that Dana over by the rail? Let's go ask her about Cal. At least she should be able to tell us if it's true that he wanted to train with her. And maybe what the deal was with him and Midnight."

We hurried over and joined Dana. She was watching as a stout woman trotted an even stouter horse around the ring.

"Heels down, Sue!" Dana called out. Then she noticed us. "Oh, hello, girls."

"Hi," I said. "We were just wondering something."

Dana didn't seem to hear me. "More impulsion!" she yelled at the woman. "He's moving like a slug, not a horse!"

"Sorry!" the woman's cheerful voice drifted back.

I watched as the rider kicked at the horse's sides.

The horse totally ignored her, trucking along at the same leisurely pace.

Dana sighed, then glanced at us. "What was that?" she said. "Did you girls say something?"

"I wanted to ask you about someone I met yesterday," I said, trying to sound casual. "His name's Cal Kidd."

Dana stiffened. "Cal? What about him?"

"We heard you might know him," George spoke up. "That he might even have wanted to train with you?"

Instead of answering, Dana turned back to face her student. "That's enough for today, Sue!" she hollered. "I've got to go."

"What?" The woman sounded surprised. "But we haven't even warmed up yet!"

"Wait," I said. "I just want to . . ."

I let my voice trail off. It was too late. Dana was already hurrying off without a backward glance.

"Okay, that was weird," George said. "As soon as you mentioned Cal's name, she totally freaked out."

Bess nodded. "So what do we do now?"

I wasn't sure. My phone buzzed, and I answered without bothering to check the caller ID. "Hello?"

"Nancy? Is this Nancy Drew?"

It was a woman's voice I didn't recognize. "Yes, this is Nancy," I said cautiously. "Who's this?"

There was a funny noise from the other end of the line. It sounded like a sob.

I pressed the phone to my ear. "Hello?"

"Nancy!" the voice gasped out again. "This is Annie—Annie Molina? We talked yesterday?"

"Yes, I remember," I said, perplexed.

Annie choked back another sob. "S-sorry to b-bother you," she wailed. "But I had to call someone, and you're the only person at the show whose name I know, and well . . . I just want to confess!"

CHAPTER ELEVEN

The Evans Edge

"THERE SHE IS." GEORGE POINTED OUT through the main gate.

Shading my eyes against the morning sun, I looked that way. Annie Molina was hurrying to meet us. My heart pounded. Could this really be so easy? Was Annie about to solve the case for us by confessing?

"Nancy!" the woman blubbered. She was a mess. Mascara dripped down her splotchy cheeks, and more tears were welling up in her eyes. "I'm so glad I tracked you down. I feel just terrible about all this!"

"Okay," I said. "Why don't you tell us about it?"

Annie nodded, wiping her nose on her sleeve. "I just wanted to help the animals," she said. "And horses are so darling and magical—when I read on PAN's website that they were coming here to protest, I just knew I had to help."

"So this was the first horse show you protested with them?" George asked. "Or was there another one a few weeks or so ago?"

Annie blinked at George as if wondering who she was. "No, this was my first one," she said. "I'd never worked with PAN before. They don't come to this area much."

"But this time they decided to come and protest the River Heights Horse Show," I prompted, poking George in the side to shut her up. I didn't want her questions to confuse Annie, who seemed a little confused already. "So you joined in to try to help the horses."

"That's right." Annie sniffled loudly. "Only I thought we'd just be carrying signs and so forth. It was bad enough when Bill threw that tomato, but then yesterday—oh, dear!" She shuddered.

"Yesterday?" I said.

Annie nodded. "I swear, I only distracted the guard so the others could sneak in," she insisted, the tears starting to flow again. "I didn't even want to do that—the whole plan just seemed too risky—but they convinced me that none of the horses would be hurt!"

"Hold it." I was starting to catch on. "You're talking about those horses getting loose from their stalls, right? Your PAN buddies were the ones who let them out?"

"That's right." Annie pulled a wadded-up tissue out of her pocket and dabbed at her eyes. "Oh, I'm just so glad nothing terrible happened! Even so, I couldn't rest all night. What if one of those beautiful creatures had been hurt? I just couldn't live with myself if we'd caused any real trouble!" She shook her head. "That's not what I thought PAN was all about!"

As far as I knew, that was *exactly* what PAN was all about. But I didn't bother to say so.

"I see," I said. "So what about the other incidents?"

"What other incidents?" Annie looked worried.

"Did something else happen? I just got here myself."
She stared wildly around the parking lot.

"So you don't know anything about Payton Evans
and her horse's drug test?" Bess put in.

"Who?" Annie said blankly.

Yeah. Maybe Annie wasn't going to solve the case
for me after all. All she was confessing to was the
loose-horse incident and the tomato throwing.

Just to make sure, we asked her a few more questions. But it soon became clear that we were wasting
our time.

After that, it took several minutes to extricate ourselves from Annie's sobbing confession. But finally my
friends and I escaped into the show grounds.

"Okay, that was a waste of time," George said as we
walked past the snack bar.

"Not really," Bess pointed out. "At least now we
know for sure that the tomato thing and the loose
horses are red herrings."

I nodded. "And I think we can cross Annie and PAN
off the list for the other stuff. It's pretty obvious they're

not organized enough to pull off anything too devious."

"Great." George clapped her hands. "Then what are we waiting for? Let's go find our other suspects!"

We spent the next few hours wandering around the show grounds, trying to do just that. Unfortunately, luck seemed to be against us. When we finally located Cal Kidd, he was schooling one of his horses in an out-of-the-way ring. We wasted at least half an hour watching him before giving up and moving on to Lenny Hood. But when we tracked him down, he was surrounded by students—and seemed to be staying that way. As for Dana, she appeared to be actively avoiding us. Was it because of our questions about Cal, or just because she was busy? It was hard to tell.

"This is ridiculous," George said as we leaned on a fence and watched Lenny canter an ornery-looking chestnut over a low fence while the horse's young rider watched from nearby. "The Grand Prix is starting in about an hour, and we haven't made any progress at all!"

"I know." I checked my watch. "Let's go see how Payton's holding up."

Halfway to the barn, we heard shouts coming from behind a shed. Bess looked worried. "That sounds like Dana," she said.

"Exactly what I was thinking." Putting a finger to my lips, I gestured for them to follow as I crept closer to the shed. Dana was still yelling—something about her reputation and how she didn't want to look bad.

". . . and trust me, having you hanging around all the time isn't doing me any favors!" she finished.

By then I was close enough to peek around the edge of the shed. I carefully did so, expecting to see Payton cringing before Dana's fury.

But Payton was nowhere in sight. My jaw dropped when I saw who was facing off against Dana. It was Cal Kidd!

"Whoa!" George breathed in my ear.

I shot her a warning glance. Luckily, Dana hadn't heard a thing. She was glaring at Cal.

"So what do you have to say for yourself?" she demanded.

"I don't know why you're so mad at me," Cal said

in a surly tone. "I'm the one who should be mad. I mean, what kind of person won't even help out her own brother when he needs a hand?"

"*Half* brother," Dana snapped. "And as usual, you're not listening to me. I don't care if we're family—I'm not going to be your shortcut back into the show world. Not until you prove to me that you've cleaned up your act for good." She poked a finger in his face. "And bad-mouthing Payton all over the place isn't helping your cause. I don't care *how* badly she beats you in every class!"

I stepped back, pushing my friends with me. My head was spinning with what I'd just heard.

"I can't believe this," Bess exclaimed once we were safely away. "Dana and Cal are brother and sister?"

"*Half* brother and sister," George corrected. "And now that she mentions it, I can sort of see the family resemblance."

I didn't say anything for a second. What did this mean? As far as I could tell, it just added one more wrinkle to an already rumpled and confusing case.

"Do you think they could be in cahoots?" I wondered at last.

"Dana and Cal?" Bess shrugged. "Maybe."

George glanced back toward the shed. "Although they didn't sound too chummy just now," she added. "Dana actually seemed upset that Cal doesn't like Payton."

"This probably explains why Cal was hanging around Dana's stalls the other night," I mused. "And why he wouldn't tell Mickey what he was doing there. He must've been trying to catch Dana alone to try to talk her into training him or whatever."

"So you don't think he has anything to do with our case?" Bess asked.

"I didn't say that. We *did* see him freak out after Payton did so well in that jumper class they were both in. And there's still the Midnight connection." I rubbed my forehead as if trying to jump-start my brain. The more information we got, the more muddled this case seemed.

We continued to discuss it as we resumed our walk.

Unfortunately, we didn't reach any new conclusions, and by the time we neared Dana's barn, I was feeling frustrated. Why couldn't I figure this one out? I had several distinct and troubling incidents, several promising suspects. But none of the pieces fit together!

When we reached Dana's section of the barn, we saw a horse cross-tied in the aisle. Jen was hard at work currying the animal's already spotless gray coat.

"Hi," I said as we reached her. "Have you seen Payton lately?"

The young groom looked up with a smile. "I think I saw her go into the tack stall," she said, gesturing with the curry comb she was holding. "She's probably getting ready to tack up for the Grand Prix."

"Thanks." I led the way toward the tack stall.

"You're not planning to talk to Payton about the case, are you, Nancy?" Bess asked as soon as we were out of the groom's earshot. "Because she probably needs to focus right now with the Grand Prix coming up so soon."

I frowned, realizing she was right. "Okay, we'll just wish her luck and then leave her alone." I sighed. "At this point it's probably too late to solve this before the Grand Prix anyway."

"That's the spirit," George joked.

I was rolling my eyes at her as we stepped into the tack stall. Out of the corner of one of those rolling eyes, I saw Payton bent over a saddle rack. She jerked back in surprise and straightened up when she heard us.

"Oh!" she exclaimed. "You startled me."

"Sorry." Noticing that she was holding a pocket-knife with the blade open, I glanced at the rack in front of her. It held a saddle with a white pad and leather girth slung over the seat. "What are you doing?"

"Nothing," she said, reaching over to fiddle with the pad. Then she glanced at the knife. "I mean, I was just scraping some dried mud off my backup saddle, since my regular one got ruined. Dana doesn't like seeing dirty tack, especially in the bigger classes." She smiled weakly, then snapped the knife shut.

"Speaking of your ruined saddle, where did that knife come from?" Bess stared at it. "Did you leave it anywhere that someone could find it?"

Realizing what she was driving at, I shot her a smirk. "I thought we weren't going to bug Payton about the case before her big class, detective," I joked.

"Sorry, you're right," Bess said quickly. "Don't pay any attention to me, Payton."

"No, it's okay." Payton smiled uncertainly. "Um, this isn't my knife. I just borrowed it from one of the grooms. They all keep them around to cut hay twine and stuff."

That made sense. "So whoever slashed your other saddle probably didn't have any trouble finding a knife to do it with." I shook my head. "Just one more clue that's not as useful as it seems, I guess."

Just then Jen stuck her head into the room. "Payton," she said. "Dana just texted me to see where you are. She wants to start warming you and Midnight up in ten minutes. Should I text Mickey so he can come help you tack up?"

"No thanks, I've got it. Tell Dana I'm on my way." Grabbing the saddle and other stuff off the rack, Payton headed for the door.

"Good luck!" my friends and I called in unison.

"Thanks!" She tossed us one last smile, then disappeared.

Bess perched on the edge of a tack trunk. "We should probably find Ned and then grab seats for the Grand Prix before it gets crowded."

"Yeah." George sounded distracted. She bent down and picked something up from under the empty saddle rack Payton had been using. "Hey, no fair!" she complained, holding up an empty candy wrapper. "Payton was eating a Chocominto bar and didn't share!"

I grinned. Chocomintos were George's favorite candy. "Too bad for you," I said. "But how do you know it was even Payton who dropped that wrapper? We didn't see her eating any candy. She didn't even have chocolate smeared around her mouth like you always get when you pig out on those things."

George made a face at me. "You know, sometimes having a detective for a friend is a real drag." Tossing the candy wrapper into the trash bin in the corner, she headed for the door. "Let's go. I want to make sure we have good seats for the Grand Prix."

...

"Wow," Ned said. "So Dana and Cal are related? That's wild."

"Shh. It seems to be some kind of secret—I don't think even Payton knows." I glanced around to make sure nobody had overheard. Luckily, the people sitting in the stands around us were all focused on their own conversations. Everyone seemed excited for the start of the Grand Prix.

The bleachers set up around the main ring were crowded and getting more so every minute. My friends and I had arrived early enough to snag seats in the second row, which gave us a spectacular view of the course. The huge, colorful jumps had actually taken my mind off the case for a few minutes. There were brightly colored rails, a fake brick wall, even a pair of jump standards shaped like riverboats in honor of our town's riverside heritage.

"It's hard to believe someone we know is actually going to jump a horse over those, huh?" Bess said, her gaze wandering to the jumps.

"Yeah." I shivered with anticipation. "I just hope Payton isn't distracted by everything that's happened." I glanced around, wondering where the Olympic chef d'équipe was sitting.

"Payton seems like a pretty cool customer when it comes to competing," George said. "I'm sure she'll be fine."

"Still, I wish we could've figured out this case before now." I sighed.

"Me too," Ned agreed. Bess, George, and I had just finished filling him in on everything that had happened that day—not that there was much to tell. "So back to Cal—if he's Dana's brother, does this mean he's off the suspect list?"

"No way," George said. "He might still want Midnight back. What better way to make a big splash in his return to show jumping than by riding a star horse? There's your motive right there. And Cal definitely had the opportunity to do most of the bad stuff, since nobody would think twice about seeing him around the barn. He could've easily slipped something into Midnight's feed bucket. And slashed Payton's saddle, too."

"So could Lenny Hood," I said. "Or Jessica Watts. Or Dana herself. Or Mickey." I shook my head. "The thing that keeps bugging me is those threatening notes—especially the second one."

"What do you mean?" Bess asked.

"I mean, I can see how most of our suspects might be able to figure out which car belonged to Payton's family and leave a note there." I glanced around at my friends. "But how in the world would any of them know she was staying at Ned's—or that she'd ever find a note left inside the beat-up old grill at his house?"

"Don't let my dad hear you talk about Bertha that way," Ned joked. Then his expression went serious again. "But actually, that's a good point, Nancy."

"Maybe someone at the show overheard us talking about the barbecue," Bess suggested.

"I suppose it's possible. Although that makes it more likely to be Dana or Mickey, right? Do you remember seeing either of them hanging around while we were talking about the barbecue?" I asked.

George shrugged. "I don't even remember when we mentioned the barbecue."

Just then the crowd roared as the first rider entered the ring. "It's starting," Ned said. "We'll have to talk about this later."

For the next half hour, I did my best to focus on the action. The Grand Prix was exciting, but I couldn't help feeling distracted. Why couldn't I crack this case? There had to be something I was missing. . . .

I tuned back in when I heard the crowd gasp. An older male rider on a fractious black horse had just knocked down the top pole on a jump. Another jump was coming up fast, and the horse was racing forward with its head straight up in the air, looking completely out of control. Sure enough, it veered sideways as it approached the next obstacle, a large, solid-looking jump with a pair of fake stone columns as standards.

"Oh!" I exclaimed along with everyone else as the horse crashed sideways into one of the columns, sending it flying. The horse stumbled over a pole and almost went down. The rider came off, hitting the ground hard and rolling out of the way of his mount's flying hooves.

"Yikes," Bess said. "I hope the rider's okay."

"He's already getting up." I clutched the edge of my seat and leaned forward, my gaze shifting back to the horse. It leaped over the scattered poles and glanced off the other standard, knocking that one over as well. Then it started galloping wildly around the ring, reins and stirrups flying, veering around the people who hurried in to try to catch it. Everyone gasped again as the horse headed for one of the other jumps, leaping over it wildly and knocking down a couple of more poles.

George squinted down toward the in-gate. "Check it out, there's Payton. Let's hope Midnight doesn't see that other horse and get any ideas, huh?"

I turned to look. Payton was riding Midnight toward the gate. The big gelding looked magnificent— his bay coat gleamed, set off by his crisp white saddle pad. Dana was scurrying along beside the horse, talking a mile a minute, though we were way too far away to hear what she was saying.

Payton halted a few steps from the gate, watching with everyone else as the people in the ring finally caught the black horse. Meanwhile Dana stepped toward Midnight's midsection, her hand reaching to move Payton's leg aside. But Payton nudged her trainer's hand away with her boot, then swung the horse aside and leaned forward from the saddle, slipping her own hand under the girth. I was too far away to see clearly, but I was pretty sure Dana had a frown on her face, though she stepped back as Payton straightened up again.

My friends were watching too. "What was that all about?" Ned wondered.

"Dana was trying to double-check that the girth is tight enough, I think," I said. "When I was a kid, my riding teacher used to do that before I rode. It's a safety thing—you don't want the girth to be too loose, or your saddle might slip."

"I guess Payton wanted to check it herself," Bess said. "Maybe she's still mad at Dana from that blowup we overheard yesterday."

"I wouldn't blame her," George put in.

"Maybe that's it." I frowned slightly as I glanced from Payton to Dana. "Or maybe there's a reason Payton doesn't trust Dana when it comes to her safety equipment."

Ned shot me a worried look. "Do you think so?"

"It might be worth asking Payton about later," I answered thoughtfully.

"Hey, Ned, here come your parents." Bess pointed.

Ned stood for a better look. "Payton's folks are with them," he said. "That's good—Mom was afraid their plane would be delayed and they'd miss Payton's big moment."

Cupping his hands around his mouth, he called out to his parents, then waved so they could see where he was sitting. Moments later, the Nickersons and Payton's parents were squeezing in beside us. Mr. Evans was a big man with a booming laugh, while Dr. Evans was petite and delicate-looking like her daughter.

"Made it in the nick of time!" Dr. Evans exclaimed, peering down at the ring.

Mr. Nickerson nodded. "Looks like Payton's on deck."

"Right," I said, glancing out at the ring. The black horse was gone, and Payton was riding in. She started walking Midnight around at the end of the ring as the crew reassembled the jumps the black horse had knocked over.

"She's looking good, isn't she?" Mr. Evans said. "Focused. Strong."

"You must be very proud of her," I said with a smile. "It's amazing that she's competing at this level at her age. That Evans Edge stuff is really working!"

Payton's father chuckled. "She told you about that, eh?"

"Uh-huh. She seems to take it pretty seriously." I couldn't help thinking that a certain aspect of the Evans Edge had almost ended up causing her to be suspended from competing. "Especially the part about signing her own paperwork at the shows instead of having Dana do it."

"Oh, that." Mr. Evans rolled his eyes. "Yeah, that's a pain in the neck if you ask me—it means I've had to fax my signature to every dang show for the past three or four months, since she can't legally sign on her own yet." He smiled and shook his head. "Still, once Payton gets an idea in her head, there's no changing her mind."

His wife heard him and chuckled. "Yes, I wonder where she got that from?" she quipped, reaching over to squeeze her husband's hand.

"Wait a minute," I said, a little confused. "You mean signing as her own trainer was *Payton's* idea? But I thought she said—"

"Look!" Ned exclaimed, cutting me off. "Payton's starting!"

While I was talking with Mr. Evans, the crew had finished rebuilding the jumps. We all watched as Payton finally nudged her horse into a relaxed trot, beginning a big, loopy circle around part of the ring. From watching previous rounds, I knew she was waiting for the buzzer to sound so she could begin.

I glanced over at Mr. Evans, who was chatting with Bess. Why was his last comment bugging me so much? Okay, so Payton put as much pressure on herself as her parents did. That was obvious. It didn't have anything to do with the case—did it?

My mind sorted through the clues and incidents again, looking for patterns. Any of our suspects could be the culprit—right? Except I kept getting stuck on that note in the grill. I tried to picture Lenny Hood following Payton home from the show grounds, then sneaking into the Nickersons' backyard. Or Jessica. Or Cal or Dana or Mickey.

It just didn't compute. How on earth would any of them pull it off? Perhaps more important, *why* would any of them hide a note in such an out-of-the-way place?

There was only one logical answer. They wouldn't. That meant somebody else must have done it.

I glanced over at Dr. Evans and Mrs. Nickerson, who had their heads close together as they chattered and laughed while waiting for Payton's round to start. A new idea crept into my mind. Could it be . . . ?

The buzzer sounded, startling me out of my thoughts.

"Here she goes!" Mr. Evans exclaimed as Payton cantered Midnight around to the end of the ring, picking up speed as she aimed him toward the timer flags.

There was a loud whoop from down by the gate. Glancing that way, I saw Dana standing there, watching Payton.

I gasped as the answer hit me like a horse's hoof to the gut. "Stop!" I shouted, leaping out of my seat so fast I almost tripped over Bess. "Stop her!"

"Nancy!" Mrs. Nickerson cried. "What are you doing?"

The others were gasping and crying out too, but I ignored them. I lunged down the bleachers, almost stepping on the hand of the man sitting in front of me.

"Stop her!" I yelled as loudly as I could, waving both hands over my head. "Please! You have to stop this round!"

CHAPTER TWELVE

⁓

Driven

I RACED FOR THE RING, IGNORING THE shouts and stares from people around me. I had to stop Payton before it was too late.

There were too many people between me and the gate, so I pushed aside some spectators standing at the fence and vaulted over. I was vaguely aware of people running toward me—jump crew, probably, trying to stop the crazy girl from ruining the show—but I had a head start as I dashed across the ring. Midnight was just a few strides out from the first jump on the course, his ears pricked forward. Was I already too late?

"No!" I howled, pushing my legs to pump faster.

Payton heard me and glanced over. A look of confusion crossed her face as she saw me running toward her.

Midnight heard me coming too. He spooked away from me, losing speed as he lurched sideways.

"Go!" Payton urged, kicking the horse to get him moving again.

But the horse's hesitation had given me the time I needed. I threw myself forward, grabbing for the reins. Midnight tossed his head, almost dragging me off my feet. But I held on, and the horse came to a prancing, snorting halt.

"Nancy, what are you doing?" Payton's face was very pale beneath her black riding helmet. "Let go!"

I met her eye, not backing off. "You don't have to do this, you know."

Someone grabbed my shoulder from behind. "Come with me, young lady," a gruff voice said.

Glancing back, I saw a particularly burly member of the jump crew. A man in a suit was hurrying toward me as well—some sort of official, I assumed.

"Get her out of here," the official snapped. He glanced up at Payton. "I'm sorry about this, Ms. Evans. If you need a moment to regroup or settle your horse, of course it's no problem."

"What's going on?" Dana demanded, rushing over to us. "Payton, are you okay?" Without waiting for an answer, she whirled to glare at me. "What in the world are you doing?" She shoved me back away from Midnight and grabbed his reins herself, running her free hand down the horse's neck soothingly. Then she glanced at the jump-crew guy. "Get her out of here already!"

"Wait." I resisted as the guy started to pull me away. "Look at this, Dana."

Slipping out of the man's grasp, I stepped forward and slid my hand under the girth, giving it a hard yank.

SNAP! It broke apart just under the saddle flap. The loose end flopped down against Midnight's front legs, making him jump in surprise.

"Whoa!" Dana exclaimed, her eyes going wide with alarm as Payton's saddle, suddenly left with nothing but gravity holding it on the horse's back, slipped to one side. "Easy, boy . . ."

I stepped back, shoulders slumping. My hunch had been right. I sort of wished it hadn't been.

Dana managed to keep Midnight still long enough for Payton to slide down before the saddle could slip any further. Then the trainer grabbed the girth for a closer look, her expression going grim as she examined it.

"It looks like this girth was cut almost all the way through. If it had broken while Payton was going over a jump . . . But how did this happen?" she blustered. "I always check all tack myself before my clients go in for—oh. Wait." She shot Payton a confused look. "Except this time I didn't . . ."

"Let's get out of here," I urged, suddenly aware of the murmurs of the crowd as they watched. "We don't need an audience for this." Noticing that the jump-crew guy was moving toward me again, I gulped. "Um, Dana, can you tell them to back off? Please? I can explain."

Dana frowned at me, seeming undecided for a second. Finally she shrugged. "It's okay," she told the men. "I'll sort it out and let you know if we need help."

By the time we got out of the ring, my friends, the Nickersons, and Payton's parents were waiting for us. "What happened?" Dr. Evans cried, wrapping her daughter in a hug.

"Oh my gosh, Payton!" Bess exclaimed at the same time. "If your girth had broken over the top of one of those huge jumps, you could've been killed!"

George was staring at me. "Nancy, how did you know that was going to happen?"

"Because I finally figured out who's behind everything that's been happening," I said.

Ned gasped. "You mean the same person who drugged Midnight and slashed Payton's saddle did this, too? Messed with her girth so she'd fall off?"

"That's cold!" George shot Dana a suspicious glance. "So who was it?"

"Not any of the people you're thinking of." I turned and gave Payton a meaningful look.

She met my eye, her lower lip trembling slightly. Then she nodded and squared her shoulders.

"It was me," she said. "I did it. All of it."

"What?" several voices exclaimed at once.

"That's right. I messed up my girth, and my saddle, too." Payton took a deep breath. "And I fed Midnight chocolate to make him flunk that drug test."

Dana looked grim. "Payton, you're the *last* person I ever thought would cheat to give yourself an edge."

"That's not why I did it!" Payton protested quickly. She pulled off her helmet. "Please, just let me explain." She shot her parents an unreadable look.

"Payton?" her father prompted. "What's this about?"

"I just wanted a break, you know?" Payton blurted out. Her eyes filled with tears. "From the pressure, the need to be the best at all costs. From not having a life outside of showing. From always being afraid I was going to let someone down." She paused. "And especially from feeling like I was pushing my horses way too hard. Especially this guy."

Midnight had turned his head to stare at the ring as another horse-and-rider pair entered. At Payton's touch, he turned and nuzzled her hair, the rings of his bit clanking against her head.

There was a babble of voices, some confused and some angry, as everyone reacted to Payton's revelation. I ignored them, watching Payton.

"So you decided to frame yourself," I said. "Make everyone think you were in danger so they'd let you quit. Maybe even *insist* you quit."

Payton ran her fingers lightly over Midnight's face. "That wasn't my first plan," she said. "First I tried to get myself suspended. I've been slipping chocolate to any of my horses that'll eat it for months."

"Ever since you first started signing as your own trainer?" I guessed.

She nodded. "I definitely didn't want Dana to get in trouble. . . ."

After that, the words poured out of her like water out of a broken dam. At first she'd been willing to wait however long it took for one of her "drugged" horses to be selected for random drug testing. But then the chef d'équipe had announced that he was coming to the River Heights show—and Payton's parents and Dana insisted that Payton skip her cousin's wedding to attend.

That had made Payton desperate enough to plant that note on her father's car. That hadn't done the trick either, obviously. Payton ended up in River Heights anyway. Even so, she'd decided to do whatever it took to avoid riding in front of the chef d'équipe, which she seemed to see as the point of no return. First she'd called in that anonymous tip to the stewards about herself. Then she'd sneaked the second note into the grill, hoping that when Mrs. Nickerson saw it, she'd put pressure on her old friend to pull Payton from the show.

That didn't work either, so next Payton slashed her own saddle. She tried calling Ned and me, pretending a shadowy man was stalking her. She even let the news about Midnight's drug test slip to Jessica Watts, knowing the gossip would be all over the show grounds in a heartbeat, which Payton hoped would influence the decision of the officials.

But when even the long-awaited failed drug test failed to stop her from reaching the Grand Prix ring, Payton had really panicked.

"I didn't want to hurt Midnight," she said, still stroking her horse's neck. "So I figured it was going to have to be me."

Dr. Evans gasped. "Oh, Payton . . ."

"So that's what you were doing when we came into the tack room earlier," George said. "You weren't cleaning dirt off your saddle with that knife. You were using it to slice through your girth."

Payton nodded. "You guys almost caught me."

Mr. Evans looked grim. "I wish you'd come to us about all of this, Payton."

"I'm sorry, Daddy," Payton whispered. She looked around at all of us, her gaze finally settling on Dana. "I'm really, really sorry. For everything."

Dana looked uncertain. "Payton . . ."

"Will you take Midnight back to the barn for me?"

Payton asked her trainer. "Please? I left some carrots for him in my tack trunk." She stroked the horse's face one more time. "No more Chocomintos for you, buddy."

Mr. Evans turned to face me. "Thank you for stopping her, young lady," he said. "I—we—really appreciate it. If she'd gone through with her crazy plan . . ." His voice trailed off as he glanced at his daughter with a hint of uncertainty in his eyes. "Well, thanks. Now if you'll all excuse us, I think it's time we had a serious family talk."

"Are you sure you're not in the mood for brunch?" I poked my head into my father's home office. "I could call and see if they have a table for us at that little café on River Street. You love that place."

Dad glanced up from his computer. "Sorry, Nancy," he said. "I already told you, I've got to get through these briefs before tomorrow."

I frowned, feeling restless. That often happened after I wrapped up a tough case. Not that this one felt very wrapped up. Sure, I'd figured out who was behind all the mischief. But what was going to happen with Payton's riding career now? That remained a mystery.

"Well, maybe I'll just go out for a run, then," I said, turning away.

"Wait," Dad said. I spun around, hoping my father had changed his mind about brunch. But he was frowning slightly. "Actually, would you mind tossing a load into the washer? I'm all out of clean socks, and since it's Hannah's day off today . . ."

I sighed loudly. It was a beautiful day, and I wasn't in the mood for laundry. Still, Dad rarely asked me to pitch in with extra housework, since our housekeeper, Hannah Gruen, took care of most of it. So I didn't feel right saying no.

"Sure," I said. "I'll go take care of it right now."

I trudged upstairs to grab the hamper. The doorbell rang when I was halfway back down the stairs.

"I'll get it!" I shouted in the general direction of Dad's office. Hurrying over to the front door, I swung it open. "Payton!" I blurted out in surprise.

Payton smiled at me. "Hi, Nancy," she said. "Hope

you don't mind me stopping by without calling first."

"No, not at all." I stepped aside. "Would you like to come in?"

"Actually, I was wondering if you wanted to go for a ride." Payton waved a hand at the car parked by the curb. "My parents are letting me use their rental car, and I could use a change of scenery. And someone to talk to."

"Sure. Let me grab my purse."

Soon we were on the road. I wasn't sure where Payton was heading, and I didn't ask. It didn't really matter.

"So I wanted to say thanks," Payton said as she eased the car to a stop at a traffic light. "I mean, at first I was kind of mad at you for stopping me. But it was the right thing to do." She shot me a look. "I guess I went a little crazy."

"I understand," I said. "And you're welcome."

She drove across the intersection as the light turned green. "Anyway, my mom calls what I did a 'cry for help.' I think that means she thinks I wanted to get caught." She shook her head. "I just couldn't think of another way to get my parents' attention—to convince them to let me slow down. They don't believe in giving up on anything they start."

"The Evans Edge," I murmured.

She nodded. "Right. That edge can be sharp, I guess. Anyway, they're paying attention now. I think they're starting to understand how I feel. Or at least trying."

"So they're going to let you give up showing?"

"If that's what I want." Payton hesitated. "I'm not sure if I want to give it up for good. I mean, I used to love it."

She glanced out the side window. We were heading out of town by now, passing by larger properties and small farms. Horses were grazing in some of the fields we were passing.

"Giving up showing doesn't mean giving up horses, does it?" I asked.

"That's exactly what I've been thinking," Payton said. "I think I'm going to take a break from competition and try just riding for fun for a while. See if I can remember what I used to love about it."

She hit the turn signal. There was no intersection in sight—just an unmarked gravel driveway.

"Where are we going?" I asked.

"You'll see." She smiled as she spun the wheel to turn into the driveway.

I glanced down the lane. It ended at a cute little red barn. Was Payton planning to start rediscovering the joy of riding right now?

Payton brought the car to a stop near the barn. "Look!" she said.

I looked where she was pointing. My jaw dropped as a gorgeous horse and carriage came into view. A woman I didn't recognize was holding the reins. Sitting beside her was someone I *definitely* recognized.

"Ned!" I blurted out.

Payton grinned. "Surprise!"

"What? But I don't understand . . . ," I began.

"It's your anniversary gift," she explained as we both climbed out of the car. "Dana knows the woman who owns this place. I know I ruined your dinner the other night, and Ned mentioned that it was originally supposed to be a picnic. So I figured I'd help him arrange a nice, romantic makeup picnic today."

"Oh!" Suddenly something else made a lot more sense. "Wait—was my dad in on this too, by any chance? Was that why he wouldn't let me leave the house?"

Payton nodded, still grinning. "Don't worry, she's definitely surprised," she called to Ned proudly as we approached the carriage.

"Impressive. It's not easy to pull one over on River Heights's greatest young sleuth." Ned winked at her.

I laughed. "Yeah, you got me," I admitted. "And I love it!"

Payton stepped over to pat the horse, a stocky palomino with a sweet face. "Well, what are you waiting for, Nancy? Your carriage awaits!"

"Thanks, Payton." I smiled at her, glad to see real happiness in her face as she patted the horse. I hoped she would be able to rediscover the joy in riding—and maybe even in showing. Considering some of the characters I'd met over the past few days, I had a feeling the show circuit needed as many people like her as possible.

But I wasn't going to focus on that right now. I took the hand Ned was offering me, climbing up into the carriage.

"Ready to ride off into the sunset with me?" Ned asked, squeezing my hand. "Or at least the midday sun?"

I squeezed back. "I'm ready."

Dear Diary

POOR PEYTON.

The pressure she was under to perform and be number one was too much for her. It would have been too much for anybody, really. It's too bad she just couldn't talk to her parents and tell them how she truly felt.

But harming Midnight sure wasn't the answer.

Hurting anybody—or anything—never is.

READ WHAT HAPPENS IN THE NEXT MYSTERY
IN THE NANCY DREW DIARIES,

Once Upon a Thriller

AS WE HEADED OUT TO THE CAR, GEORGE and I quickly filled Bess in on what she had missed.

"Weird!" Bess exclaimed. "What do you think 'nine-one-fourteen' means?"

"I don't know," I replied. "Some sort of a code? A date?"

"September first, 2014," George stated matter-of-factly.

"Could be," I mused.

We drove back to the cabin in silence, mulling it

over. Then we unloaded our groceries and put every-thing in the fridge, put on our bathing suits, shorts, and tank tops, and headed outside. Bess unlocked the equipment shed near the cabin, and retrieved the paddles while George and I carried the canoe down to the tiny stretch of rocky sand just behind our cabin.

Bess pulled a bright orange life vest over her head, then handed one each to George and me.

"Ugh," she sighed. "Why do they have to make these so ugly?"

"So they can be spotted in a storm," I replied simply.

"Thanks, supersleuth," Bess joked. "It was a rhetorical question, though."

She squinted at the sky as she donned her life vest. "Speaking of storms, it looks a little dark off in the distance, doesn't it?" she asked. "Maybe we should wait until tomorrow to take out the canoe."

She was right—the sky above the horizon was defi-nitely gray. I pulled out my phone to check the weather.

"Well, there's no rain predicted for this afternoon,"

I assured her. "I think we should be okay. And I'm really curious to check out Lacey O'Brien's cabin."

"I'm not sure I agree, but all right," Bess grumbled. George just shrugged and followed us down to the shore. We climbed into the canoe and pushed off. As George and Bess paddled, I looked around at the many different green shades of the trees next to deep blue of the water. It should have been soothing scenery, but it wasn't.

I couldn't turn off my brain.

"Stop fidgeting, Nancy. What are you thinking about anyway?" Bess asked.

"Just the bookstore fire," I replied. "I'm really curious to hear what the fire department says. Paige seemed awfully certain it was accidental, but I'm not so sure. And she seemed so jumpy when I picked up that slip of paper. And where was Lacey O'Brien's this morning. I know she's a recluse, but why didn't she shown up for her book signing?"

Bess nodded. "Good questions."

I continued. "And what about Alice Ann? I

overheard her talking to the baker in front of the Cheshire Cat before I bought the books, and she didn't seem particularly fond of Paige or Lacey."

"Wait, who's Alice Ann?" George asked. She handed the paddle to me as we carefully switched places.

"That woman at the inn who returned my wallet and gave us directions to Lacey O'Brien's cabin," I explained as I started paddling.

"Oh, right," George answered. Then she glanced down at her phone, which was open to a compass app. "Speaking of directions, that's the northwest corner of the lake right there."

George looked from her phone back up at the gray sky.

"I'm wondering if maybe we should turn back, though," she said worriedly. "It's gotten a lot darker and my hair's suddenly standing on end because of all the static electricity in the air. I don't like the idea of being on the water in a lightning storm, no matter who we're looking for."

"I agree," Bess said nervously. "And the wind is

changing—I can feel it. I'm getting goose pimples on my arms."

The sky definitely did look more menacing than it had before, but suddenly I caught a glimpse of a dark figure on the beach.

"Look!" I cried out. "Over there on the beach. You think it's Lacey O'Brien?"

I gave George and Bess a pleading look.

"We're actually closer to this shore of the lake now than we are to our cabin," George said with a sigh. "I'd rather be near the shore—any shore—than in the middle of the lake if we do run into trouble."

"Maybe . . ." I began. "Maybe we can land on the beach there and ask for some temporary shelter if it starts to storm."

Bess sighed.

"You're both right," she agreed. "But next time you'll listen to me. Turning back now would be more dangerous than going ashore here."

Bess and I paddled hard. The gusts picked up while George gripped the sides of the canoe. The wind was whipping at us from every direction, but there was nothing else to do but press on.

The shadowy figure on the shore loomed larger as we got closer. I put my head down and used all my strength as I pulled on the paddle. The waves were getting bigger, and every time one hit us we rocked unsteadily from side to side.

"Whoa!" Bess cried out.

"Ugh," George moaned. "This rocking motion is making me feel ill."

"Try to keep the canoe cutting through the water perpendicular to the waves!" I called to Bess over the howling wind. "That way we won't tip over."

"Okay!" Bess called back as she and I both maneuvered to turn the canoe so the bow of the boat was slicing through the waves at a right angle. Suddenly the wind changed and a swell of water hit us hard from the left, causing us to tip toward the right.

"Yikes!" Bess screamed. At that moment George pointed to a floating dock that had come up seemingly out of nowhere.

"Nancy! Bess!" she shouted. "Watch out!"

In trying not to hit the dock, Bess and I managed to turn the canoe so that we were once again parallel to the waves. A second later, we were hit from the left with another giant swell.

Before I even realized what was happening, the boat lurched wildly to the right, throwing us into the dark, churning water.

FOR ACTIVITIES, STICKERS, AND MORE, JOIN THE ACADEMY AT GODDESSGIRLSBOOKS.COM!

NANCY DREW DIARIES™

Once Upon a Thriller

#4

CAROLYN KEENE

Aladdin

NEW YORK LONDON TORONTO SYDNEY NEW DELHI

ALADDIN

An imprint of Simon & Schuster Children's Publishing Division

1230 Avenue of the Americas, New York, NY 10020

First Aladdin paperback edition September 2013

Copyright © 2013 by Simon & Schuster

All rights reserved, including the right of reproduction in whole or in part in any form.

ALADDIN is a trademark of Simon & Schuster, Inc., and related logo is a registered trademark of Simon & Schuster, Inc.

Also available in an Aladdin hardcover edition.

For information about special discounts for bulk purchases, please contact Simon & Schuster Special Sales at 1-866-506-1949 or business@simonandschuster.com.

The Simon & Schuster Speakers Bureau can bring authors to your live event. For more information or to book an event contact the Simon & Schuster Speakers Bureau at 1-866-248-3049 or visit our website at www.simonspeakers.com.

Designed by Karina Granda

The text of this book was set in Adobe Caslon Pro.

Manufactured in the United States of America 0316 OFF

10 9

Library of Congress Control Number 2013944613

ISBN 978-1-4169-9074-1 (pbk)

ISBN 978-1-4424-6612-8 (hc)

ISBN 978-1-4424-6572-5 (eBook)

Contents

Dear Diary,

IT'S NO SURPRISE THAT MY NOSE IS always stuck in a book. I can't get enough of a good biography, historical novel, or fantasy story. But my favorites are edge-of-your-seat, page-turning mystery stories. And when Bess, George, and I were in the middle of a raging storm on Moon Lake, I wished I were just reading a mystery, not smack in the middle of one.

CHAPTER ONE

Burned

"COME ON. HURRY UP AND LET'S GO!" I called to Bess and George as I popped open the trunk of my car. I had parked in front of George's house and was in a rush to get going.

"Leave it to you to be right on time, Nancy," Bess teased as she and George walked down the front steps of the porch and headed toward me, overnight bags in hand. George glanced at her watch.

"Whoa, Bess is right!" George said. "It's nine a.m. on the dot." She grabbed Bess's bag and tossed it and her own into the trunk before slamming it shut.

"Well, that's when I told you I'd be here," I answered. "And I'm really looking forward to getting to the lake early so we can settle into our cabin and go for a hike before it gets too hot."

"Ugh," Bess groaned. "Not a hike! You and George promised me this would be a relaxing weekend."

"And it will be," I said. "A short hike this morning, followed by a canoe ride this afternoon. Then tomorrow we can sleep in and read and relax before we go waterskiing after lunch."

Bess rolled her eyes at me. I could tell she would have preferred spending the entire weekend doing nothing but sitting on the shores of Moon Lake with a magazine and a bottle of nail polish to touch up her manicure and pedicure. But there's no way I could manage that—I would get way too antsy.

Besides the outdoor activities, I also planned to read the latest Miles Whitmore mystery, *Terror on the Trail*. Lately, I couldn't get enough of his books. I never figured out "whodunit" till the very end, and I'm an amateur detective. That's how crafty a writer he is.

I pulled away from George's house and maneuvered my car toward the highway. Once we got going, it was only about fifty miles to Avondale, which is where Moon Lake is located. If we didn't hit any traffic, we'd be there in under an hour.

"We'll make it up to you, Bess," George said. "You have complete control over music for the entire weekend."

"Really?" Bess asked, incredulous. "I'm not sure I believe you. You always hate any group I like."

"Really. I promise," George said. I was impressed. George can be incredibly opinionated when it comes to music. She and Bess are my best friends, and they also happen to be cousins. But the two are as different as Beethoven and The Rolling Stones. Sometimes it's hard to believe they're related.

"Well, I suppose that's something," Bess said with a sigh. She plugged her MP3 into the radio and out blasted Grayson & James, her latest favorite group.

I saw George in the rearview mirror, and I knew she was working hard to restrain herself. I saw her putting on her own headphones to drown out Bess's music.

"I know, I know," Bess half apologized, sensing George's frustration. "But this is great driving music, isn't it, Nancy?"

"I actually like this song," I admitted sheepishly. I was trying to keep the peace between my friends, but I was also being truthful—the song was catchy and fun. And with that, we all settled in to enjoy the ride.

We pulled up to our rental cabin on Moon Lake almost exactly an hour later. Towering green pines surrounded the cabin, and the setting looked inviting. I couldn't wait to get started—within minutes, the car was unpacked and our hiking boots were on.

"I promise it will be a short hike, Bess," I told her as I pulled my hair into a tight ponytail. "Let's just do one loop around the lake. We'll be back in time for lunch."

"All right," Bess grumbled. "Let's get this over with." She tightened the laces on her boots and the three of us headed for the trailhead, which happened to be just a few paces from our cabin.

As we hiked, I took in the beautiful scenery and

tried to let my mind wander. That can be tough for me, as I always have some mystery on my mind—a real one or one in a book.

But this weekend at the lake I really planned to focus on my friends and the great outdoors.

"Right, Nancy?" I heard George say. She was looking at me as though she'd been talking to me for five minutes without a response. Which, come to think of it, was quite possible.

"Oh, uh, sorry, George," I replied. "I guess I was lost in my own world."

"I said, that's our cabin right there, isn't it?" George repeated, pointing to the little wooden structure peeking through the trees a few hundred yards ahead of us.

"It is," I replied, glancing at my watch. "Wow, that was quick." It had taken us less than an hour to hike the three-mile loop around the lake. Even Bess agreed that it had been pleasant and not particularly taxing.

"Great!" George said. "Because I'm ready for Hannah's lunch."

Back at the cabin, I went into the kitchen to get the

basket Hannah had packed for our weekend. Hannah Gruen is my dad's housekeeper, and she loves to keep all of us well fed and nurtured—she's got lots of love to share. I couldn't wait to dig into some of her famous fried chicken and homemade coleslaw.

But the basket was nowhere to be found. Suddenly an image of it popped into my head. It was sitting on the counter—the counter at my house in River Heights, that is.

"Bad news," I groaned. "I left the lunch basket Hannah packed for us at home."

"That's because you were rushing like crazy to get up here," George said. "What's my stomach supposed to do?" she joked.

Bess smiled broadly. "I guess we'll just have to make a trip into town, then," she suggested. "It's not far away, and I'm pretty sure Avondale has a bunch of cafés and cute stores."

She emphasized the word "stores," and knowing Bess, she was eager to squeeze in some shopping along with lunch.

"Great," I agreed. "Because I also left *Terror on the Trail* at home, so now I have nothing to read. Hopefully there's a bookstore in town too."

"Terror on the what?" George asked. "Do you ever stop trying to solve mysteries?" She tapped her tablet, which was perched on a nightstand. "You know, Nancy," she continued, "you wouldn't have this problem if you weren't so resistant to e-books. You could take ten books with you at once."

"As long as she remembered to actually bring the reader," Bess pointed out.

"Ha, ha," I said drily. "But you know what? When it comes to books, I like the feel of the pages in my hands, and even the smell of them."

"That's Nancy," George teased. "Always with her nose in a book—literally. Now let's go—I'm starving!"

Ten minutes later we pulled into the town of Avondale. And Bess was right—there were plenty of quaint stores and shops. But that's not what caught my attention. Two fire trucks were stopped in the middle of the street, and an acrid smell filled the air.

We parked and quickly made our way toward the crowd that had formed.

"Was there a fire?" I asked a man with a golden retriever close by his side.

"Looks that way," he replied, shaking his head and gesturing toward a nearby building. A sign in front of the shop was in the shape of an open book. "And at Paige's Pages, of all places."

Nearby, three young women had their heads together, whispering—but loud enough that we could hear them.

"And now we won't get to meet Lacey O'Brien," one of them said.

"I can't believe it, Carly!" another replied. "And I've read all her mysteries."

That word got my attention. I moved closer to the girls.

"Excuse me," I said. "Do you know what happened? We're just here for the weekend, but what's going on here? I was trying to get to the bookstore, but it looks like that's going to be, uh, difficult."

"We were here for the bookstore too," the first girl replied. "Lacey O'Brien was supposed to do a reading and a book signing—you know, the mystery writer?"

"I've heard of her, sure," I replied.

"She's like a local celebrity around here," the second girl, who had dark, curly hair, said. "Well, except that people hardly ever see her. I heard this book signing was the only one she was doing all year."

"And now we're out of luck, aren't we, Mandy?" the third girl added. "No signing today."

The girls continued chattering, and I took a few steps back. But I could still hear them clearly. In fact, everyone around us could. A firefighter near us was talking with a distraught-looking woman with graying hair who was pointing to the store.

"Did you realize there was a fire in her latest book, *Burned*?" Mandy whisper-shouted to her friends.

"You're right!" Carly answered. "That's a weird coincidence. You don't think Lacey had anything to do with this fire, do you?"

"Well, at least something finally happened here. Nothing exciting or mysterious ever happens in Avondale," Mandy said.

I wouldn't be so sure, I thought. That's what everyone thinks until something actually happens.

At that moment, one of the other firefighters approached us.

"Everyone, please step back," he announced. "We need to get our equipment out of the store."

"Sure, no problem," George said. We all moved back, but Mandy had ideas of her own and went right up to the fireman.

"What happened?" she demanded. "We really, really wanted to see Lacey O'Brien today. And now we might have to wait another year until we do."

I could have sworn the fireman rolled his eyes. But he patiently answered her question. "From our initial investigation, it looks like some faulty wiring in an old chandelier," he replied. "That happens a lot in older buildings like this one."

Mandy gasped. "It does?" she asked, an amazed

look on her face. "Because that's exactly how the fire started in Lacey O'Brien's last book! Except the wiring in the chandelier hadn't really caused the fire. It was arson!"

CHAPTER TWO

The Missing Wallet

I TURNED TO GEORGE AND BESS TO SEE if they had been listening. One glance at their faces told me they had heard everything. In fact, there was an almost collective gasp from the crowd around us.

"Hmm," the firefighter replied. "That's very interesting. But until we do a more complete investigation, we can't make that assumption, miss."

Mandy turned back to her friends. "Well, I can, and I will," she whispered to them.

The crowd broke up and Bess, George, and I walked slowly down the main street.

George cleared her throat. "Nancy, if this is arson, then it's really none of our business, right?" she began. "We can just go about our weekend plans, can't we?"

"Without you looking under every rock," Bess chimed in.

My mouth dropped open, but I wasn't really surprised. My friends knew me better than anyone, except maybe for Ned. And they knew it would be close to impossible for me to resist a suspicious fire and a well-known writer who happened to specialize in mysteries.

"I guess I'm an open book," I agreed with a soft laugh. "No pun intended."

"Well, before we start," George said as we walked, "can we grab some lunch first? I won't be much help unless I eat."

"Why don't you and Bess find someplace, while I ask a few more questions? Just text me where you go, and I'll meet you there in about ten minutes. Okay?" I said.

"Perfect," George agreed as she and Bess headed down the street.

I turned back toward the spot where the firefighter had been talking with Lacey O'Brien's fans. Most everyone who had gathered was gone, except for the firefighter who Mandy had questioned. He was busy talking on his phone and I waited a moment until he seemed like he was wrapping up his conversation.

"Excuse me," I asked. "But do you know when the bookstore might reopen? And when Lacey O'Brien will be signing her books?"

"I think you're out of luck," he replied. "The store won't be reopening for a few weeks at least. It wasn't a bad fire, but there's a lot of smoke and water damage. The owner, Paige Samuels, has quite a mess on her hands."

"Do you think those girls were right?" I asked innocently. Then I thought fast. "My brother's a volunteer firefighter and has never dealt with arson before."

"I really don't know and can't say just yet," he replied. "It looked like bad wiring to begin with, but it could have been anything. As I said, we'll be doing a full investigation, but it's too soon to tell right now."

He excused himself and headed over to the other firefighters. I nodded and backed away. Then I pulled out my phone to see if George or Bess had texted me. I had one new message from George: MEET US AT THE AVONDALE DINER, CORNER OF PARKSIDE AND MAIN.

I headed up the street, passing an eyeglasses store and a bakery. Baskets of purple and pink impatiens hung from the streetlamps, and I had the feeling that Mandy was probably right that nothing exciting ever did happen in Avondale. It was quiet and quaint with a small-town feel. So why now—why a fire? And who? And did the fire really have anything to do with Lacey O'Brien's book? Or maybe even Lacey O'Brien herself?

At that moment I passed the Cheshire Cat Inn. In front a woman was sweeping the sidewalk, mumbling to herself. She had curly, dark-brown hair with a distinctive streak of gray in it. As I got closer, I realized she was talking to someone—an older man in an apron who stood half-hidden in the doorway to the bakery.

"She had it coming to her, if you ask me, Arnold," I heard her say.

"Now, now, Alice," the man scolded gently. "I know you and Paige have never been the best of friends, but no one deserves to have her shop practically burned to the ground."

I couldn't believe my luck. They were talking about the bookstore and the owner. I had to find out more.

"I'm sorry to interrupt," I said. "But I think I'm a bit lost. Is this the way to the Avondale Diner? Parkside and Main?"

"You're going in the right direction," the man—Arnold—replied. "This is Main Street here. Just keep walking two more short blocks and you'll come to Parkside. The diner's on the other side of the street. Best peach pie around, by the way," he added, and smiled.

"Thank you," I said, and started walking, but then turned back.

"One more thing. I was hoping to get a copy of Lacey O'Brien's latest mystery at the bookstore, but her signing was canceled." I gestured toward the few people still lingering in front of Paige's Pages. "Do either of you know of another place in town that sells books?"

The woman stopped sweeping. "I sell all of Ce—I mean, Lacey's—novels in my gift shop," she replied, somewhat too cheerily. She stepped into the lobby of the inn and motioned for me to follow her.

"Thanks, that's perfect," I said. I followed her into the lobby, which was dim, dark, and covered in ornate, flowery wallpaper. An enormous antique grandfather clock stood against one wall. Just beyond it was a small arched entryway that led to a tiny nook of a room. In addition to a wide variety of antiques, it was packed with Cheshire cat–themed gifts, from salt and pepper shakers to clocks to tea towels and Alice in Wonderland books and toys.

"This is a lovely place," I said as I studied an antique Tiffany lamp in the entryway to the gift shop. "It's so charming."

"Thank you," she answered. She seemed surprised at the compliment. "It's nice to see a young person like yourself appreciates dusty old antiques the same way I do. Most girls your age are more interested in cell phones and technical gadgets." She wrinkled her nose in disgust. "I'm Alice Ann Marple, by the way. Lacey O'Brien's from around here, you know. Tourists know she's a local writer, so guests are always asking for her books."

"Nice to meet you. I'm Nancy Drew," I said. "I'm a writer myself," I fibbed. "And a big mystery fan." I gestured to the rack of Lacey O'Brien's novels, which was tucked between a display of antique picture frames and a shelf of cat figurines. There were at least ten different titles to choose from.

"I'm sure you know, but this one's her latest," Alice Ann began, picking up a copy of *Burned*. The front cover showed an old house lit up in bright flames. "But this one's my favorite."

She handed me a copy of a book called *Framed*, which had an image of a shadowy figure in an oversize picture frame on the cover.

"You know, all of her books are set in a town that's similar to Avondale," Alice Ann continued. "Some people even think they're based on real crimes, but I think that's just ridiculous. I went to high school with her, and she had quite an active imagination."

What was Alice Ann saying? Did she know something about the fire today? "Are you still close friends?" I asked.

"Friends? Close?" Alice Ann scoffed. "We were never really close. I wouldn't even say we were friends. We were foe—" Alice stopped. And then she went on but in a more measured tone. "Lacey was—well, she kept to herself. Still does, as a matter of fact."

I nodded. "Well, it would have been nice to see Lacey today, especially since I hear she rarely makes public appearances to promote her books. And how awful about the fire. I really feel bad for the owner." I hoped Alice would continue talking about Paige.

But she just gave me a tight-lipped nod. It seemed like she had remembered that I was a stranger in town and not an old acquaintance to gossip with. I guessed I wasn't going to find out why Alice felt Paige had something coming to her.

"Yes, it's quite a tragedy," she replied. For a moment

I thought I heard sarcasm in her voice, but I couldn't be sure because she moved on.

"Have you decided on a book?" she asked, gesturing to the two paperbacks I was holding.

"I'll take them both," I replied. "Thanks again for the help."

"Of course," she said. "I'll ring them up for you." It was clear our chat was over.

A few minutes later I was sitting in a booth at the diner with George and Bess, who were finishing dessert.

"We almost started to worry about you," Bess said. "But we went ahead and ordered you an avocado-and-cheddar wrap with hummus. Hope that's okay."

"Well, it's not Hannah's fried chicken, but it still sounds pretty good," I replied. "I'm starving."

"So, what did you find out?" George asked.

"Only that Lacey O'Brien grew up here and keeps to herself, and that Alice Ann Marple, owner of the Cheshire Cat Inn, is no fan of Paige Samuels or Lacey

O'Brien. I overheard Alice saying that Paige had it coming to her, and then she started to say that she and Lacey were more enemies than friends." I knew it would be way too easy if Alice Ann was the one to set the fire, but what did she mean by her remarks?

I took a sip of water from the glass in front of me.

"And I bought two Lacey O'Brien books," I said. I pulled out my copies of *Burned* and *Framed*.

"Nice work," George said. "Why don't you give me *Burned* and you take *Framed*, and we'll see if there's anything to what those girls said about the bookstore fire."

"Well, it's a first step at least," I said. "But I think we're just getting started. You don't think *she* could have been behind the fire, do you?"

Bess started to answer, but the waitress arrived with my wrap, and as she placed it on the table, she noticed my books.

"I loved *Burned*. I think it was her best yet," she commented.

"I just started it, but so far it's terrific," I agreed.

"Lacey O'Brien lives in town, right?" Bess asked innocently. "Does she ever eat here?"

"Never has on any of my shifts," the waitress replied. "She doesn't live in town, though—she has a cabin on Moon Lake. And she's one of those reclusive writer types. She does one signing a year at Paige's Pages, but that's it. No one around here sees her for the rest of the year."

So the girls who we saw at the fire and Alice were in agreement about Lacey—she really didn't show up in town often.

"We're staying in a cabin on the lake. Maybe we'll bump into her up there," Bess said to the waitress.

"You never know," she said with a shrug. "But her cabin is almost completely hidden. You can't even see the place from the road. I've heard that her lakefront is decorated with a huge carving of a brown bear. I've never seen it myself, but that's what a customer told me."

Then the waitress leaned into our table and said, "I don't think folks from around here like her too much.

Like she thinks she's better than everyone who lives in Avondale."

She tucked the check under the saltshaker and moved on to take the order of the couple seated at the table behind ours.

"Wow," Bess whispered. "I wonder what she meant by that. And I'm totally intrigued by this hidden cabin."

"And the bear," George said. "That's a great way for us to find the cabin from the lake."

"If we could score an interview with Lacey O'Brien, that would be terrific," I remarked.

George nodded. "We can still take the canoe out this afternoon," she suggested. "Maybe, just maybe, we'll be able to spot that bear and Lacey's cabin."

"Sounds like a plan," I said as I picked up the check. "By the way, lunch is on me."

I opened my backpack and reached inside for my wallet.

Then I gasped.

"What is it?" Bess exclaimed.

"My wallet," I groaned. "It's gone!"

CHAPTER THREE

Capsized!

"I THOUGHT NOTHING EVER HAPPENED in Avondale!" George cried. "First a fire and now a lost wallet? Did we bring this bad luck with us?"

"Oh no," Bess said. "Do you think it was stolen?"

"Anything's possible," I said, sighing and searching through my backpack again. "I hope not. I'll have to cancel all my credit cards and get a new license. What a pain!"

"When did you last have it?" George asked, not wasting a second.

It took me a moment to retrace my steps, but it came to me pretty quickly.

"The Cheshire Cat," I said. "At the gift shop."

"Oh, is that where you bought the books?" Bess asked.

I nodded, breathing a sigh of relief as I pointed to the novels still sitting on the table. My wallet probably hadn't been stolen—more likely I had flaked out and left it on the counter while talking to Alice Ann.

"Let's go. We'll stop there on the way back to the car," George said as she went to pay the bill.

"Thanks, George." I smiled. For someone with such a great memory when it came to mysteries and clues, I could sometimes be surprisingly absentminded about everyday things like wallets and car keys.

As soon as we entered the inn, Alice Ann cried out, "I'm so glad you came back! You left your wallet on the counter when you paid for those books. I've been waiting for our front desk clerk to return from her lunch break so I could dash up to the diner to return it to you."

"Thanks so much," I said, relieved. "I can be such a scatterbrain sometimes."

"Happy to help," Alice Ann replied. Then she noticed George and Bess behind me. "I didn't know you had friends with you. Any chance you need a place to stay? We've had a few cancellations, so there's plenty of room here at the Cheshire Cat."

"No thanks," Bess said. "We've already rented a cabin on the lake."

Suddenly I had an idea. Maybe I could get Alice Ann to open up a bit more after all.

"Speaking of the lake, the waitress at the diner mentioned that Lacey O'Brien lives up there," I began. "I know you said she keeps to herself, but any chance you know which cabin is hers? Of course, we wouldn't bother her, but we're taking a canoe ride this afternoon, and it might be fun to just pass by."

Alice Ann hesitated for a moment.

"Well, I'm not in the habit of advertising her whereabouts to tourists," she said. "We may not have ever been close friends, but I suppose the woman is entitled to her privacy."

She paused again. I waited, sensing that she was about to give in.

"Well, I suppose it won't do any harm . . . but hers is the cabin on the northwest corner of the lake. And you won't be able to miss it from the water because there's a massive carving of a grizzly bear on the shore. That monstrosity must have cost her a fortune," Alice said, and pursed her lips. "I don't know what she was thinking when she commissioned that piece."

"Ummm . . . thank you, Alice. We'll just paddle by and get a peek at the place from afar," I told her, knowing full well that Bess, George, and I had other plans.

Alice Ann nodded curtly. Once again she was acting as though she might have opened up and said too much.

"You enjoy your books, now," she said as we thanked her again and headed back out the door and to the car.

On our way back to the cabin, we stopped at a grocery store to pick up a few supplies. Bess headed to the produce aisle for fruit and vegetables, while George and I picked up some bread, cereal, and milk for break-fast the next morning.

The three of us met in the checkout line. We were right behind a nervous and tired-looking woman who was speaking with the checkout clerk in hushed tones.

"—so sorry about the fire, Paige," I heard the clerk tell the woman.

With a start, I realized we were behind Paige Samuels, the owner of the bookstore! I glanced quickly at the items she was purchasing, which included a box of heavy-duty trash bags, a large flashlight, a heap of batteries, and a case of bottled water. Then I elbowed George in the side and silently gestured to the woman. George glanced at the supplies and gave me a quick nod, and we both leaned in a bit to hear more.

"Thank you," Paige said to the cashier in a quiet voice. "It's quite a shock."

"Do you know what happened?" the clerk replied. "A few people have said that it might have been arson. What do you think?"

Paige seemed surprised by the suggestion. "No,

no," she replied hastily. "The building is very old, you know. I'm sure it was just an old faulty wire, which is what the fire department thinks. Besides, Carol, why would someone want to deliberately set fire to my store? Alice Ann doesn't dislike me that much, does she?" And then she laughed.

George and I looked at each other. Alice Ann? And Paige was laughing? This was too weird. Paige paid the cashier and quickly headed for the exit. As she pulled her car keys out of her pocket, a slip of paper fluttered to the ground. I leaned down and snatched it up. It read: 9-1-14.

"Excuse me!" I called after her. "You dropped this."

She turned back, a startled expression on her face. Then she saw the slip of paper, snatched it from me, and fled without saying thanks.

"Whoa," George said as she appeared at my side. "That was beyond strange."

"Tell me about it," I agreed. We headed back to the checkout line and joined Bess, who was busy loading our groceries onto the conveyer belt.

"What was that all about?" Bess asked.

"Nothing," I said softly, not wanting to speak freely in front of the cashier. Bess gave me a puzzled look, but she just shrugged and began bagging the groceries.

As we headed out to the car, George and I quickly filled Bess in on what she had missed.

"Weird!" Bess exclaimed. "What do you think '9-1-14' means?"

"I don't know," I replied. "A date? It could be some sort of code, though."

"I bet it is a date: September 1, 2014," George stated matter-of-factly.

"Could be," I mused.

We drove back to the cabin in silence, mulling it over. Then we unloaded our groceries and put everything in the fridge, put on our bathing suits, shorts, and tank tops, and headed outside. Bess unlocked the equipment shed near the cabin and retrieved the paddles, while George and I carried the canoe down to the tiny stretch of rocky sand just behind our cabin.

Bess pulled a bright-orange life vest over her head and handed one each to George and me.

"Ugh," she sighed. "Why do they have to make these so ugly?"

"So they can be spotted in a storm," I replied simply.

"Thanks, supersleuth," Bess joked. "It was a rhetorical question, though." She squinted at the sky. "Speaking of storms, it looks a little dark off in the distance, doesn't it?" she asked. "Maybe we should wait until tomorrow to take the canoe out."

She was right—the sky above the horizon was definitely gray. I pulled out my phone to check the weather.

"Well, there's no rain predicted for this afternoon," I assured her. "So I think we should be okay. And I'm really curious to check out Lacey O'Brien's cabin."

George just shrugged and followed us down to the shore. We climbed into the canoe and pushed off. As Bess and I paddled, George sat back and closed her eyes.

I looked at the expanse of sky and the deep-green fir trees that ringed the lake. It should have been relaxing, but it wasn't. I couldn't stop thinking about the fire and the odd facts and timing surrounding it.

"I'm really curious to hear what the fire department says. Paige seemed awfully certain it was accidental, but I'm not so sure. And she was so jumpy when I picked up that slip of paper. And I know she's a recluse, but even though there couldn't have been a signing, I'm a bit surprised Lacey stayed away."

Bess nodded. "Good points."

I continued, "And what about Alice Ann? Even Paige pointed out that Alice wasn't too fond of her."

George glanced down at her phone, which was open to a compass app. "We're here—well, the northwest corner of the lake anyway."

She looked from her phone back up at the sky.

"I'm wondering if maybe we should turn back, though," she said worriedly. "It's gotten a lot darker out here, and my hair's suddenly standing on end because of all the static electricity in the air. I don't like the idea of being on the water in a lightning storm."

"I agree," Bess said nervously. "And the wind is

changing—I can feel it. I'm getting goose pimples on my arms."

The sky definitely did look more menacing than it had before, and the wind had picked up. It was growing increasingly more difficult to paddle through the choppy water. But suddenly, out of nowhere, I caught a glimpse of a dark figure on the beach. Two figures, actually: one in the shape of a bear, the other, a human.

"Look!" I cried out. "Over there. Someone's on the beach."

I gave George and Bess a pleading look.

"We're actually closer to this shore of the lake now than we are to our cabin," George said with a sigh. "I'd rather be near the shore—any shore—than in the middle of the lake if we do run into trouble."

"Maybe . . . maybe we can land on the beach and ask for temporary shelter if it starts to storm," I said.

Bess sighed.

"You're both right," she agreed. "Turning back now in this wind would be more dangerous than going ashore here."

Bess and I paddled hard. The gusts picked up while George gripped the sides of the canoe. The wind started whipping at us from every direction, but there was nothing else to do but press on. If we could make it to the beach, we'd be safe from the storm.

The shadowy figure watched us from the shore. He or she didn't wave or yell out to us. It just watched us struggle. I put my head down and used all my strength as I pulled on the paddle. The waves were getting bigger, and every time one hit us, we rocked unsteadily from side to side.

"Whoa!" Bess cried out.

"Ugh," George moaned. "This rocking motion is making me feel ill."

"Try to keep the canoe cutting through the water perpendicular to the waves!" I called to Bess over the wind. "That way we won't tip over."

"Okay!" Bess called back as she and I both tried hard to turn the canoe so the bow of the boat was slicing through the waves at a right angle. Suddenly the wind changed, and a swell of water hit us hard from the left, causing us to tip toward the right.

"Yikes!" Bess screamed. At that moment George pointed to a floating dock that seemingly just appeared.

"Nancy! Bess!" she shouted. "Watch out!"

In trying not to hit the dock, Bess and I managed to turn the canoe so that we were once again parallel to the waves. A second later we were hit from the left with another giant swell. Before I even realized what was happening, the boat lurched wildly to the right, throwing us into the violent waters.

"Help!" I yelled out.

But my screams were lost in the wind.

CHAPTER FOUR

No Trespassing

I GASPED WHEN I HIT THE LAKE, SUCK-ing down a mouthful of frigid water. Luckily, the life vest kept me afloat as I coughed and spluttered until I had spit most of it out. George and Bess bobbed next to me.

"Are you both okay?" George yelled, wiping a handful of weeds off her face.

"I'm fine," I yelled back as I grabbed hold of the side of the canoe. "Just drank about half the lake, but other than that, I'm okay."

"Ugh!" Bess screamed. She combed a muddy twig

out of her hair with her fingers, and she was covered in lake gunk. She swam around to the other side of the canoe and grabbed hold as well.

I glanced toward the beach to wave for help, but the person who was there before had disappeared. That was strange. Whoever it was had just been there a moment ago. Had the person really watched us capsize and then vanished without offering to help? I was certain since we had also spotted the bear that this was Lacey O'Brien's house.

"Looks like we're on our own," I told my friends. I studied the canoe I was gripping. After we capsized, the canoe had flipped right side up again, only it was now full of water. Then I felt raindrops. So much for getting an accurate weather forecast before we'd set out.

"Hey! Where did that person go?" George asked, incredulous. "What if we were in real trouble out here?"

"Maybe they're going to get help?" Bess said.

George shook her head. "Doubt it," she replied. "Nancy's right—we're going to take care of this. Do either of you have any idea how to empty a swamped canoe?"

I could barely hear her above the wind, and we kept screaming back and forth to one another.

"Well, I did see it in a movie once," I admitted. "First we'll have to dump out most of the water. I guess we'll have to turn it over to do that."

George shook her head. "We're only about thirty yards from shore," she said. "Let's swim in and tow the canoe behind us. We'll wait out the storm on the beach."

Amazingly, we made our way to shore, kicking hard as we towed the boat through the thickening sheets of rain. Luckily, we didn't see any lightning or hear any thunder as we slogged through the lake. It was slow going, but we finally got close enough to the shore so we could stand and dump the water out before we pulled the boat the rest of the way in.

We collapsed on the ground, soaking wet and exhausted. Dragging that canoe was one of the most physically challenging things we had ever done together. Once we were somewhat rested, I stood up, looked around, and saw that the property was covered in NO TRESPASSING signs.

"Not exactly rolling out the welcome mat, right?" Bess commented. "I guess I understand why that person on the beach disappeared."

"Well, I'm not going to let those signs stop me," I replied. "If that was Lacey—or someone else—I want to meet whoever wouldn't help three people stranded on a lake in the middle of a storm."

"And we've got to make it back to our cabin," Bess said, which was something I hadn't actually considered.

The rain had let up somewhat, so George and Bess parked themselves under a tree, while I climbed the wooden steps that led from the shore to the cabin.

I pounded on the back door, waited a good two minutes, and then pounded again. "Hello? Ms. O'Brien?" But nobody came to the door.

When I backed away from the cabin, though, I caught a flutter of curtains at the window beside the back door.

"Hello?" I called out loudly. "Is someone there?

We're just looking for a place to dry off for a few minutes until the storm passes. Hello?"

Still nothing. I waited another minute, but the door remained firmly closed. The curtains didn't move again.

I returned to the beach and to George and Bess. The canoe was emptied, leaning on its side. Just as quickly as the storm had formed, it had let up.

"I thought I saw the curtains flutter when I knocked on the door, but I could have been mistaken," I told them, shaking my head.

"What now?" Bess asked.

"We get back in the canoe and then head back to our cabin," I replied with a shrug. "And we try to figure out why Lacey O'Brien or whoever that was on the beach earlier refused to help us. If that was her, no wonder she has a terrible reputation in town."

George bit her lip thoughtfully. "It was pretty rude," she agreed. "Maybe the fire was set to sabotage her book signing—she may have enemies right here in Avondale."

At that moment, a small motorboat with two men

aboard headed toward the shore. I could see the words AVONDALE POLICE stenciled on the hull.

"You folks okay?" one of the men shouted. "We received a call that a canoe had capsized in the storm. And that trespassers were on this property."

"We're fine," Bess called back. "Just cold, wet, and exhausted."

The boat pulled up to a small dock, and the second officer climbed out. He was much younger than the first and had dark brown hair and eyes. More importantly, he was carrying an armload of thick, heavy blankets.

He walked across the beach and handed one to each of us.

"Thanks!" Bess said, a smile crossing her face. "I haven't been so happy to see a blanket in a long time."

He smiled back at her, blushing slightly and revealing two enormous dimples. The sun peeked out from behind the clouds for a second. Bess lowered her eyes and her cheeks reddened. It was all a little ridiculous, considering what had just happened to us.

George rolled her eyes.

The other officer started talking. "Ladies, I'm Sheriff Garrison. I'm relieved you are all okay, but you must have known how dangerous it was for you to be on the lake with a storm of this magnitude. And trespassing is a serious offense in Avondale. What were you doing here, anyway?"

"The storm came up suddenly and we headed for the nearest shore. Then we tried to get help from the owner of the cabin. We didn't mean to trespass."

"I understand, but the 'No Trespassing' signs are there for a reason. The owner of this cabin likes her privacy and is very wary of any strangers who could be stalking her," said the sheriff.

Bess spoke. "We really didn't mean anything by this, sir. We promise to steer clear for the rest of our visit. I apologize for all of us."

The sheriff nodded. "I will let you off with a warning—this time. But if I hear another complaint about you three, I'll bring you into the precinct. That's a promise."

He walked away and started talking on his phone,

leaving us with the younger officer. We were speechless. How had this weekend taken such a disastrous turn?

He smiled. "I'm sorry my uncle was so rough on you guys," he apologized. "But folks in Avondale really take their privacy seriously. I'm Ian Garrison, by the way. I'm interning over the next couple of months for the sheriff's office. It looks like you could use help getting back to wherever you're going. Right?"

I nodded. "We're heading to our cabin on the southeast corner of the lake," I explained. "I think we'll be fine. But if you're going in that direction, we wouldn't mind the company."

"We're heading that way too. Just consider us your police escort."

"Nancy," I replied as I took his hand. "And that's Bess and George." I pointed to my friends.

"Nice to meet you all," he said.

George and I portaged the canoe down to the shore, Bess carried the paddles, and we climbed in and pushed off. We got back, slowly but surely, the motorboat officers watching our every move.

By the time we got back to our cabin, the weather had cleared. And I couldn't believe it, but it was close to dinnertime. What a day it had been.

"Can we get you anything to drink before you leave?" I asked Sheriff Garrison.

"No thanks," he replied. "I have to get back. But remember, stay out of trouble while you're here." Then he smiled and said, "But barring an emergency, Ian here is done for the day." He gestured to his nephew.

"That would be great, thanks," Ian replied with a shy smile in Bess's direction.

Sheriff Garrison took off, and Bess and I went into the kitchen to get the drinks.

As I sliced some lemons to add to a pitcher of iced tea, I said to Bess, "I was hoping you might be able to pump Ian for some info on the fire." I smiled at her in what I hoped was a winning fashion. "You know, since he seems to really like you."

"He does not," Bess protested. "But I'll ask a few questions if it helps."

We headed back out onto the porch with the ice-filled pitcher, four glasses, and some snacks.

"This is great, thanks. So, where are you all from?" Ian said.

"River Heights," George replied. "We're just up here for the weekend."

"What do you think so far?" Ian asked.

"The lake is beautiful if you can manage to stay in the canoe," I joked. "And we got to check out Avondale earlier today as well. That bookstore fire looked really terrible."

I glanced at Bess to see if she would take the lead.

She turned to Ian and asked, "Who would want to torch a bookstore? We heard some people say that Lacey isn't too popular around here, even though she's a famous mystery writer. And Paige seems to have an enemy or two as well."

"Well, I'm not supposed to discuss ongoing investigations, but we really don't know that much yet. I'm sure it wouldn't hurt," Ian said. "The fire chief and Uncle Bob—uh, I mean the sheriff—were in the bookstore all morning collecting evidence. They still have to evaluate everything officially, but just between us, that fire was definitely not an accident.

"They found traces of kerosene, though they also found some frayed wires on an old chandelier," he continued. "It looked like someone cut through the wires to make it look like that's what started the fire. Now they've launched a full investigation."

So it was official: Someone had started the fire on purpose. But who was the target? Paige? Lacey? Or someone else? I was contemplating my next move when the ringing of Ian's cell phone cut through my thoughts.

"Hey, Uncle Bob," he answered. "Is everything okay?"

The sheriff. It was difficult not to eavesdrop, since Ian was sitting just a few feet away.

"Really?" he asked. "Of course . . . I'll be there as soon as I can."

The call over, he looked at us, seemingly in shock.

"Thanks for the iced tea," he said, nodding his head at Bess as he spoke. "But our small town has been hit again. Someone stole a valuable, one-of-a-kind statue."

He shook his head. "I just don't understand why this is happening."

CHAPTER FIVE

Cracking the Code

BESS WAS UP FROM HER CHAIR IN A second. "Come on, Ian," she offered. "I'll give you a lift back."

George and I walked Bess and Ian to the car. "Do you have any more details?" I asked.

He opened the car door and said, "The piece was by artist Rick Brown. It was taken from one of the small art galleries in town. *The Bride of Avondale*, I think my uncle said."

"Two crimes in less than twelve hours?" George questioned once they drove off. "I know that may not be much for River Heights, but from what we've heard about Avondale, it's pretty suspicious, isn't it?"

"I agree," I said. "I know I've heard the name Rick Brown, but I can't remember where."

"Maybe you saw one of his pieces in a museum, or read about him in art class," George suggested.

"Wait a sec," I said. "I remember." I jumped up and ran into the house to grab the two Lacey O'Brien books I had bought earlier in the day. I came back to the porch and opened one of them to the "About the Author" page and skimmed it quickly.

"I knew it!" I said triumphantly. "I read about the author on the way to the diner before. Rick Brown is Lacey O'Brien's husband."

"That's too much of a coincidence, isn't it?" George said. "I mean, first Lacey's supposed to appear for a reading but there's a fire at the bookstore. Then her husband's statue is stolen from an art gallery on the same day."

I took a sip of tea and closed my eyes for a second.

"Do you remember those two girls at the bookstore fire this morning? One of them mentioned that it seemed awfully similar to the plot of Lacey O'Brien's book *Burned*."

George nodded. "Right," she agreed. "But what does that have to do with the stolen sculpture?"

"Well, *Burned* is about a fire in an old building, and *Framed* is about a theft from an art museum," I told her.

"Seriously?" she said.

I nodded. "And another one of Lacey's mysteries is *Drowned*. Think about what happened to us on the lake before. It sounds like someone's copying the crimes from her mystery novels," I said.

George gave me one of her George looks and said, "Okay, so we could have drowned today in Moon Lake, but why would anyone target us? No one knows who we are. And besides, how could anyone have known we'd go out on the lake and be caught in a storm?"

"But remember Alice Ann—and that waitress— told us where Lacey lives. I just have a feeling it's connected somehow. I know you're beat, but maybe we should start reading *Burned* and *Framed* now.

There just might be more clues to what's next."

"I'll tell you what's next for me, Nancy: sleep. You can wait up for Bess, but I'm going to bed."

The next morning I woke up early and waited to tell Bess and George what I had discovered. I had looked at both books, letting George get her beauty sleep. *Burned* opens with a mysterious fire at an antiques store. The arsonist tampers with the wiring in an old chandelier to make it look as though the fire is acciden-tal. The rest of the plot involves an international ring of criminals who traffic in fake and stolen antiques. The heroine in the novel—a journalist named Lucy Luckstone—breaks the story and eventually solves the case with the help of Detective Buck Albemarle.

The two characters appear again in the novel *Framed*. This time a thief steals a valuable painting from an art museum while Lucy Luckstone is on a behind-the-scenes tour. Lucy is framed for the theft, and Detective Albemarle has to clear her name.

I didn't know if *Drowned* would have revealed

anything helpful, but I didn't have a copy of it.

I was on my second cup of tea when Bess came into the kitchen.

"So, what did you find out?" Bess asked eagerly as she helped herself to a mug of coffee. "Any insight into the Avondale crime spree?"

"Well, I think there's a pretty good chance I'm right about someone borrowing crimes from Lacey's books," I explained. "But I don't even know where to begin in terms of motive."

"How about Alice Ann?" George said as she shuffled into the living room. "You said she didn't seem to like Lacey or Paige all that much."

I nodded. "Could it really be that easy? Who else? Lacey?"

Bess yawned from the couch. "It sounds crazy, but who else knows her books better than the one who wrote them?"

Bess had made a good point. But as much as I would love to talk to Lacey, we had already been warned by Sheriff Garrison to stay away, far way. I wasn't sure if anyone would be willing to talk to strangers from out of town, no matter how friendly people from Avondale appeared.

George looked thoughtful. "Well, you're probably the only person in town who's made the connection between the two crimes," she said. "Ian and the sheriff might figure it out as well, but something tells me you have a leg up on those two, at least for a little while. The sheriff thinks we're stalkers, remember?"

I answered, "I know. But the girls in town did know that the Paige's Pages fire sounded similar to *Burned*. Maybe it would make sense if we let people know about the connection between the two crimes. What do you think?"

George didn't look too happy. "Do we really have to get involved in this, Nancy? Can't we let the sheriff take charge, for once?"

My friends knew me better than that. If there was even a possibility that these occurrences were copy-cat crimes, then I couldn't ignore them. And it didn't mean they would stop—Lacey O'Brien had written a number of mysteries, and the person or persons behind the fire and the theft had more than enough material to keep them going.

I frowned at George.

She and Bess both sighed. "Okay, Nancy," Bess finally said. "What do we do next?"

I got up from my chair and walked into the kitchen area to pour myself another cup of tea.

"I was thinking I might give Ned and his dad a story for the *Bugle*, and if they want to run it, they would be free to do so."

Bess nodded. "And you'll get this story by . . ."

"Saying I'm a *Bugle* reporter, of course. And that I'm following Lacey O'Brien's rare appearance and book signing in the quiet hamlet of Avondale."

"Hamlet?" George said.

"I'm going to give Ned a call right now," I said. "And then I'll do the dishes. Promise."

My boyfriend, Ned Nickerson, is a part-time reporter and news editor at the *River Heights Bugle*, his dad's paper. The *Bugle* covers a wide area encompassing three counties, including Avondale, so the chances were good that Ned and his dad would be interested in the story.

I quickly filled him in on what had happened yesterday, and he agreed that both crimes sounded newsworthy.

"I'll have to clear it with my dad, but if you write the story, I'll edit it and get my dad to publish," he told me on the phone. "When will you be back in River Heights?"

"I'm not sure. But Bess and George are coming home first thing tomorrow," I replied. "I hope to do the interviews tomorrow morning and write the article tomorrow night so you can post the story ASAP. Sound good?"

"Yes, sounds great," he replied.

After I hung up the phone, I cleaned up the dishes as promised. And because yesterday had been such an unplanned adventure, we decided to relax the rest of the day at the cabin—snacking, napping, reading— before George and Bess took off for home.

After dinner, we decided to play one of our favorite games, Scrabble.

George was easily the best player among us, and

just fifteen minutes into the game, she was well ahead of Bess and me.

"Triple word score!" she shouted gleefully as she played the word ZEBRAS.

"Ugh, and you even have a Z in there," Bess groaned.

"Not only that, but the Z is on a double-letter-score square," I added with a pained sigh.

"Sorry, girls," George said apologetically, though the smile on her face made it hard to believe she was being sincere.

I played the word YEAR and was left with the letters A, D, K, and O. I selected a Q and then two Os in a row.

"Really?" I exclaimed, exasperated. "Two more Os?"

"Nancy, you just totally gave away your letters!" Bess laughed.

I shrugged. I was losing badly by this point anyway. I placed the tiles on my stand with a sigh and started rearranging them. Suddenly I remembered the scrap of paper from yesterday.

"Oh!" I exclaimed, practically knocking my tiles over. "I think I know what that number might have been!"

George and Bess both gave me puzzled looks.

"Number?" Bess asked. "What number?"

"The one on the paper Paige dropped in the super-market," I reminded my friends.

"What do you think it means?" George asked.

"Well, I was rearranging the letters on my stand, and I was looking at the number of points assigned to each letter instead of at the letters themselves," I explained. "Maybe each of those numbers corresponds to a different letter of the alphabet."

I spun my stand around to show them.

"Well, I guess the game's over if you're showing off all your letters," George joked.

I glared at her.

"Sorry, sorry!" she said, waving her arms in apology. "Please, go on."

"George, I know you thought the number might be a date, but what if it's a word?" I continued. "The numbers were 9-1-14, so we should try the ninth, first, and fourteenth letters of the alphabet."

Bess had been keeping score, so she quickly grabbed a scrap of paper and a pencil and jotted down the numbers one through fourteen on the paper with the letters of the alphabet below them. She studied the paper for a second and then gasped.

"The letters spell the name 'Ian'!" she cried.

"Really?" I asked, intrigued.

"It's a good theory, but why would someone write down numbers instead of letters for someone's name?" George asked. "I admire your sleuthing skills, but maybe the number is just a number."

"You have a point," I admitted. "People sometimes write things down if they're likely to forget them, and 'Ian' doesn't seem like a name that would be hard to remember."

"Or necessary to disguise," Bess pointed out a bit defensively.

"Well, we don't know about that, do we?" George joked. "Maybe he's an undercover spy and his cover is that he's the sheriff's nephew-slash-intern."

"Ha, ha," Bess replied, rolling her eyes.

"Wait a minute," I said. "If it is just a number, a number that someone wouldn't want to forget, it could be a combination—maybe to a safe?"

"And that would explain why the bookstore owner looked so alarmed when you picked it up," George pointed out. "Maybe it's the code to a safe she has in the bookstore."

I nodded. "It's a possibility."

"Are we done with this game, then?" George asked as she gestured at the abandoned Scrabble board. "Or are we still playing?"

Bess threw up her hands. "It's no use, George," she admitted. "You'll win anyway. Let's call it quits."

"I agree," I chimed in. "You are truly the champ, George."

With that, we packed up the game and headed to bed.

I fell asleep as soon as my head hit the pillow. But I was startled awake in the middle of the night by a rustling noise outside the cabin. I sat straight up. Bess was still sleeping soundly in the bed next to mine, but I saw George shift in her bed across the room. She sat up too.

I tiptoed over in the dark and perched on the edge of her bed.

"Did you hear that?" I whispered.

She nodded. "It sounds like someone's out there," she said in a hushed tone.

I stood up and dashed back to my bed to grab a sweatshirt and my cell phone—just in case. I pulled the sweatshirt over my head and stepped into my flip-flops. George did the same, and then we quietly went out into the cabin's main room.

A shadow darted past the window next to the front door. George and I both held our breath.

"Maybe we should call the police," she said quietly.

Suddenly the hairs on the back of my neck stood up, and I clutched George's arm.

What I had seen outside was now behind me, but inside.

CHAPTER SIX

Shadowed

THE MOONLIGHT CAST THE FIGURE'S shadow on the wall in front of me. I grabbed a ceramic frog that was perched on the sideboard and whirled around, my heart pounding. I raised the frog, ready to bash the intruder.

"Stop! Don't touch me!" the voice screamed.

Bess?

I lowered my arm. "Bess! You scared the daylights out of us!"

Bess flinched and then scowled. "You almost hit me with that—that ugly frog."

I smiled apologetically. "Sorry," I said sheepishly, glancing at the painted ceramic figurine. "I thought you were an intruder."

"I did too," George added.

Bess glared at us both. "Well, you two are the ones who are out of bed in the middle of the night," she said accusingly. "I heard the floorboards creaking and both of your beds were empty, so I didn't know what was going on. What's up?"

"George and I heard something outside the cabin," I explained, leaning over and flicking on the light switch. "We wanted to check it out."

George nodded. "And then we saw a shadow on the front porch. We were about to call the police when you came up behind us."

"Well, let's call, then. It's possible the intruder is still around." Bess shuddered. "I still don't know why anyone around here is interested in us."

She picked up the phone and dialed 911.

About ten minutes later, Sheriff Garrison appeared at our front door.

"What seems to be the problem, ladies?" he asked. "I didn't expect to see the three of you again so soon."

George said, "We heard a noise outside the cabin. Then we saw a shadow flit across the porch. We thought someone might be trying to break in."

The sheriff looked concerned. "I'm glad you notified us," he replied. "This is the third call we've received tonight from the cabins around Moon Lake. It seems there have been a few sightings."

Bess, George, and I exchanged a look. First a fire, then a theft, our almost drowning, and now three calls to the police in one night? Was that also a plot from one of Lacey's books?

The sheriff's walkie-talkie crackled.

"Unit One, come in."

The sheriff pulled the handset off his belt and replied, "Sheriff Garrison here."

"We're sending the chopper over Moon Lake. Looking for a perp in the southeast quadrant."

"Copy that," the sheriff replied. He turned back to us. "You ladies okay? We're sending the helicopter out over the lake, so if there's anyone still out there, he or she should flee quickly or be caught in the floodlights. In the meantime, lock all the windows and doors and turn on any lights around the outside perimeter of the cabin. I doubt the perp will come back this way, but if you see or hear anything suspicious, just give me a call."

He handed me a card. "This is my cell number. Feel free to call me directly and I'll send someone out ASAP."

"Thanks a lot, Sheriff," Bess replied as she held the door open for him. "And sorry to bother you twice in two days. At least we weren't annoying anyone this time." She smiled.

"No bother," he replied. "That's what I'm here for."

Once the sheriff had gone and we had double-checked to be sure all the doors and windows were locked, we returned to the bedroom and climbed back into our beds.

"Whew," Bess said as she slipped under the covers. "I feel like these two days have been like a roller coaster."

"I know," I said as I lay back against the pillows. "I'm really sorry this visit to Moon Lake hasn't been restful."

I closed my eyes and mulled things over for a few minutes. Could the would-be intruder be connected to the fire and the art gallery theft? I had to check the plots of some of Lacey O'Brien's books to find out if an intruder in the woods was a character who appeared in any of her stories.

I opened my eyes to see that Bess and George were both asleep. I quietly slipped out of bed, grabbed my laptop from my bag, and tiptoed into the living room. Once my computer was running, I did a search on Lacey O'Brien's books. Up came *Framed*, *Drowned*, *Consumed*, *Shadowed*, *Snatched*, *Dragged*, *Ditched*, *Stalked*, *Nabbed*, and *Burned*, with plot summaries of each novel.

I read through the summaries, and my breath caught when I got to *Shadowed*. Lucy Luckstone is the protagonist again, and this time she's spending a week on vacation in a rented cabin on a lake. On the first day of her trip, her wallet is stolen, and for the rest of the week, she feels as though she's being followed. Then one night someone tries to break into her cabin. It turns out she has a doppelgänger who's trying to steal her identity.

My skin prickled. It was as if I was reliving the book. How could that be?

Had I really left my wallet at the Cheshire Cat Inn, or had someone—Alice Ann?—lifted it from my purse and then returned it to me after finding out my background?

I dug through my bag and grabbed my wallet, popping it open to check its contents. My credit card, ID, and cash were still inside. I laughed nervously. Of course Alice Ann hadn't stolen my wallet—she was the one who had brought up my missing wallet when Bess, George, and I returned to the inn, not the other way around. But just because everything was accounted for didn't mean Alice Ann—or anyone, really—hadn't looked through my wallet.

Now I was really being paranoid. But I couldn't

help feeling that I had become the copycat criminal's target.

A wave of exhaustion washed over me. My head hurt from thinking too much about all the different possibilities. I had to get some sleep or I'd never be alert enough to track down the owners of the bookstore and art gallery, and possibly Lacey O'Brien the next morning. With heavy eyelids, I headed back to bed and quickly fell into a deep sleep.

The next morning we were all awake bright and early. George and Bess were packing up to return to River Heights. Meanwhile, I would stay here in Avondale and try to interview as many possible suspects as I could.

I decided to leave our rental cabin on the lake, which, without Bess and George, would be too isolated for me to stay in alone. I thought I'd stay in town at the Cheshire Cat. I'd be able to keep my eye on Alice Ann and anything else that happened.

"Nice to see you again, Nancy," said Alice Ann as she checked me in. "So glad you decided to stay here after all. I think Two-B would be perfect for you. Just up the staircase, second door on your right."

Two-B was decorated with everything related to famous writers, from Edgar Allan Poe to Emily Dickinson. A bust of William Shakespeare sat on the night table, and a framed needlepoint of the Robert Frost quote, "Two roads diverged in a wood, and I—I took the one less traveled by," hung on the wall above the bed.

There was even an old typewriter on a desk in front of the windows. I looked for a memento of Lacey O'Brien, but there was nothing honoring her in the room. That would be odd, if I didn't already know Alice Ann's true feelings about her.

I headed to Paige's Pages bookstore first. It was still closed, of course, but I was hoping Paige might be around cleaning up after the fire. The store was locked up tightly, though, and there was still police crime-scene tape across the front door.

I headed around to the back of the store, where a woman with dark, graying hair in a messy bun was loading large trash bags into a white pickup truck. I recognized her immediately as the woman from the grocery store—Paige.

I cleared my throat softly and she whirled around, clutching her chest.

"Oh!" she exclaimed. "You scared me. Can I help you?"

"My name is Nancy Drew, and I'm on assignment for the *River Heights Bugle*," I introduced myself, holding out my hand. "Are you the owner of the bookstore?"

She studied me carefully, taking in my notebook, sunglasses, and reddish-blond hair.

"Have I met you before?" she asked, genuinely perplexed. "Have you been to my store?"

I figured she might recognize me from the grocery store, and it seemed like the best thing to do was just fess up.

"I think our paths crossed at the grocery store on Saturday," I admitted. "You dropped a slip of paper and I handed it back to you."

She smiled.

"Oh, yes, of course," she replied. "Thank you for that. And I apologize if I was abrupt. I was a bit out of sorts that day, with the fire and everything. I still am today, I'm afraid. I didn't sleep much last night."

She wiped her hair out of her eyes with the back of her hand, and I noticed the dark circles under her eyes. Then she said, "I know the investigators said it may be arson, but who would do such a thing? We're a quiet town, with law-abiding citizens. This is quite disturbing."

I thought back to my busy night and didn't blame her for not being able to sleep much, given what she had been through.

She took my hand and shook it firmly. "I'm Paige Samuels," she said.

"I realize it must be difficult, but I'd like to speak with you for a few minutes about the fire," I explained. "I'm doing a story about a few crimes that have taken place around town over the last few days."

"A few crimes?" she asked, her eyebrows raised. "I didn't know there were others."

I nodded. "There was a theft in town Saturday as well, and sightings of an intruder near Moon Lake last night. I think the crimes may be related. Do you have a minute to talk?"

Paige nodded. "Let me just put this last bag of trash in the back of my truck and then we can grab a coffee at the diner. The firefighters let me bag up some debris on Saturday before they began their investigation. I figure there's still plenty more to do inside the store, but for now, I may as well clear away as much of this trash as I can."

"No problem," I said. "Should I meet you there in about fifteen minutes?"

Paige nodded. "Sure, that works."

I got back in my car, drove up the street, and parked in the lot across from the Avondale Diner. Standing on the curb, I quickly glanced to the left and right before stepping into the crosswalk.

Suddenly a black car raced around the corner, tires squealing, heading straight for me!

CHAPTER SEVEN

Close Call

THE CAR SWERVED TO THE LEFT JUST as I jumped to the right, landing in a planter full of impatiens. The flowers managed to cushion most of my fall, though my right thigh was somewhat scraped and bruised from where it hit the edge of the planter.

Slowly I stood up, and as I brushed myself off, I saw that the black car had screeched to a stop and pulled over to the curb ahead. A man and a woman got out and approached me hurriedly. The woman was tiny and wore an oversize hat and sunglasses. The man, in a dark, ill-fitting suit, was extremely tall. Both were pale and looked completely shocked at having come so close to hitting me. The woman grabbed both of my hands and looked me straight in the eyes.

"Are you okay?" she asked a bit hysterically, her voice rising in pitch at the end of the question.

I nodded. I was a bit shaky, but I was otherwise fine. I hadn't even torn or dirtied my shorts, despite the scrape on my thigh. *Wait until Bess and George hear about my latest brush with death,* I thought. *They'll never believe it happened in Avondale.*

The woman turned to the man and poked him in the arm, hard.

"I told you to slow down, Rick," she shrieked, almost in tears. "You almost ran this woman over. You could have killed her!"

"I know, I know," he lamented, wringing his hands.

He turned to me. "Words cannot express how sorry I am, and how thankful I am that you're okay," he said genuinely.

"It's all right," I replied, giving them both what I

hoped was a reassuring smile. "I'm fine, really. It was clearly an accident."

"Do you need us to call an ambulance or the police?" he asked.

"No need for that," a loud voice replied from behind me. "The police are already here."

I turned to see Ian and Sheriff Garrison heading toward us.

Oh no, I thought. Not another encounter with the Avondale police! This was getting a bit absurd.

Sheriff Garrison interviewed the couple and me and took down a full report, while Ian tended to my leg using a first aid kit that looked like it was at least ten years old.

"Are you sure that adhesive is still sticky?" I joked as he placed some gauze over the scrape.

"Are you kidding?" he replied. "They don't make this stuff like they used to. I'll bet this will still be stuck to your leg a year from now."

Once Ian was done patching me up and Sheriff Garrison had completed his report, I assured everyone for the tenth time that I was just fine. Then the woman reached into her purse with shaking hands and pulled out a small notebook. She wrote down a phone number and address, tore the sheet out, and handed it to me.

"We're on our way to an appointment outside of town, but please call on us later today if you need anything at all," the woman said.

I glanced at the slip of paper before putting it in my pocket.

"Sure, thanks," I replied, though I doubted I would ever call. I had a full day planned, and though I was still a bit shaken, I was fine.

The couple climbed back into their car and drove away, and Ian and the sheriff turned to me.

"Are you sure you're all right?" Ian asked yet again.

"Of course!" I replied, smiling reassuringly. "You did a great job patching me up."

"I'm going to stop by the cabin later this afternoon, if that's okay," Ian told me. "You know, just to make sure."

I smiled. "Since Bess and George went back to River

Heights, I checked into the Cheshire Cat Inn. It's not necessary, but that's where I'll be if you want to stop by."

I waved a quick farewell and hurried across the street to the diner. Paige was waiting for me at a windowed corner booth.

"Are you okay? I just saw that car almost take your life," she said.

I smiled sheepishly. "Really, I'm fine. No worse for wear," I said as I settled in across from her and began the interview.

"What can you tell me about the fire Saturday morning?" I asked as I opened my notebook. I would have taped our interview, but thought I would be less threatening just taking notes.

"Well, we had a book reading and signing scheduled for ten a.m. with Lacey O'Brien. We're not particularly close, but we were in the same class in high school. Once a year, I'm able to convince her to come out for a special event. Well, her husband convinces her. I knew him back then too. They're high school sweethearts, you know."

She paused and looked off in the distance distract-edly for a moment before she continued. "Of course, as you know, the event never happened. When I showed up at eight to open the store, the firefighters were already there. It looks like the blaze broke out in the early morning, and the firefighters think it was caused by old electrical wiring."

I jotted everything down in my notebook.

"I thought the firefighters were investigating the possibility that the fire was caused by an arsonist," I pointed out. "Isn't that why there was police tape up around the store?"

Paige sighed heavily. "I was hoping you wouldn't have to print that in your article," she explained. "The bookstore hasn't been doing too well lately, and I didn't want the bad publicity. But you're right—the sheriff and the fire chief are investigating the matter. I hope it wasn't arson and that the fire was accidental."

I nodded as I made a few more notes, thinking back to what Ian had said about the sheriff and the fire chief finding the kerosene and frayed wire in the bookstore. Clearly Paige was in denial about the cause of the fire. "Ms. Samuels, if it was arson, do you have any idea who would want to torch your shop?"

"Please, call me Paige," she said. "Oh, my. Absolutely not. As I said before, this is a very small town, and everyone here gets along."

Hmm, I thought. *Not exactly.* I thought of Alice Ann, and how she didn't seem to care much for either Lacey O'Brien or Paige. I still found it hard to believe that Alice Ann was behind the fire or the theft, but stranger things had happened. But I still couldn't figure out what her motive would have been. And was it Alice Ann who'd been on the porch of our cabin? If it was, she sure knew how to cover up her feelings, as she couldn't have been nicer to me when I got a room at the inn.

I caught Paige glancing at her watch, so I quickly moved on to the next topic.

"Did you call to tell her about the fire?"

Paige nodded. "After I'd spoken with the firefighters, I did call her to let her know what happened.

We briefly discussed rescheduling the appearance for later in the year, after the store reopens."

"And her husband, Rick Brown. Do you know him well?" I asked.

Paige shrugged. "Not really. Like I said, we went to high school together, but that was ages ago."

"You do know that one of his sculptures was taken?" I said.

"I just heard about it on my way here," Paige answered. She shifted in her seat and glanced at her watch again.

"For the life of me, I don't have a clue as to who would be targeting Avondale's fine arts," she said. "Books and paintings and sculpture are important tourist attractions for us and add so much to our community. I do hope the police get to the bottom of this and fast."

She paused, then said apologetically, "I should probably be getting back. I have so much cleanup work to do."

"Of course," I answered. "Just one last thing. Some

people have theorized that the arsonist and the art gallery thief may be perpetrating crimes based on some of the plotlines in Lacey O'Brien's books."

Paige looked startled. "Really?" she asked. "You mean, like a copycat criminal?"

"Exactly," I explained with a nod. "Do you think you could help me contact Lacey? I'd like to speak with her about her books, but I know she's reclusive. I'd also really like to interview her husband about his art piece."

Suddenly Paige's face lit up.

"Did you happen to catch the names of the couple from your accident?" she asked.

I thought back to the police report the sheriff had filled out, wondering what this had to do with Lacey O'Brien.

"I think they were Richard and Cecilia Brown," I told her. "Why?"

She leaned in and whispered, "Well, the couple that tried to run you down was none other than Lacey O'Brien and her husband!"

CHAPTER EIGHT

The Secret Door

I PULLED THE SLIP OF PAPER THE woman had handed me earlier out of my pocket. It read:

555-0192

34 Crescent Lane

"Cecilia Brown is Lacey O'Brien?" I asked, incredulous.

Paige nodded. "Lacey O'Brien's been her pen name since we were in high school," she explained. "She always hated the name Cecilia Duncan. She was named for her grandmother, and Lacey thought it sounded old-fashioned. It didn't help that most of the kids in school called her CeeCee, even though she despised the nickname. She almost always goes by Lacey these days, but it makes sense that she gave her real name to the sheriff."

"But he acted like he didn't even recognize her," I said. I couldn't believe that the sheriff hadn't known that Cecilia Brown and Lacey O'Brien were one and the same person.

Paige shrugged. "He probably didn't," she said. "Most folks in Avondale have only heard of her as Lacey O'Brien, the local mystery writer, and don't know her personally. Aside from her close friends and people who grew up with her, not many local residents would recognize her. I only know her real name is Cecilia because of our high school days. So it's no surprise the sheriff didn't know who she was. He's only been in office a few years, anyway."

I glanced back down at the slip of paper. What luck! As crazy as it sounded, almost getting hit by a car was turning out to be my best break of the day. I was all but guaranteed an interview, or at the very least, a meeting with the famous author later that afternoon.

For now, I had one more place to visit in town—the art gallery.

"Thank you again for your time," I told Paige. "The story should be in both the online and paper edition of the *River Heights Bugle* tomorrow morning."

"Of course," she replied. "I'm happy to help. And thank you for looking into the fire. If it was arson, I'm eager to find out who's behind it."

"Me too," I assured her. "And I won't stop investigating until I do."

Paige offered to pay for our coffees on her way out, and I headed to the ladies' room.

On my way there, I realized someone was in the booth right behind ours. Oddly, he or she—I really couldn't tell—was hunched down in their seat and seemed to be hiding behind a large menu. But I was able to glimpse a shock of curly brown hair with a streak of gray.

"Alice Ann?" I asked tentatively.

She lowered the menu and seemed surprised to see me there. An empty coffee cup and a plate with the remains of a slice of pie sat on the table in front of her. Since I hadn't seen her come in, I figured she had been there the whole time Paige and I had been talking, which meant she had likely heard our entire conversation. And considering she was my number one suspect—maybe my only suspect—I wasn't thrilled that she was pretty much spying on us.

"Nancy!" she replied a bit too cheerfully as she jumped up and grabbed her check from the table. "I didn't know you were here."

She waved the bill in front of me as she headed for the cashier.

"In a hurry!" she cried. "I've got to get back to the inn!"

I walked out the door, shaking my head. In addition to being one of the town's biggest gossips, it seemed Alice Ann was also an expert eavesdropper. Or was it more than that? I thought back to the wallet incident on Saturday. Was it possible that Alice Ann was really shadowing me? I was glad that my stay at the inn would keep her close to me.

I headed outside, and after quickly checking directions on my phone, I realized I could walk the few blocks to the art gallery. I glanced behind me a few times on the way just to be sure Alice Ann wasn't tailing me. I was fairly confident I was on my own, but I felt jumpy all the same. I couldn't shake my suspicions about that woman.

The Clancy Tate Gallery was cool and bright, though the scene that greeted me was anything but cheerful. A thin, tight-lipped man in a dark turtleneck and thick glasses with tousled hair was standing in front of a desk in the corner, having a heated argument with a woman in a blue suit standing opposite him.

"Mr. Tate, please, I ask you not to raise your voice!" she implored him. "I assure you that it won't help the situation."

The man sat down in his chair abruptly and slumped back, looking completely dejected.

"I'm ruined!" he wailed.

"Now, now, Mr. Tate," the woman replied in a clipped voice. "There's no need to be so dramatic."

The man stood back up and squared his shoulders proudly before he addressed her again.

"Excuse me," he began softly. "But you've just come into my gallery and informed me that my insurance policy lapsed three days ago, and that no one from your agency had the decency to send me a renewal notice. So for the last three days—including the day before yesterday, when a valuable piece of artwork was stolen from this gallery—I have had absolutely zero insurance coverage! Which means that I am solely responsible for the cost of the piece! And you dare to accuse me of being overly dramatic?"

He was shouting loudly by the end of his brief speech.

The woman retreated sheepishly.

"I do apologize, Mr. Tate," she replied. "Perhaps I should come back tomorrow so that we can discuss this further."

She turned to leave and saw me standing near the entrance.

"And I see you have a customer as well, so I'll be out of your hair now," she said as she quickly darted past me and out the door.

The man sighed loudly.

"Thank goodness that vile woman is gone," he muttered, more to himself than to me.

Suddenly he seemed to notice me standing there.

"Oh, excuse me," he apologized, a dazed look on his face. "Can I help you?"

"I hope so," I replied. "Are you Clancy Tate?"

He grimaced. "I'm afraid so."

"My name is Nancy Drew," I introduced myself. "I'm on special assignment for the *River Heights Bugle*, investigating the recent Avondale crime spree. Would you have a moment to answer a few questions about *The Bride of Avondale* for my article?"

"Would I?" Mr. Tate asked. "If your article can help get the statue back, then I've got all the time in the world."

We sat at a glass-topped table, and once again, out came my notebook.

"When did you first notice that the sculpture was missing?" I asked.

"I was the only one here. One of my co-workers had the day off and another called in sick." Mr. Tate paused and then went on. "Lacey O'Brien's fans were in town for her signing at the bookstore. I guess a few of her 'super fans' know she's married to the sculptor Richard Brown, so they came flooding in to see one of his most beloved works. It's not a large piece—in fact, it's rather delicate—but the detail and intricacy is meticulous.

"We had about twenty more people than usual sign the guest book on Saturday. At one point, I must admit, I did go in back to look for a sepia photograph of Moon Lake by Ethan Jenkins, another of our local artists." He took a deep breath and continued. "After that, I was busy making a sale of a few posters to a woman from Louisiana. When I realized the statue was gone, I called the police immediately, and they were here within minutes. But it was too late. The thief was long gone—it could have been anyone."

"May I see the guest book?" I asked. I didn't think a thief would actually sign in, but I still had to check.

"Go right ahead," Mr. Tate replied. He handed me a thick, oversize leather book and opened it to the most recent page.

I scanned down the list of names and addresses. A few were locals, but most of the addresses were from neighboring towns. Ian Garrison . . . the sheriff's nephew? Arnold Edwards . . . was that the man in the apron talking to Alice our first day? But one name stood out more than the others: Alice Ann Marple.

Hmm. If Alice Ann was the thief, she was either the dumbest thief in the world for signing the book or incredibly shrewd.

"Do you mind if I take note of these names and addresses?" I asked.

"No, not at all," Mr. Tate replied. "Like I said, if your story helps get that statue back, I'll be in your debt forever. And you know what they say about publicity— it's never a bad thing, at least in the art world. Do you want me to make a copy of that page for you?"

"Nope, I've got it," I replied. I used my cell phone to take a photo of the register before I handed the book back to him. I started to put my notebook away, when Mr. Tate cleared his throat.

"There's one thing I forgot to mention, and it involves Lacey O'Brien. But I can only tell you off the record. It would be a security risk for me if you printed it in the paper."

I was immediately intrigued.

"Of course," I assured him. "From now on, everything you say is one hundred percent off the record."

"There's one other way to get into the gallery. Only a few people know about it. I mentioned it to the police, and they've concluded that's probably how the thief came in and exited."

"Go on," I prodded. I sure wished Bess and George were here. I could have used some extra eyes and ears.

"The gallery actually shares space with a mystery writers' retreat and workshop," he explained. "As a wealthy local artist, Richard Brown has always been a huge investor in and supporter of the gallery. A few years ago Lacey had the idea to fund a dedicated writing space for fledgling mystery writers. She and Richard didn't want their names attached to it, since she so closely guards her privacy. But Lacey still believes beginning writers should get a break, especially mystery writers."

Gee, I thought. That didn't sound like someone who thought she was better than everyone in town.

Mr. Tate went on. "Anyway, Richard proposed closing off the back half of the gallery that faces Oakwood Lane and turning it into the writers' space. There would be a separate entrance, and Lacey would rent the space from me. She and I are the only two people with a key to the door between the gallery and the writers' space."

My mind raced as I quickly processed the new information.

A place just for writers? Mystery writers? Even though Lacey didn't want anyone to know the space was her brainstorm or that she was paying for it, I wonder if she ever dropped in as her "former self," Cecilia Duncan. Most people probably wouldn't guess that their writing mentor or coach was the bestselling Lacey O'Brien. It was as if she was hiding in plain sight.

Whoa—besides Mr. Tate, Lacey was the only person with access to the gallery through the secret entrance. But why would she have stolen her own husband's sculpture? Was it some sort of strange publicity stunt? As Mr. Tate had said, no publicity is bad publicity in the art world—or the world of publishing.

"Who owns *The Bride of Avondale*?" I suddenly asked Mr. Tate.

"Lacey does. I put it on exhibit to coincide with her book signing."

"Wait a minute, the sculpture that was stolen was one of Lacey O'Brien's, and she's the only one—other than you—who has access to the gallery through a secret entrance?" I asked.

At that moment a crash sounded from a back room. Could Lacey be in the writers' room now?

A voice called out, "Sorry, Uncle C. I was standing on a stool in the supply room and lost my balance." Into the gallery walked a girl with a familiar-looking face.

"Mandy!" I said. "What are you doing here?" It was the girl who was with her friends the other day, standing outside Paige's Pages after the fire.

Mr. Tate asked, "Do you two know each other? How can that be?"

Mandy looked at me quizzically at first and then had a "lightbulb" moment of recognition. "Hey, you're the person who was asking me and my friends Carly and Rachel all about the bookstore."

"That's right. I'm Nancy Drew. I'm writing an article about the recent crimes in Avondale and have been interviewing Mr. Tate about the theft of the statue," I explained.

"Well, my uncle C is totally clueless about it," she said. "But I think someone is definitely lifting their ideas from Lacey O'Brien's books—just like I said the other day. And my friends and I think it might even be Lacey O'Brien."

I might not have thought Mandy knew what she was talking about the other day, but right now we were on the same page.

CHAPTER NINE

Framed

I RAN OUTSIDE AND CALLED GEORGE, quickly updating her on what I had discovered. "What do you think?" I asked.

"I don't buy it," George said. "It's just too, I don't know . . . convenient."

I agreed. I didn't actually believe Lacey had stolen the statue either, but clearly she had to be considered a suspect.

George continued, "Since the statue was just on loan to the gallery, Lacey doesn't have a real motive for stealing."

"You're right," I said. "The motive question is definitely a problem. But that doesn't change the fact that she had ample opportunity."

"But it's all so obvious," George replied. "It's almost as if someone chose stealing the sculpture because it would make Lacey a prime suspect."

"Exactly! Lacey's being framed, just like the character Lucy Luckstone in her novel *Framed*."

"That makes sense," George answered. "Kind of. Do you think she's also being set up with the fire? Who would want to frame her, Nancy?"

I kept walking down the street and noticed the Avondale Library. I sat down on a bench in front to continue our conversation.

"I understand those crimes could be connected to Lacey and her books, but what about the intruder at our cabin, and the canoe, and me almost being run over?" I asked her.

Nothing answered me.

"Hello? George? Are you still there?" I asked.

George spoke. "Nancy, when were you almost run

over? Are you okay? See what happens when Bess and I aren't around to chaperone you?"

Oh no . . . I'd never told them about my near accident. "I'm fine. Really. But because of it, I'm hoping to get a face-to-face meeting with Lacey O'Brien."

George laughed a bit on the other end of the phone. "Only you, Nancy, only you could have that happen. But nice work. If you need us to come back to Avondale, just say the word."

We hung up, and I walked back to my car. Instead of first calling Lacey, I decided to drive right to her house. Maybe by surprising her I would get more information. Or perhaps a confession?

I used my phone's GPS to navigate from town back to Moon Lake and 34 Crescent Lane. Lacey and Richard's cabin was set back from the road, covered, it seemed, by giant oaks and pine trees. I pulled into the long driveway and in two minutes was knocking briskly on the front door.

Within seconds, Cecilia Brown—aka Lacey O'Brien—flung open the door and greeted me by grabbing both of my hands tightly in hers and squeezing them, hard.

"Please tell me you're still feeling okay, dear," she gushed as she swiftly pulled me into the house.

"Of course!" I replied. "I'm feeling just fine. Honest."

Her cheeks reddened, and she looked down at her feet in what seemed to be embarrassment.

"I'm afraid I owe you an apology," she said softly. "I know who you are."

Wow. Did she know I was writing an article? And that I suspected her of staging her crimes from her books?

She continued, "I recognize you from the lake on Saturday. You had two other young women with you. I'm so very sorry Rick and I didn't come out to help you. I truly regret it. It's just that—well, we've had people stalk us from Moon Lake in the past, and we're never sure who to trust."

Lacey wrung her hands nervously, then said, "We did call the sheriff, but there's still no excuse for our not coming out there ourselves to make sure you were okay."

I was stunned. That Lacey—Cecilia—was so honest and forthcoming took me by surprise. Could this truly be someone masterminding a local crime spree?

"Thank you, Mrs. Brown," I answered. "Luckily, we were just drenched to the bone, shaken up somewhat, but nothing more serious."

"Why don't we sit down and make ourselves comfortable," she replied, and I followed her into a warm and comfortable living room, with floor-to-ceiling windows overlooking the lake. We settled in on an overstuffed couch.

"We were not stalking you, but we did hear that this is where Lacey O'Brien lives. And when you and I had our run-in in town, I had no idea you were Lacey O'Brien."

I paused and then admitted, "I'm not here about our run-in this morning, though. I'm here because I'd like to interview you for an article I'm writing for the *River Heights Bugle*."

Again, Lacey looked embarrassed. "I see it wasn't hard for you to connect the dots about who I am. I'm so sorry, but I don't grant any interviews about my work," she explained. "I made a decision many years ago not to allow interviews, so now I'm afraid I'm stuck. If I make an exception for one paper, the floodgates would open. I hope you understand."

Once again, she seemed genuinely sorry.

"The story isn't about your writing," I said. "It's actually about a number of crimes that have taken place around Avondale this weekend."

"What does that have to do with me?" she asked, looking me squarely in the eyes.

Truth time. I was a little nervous to directly confront Lacey and was hoping she wasn't currently writing a mystery entitled *Murder at Moon Lake*, but I had to take the chance. I probably should have looped in Sheriff Garrison and Ian, but I kind of knew they wouldn't approve of what I was doing.

"My article reports the ways the perpetrator of the crimes is stealing ideas from your books—*Burned* and *Framed.* The police and the fire department have determined that the bookstore fire started due to wiring in an old chandelier that had been tampered with—exactly like what happened in *Burned*. And besides Mr. Tate, you're the only one with a key to the gallery's back room and easy access to the statue. I'm afraid that you're at the top of my suspect list."

Lacey paled. And then grew angry.

"That's awful," she said. "And, frankly, I resent your accusations. However, for your information, I was home the morning of the fire—Paige called me to tell me about it. I certainly couldn't be two places at once!"

She went on heatedly, "There is no way I could be your culprit."

I exhaled. What a relief.

"Now I'm the one to apologize, Lacey. But I hope you understand that I had to play my hunch," I said.

There was somewhat of an awkward silence before I spoke again.

"It's quite possible then that you're being framed."

"Me, framed?" She laughed lightly, and I realized

it was the first time I had seen her smile. But then she paused as though trying to determine whether she should reveal something.

"About ten years ago a big fan of my work called me every day. He figured out where I lived and trailed me around town for a number of weeks. He was basically harmless, but I ended up getting a restraining order because it was very unsettling. The last I heard, he had retired to Florida and was doing well. That's the main reason Rick and I became so reclusive and protective of our privacy. We didn't want to go through something like that again," she said.

"Have you heard from him recently?" I asked.

"No, I haven't," she replied with a shake of her head. "I actually have no reason to suspect him, but we do have a history, so it's one possibility."

"Anyone else?" I said.

She shook her head again. "I'm afraid there's no one I can think of."

I took down the former stalker's name anyway. Though it didn't sound like a promising lead, I intended to look into it. Then I gave her my number and asked her to call if she thought of anything else. "If anyone comes to mind, please let me know. Who knows what they'll do next to set you up?"

"I'll definitely be in touch if I think of anything," Lacey said. "Nancy, I should let you know that I'm going to tell my husband Richard what's transpiring. I don't want either of us letting down our guard."

She walked me to my car and warned me to be careful.

"I know Avondale has a peaceful facade, but one never knows what lies beneath."

Even though it was warm outside, Lacey's words chilled me to the bone.

Another exhausting day. I drove back to town, looking forward to the quiet of my room at the inn. Now I had to write the article, and by the time I was done with it, I realized I hadn't solved a thing and had actually created more questions than I had answered.

Just after seven thirty, I hit send with my article to

Ned. Then I called to let him know it was on its way.

"You sound beat, Nancy," Ned said. "Maybe I should drive to Avondale tomorrow and help you out."

"I'm fine. If I can't figure this case out in the next two days, I promise to turn it over to the sheriff," I told him. I was about to hang up, when there was a knock at my door.

"Hold on a minute, Ned. Let me see who this is." I padded past the Dr. Seuss chair and opened the door.

Nobody was there.

But on the ground was an envelope with my name. I opened it, wondering what it could be, a thin slip of paper fluttered out. I picked it up and read the type-written note:

STOP PRESSING YOUR LUCK. IF YOU KNOW WHAT'S

GOOD FOR YOU, YOU'LL GET OUT OF TOWN NOW.

CHAPTER TEN

Stalked

"NED, I'LL CALL YOU RIGHT BACK," I SAID, and hung up.

I peered at the note and realized it had been typed on an old-school typewriter rather than printed out from a computer. I looked at the letters closely and realized that all the *T*s were more faded than the other letters, as though that key on the typewriter didn't work quite so well.

I looked up and down the hallway and didn't see or hear a soul.

Suddenly my phone rang, and I jumped. "Hello? Who is this? What do you want?"

"Nancy? It's me, Ned. You said you'd call back in a minute—what happened?" He sounded panic-stricken.

"Ned! I'm sorry—but I think I will take you up on your offer. Can you come to Avondale first thing tomorrow?" I said.

"Of course I'll come. But are you all right tonight?" Ned asked.

I assured him I would lock my door, not open it for anyone, and meet him at the Avondale Diner at eight a.m. We said good night and I got into bed, still tired and now a bit scared.

Not surprisingly, I had trouble falling asleep. A million thoughts filled my head. I must have been closer to who was behind this mystery than I realized. Who'd left that note, written with a typewriter?

I sat up in bed. Typewriter . . . there was one right on the desk in my room. I turned the night table lamp on and walked over to the desk. I took a sheet of the Cheshire Cat Inn stationery and put it in the roller.

I typed the same words in the note: STOP PRESS-ING YOUR LUCK. IF YOU KNOW WHAT'S GOOD FOR YOU, YOU'LL GET OUT OF TOWN NOW.

I ripped out the paper, inspected the *T*s, and almost started crying, but from relief: This wasn't the same typewriter used to write the note sent to me. I'd been so worried that someone had snuck into my room. But maybe, just maybe, if I found the typewriter that was used for the letter, I would find out who was behind the crimes.

The next morning I was already on my second cup of tea, reading my article in the *River Heights Bugle*, when Ned arrived at the diner. He listened closely while I filled him in on everything that had happened—everything I hadn't written about in the article, that is—over the last few days.

"So you've talked to Paige, Lacey, Alice Ann, and Mr. Tate. It could be any of them, Nancy," Ned said.

It was great seeing Ned. And great to be able to bounce theories off him. After we talked, we both were in agreement about two things: We didn't think Lacey was the culprit. And in order to find who was, we had to find the broken typewriter.

I figured we'd swing by Paige's Pages first, and then stop at the Cheshire Cat Inn. Both seemed to be likely spots for an antique typewriter. But the bookstore was dark and the web of police tape still decorated the front door. I cupped my hands around my face to block out the bright sunlight and peered inside, but the store looked deserted. I realized I didn't know how to reach Paige other than by stopping by the shop, but then I remembered Alice Ann. Maybe she would be able to tell me where to find the bookstore owner.

"Nothing?" Ned asked as I backed away from the darkened window.

"Nope," I replied, shaking my head. "Let's walk up the street to the Cheshire Cat Inn. Wait till you see this place."

When we entered the inn, Alice Ann was front and center behind the receptionist's desk, chatting with someone on the phone. When she saw me come in, her face lit up. She gestured that she would be just a moment, and I nodded before Ned and I ducked into the gift shop.

"Wow, she sure has a thing for cats," Ned remarked as he took in the array of cat-shaped knickknacks crammed into the tiny space.

"Mm-hmm," I replied absently as I surveyed the space for typewriters. Antiques and old-looking memorabilia were everywhere. My eyes took in a shelf of antique scissors (strange items for an inn gift shop, I thought) and old-fashioned writing devices like fountain pens and quills. In addition to the spinner rack of paperbacks that housed all of Lacey O'Brien's books, there was a shelf of dusty old dictionaries, encyclopedias, and Avondale High School yearbooks. But there was no typewriter.

"Nancy!" a voice cried out behind me, and I turned to see Alice. Shockingly, she grabbed me and gave me a friendly hug.

"Oh!" I exclaimed. "Hi, Alice. Good morning."

She laughed. "I hope you had a restful night. I was looking for you this morning, but you were out bright and early. But now I can thank you in person."

"Thank me?" I asked, genuinely perplexed. "For what?"

"Ever since your article was published in the *River Heights Bugle* this morning, my phone has been ringing off the hook," Alice replied, a huge grin on her face. "We've had a tough summer at the inn, and it's been hard to book rooms. But it seems that people all over the county are curious about Avondale and Moon Lake since your story came out. We're completely booked for the next three weekends, and I imagine we'll be full for the rest of the summer by the end of the day. It seems people want to make a weekend trip to Avondale so they can retrace the steps of the copycat criminal. And relax by the lake, of course."

"That's a little disturbing," Ned replied, a troubled look on his face.

"Well, yes, I suppose it is," Alice admitted, and her brow wrinkled for a moment in dismay. Then she shrugged. "But it's been great for business."

At that moment the phone rang again, and Alice dashed back to the reception desk to answer it. Ned and I continued to browse the shop while she finished the call. About fifteen minutes later she returned.

"Sorry about that," she explained a bit breathlessly. "Now, what can I do for you two?" She studied Ned carefully and raised her eyebrows questioningly at me.

"This is Ned Nickerson," I replied. "Ned, this is Alice Ann Marple."

"Very nice to meet you," Alice said as she shook his hand.

"You too," Ned replied. "Nancy told me about your little shop, and I know how much she loves antiques."

"Actually, I was really looking for an old-fashioned typewriter," I jumped in. "Would you happen to have any of those?"

I watched her closely to see her reaction, but Alice Ann barely blinked.

"No, I'm afraid not," she replied. "But I do have some vintage typewriter ribbon tins. They're very collectible." She pointed to a shelf of colorful lidded tins.

I shook my head. "But who buys the ribbons without the typewriter?" I asked. "I was really hoping for a typewriter. I couldn't recall whether you had one in here or not."

I smiled, and Alice did as well. She didn't seem rattled at all when I mentioned looking for a typewriter.

"You might try Memory Lane on Oakwood," she suggested. "Stephen Grey is the owner, and he might have something like that in stock. Just tell him I sent you."

"Okay, thanks," I replied. "I appreciate it."

"It's no problem at all," Alice Ann gushed. "I really am so grateful for your article. Not that I'm pleased about the crimes that have taken place, of course," she added, her face growing serious. "I hope you don't think I'm an opportunist like all these tourists who have been calling this morning."

"No, no, not at all," I murmured.

"I mean, I'm not at all happy about the reason I'm

seeing so much new business. It's just that the inn has been struggling so much recently I've thought about throwing in the towel and retiring early. But this new business should be enough to keep us afloat at least through the end of the year, which is when we usually see a bump thanks to the ski resort in nearby Sugarville."

"I understand," I told her. "Don't worry, we don't judge you."

"Well, thank you," she replied, her cheeks reddening a bit. "I'm a little embarrassed to be profiting from the crimes, but what can you do? It is what it is."

Ned and I nodded in agreement. Truthfully, I did agree with her. If she hadn't committed the crimes, then it wasn't her fault that was the reason tourists were flocking to the Cheshire Cat.

"Well, thanks for your time," I told Alice as we headed for the door. "Oh, one more thing. Any idea where I can find Paige Samuels? I wanted to ask her when she thought the bookstore would be reopening and if she was going to reschedule the Lacey O'Brien signing."

"Really?" Alice Ann replied, looking more than a little curious. "Well, she often has lunch at the diner, so you might try to find her there. Or you can swing by her place. She lives in an apartment on Oakwood Lane, right above the antique shop, in fact."

Alice prattled on. "I don't know where she's been keeping herself. I know the fire put her store out of commission for a time, and she's probably mad as blazes at Lacey . . . for so many reasons dating back to high school that I couldn't even begin to tell you about, but, no, I haven't seen her."

"Thanks, Alice Ann," I said. I was grateful when the phone rang and Alice Ann stopped gossiping.

Ned and I headed out into the warm morning.

"Well, she sure is something," Ned said softly as we left the inn. "Doesn't want to profit off the crimes, huh?"

"How can't it be Alice Ann?" I whispered to him. "We've got a motive now—her business was suffering and now it's booming. She doesn't particularly like Lacey or Paige, either." I paused. "But we still need actual proof. We've got to find that typewriter."

Ned nodded.

As we walked past my car, he plucked a piece of paper from the windshield and held it out to me. "Hey, what's this?" he asked.

Oh no! Not another note. Again, it was typed in all caps:

MS. DREW: YOU SEEM TO HAVE TROUBLE

FOLLOWING DIRECTIONS. DON'T SAY I DIDN'T WARN

YOU. . . .

CHAPTER ELEVEN

Opportunity Knocks

MY STOMACH DROPPED TO MY FEET.
Who was watching me?

"There goes that theory," I said with a shudder.
"There's no way Alice Ann could have put that note on
my car; she was with us the entire time. And we just
passed my car on our way from the bookstore to the inn."

I chewed my lip as I thought things over. Then
I glanced down at the latest note again. I needed to
find that typewriter—it was our best clue. And I was
worried about what would happen next . . . to me, or
someone else in Avondale.

"Let's go to Memory Lane, then," Ned suggested. "Maybe the owner knows of someone in town who's a collector."

"Sounds like a plan," I agreed, giving him a grateful look. "Thanks again for coming along today."

"Happy to help," Ned said, reaching over and giving my hand a squeeze. "You'll get to the bottom of this. I just know it."

A few minutes later I parallel parked in front of Memory Lane. There was a doorway just next to the entrance that had two buzzers. The top one was labeled SAMUELS. I rang and waited a minute or so before ringing again. When there was no response after the third ring, I gave up, and Ned and I headed into the antique store.

The shop was dim, dusty, and absolutely crammed from floor to ceiling with antique furniture, light fixtures, candlestick holders, china, cameras, and clocks. Ned and I made it about two feet before we were stopped by an enormous antique bookshelf filled with crumbling old books. We couldn't figure out how to get around it, so instead I called out for help.

"Hello, Mr. Grey?" I cried. "Is there anyone here? We could use some—uh—assistance."

"Coming, coming!" a muffled voice replied from what sounded as though it was somewhere below us. A minute later a man with horn-rimmed glasses popped up behind me.

"Hello! So sorry to keep you waiting," he said. "I was just in the basement organizing some stock. What can I do for you?"

"Alice Ann Marple sent us over. We're looking for any old or antique typewriters you may have."

He scratched his head and looked around at the piles and piles of stuff surrounding us.

"Typewriter . . . typewriter," he muttered. "Let me check my inventory. Come right this way."

Mr. Grey darted to the right and squeezed his way past the enormous bookshelf. Then he weaved his way through a row of wicker chairs and around a mirrored door that was leaning against the wall until he came to a rolltop desk that was completely covered in more paper. He picked up a large notebook and began to thumb through pages that were covered in rows of nearly illegible scrawls of ink.

"Ah, yes!" he exclaimed, pointing at a row in his ledger. "We do not have a typewriter."

"Uh, okay," Ned replied, glancing at me. *How is this helpful?* he mouthed.

I just shook my head at him. *Trust me,* I mouthed back.

"Does that mean you used to have one but it's been sold?" I asked.

"Indeed it does," Mr. Grey said with a nod.

"That's too bad," I replied, thinking quickly. "Did you happen to sell it to someone local? I'm a collector and would pay top dollar."

Ned raised his eyebrows at me. *Nice,* he mouthed.

"Of course, of course," Grey replied without hesitation. "I sold it to that famous writer. What's her name again? Lacey O'Neil? She was wearing a big hat and sunglasses so I wouldn't recognize her, but I knew who she was."

He shook his head before he continued, "That typewriter wasn't even in very good shape. In fact, there were a few keys that were broken when she bought it."

Ned and I looked at each other and quickly said good-bye. I grabbed his hand and hurried him out the door. "We've got to question Lacey again—come on, we're driving to Moon Lake."

I was glad to leave the dust and papers behind and be outside in the sunshine.

"One more second, Ned. Let me ring Paige's buzzer again. Maybe she came home while we were talking to Mr. Grey," I said. But Paige still wasn't home, or just not answering. We started to go to my car when I noticed the storefront on the other side of Memory Lane. It was unmarked, but there was a logo of a quill and a jar of ink etched into the glass door. That had to be the writers' space that was connected to the art gallery. We didn't have time to check it out—we had to get to Lacey.

I was sorry that Ned and I couldn't enjoy the

scenery or a hike as we drove out to Moon Lake.

Right before we pulled into her driveway, Ned asked, "What about Lacey's stalker? Did you check him out? These notes seem to have 'stalker' written all over them. No pun intended."

I had to smile at Ned. I knew he was trying to calm my nerves. "I did check up on him. I placed a few calls before you came this morning and confirmed that he's still in Florida."

We got out of my car, and it took all my self-control not to run to the porch. I rang the bell and we waited. I rang again, willing Lacey to be home.

Finally the large oak door opened. Lacey looked at me like she didn't recognize me. But an instant later she exclaimed, "Nancy! It's lovely to see you again so soon. Is everything all right? Have you found the guilty party?"

But I wasn't as warm and friendly to her. "May we come in, please? This is my boyfriend, Ned Nickerson."

"Please do. Come in and have some tea," Lacey

said. "Rick's in his studio working, but I'll go get him."

Just like yesterday, Lacey didn't act uncomfortable or guilty in the least. Ned and I sat down in cushy green armchairs in the living room, while Lacey disappeared into the back of the house. She returned a few minutes later with a tray of tea and her husband.

"Nice article, Nancy," Rick remarked as he shook my hand. "Are you any closer to solving this mystery and recovering the stolen statue?"

"Rick!" Lacey scolded him. "Isn't clearing my name more important?"

"Of course," he replied. "But I'm sure that finding that statue will clear your name."

He turned to Ned and me. "The sheriff and his assistant were here earlier today with a search warrant. They were looking for the sculpture."

I looked at Lacey expectantly.

"Of course they didn't find it, because it's not here," she told me. "But they're getting a warrant to search my writers' space next."

As Lacey fixed herself a cup of tea, I took out the

typewritten notes I had received. I took a deep breath and began.

"I know you were adamant yesterday defending yourself. But not only did someone make sure I got these notes"—I paused and held them up—"but we found out from Stephen Grey that you were the one who bought the typewriter they most likely were written on."

Lacey and Rick exchanged glances. "May I see those, please?" she asked. She took the papers and slowly read the messages.

"I didn't write these notes!" she exploded. Her face turned red.

I held my breath as I waited for her to explain.

"The typewriter is at Oakwood Writers' Workshop, of course," she replied. "But no one uses it. It's there merely as decoration. And perhaps inspiration for the writers. You must know, Nancy, that hardly anyone uses typewriters anymore."

I nodded. "True. But anyone who uses the space had access to the typewriter and to the secret entrance to the art gallery."

"No one has access to the art gallery through that entrance except Lacey and Clancy," Rick chimed in.

"For both your sakes, I really hope you're wrong about that," I said.

Again, Rick and Lacey glanced at each other. What was in that look? Did they seem concerned about something? Maybe I had been right about Lacey's innocence, but could Rick have been involved?

"How can we help?" Rick asked.

"I think Nancy really needs a list of people who are members at Oakwood," Ned suggested helpfully.

I nodded.

"Just give me a few minutes and I'll print the membership list from my laptop," Lacey said.

The next five minutes seemed to take an eternity.

When Lacey returned with the sheet of paper in her hand, I jumped up from my chair. I scanned the list from top to bottom three times. One name made me stop—and I realized I had to get back to town, now.

CHAPTER TWELVE

The Final Clue

I DIDN'T WANT LACEY—OR RICK—TO know I suspected anyone on the list, so I handed it back to her and thanked her.

As they walked Ned and me out, Lacey told us about a last-minute fund-raiser that they were holding tonight at Mr. Tate's art gallery. With the theft of the *Bride of Avondale* statue, his gallery was in jeopardy of closing because of the lapsed insurance policy, and the local art community had organized the event.

Rick glanced at me and said, "You and Ned should come. Lacey and I will get you tickets. And you can ask your friends who had the canoe mishap the other day to come as well. It's the least we can do."

"Thank you," I answered. "We'll try to be there."

Once we were in the car, I turned to Ned. "We've got to hurry," I told him. "We have to get back to the Cheshire Cat Inn and then to that fund-raiser!"

"The Cheshire Cat?" Ned looked at me, incredulous. "But it can't possibly be Alice Ann—you said so yourself!"

"Trust me on this one," I said. "There's something there that I need. Let's go!"

I drove carefully but quickly, hoping Alice Ann hadn't locked up the gift shop for the day. I figured she was attending the fund-raiser that evening too, and she probably needed some time to get ready. As I drove, Ned called Bess and George to see if they could make the trip to Avondale in time for the fund-raiser. I figured Ian would be there, so it wouldn't be hard to sway Bess, but I wasn't so sure about George.

"Neither of them answered their phones, but I left messages," Ned said.

"Perfect," I replied. "Hopefully they'll be able to make it."

We drove the rest of the way in silence as I puzzled over all the clues. I was pretty sure I had figured out who was behind the crimes, but there were still a few loose ends that needed tying up.

"Penny for your thoughts," Ned said, breaking the silence.

"You'll know soon enough," I replied.

Before I knew it we were back in town. I parked in the lot behind the inn and hurried inside, Ned struggling to keep up with me.

I slipped into the dark lobby and headed straight for the gift shop, almost crashing into Alice Ann as she turned the key to lock the door to the tiny room.

"Wait!" I cried. "Don't lock up just yet. Can you let me back into the shop?"

"Nancy?" Alice Ann asked. "Whatever for? I'm running late for a fund-raiser at the Clancy Tate Gallery."

"I know," I replied. "I am too. But first, there's

something in your shop that I need to borrow, just for the evening."

"Borrow?" Alice Ann asked, raising her eyebrows. "This isn't a library, you know. People tend to buy the things they like, especially if it's something to wear to a fancy event."

"It's nothing like that," I explained. "I need to look at your Avondale High School yearbook collection. I'm this close to solving the mystery of the bookstore fire, the art gallery theft—oh, everything!"

Alice Ann smiled brightly.

"Well, why didn't you say so?" she asked. "In that case, go right in."

She unlocked the door and pushed it open, practically shoving me inside. Then she flicked the lights back on and hustled me over to the bookshelf where I had seen the yearbooks earlier that day.

"Which one do you need?" Alice Ann asked. "And I knew you weren't just a reporter working on a story— you're really a detective, aren't you?"

"Well, yes," I replied. There was no sense keeping

up my cover story when I was this close to solving the case and knew that Alice Ann wasn't who I was after. "I am. And right now I'm really hoping you have the yearbook from the year you graduated. That's the year that Paige, Rick, and Cecilia graduated too, right?"

"Yes, that's right," Alice Ann replied, a puzzled look on her face. She pulled a dusty book off the shelf. "Here it is. But our high school days were years ago. I really don't see how that's going to help you," she said.

Suddenly I had a pang of doubt. What if I couldn't find the proof I was looking for? What if the hunch I had was just that—a hunch?

Alice let me take the book back to my room, and she closed up the shop. Back in room Two-B, I sat down on the Dr. Seuss chair and began flipping through the yearbook.

"Who—or what—are you looking for?" Ned asked, looking over my shoulder.

"Pictures of Rick Brown," I replied.

I turned a page, skimming captions of sports teams and school clubs. But finally I found him: an image of

Rick in a tuxedo, standing arm in arm with a pretty girl with curly hair in a lovely, off-the-shoulder evening gown.

I had never been so happy to see an old prom picture in my life!

Luckily for Ned and me, the Clancy Tate Gallery fund-raiser wasn't a black-tie affair. Since it had been planned at the last minute, everyone was dressed casually, so we didn't stick out too much in our khakis and sneakers.

It was wall-to-wall Avondale when we walked in. In just a few days, I already recognized faces, from Alice Ann to Lacey to Paige and even Mr. Tate and Mandy. It seemed like there was a great deal of support for Mr. Tate and his gallery.

I knew that the fund-raiser was the perfect cover for me to finally get to the back writers' room. I would try to convince Mr. Tate to give me the key so I could look around for myself.

"Ned, you stay here and mingle," I told him. "I'm going to talk to Mr. Tate alone."

But I couldn't get close to him with the all the people who were listening to his story of the statue's theft.

I walked to the rear of the gallery, to the locked door to the writers' space. I wanted to will it open and wished there was a magical phrase like "open sesame" that would somehow make it so.

But something magical did happen: The door opened and out walked Mandy.

"Mandy! What are you doing here?" I started to shriek, but quickly lowered my voice. "I mean, what are you doing in there?" and motioned my head toward the door.

"Hi, Nancy." Mandy smiled. "I had to escape this crowd. Really, how boring can it get? People just telling Uncle C how wonderful they think this boring gallery is, over and over again," she said. "I couldn't stand it."

"But I thought only your uncle and one other person had the key to this door. Was it left unlocked?" I asked.

"Unlocked? No," Mandy answered. "The writers'

room isn't a secret to me. I know where the key's hidden, so I take it anytime I want. Like I said the other day, my uncle is pretty clueless. Nice, but clueless." She laughed a little bit.

And then she said, "I hang out here a lot. Sometimes with my friends, sometimes with the writers. Ms. Samuels is even there right now."

"Paige? Paige is in the room?" I said.

Mandy nodded and then took off. So I slowly, quietly opened the door and couldn't believe my eyes: Paige was there, just as Mandy had said. And in her hands was *The Bride of Avondale*!

"Sheriff Garrison," I screamed. "HELP!!!"

CHAPTER THIRTEEN

Facing the Facts

PAIGE TURNED AROUND AND GASPED.

There stood not only me, but Sheriff Garrison, Ian, Ned, Lacey, Rick, Mr. Tate—and what seemed like the entire population of Avondale.

"Ms. Samuels, just what do you think you're doing?" asked the sheriff.

"I'm—I'm—," she sputtered.

"Caught red-handed, I'd say," Lacey said, and walked into the room.

I thought Paige was going to pass out, but instead she placed the statue on a shelf—right next to an old typewriter—and then she sat down at one of the writer's desks.

"I'm sorry," she began. "I didn't mean for—"

Sheriff Garrison interrupted her. "Stop right there, Ms. Samuels. You have the right to remain silent."

And then he and Ian walked calmly over to the owner of Paige's Pages and escorted her to their police car.

One week later Bess, George, and I were sitting in my kitchen, having apple pie and chocolate butterscotch cookies—just the treats we were craving.

George took a sip of lemonade and said, "So Sheriff Garrison was ready to arrest Lacey O'Brien for the crimes? The 'intruder' at our cabin turned out to be a bear—that's what he said, right? See, Bess. I told you he and Ian needed help. It's a good thing Nancy was there."

Bess rolled her eyes but smiled at her cousin. "And Paige was so jealous of Lacey's success and her marriage to Rick. But still, to go to those lengths?"

I sighed. After Paige's arrest, Alice Ann had actually visited her in jail. I don't know if she went just to find out more gossip or to finally be a friend, but Alice found out that Paige had always felt she was competing with Lacey, as far back as high school. But she never came out ahead—even though she had attended the prom with Rick. That's the photograph I saw in the old yearbook.

When the bookstore started doing poorly, Paige planned to close it. But then she devised a plan to make money from the insurance company—an idea taken straight from Lacey's mysteries. The fire was meant to look like an accident. But once she realized that the fire and police departments suspected foul play, she started to cover it up.

I took my plate to the sink and let the water run over the leftover crumbs.

"I think there was a part of her that wanted to get caught," Bess added. "Why else would she join the writers' space and hide the statue in her own locker? She was bound to be found out, especially after getting the writer's room key from Mandy."

Bess had a good point. I wondered whether, when I'd picked up the paper with her locker combination on it at the grocery store, Paige had been deliberately dropping clues.

"Well," I told my friends, "I'm glad no one got hurt. Broken hearts, maybe, but nothing else. And now I've got one more mystery for you to solve."

George groaned. "Please, Nancy. Say you're joking. How much more can we take?"

I started to laugh. "Where do you think I put the latest Lacey O'Brien mystery? I can't find the book anywhere!"

Dear Diary,

A few months later, Ned and I took a day trip to Avondale. We had read that Lacey and Rick Brown bought the bookstore—now called Brown's Books—and completely renovated it, expanding the mystery and children's sections.

And inspired by the town's new notoriety, Alice Ann began hosting Murder Mystery weekends at the Cheshire Cat Inn to continue to draw new tourists. I hear they're a smashing success. But as far as I'm concerned, I think I've had my fill of mysteries at Moon Lake.